CHARLES NATON

THE CRONUS EQUATION

A Cortlandt Publication

Published by Cortlandt Publications 2016

ISBN 978 0 9933103 2 4

Cover design by Adrijus Guscia at
www.rockingbookcovers.com

For Dad

1

The lonely glow of a cigarette was barely visible through the freezing fog, that tiny incandescence in the December darkness providing the only clue that the skulking truck was occupied.

Inside the cab, George Tooley used his sleeve to clear a sparkling sheen of condensation from the windscreen before rolling down his window to let the smoke escape. Ever vigilant, he peered into the night and surveyed the silent cobbled street once again. He'd waited for half an hour and seen no movement outside, not that he'd expected to in this ruined part of the city.

Finally satisfied that he was alone, Tooley quietly opened the door and clambered out of the truck, throwing his cigarette into the darkness. His army boots crunched and clinked on broken glass as he surveyed the skeletons of ruined warehouses stretching away into the misty darkness. The blackout had been partially lifted since September, but that made little difference here in Silvertown. Hit hard by the Luftwaffe, some of the more badly damaged areas had been abandoned altogether, leaving a gangrenous hole at the very heart of the Empire. Perhaps someday, life might bustle among the docks and warehouses once more, but Tooley doubted it. He was one of the few who truly understood that this wasn't just another war, but the beginning of a new era. With a little luck, nothing would ever be quite the same again.

He paused briefly to check his shadowy reflection in the truck's side mirror, adjusting his beret and buttoning his top pocket. The Royal Engineer's uniform and unexploded bomb story never failed to keep nosy parkers away, but Tooley knew he still had to be cautious. After all, he wasn't the only man doing business behind the cloak of officialdom. Coppers and soldiers had gotten a lot more suspicious over the last couple of years, so it paid to be extra careful.

Glancing around one final time, Tooley took a deep breath and strode purposefully towards the back of his drab green Bedford truck, an invaluable asset which deflected awkward questions about petrol rations and unauthorised journeys. He quickly lowered the tailgate and hauled out a heavy canvas bundle tied with ropes. It hit the rubble-strewn cobbles with a heavy thud and immediately began thrashing and yelling muffled obscenities.

Ignoring the half-audible shouts and threats issuing from the tightly bound parcel, Tooley grabbed a handful of rope near the man's feet and began dragging his victim across the slippery cobblestones. It was hard work and he wished he had some help, but there were some jobs you just had to do on your own. Big Frank would've been useful in a situation like this, but Tooley knew better than to involve his much larger and simpler sibling in such affairs. It wasn't that Frank couldn't be trusted, quite the reverse. It was just that the lad didn't really understand the subtleties of politics, and probably never would.

A final heave over a half-demolished wall and Tooley let go of his struggling bundle, panting with the exertion and glad to feel the freezing drizzle on his face. He tensed as he heard a clatter of rubble nearby, his hand darting to his coat and quickly extracting his pistol. As he crouched in the darkness, Tooley began to wonder if he was getting a little nervous; even paranoid. The Ministry of Information's admonishment that walls have ears had never seemed so pertinent, although he was pretty sure they didn't have *him* in mind when they'd dreamed up that catchy slogan.

Tooley glanced down at the now quiet bundle beside him, and a dark smile played across his lips as he realised this wasn't the first, and it probably wouldn't be the last time he'd have to dig for victory.

Satisfied that the nearby noise was simply the constant shifting of loose rubble, Tooley pocketed his weapon and took a firm grip on his captive's ankles once more.

The inert bundle sprang into life again, and the half-coherent threats and curses resumed as Tooley doggedly dragged his prisoner across the floor of what had once been a busy import warehouse.

At last he reached his destination, a rectangular hole carved into the base of a large mound of masonry. Tooley rolled the mummified man over before drawing his pistol once more, his fingertips tracing the smooth machined surface of his army Colt. It was a good gun, bartered from a Yank deserter in exchange for a new identity. He aimed the pistol at the struggling bundle, thumbing off the safety as he fought temptation to pull the trigger, just to see what damage the forty-five calibre rounds would cause at close range.

Tooley's captive stopped struggling again, seeming to sense that his life hung in the balance. For a few seconds the only sounds filling the freezing night air were both men's laboured breathing.

Eventually sense prevailed and Tooley gently eased the hammer back into place. Corpses with bullet holes in them aroused suspicion, and their plans were far too far advanced to be jeopardised by such carelessness.

With business fixed firmly in mind, Tooley pocketed the pistol and set about loosening the canvas shroud around his prisoner's head. This grass's fate was already sealed, but he might offer up some useful information if a last-minute reprieve was dangled in front of him. Tooley's hopes weren't high as he loosened the ropes, but all opportunities had to be followed up.

At last the bloodied and bruised captive was able to suck in the damp December air, his expression a mixture of relief and trepidation.

The fake Royal Engineer stepped back a couple of paces and tilted his head as he studied his erstwhile partner in crime. "Now listen up, me old son..."

"Fuck you, George! I wanna see Mr Hill." The captured American's voice rebounded off the damp, fire scorched brickwork.

Tooley raised his eyebrows. "You've been working on your Cockney, me old china. Not bad, but this here's a private enterprise, nothing to do with Mr Hill. Besides, what makes you think he'll give a toss about a slag like you? He hates a bloke who'd sell out his mates, and so do I."

"Mr Hill knows me. I've found him some good deals in the past and he'll ask questions if I disappear!"

Tooley put a finger to his lips. "Quietly now or you'll bring the rozzers poking around, and they'll just hand you back to the Yanks once they find out who you really are." He leaned closer, his voice dropping to a whisper. "Is that why you've been snitching? Did the G-men offer you some sort of deal?"

A choked laugh hissed between the prisoner's swollen lips. "You've got it all wrong, buddy. If someone's leaking it ain't me, understand? It ain't me!"

Tooley shook his head sadly. "Listen mate, it's cold and I've got a busy night ahead, so I'll save you the bother of going through all the bullshit. I already know everything. I know how you've been leaving messages for that walking scarecrow down the Red Lion."

The prisoner's eyes widened. "Red Lion? Never heard of the place."

Tooley held up his hand for quiet. "A little bird told me, y'see." He crouched down and grabbed the man roughly by the hair. "If you tell me who that scruffy little bugger is right now, there might still be a way out of this."

The prisoner hissed with pain. "Oh yeah? How do you figure?"

Tooley released his grip and smiled. "Work for *me*, my son, my brother. You're not one of them, and they'll never let you be. You must know they'll kill you in the end. It's what they do, it's how they survive. They get into your mind and convince you to betray the mates you should be helping. Do you think they really give a toss about you? Do you think they'll invite you to their barbecues and cocktail parties after the war? Everything gets turned upside down sooner or later, and that's when your friends become enemies. Work for me, and you can write the reports *I* tell you to. It wouldn't be the first time."

The battered man shook his head. "Too late for that. I don't know what the hell you've been planning, but you're one crazy son of a bitch. It's over. They know all about you and they know all about your damned shopping list, so whatever you do to me won't change that. You do what you gotta do. I know I've done what's right, and that's something you'll never understand."

Tooley felt around in the darkness, his fingers closing around a jagged half-brick. "You think I'm simple because of this cor blimey accent? Don't you bloody dare lecture me about believing in something bigger than yourself! You're just a mug, a tool to be used up, broken and discarded."

"You're nothing!" The American retorted. "Behind all your fancy talk and self-justification you're just a spiv, a thief, a man who only cares about..."

The prisoner's last sentence was cut short as Tooley savagely swung the half-brick into the doomed man's temple, sending a spray of warm blood into the freezing night. Tooley smashed the makeshift weapon down twice more, grimacing as more blood spurted across his victim's canvas cocoon. That would have to be burned now, and decent canvas was hard to come by.

Tooley wiped his hands on the bloodstained wrappings and removed the restraining ropes, before rolling the battered body into the shallow grave he'd already prepared. He shook his head ruefully as he began kicking dust and broken masonry back into the hole. "We lost you a long time ago, mate. Yank or Brit, Frenchy or Kraut, don't really make no difference. You should've spent more time thinking, instead of whoring and drinking. Now you're dead, and you never even came *close* to stopping me. You bloody fool."

His grim work completed, Tooley dusted his hands and gathered up the bloodied canvas before making his way back to the truck. The poor mug would be found eventually, but by then it would be too late for the Yard to pin it on anyone, and the Snowdrops had enough on their plate without chasing down a single dead deserter. By the time the Feds discovered their informant's fate, George Tooley and his crew would be long gone.

Crossing the rubble strewn lane, Tooley quickly stowed the canvas in the back of the truck and jumped into the cab, taking a long draw as he lit another cigarette. He'd never actually enjoy killing another real person. Officers and aristocrats, well that was different. They were much bigger villains than *he'd* ever managed to be, not that the courts would see it that way if the rozzers ever fingered his collar.

There was nobody within earshot as the truck's engine coughed into life, and nobody to witness the hooded headlamps piercing the misty darkness as George Tooley left the broken citadel of the dead and began his journey back towards the still living part of London.

2

The Reverend Josiah Piggott blew pointlessly into his gloved hands, turned up the frayed collar of his overcoat and hunched his shoulders in a vain attempt to keep the freezing winter fog at bay.

He paused for breath and glanced around as he leaned heavily on a stranded gatepost marking the churchyard's entrance, the cast iron boundary fence swallowed long ago by the ever-ravenous factories of war. The fluted outline of St John's spire loomed above the cheerless Dickensian tombs, an ill-defined shadow disappearing into the darkness above a bomb-shattered roof and fire-blackened walls.

Despite terrible damage and lack of congregation, Piggott had been shown that a seemingly dead church could still shine as a beacon of redemption in an increasingly weary and war-torn world. Like a stone-carved echo of his own failing form, he knew that the building was damaged beyond repair, but he took solace from the certainty that while both he and the church remained in this world, angels still walked unseen among men. For Piggott this was not merely a matter of faith but a simple observation.

As he caught his breath and pondered the short span of his life as yet unlived, the ageing priest began to feel uneasy. He cleared his throat and tried to ignore a nagging suspicion of imminent danger; instinctively touching his neck, which felt strangely exposed and vulnerable now that his dog collar had gone the same way as so much else had done during his unusual journey through life. The atmosphere surrounding St John's had subtly shifted while he'd been out. Although the forlorn structure *looked* just the same, something insubstantial had changed. Something was wrong.

He fumbled in his pocket and brought out a US Army torch, its beam diffused by a paper filter covering the lens. It was hardly a searchlight, but at least the dim glow around his feet prevented him tripping on cracked paving slabs as he began a slow circuit of the churchyard. Clockwise of course.

As he carefully made his way along a furrowed stone path that sparkled with puddles, Piggott reflected on how he'd never fully reconciled himself with this particular churchyard. Not a single blade of grass grew between the soulless sepulchres where the departed slumbered in mouldering brick vaults, rather than cradled in the soft, natural earth. Although Piggott had never quite worked out why, the idea just didn't sit well somehow.

The Reverend wondered if morphine had finally dulled his senses to a point where he could no longer discern simple imagination from his heightened awareness of...other things. Perhaps he was wrong. Perhaps St John's was just the same as he'd left it and *he* had changed just a little. Perhaps he'd finally fallen prey to the slow erosion of hope and faith in justice he'd sensed throughout this poorer and rougher part of the city. After several hungry winters, London was just that bit more tired, thinner, sicker, colder and more cynical. The hope and elation following the D-day invasion had quickly become bogged down in a quagmire of doubt and anxiety as the Allies had faltered in Holland, and now again in the frozen French mountains. Another Christmas of shortage and uncertainty in the bitter cold.

Piggott stopped abruptly as he rounded the corner of the church. Even though the weak glow of his torch revealed nothing, he could tell something was amiss. He crept forward and gingerly leaned over the seemingly fathomless hole where iron railings had once guarded the steps leading to St John's crypt. Someone was inside. The almost imperceptible glimmer of a shielded candle spattered sporadically from beneath the crypt's stout oak door.

It was probably just some poor soul looking to shelter from the freezing winter night, bombed out of his home and fallen through the cracks in the bureaucracy. Still, experience had taught Piggott to expect the unexpected and so he fished inside his coat to retrieve his heavy Webley revolver.

The armed priest's well-worn shoes were silent on the well-worn steps as he descended into the darkness of the dead's domain. Josiah Piggott might have seen service more than twenty years ago, but he could still shoot straight if he had to. He didn't actually like the idea of firing on an intruder, or even carrying a gun for that matter, but these were strange times and there was no telling who might be prowling London's shadowy streets on the lookout for him. He knew he was blessed by Divine protection, but he'd also learned first-hand that God favoured the strong and the decisive.

Hoping the laudanum wouldn't slow his reactions too much, Piggott took a deep breath and pushed the crypt door open, immediately advancing inside with his pistol held steady. "Who's down here?" His gaze was drawn towards the stub of a candle stuttering beside a stone sarcophagus.

There was no response, so Piggott spoke again. "Listen mate, you might as well come out, and slowly so nobody gets hurt." He tensed as a shadow shuffled into the dim pool of candlelight. At first Piggott thought he'd cornered an animal as the indistinct shape stayed low to the floor, its eyes two matching orbs glistening in the gloom. It wouldn't be the first time he'd found a fox or a badger sheltering from the cold. The priest dismissed that thought as quickly as it had entered his mind because foxes and badgers didn't use candles. He squinted down the Webley's sights as he moved forward for a clearer view. A brief glint of metal confirmed that Josiah Piggott had in fact cornered a man. An armed man.

The intruder rested on one elbow while a Yank forty-five wavered in his unsteady hand, shaking violently as a fit of phlegmy coughing shook his body.

Piggott slowly stepped forward, keeping his Webley trained firmly on the figure in the shadows. As he drew nearer he breathed a sigh of relief and lowered his weapon. Throughout his eventful life, Piggott had stared into the faces of both trained soldiers and desperate criminals. Whichever this man turned out to be, he was certainly no threat at the moment. The feverish pallor of his skin and shortness of breath confirmed that the man was ill, and frightened.

For a moment the priest found himself staring directly into those oddly reflective eyes, instinctively searching for some inner source of illumination. Dismissing the impression as a conspiracy between the candlelight and his own senses, Piggott slowly moved further forward. "Hope you've got the safety on that, me old son. It's liable to go off if you keep waving it around."

"Who are you?" The voice was husky, weak, and American.

"I live here. I was...I *am* the Reverend Josiah Piggott, and who might *you* be?" Increasingly confident that he was not confronting a man intent on theft or murder, Piggott stepped a little closer. He pursed his lips and shook his head sadly as he looked at the unwashed and unkempt civilian slumped on the freezing flagstones. The candle's yellow light revealed a pattern of scarring beneath the hair on the left side of his head, the tell-tale signs of a fairly recent injury. Whoever he might be, the scarred stranger belonged in bed if he were to survive at all.

Piggott pointed to the man's pistol. "There's no need for that, son. Plenty of shooting going on in France without adding to it over here."

A brief smile flashed across the American's darkly stubbled face before a new fit of coughing screwed his eyes tight shut.

Piggott waited patiently.

At last the coughing subsided and the unkempt intruder shoved his Colt into a grimy kitbag. "Thought you might've been someone else. Don't worry though, Father, I'm just gonna rest here tonight and I'll be on my way in the morning."

Piggott fingered his non-existent collar again. "Well, technically it's Reverend, not Father, but that doesn't really matter." He looked at the American's crumpled suit. "Are the Snowdrops looking for you?"

The Colt quickly reappeared. "What do you care?"

"Take it easy, son. I'm not going to shop you. By the looks of things, whatever you've done it won't be Uncle Sam you'll have to answer to."

Another fit of coughing. "I'll be okay. Just don't tell anyone I was here. This ain't what it looks like."

Piggott rolled his eyes. "To *me* you look like a man who needs medicine, a hot meal and a warm bed. What's your name?"

"Who are you, my fairy godmother?"

"Look son, why don't you stop waving that gun around like Al Capone and come into the church? It's full of holes but it's warm, in places, and there's even a spare cot in the vestry. I can find you some clean clothes and you can rest. We'll talk things over once you've seen a doctor and had some sleep. The coppers never bother with St John's. Nobody bothers with St John's any more."

The nameless American smiled ruefully and shook his head before hawking loudly and spitting out a mouthful of phlegm. "I'm safer here, underground, away from people. Anyway, Uncle Sam's the least of my worries right now."

Piggott folded his arms and raised his eyebrows. "That Uncle Sam's an awfully big fella and he packs a real wallop. Who's bigger than him? Apart from the obvious of course," he quickly glanced heavenwards.

A fresh fit of coughing wracked the intruder's body and his heavy pistol scraped on the stone floor. "Just leave me be and I'll be gone tomorrow. I don't want any trouble."

The priest slowly bent down and prised the weapon from the American's feeble grasp. Checking the safety, he hurriedly pocketed it and waited patiently as the stranger's eyelids began to flutter. At last he darted forward and deftly caught the sick man's head as he finally slumped to the floor.

Piggott sighed sadly as he smelled scotch and felt the scarring beneath the bedraggled stranger's damp hair. He quickly reached across and grabbed the man's greasy kitbag, sliding it beneath him as a makeshift pillow.

Piggott looked down at the unconscious fugitive while he considered his options. Once he'd made his decision, he gently covered the anonymous intruder with his own overcoat before climbing back out of the freezing crypt.

3

Dr Wilhelm Werner waited for his eyes to adjust before setting off across the cavernous chamber. Low voltage security lights strung from the vaulted brick ceiling picked out a path through the subterranean archive of things best forgotten; stored safely out of sight and almost out of mind. That shadowy maze of filing cabinets and locked cupboards hinted at ancient heresies long since consigned to the dungeon's darkness, the dissident captives of reason's tyrannical inquisition.

Wilhelm's father had taught him that secrets were at their most potent when they had all but faded from memory, and he was certainly speaking from experience. Not for the first time did the young psychiatrist's mind dwell on the symbolic convergence of his current surroundings and occupation.

The sound of a steel door slamming shut rumbled through the underground archive, confirming that the Royal Marine sentry had returned to his post at street level, leaving Wilhelm alone with the prisoner. The guards and the hidden chamber's unique construction ensured there was little danger of any conversations being overheard, even by those *with* security clearance. The tiresome but necessary precautions taken to protect the invisible archive were hopefully sufficient to secure its arcane and dangerous ideas, but Wilhelm knew that no system was fool-proof.

The underground space had originally been dug by the Romans, so the story went, and had been enlarged, changed and redeveloped countless times over the centuries. In that respect it was very similar to the city above ground, which was currently undergoing yet another transformation, only this time brought about by Hitler's newest rockets of retribution.

Measuring about one hundred yards from end to end, the hidden archive was ideal for storing awkward materials and personnel. With a concealed entrance through a street cellar and access to London's extensive underground rail network, it was perfect for the discreet provision of electricity, communications and other services while remaining safe from air attack and the scrutiny of curious onlookers; both of this world and others.

Stepping between two damp-swelled filing cabinets, Wilhelm immediately turned right and followed the cavern's side wall, passing a series of arched alcoves whose original purpose was long forgotten. The doctor stopped about twenty yards from the final alcove in the row and studied the pool of light spilling out across the stone floor. Converted into a makeshift prison cell, the space was sealed by a row of hurriedly installed but nonetheless solid steel bars. The patient confined within was obviously still awake as a distorted shadow shifted occasionally, although there were no sounds of movement.

Wilhelm quickly glanced in the file he was carrying, straightened his tie and walked forward. He waited quietly while the prisoner finished writing, knowing that whomever he might end up talking to tonight, the patient didn't like to be disturbed. As always, the hair-tingling hum of high-voltage filled the air with a thunderstorm expectancy, the heavy cables coiled around the cell's interior walls being an unusual but very necessary precaution.

At length the prisoner stopped writing, clicked the top of his fountain pen and placed it neatly on the plain wooden desk which had been fitted inside the cell.

Wilhelm cleared his throat. "Good evening, Dr Hammond."

"Dr Werner." The man in the cell extricated his wheelchair from beneath a specially adapted desk and rolled slowly towards the steel bars.

Wilhelm took a step back to ensure he was well out of reach, mindful of the special security precautions required for this prisoner.

Dr Thomas Hammond stopped a foot short of the bars and rested his gloved hands in his lap. His customary well-groomed appearance had suffered greatly during his incarceration. Both his hair and beard were longer than usual and streaked with grey, whilst the army fatigues he wore could not have been a greater contrast to the tailored suits he'd previously sported. The prisoner removed his glasses and placed them in a leather case with some effort, as his left arm was twisted at an unnatural angle and trembled alarmingly as he lifted his hand to his face. "What time is it, Herr Doctor?" Hammond began polishing his glasses with the cuff of his shirt.

Wilhelm glanced at his watch. "A little after two in the morning."

Hammond snorted. "Boys like you should be in bed at this hour, not bothering grown-ups in the middle of their work."

The young psychiatrist walked a few paces across to an emergency door and picked up an old wooden chair resting beside it. Placing it a safe distance away from the bars he sat, produced a pencil, opened his bulky file and began to scribble. "It is certainly good to see you again, Herr Doctor Hammond." He turned a page and looked up, pencil poised. "How are you feeling?"

Hammond wheeled himself a little closer. "You come trotting down here in the wee small hours to ask me about my health?"

"I'm a doctor."

"Me too, and I don't give a damn about how *you* feel! In fact, I hope you're weary, depressed and questioning your place in this world."

Wilhelm smiled and scribbled again. "I'm very glad to hear the voice of the compassionate healer we know you to be. We've been worried about you of late, Herr Doctor. You've not been yourself at all. Tell me please, do you have headaches?"

"No."

"Fever?"

"No."

"Feeling thirsty?"

"No."

"Nightmares?"

"No, no nightmares. Apart from when I wake up to find myself buried alive in this electrified cesspool." He pointed at a plywood screen which hid the Elsan toilet the corner of his cell. "I can't stand that stench any longer! Is this what you people think I'm worth now? Is it?" The pitch of Hammond's voice rose with his anger. "There was a time when the whole intelligence community would fight for access to my work. Now I'm pissing in an oversized potty, damn it! I may as well have stayed in Dartmoor."

Wilhelm nodded sympathetically. "I understand your feelings, Dr Hammond, but I've already explained that we are below the level of the sewage system. If it is any help, I too must use such a commode when I'm down here." He leaned forward, pencil still ready. "You said you had no nightmares, but you *do* dream, yes?"

Hammond sighed with exasperation. "We both know that I'll be dreaming of many things at the moment. I was working in this field while you were still wearing short lederhosen."

"Quite so, Dr Hammond. So, what was your last dream and when did it occur?"

Hammond stared defiantly back at the younger psychiatrist. "Tell me about the Americans first. When will I speak to one of their people?"

Wilhelm sat back in his chair, making himself comfortable for the set-piece conversation. "As I have told you before, Herr Doctor, the Americans will not see you until you have been given a clean bill of health by us. Meaning that we are satisfied you have turned over all pertinent information regarding the Brotherhood's activities, and we confirm that you are medically fit. Even if that were to happen, you would then be screened extensively by their senior staff and your release sanctioned at the very highest levels of our government."

"*Our* government?" Hammond echoed sarcastically.

Wilhelm ignored him and continued. "To say that your emigration is dependent upon a number of conditions would be a great understatement. If you are to progress, then our first priority is your mental state. There are still many serious questions arising from the Cedarwood episode."

Hammond smoothed his hair back with his right hand. "I need to see a barber."

"I will speak to Major Clarke. I'm sure something can be arranged."

Hammond emitted a short bark of laughter. "If I know Clarke, he'd send Sweeney Todd and sell tickets to watch."

Wilhelm's face became stern. "Dr Hammond, you know I am a great admirer of your work, and I believe I am very privileged to be given the responsibility for your care. But your attempts to form a bond of friendship will not prevent me from carrying out my duty. No more delays, and no more attempts to change the subject. We both know that I will eventually learn anything you have been attempting to hide." The younger man stared hard at the prisoner. "Please tell me about the last dream you had, with as much detail as you can recall."

Hammond's head fell slightly and his face took on a thoughtful expression. "If you must know, I dreamt of Mr Digby."

Wilhelm scribbled. "The American? When was this?"

"Last night. We were here, just as you and I are now, and he was asking me about Jacob Small, again."

The younger psychiatrist pushed his wire-rimmed spectacles back onto his nose. "And how did you react when he asked you about this Sergeant Small?"

Hammond turned his chair and wheeled himself towards the collection of freehand sketches tied to the cables lining his cell. He reached forward and removed one, staring thoughtfully at the face between his gloved fingers. "I dreamt of telling him the same thing I've already told the rest of you. I have no explanation for Sergeant Small's advanced projection abilities, and I did not have time to explore what other latent talents the man may possess. I *had* thought that such characteristics could be identified and developed only within the handful of families we've already identified."

"The Brotherhood," confirmed Wilhelm softly.

The older man nodded. "Quite so. In fact your late father was the first outsider to ever attempt any systematic study of the relevant groups." Hammond turned his wheelchair and rolled back to the bars. "A pity his research didn't survive, but he must've spoken of it."

The younger doctor took a deep breath. "We are now straying into areas of speculation which are at best unwise. You may have enjoyed a high-level clearance whilst heading up

Section 12, but that was another life in more ways than one. Please confine yourself to answering my questions in as much detail as you can."

Hammond looked crestfallen, his desire for academic conversation thwarted. He huffed and rolled himself backwards, into the shadows of his electrified cell. "All I remember is that I told that scruffy little Yank I had no idea where Sergeant Small might be hiding, even if he *were* still alive, which I very much doubt."

"Why do you think Jacob Small is dead?"

Hammond tapped his left thigh and tugged at the knotted fatigues covering the stump of his leg. "No doubt Nero would've said that Providence has seen fit to preserve me for greater things. *I* barely survived that mess in Kent, and I doubt the Sergeant, for all his raw talent, enjoys quite the same place in the grand scheme of things. After all, mother nature does have a way of dealing with freaks, mistakes and unlikely occurrences."

Wilhelm closed the file and placed it carefully under his chair. "Dr Hammond, the dream to which you refer was a real occurrence. You spoke to Mr Digby in person regarding these matters about a week ago. Don't you remember?"

Hammond frowned, squinted and then shook his head. "Impossible. I remember it clearly and it was only a couple of days ago, or at least I think so, it's difficult to keep track of time down here."

Wilhelm patiently shook his head. "No Herr Doctor, I assure you it was a week ago. Do you mean to say you have no recollection of the time between Mr Digby's leaving and my arriving here now?"

Hammond's chin jutted forward defiantly as he wheeled himself forward once again. "Do not mistake me for a simpleton, Dr Werner. I know that the removal of any means to measure time is a standard procedure for debriefing and interrogation. It's all too easy to lose track of hours, minutes and even days in a place like this. I maintain that I dreamt of Mr Digby only two days ago, and I refuse to countenance any suggestion to the contrary. I'm not sure why I'm being treated this way but I've had enough. Do you hear me young man? I don't know what you're hoping to achieve by this ridiculously clumsy exercise, but it's finished now. I will speak only to Major Clarke in future." With that Hammond abruptly spun his wheelchair around and disappeared behind the plywood screen which covered his washing area and chemical toilet.

Knowing that the interview was over, Dr Werner stood and retrieved the file. "I had hoped to avoid using more direct methods to help you see the truth, but I fear that such an approach is now necessary." With that the German psychiatrist nodded in the direction of Hammond's cell and began threading his way back through the archive.

4

George Tooley turned up his collar and folded his arms in a futile gesture against the December drizzle. Rubble and glass clinked under his boots as he leaned through the charred doorway and glanced down the darkened street.

They were late, but they were all very able, although delays were always a danger during such high-risk operations. Not for the first time did Tooley's mind dwell on the similarities between professional criminality and military planning, and he often wondered how he might've fared as an army officer, had the course of his life not been predetermined by privilege and vested interests. Nevertheless, the war had bestowed unprecedented opportunities on intelligent and determined men like him, opportunities to undertake endeavours which might even help to shape the course of history. Unfortunately, such lofty ideals cost real money, and that universal rule applied to an underworld network just as much as to a bloated Establishment.

The rumble of an engine announced his crew's arrival as partially covered headlamps slowly materialised through the freezing fog. The large V6 echoed loudly down the narrow street of terraced houses, rattling the windows of those fortunate enough not to have been bombed out. That didn't matter though, for even if the sleepers were shaken from their beds to peer blearily through their windows, all they would see was an ambulance trundling over the uneven cobbles. They would naturally assume it was on some mission of mercy to help the sick and injured, not for a moment suspecting its true purpose.

The American built Chevrolet slowed to a crawl and stopped at the prearranged pickup point. It only took a second for

Tooley to step across the pavement and through the passenger door before the driver pulled away again, the rendezvous disguised from all but the most determined observers.

Once safely inside the cab, Tooley turned down his collar, unbuttoned his army coat and loosened the camouflage scarf round his neck. "Bleedin' heck, it's bloody freezing out there again."

"You're sure right about that, Guvnor. I hate this damn country in the winter, don't even love it in the summer neither. Say, I thought you were bringing the Bedford."

Tooley looked across at the ambulance driver, an ebony-skinned deserter called Duke. At least, that's what he *said* his name was, although his forged papers told a different tale. Duke was a classic case of downtrodden man rising to claim his birthright by any means necessary. He'd grown up somewhere in America's Deep South, although Tooley couldn't remember exactly where. Starved out by the Depression, Duke had migrated north to sweat in Detroit's stinking factories and shiver in the substandard houses clustered around them. No sooner had war broken out than he was drafted to labour for Uncle Sam, coerced into risking his life for a nation which had never given a damn about him in the first place. A lifetime of frustration had inevitably boiled over and he'd finally lost his cool in a Portsmouth pub. Duke didn't like to talk about it much, but his fate was sealed during a bust up with some other Yanks whom he always referred to as *"white trash."* In the heat of the moment he'd grabbed a Snowdrop's long baton and beaten the man senseless with it. Duke knew he was facing a long stretch in the stockade at the very least, so he'd taken to his heels and made for London, the only place where he stood at least *some* chance of disappearing. Tooley liked Duke. He was tough, smart, reliable and understood the true nature of the world in which he lived.

The Guvnor reached into his pocket for his cigarettes, offering one to Duke. "The Bedford's off on a supply run. Any bother with our new friend?"

Duke's teeth flashed white in the darkness as he took one of the smokes. "Man, I love the way those guys talk. So correct and all; it's almost a shame when their face all swells up so they can't talk right no more."

Tooley sparked up his old-fashioned lighter, quickly filling the cab with aromatic French smoke. "Nothing you couldn't handle though. I assume he's had his best interests explained to him."

"No sweat, Guvnor. Yellow and Frank are in the back making sure he don't get lonely and Sam's back at the house, just keeping an eye on things."

"Where's the wife?" Tooley asked sharply, only too aware of Sam's generally low opinion of women. Although he didn't really give a damn about the jeweller's wife, he knew better than to allow Sam's proclivities to jeopardise a carefully planned operation. Sam was useful to be sure, and the terrified jeweller in the back of the ambulance had to believe that his family was in real danger. On the other hand, if their hostage thought an assault on his wife was a foregone conclusion then he might decide there was nothing to lose. Tooley was confident that his firm could handle any situation, but experience had taught him just how unpredictable angry and frightened men could be.

Duke sparked up his own lighter and cracked open his window. "It's okay, She's visiting her mom with the kids so that's a bonus."

Tooley pointed down a side road. "Left here, then take the second right."

Duke swung the American ambulance none too gently down a wide street lined with large townhouses, built at a time when the plunderers of the world wore wigs and stockings rather than bowler hats. Perhaps a more honest age in many ways.

Duke took the designated turns as instructed, steering into a narrow lane bordered by high walls protecting the gardens of elegant and expensive Georgian houses.

"Stop here," instructed Tooley as they pulled up where the back street intersected a wider thoroughfare, this one lined with elegant shops rather than elegant houses. Copperplate calligraphy and European-sounding titles left visitors in no doubt as to the kind of goods on offer to those who could still find and afford any kind of luxury, despite the years of rationing and regulation.

Satisfied they were alone, Tooley motioned for Duke to pull the ambulance up on the pavement right beside the entrance to Forsyth and Co, fine jewellers. Both men winced as they bumped up the curb and rolled to a stop. Duke immediately killed the engine and lights while Tooley donned a tin hat and jumped out of the passenger door.

The Chevrolet's rear doors were open by the time Tooley reached them and his younger but much bigger brother jumped out, leaving Yellow in the back. Like the rest of the crew, big Frank Tooley and Yellow were kitted out in stolen St John's Ambulance uniforms.

Reliable and cool under pressure, Yellow had been christened not for cowardice, but for his thatch of uncontrollable and straw-like hair.

Tooley glanced into the ambulance, nodding approvingly as he saw their hostage secured to a stretcher, a blanket covering his body and face.

Big Frank joined his brother on the pavement while Yellow set about untying the ropes preventing a pair of six inch artillery shells from sliding around and causing untold damage in the back of the ambulance. Once freed, Yellow slid the first shell to the open door before Frank tipped it forward and hefted it onto his shoulder. He carefully placed it beside the reinforced shop door before returning for its twin.

Once the shells were in place, the Guvnor retrieved a metal ammunition box from the cab and removed two pre-cut lengths of fuse. He then carefully extracted two sticks of dynamite from their sawdust packing and quickly carried them across to the doorway. The percussion tips of each shell had already been removed, leaving a hole large enough to gently lower the blasting sticks into. Once ignited, they would act as detonators for the main Amatol charges packed inside.

Big Frank had already jumped back into the ambulance by the time Tooley had finished laying the fuses, twisting the ends together so they could be lit simultaneously.

With the body of the ambulance still hiding their activities, Tooley sparked his old lighter and watched a cloud of thick smoke billow upwards as the fuses began to burn. Knowing that speed was everything, Tooley banged on the side of the ambulance as he ran into the driver's door.

Duke was already putting the vehicle into gear as Tooley yanked open the passenger door and leapt inside. A quick glance at the plume of smoke in the wing mirror confirmed that the fuses were well alight and burning steadily. "Just keep turning left and take it round the block. It'll blow any second."

Duke grinned and stamped on the accelerator. They just had time to turn at the first junction before the ground shook and a roar echoed through the genteel streets of Mayfair. The driver pushed his foot to the floor and the heavy vehicle slewed around the next two corners at speed, slowing as they approached the final turn of the square.

Tooley grinned and thumped Duke's shoulder when he saw that the road was littered with debris as they approached. Steering a little more cautiously, the ambulance pulled up outside Forsyth & Co's now demolished shop front once more.

Tooley nodded his approval, satisfied the blast had caused enough damage to ensure that confusion reigned for at least the next few minutes, and probably longer. His smile broadened when he realised that the explosion had set fire to the blackout curtains covering the windows above the shop. Even better, as a serious blaze would further help to obscure their movements.

As always, Duke stayed in the driver's seat while Tooley quickly jumped out of the cab and ran to the back of the ambulance again. The moment the rear doors were open, Big Frank and Yellow picked up a specially adapted stretcher and quickly manhandled Forsyth & Co's tightly trussed proprietor into his own shop. Kicking the remnants of metal grilles aside and ignoring the empty display cases, Tooley's men carried the stretcher straight into the back room, the pile of concealing blankets crying out with muffled pain as they dropped the stretcher on the ground.

All three men removed their tin hats and donned black balaclavas before the top blanket was snatched away, at last revealing the terrified jeweller. Yellow produced a battery torch and shone it around the smoke-filled room, quickly locating the steel safe in the corner.

Tooley pulled his Colt from his pocket and jammed it hard under the trembling prisoner's chin. Pausing for effect, he fished in his other pocket and produced his American switchblade, allowing it to glint in the wavering torchlight before letting his hostage feel cold steel as he sliced through the stifling gag.

For a moment the two men stared at each other before Tooley spoke. "All right mate, you know what we want so no messing about. Just get the safe open and nobody needs to get hurt, not you *or* your little ones. We know where they are."

"You bloody swine, why did you have to destroy my shop? You know I have the keys..." The proprietor's protestations were cut short as Tooley struck him across the cheek with the pistol's barrel, before pushing its muzzle hard into the man's temple. "You can let *me* worry about the strategy. Just do as I say while you still can." Without waiting for a response, Tooley heaved the man over and swiftly cut the ropes binding his wrists and ankles.

Clutching his throbbing face, the dishevelled shopkeeper clambered to his feet and weaved across the darkened room.

"Hurry up! We ain't window shopping here." Tooley glanced out through the ruined entrance and saw the first shapes of curious onlookers through the haze of smoke and dust. He jerked a thumb towards the door. "Clear a path, number Five. You know what to do."

Big Frank grinned as he turned his back to the hostage and removed his balaclava. "No problem, number One." He quickly pulled his gas mask from his satchel and stretched it over his head, replaced his tin hat and straightened his ambulance uniform. His voice was muffled by the thick rubber as he moved to the front of the shop and took charge of the growing group of onlookers. "Please keep the gangway clear folks. We've got an injured man in here."

Having no reason to think something amiss, the small group of pyjama-clad neighbours dutifully separated to clear a path to the ambulance.

Tooley pushed the dazed proprietor aside as he finally opened the steel door. "See, that beats having to blast it." He quickly fished in his pocket, produced a black drawstring bag and emptied the safe's sparse harvest into it. A few sovereigns, a couple of modest trays of diamond rings and a small box of gold scrap. He then turned to the frightened prisoner and jammed his pistol against the man's forehead to emphasise his next demand. "Okay Grandad, now for the moolah, and hurry up."

The shaking jeweller squeezed his eyes tight shut and shook his head. "No cash here. It goes in the bank each afternoon. That's all there is, honest. If you ever bothered to read the papers you'd know there are limits to what I can hold."

Tooley sighed and struggled to keep his patience. "Look, just give us the gold under the counter and we won't have to break up the place any more than we already have. Don't mess about, mate. You know we're serious, so just do what's good for you and your family."

"That's all there is, I swear."

Tooley shook his head and rolled his eyes before viciously back-handing the man across the temple with the butt of his pistol. The proprietor dropped soundlessly into a heap on the floor as Tooley motioned to Yellow. "Get him back on that stretcher and make sure he keeps quiet."

Yellow nodded and rolled the unconscious man back onto the stretcher before removing his own balaclava and donning his gas mask.

Tooley glanced towards the street as he heard the sound of a distant alarm bell. Could be fire brigade or police, although he hoped for the former.

Knowing that time was rapidly running out, Tooley quickly put on his own gas mask and left the back room. Crouching beneath a shattered display case, he opened the storage cupboards below and felt the floor beneath the counter. His fingers soon located a smooth hole drilled in the uncovered boards. Hooking his finger through the hole, he lifted the board to reveal a small darkened space beneath. Tooley grinned behind his mask as he reached inside and heaved out the first of two bulky drawstring bags, much like the one he'd brought with him. "Damn you, Reverend. If you don't have something of the Devil in you then I'm a Dutchman." He quickly pulled the second bag out of its hiding place, and with some difficulty carried them both into the back room.

Tooley placed all three bags on the stretcher, nestling them neatly between the unconscious jeweller's calves before pulling the blanket back over the prone man. With the jeweller's face hidden and both ambulance men in gas masks the illusion was complete, and Tooley nodded briefly to Yellow before they hefted the stretcher out through the shop and onto the pavement.

A hush fell over the small crowd as the sombre rescuers carried the jeweller's body from the shop, his mortal remains respectfully covered. Yellow, who was a Yank himself, stayed silent and let George do the talking as they carefully lifted the stretcher into the waiting ambulance. "Daft old bugger. Don't know what he was doing here in the first place. He should've been home in bed. These bloody rockets are a dishonourable way to fight a war. There's no warning for *anyone*; old men, women, children. It just ain't right." Tooley shook his head sadly as he beckoned Big Frank into the back of the ambulance before rapping on the driver's partition.

Duke immediately started the engine and slowly bumped the heavy vehicle off the curb, just in time to see the hooded lights of an approaching fire engine appear at the end of the street. The clamouring warning bell rose to a crescendo before fading as it passed by the ambulance, both drivers exchanging grim nods of solidarity.

Inside the ambulance, Tooley quickly whipped back the blanket and dragged the heavy bags off the stretcher as the jeweller began to groan.

Big Frank grabbed the blanket and held it tight over the confused hostage, pinning him down and obscuring his vision as George delved into one of the larger bags and retrieved a handful of gold sovereigns. He playfully poked the semiconscious man in the thigh. "You're a naughty boy. What would the Treasury say if they'd gotten wind of this lot? You must know that hoarding's a serious offence, you greedy bugger." He tutted reprovingly. "You'd have got quite a stretch for this I'll bet, so it looks like we've done you a favour, me old mate. Don't worry, we'll keep the gold and you can go back to your kids, safe in the knowledge that they'll not be deprived of their honourable, hardworking dad; unless his memory gets a little too sharp." He rapped on the driver's partition again.

Yellow chuckled as he opened the rear doors.

The ambulance rounded the corner of a quiet residential street and made the briefest of stops. The vehicle had barely come to a halt before Big Frank picked up one end of the stretcher and tipped the now penniless proprietor onto the freezing wet road.

Tooley rapped on the partition once more and Yellow pulled the rear doors shut as the rogue ambulance vanished into the freezing night.

5

With a frustrating sense of familiarity, Sergeant Jacob Small of the Fourth Infantry awoke only to realise that he was actually still asleep. He'd become increasingly fearful of "jumping out" since the Cedarwood episode; and scotch, or gin, had become pivotal in his struggle to keep body and soul; spirit, or whatever-the-hell-else you wanted to call it bound together in the same place. A liberal helping of black market booze remained his preferred remedy for such spontaneous nocturnal wanderings, but a near miss with Pete Finch's henchmen and a delirious fever had disrupted his routine.

He sighed - if it were possible to sigh without lungs - and looked around to get his bearings. Wherever in the world his disembodied consciousness had jumped to, it wasn't any place he immediately recognised.

Having accrued some experience of that rare, intangible state of being, he'd learned that his overriding concern was to remain calm. Waking up lost in the "real" world was bad enough, but in that gently sparkling replica of the material realm it was especially unsettling, and nothing short of terrifying if you were just a kid. Memories of a forgotten child's incorporeal panic rushed unbidden to the forefront of Jake's mind, and he fought to stay focused on the present as he suddenly recalled "waking up" in the servant's quarters; and then there was that frightening and confusing night in the gardener's lodge when he'd strayed much further afield than usual.

Jake mentally dug in his heels and reigned in the recollections stampeding through his consciousness. *Servant's quarters? Gardener's lodge? Wise up, shaky Jakey. The only servants at St Alphonsus were us kids.*

It was happening again, and this time his obviously false past was painted in far greater detail than ever before. Objectively impossible and yet completely convincing recollections from a different life, a stranger's history, had somehow entwined themselves around the limbs and branches of Jake's own consciousness like a psychic bindweed. He tried to dismiss the nagging worry that they might one day overwhelm the weakened structure of his own past and replace it with an altogether different and alien history, like a metaphysical editor busily rewriting his most intimate, unspoken memoirs.

When you can't trust anything else, trust your own senses. Concentrate on what is right in front of you. The wise words of an insane man suddenly replayed themselves inside Jake's head. Peter van Cortlandt might be dead, but that fact did little to stop the old man's memories reaching out from the abyss and into the magical glowing world of Jake's own projected consciousness.

He began reciting a hastily devised and rather clumsy mantra in his mind. *My name is Sergeant Jacob Small, assuming I haven't been court martialled by now. I was born in Detroit and lived at the St Alphonsus orphanage. Never had servants, or gardeners or fine silverware or an impressive private library. That couldn't have been me. Those memories belong to a dead Dutchman, and God only knows who else.*

Satisfied that for the moment he'd maintained a firm grip on his sense of self, Jake made systematic mental survey of his surroundings. As he took stock, he figured he must've passed out from fever rather than bootleg booze. After all, he'd only been thinking half-straight when he'd staggered into that musty old crypt to shelter from the cold, hoping that the fat smuggler's men wouldn't think to look for him there. Whorehouses and gambling dens were more to their taste, and there were plenty of those to search in London.

Jake vaguely recalled meeting someone, a stranger, maybe a priest, as he studied what he assumed was a room inside the shattered church above the crypt. The small pointed doorway, stone walls and clutter of threadbare furniture all gently pulsed with a familiar ghostly glow, confirming that his consciousness had indeed crossed over to the astral plane. At least that was what some occultists called that inexplicable facsimile of the physical world, painted by an insane artist who worked only in semi-luminous shades.

A knot formed in Jake's stomach - if he actually had one in this state - as he turned to see an old man bent over a narrow cot in the corner of the tired room. The stranger's form was suffused by a light green aura tinged with yellow, radiating out to merge with the angry red glow surrounding a potbellied stove skulking in the corner. The heat from the glowing coals was plainly visible in this version of reality, where it was expressed as just another frequency within that endless spectrum of universal energy.

Jake tried to keep calm as he saw there was no trace of life emanating from his own physical shell as it lay helpless on the cot. He quickly consoled himself by speculating that his body's weakened energies were obscured by the brighter broadcasts of the so-called priest and his glowering stove.

He turned away, unaccustomed to seeing his corporeal form in such a vulnerable state, yet also thankful to be free from the anguish and restriction of ill health, at least for a while. Silent and invisible on his parallel plane, Jake could enjoy a welcome respite from the agonies of the flesh, and he felt a sudden pang of pity for the multitude of suffering souls trapped inside their own prisons of pain.

While taking stock of his situation, Jake soon realised that he knew nothing about his mysterious benefactor, aside from the fact his name was Piggott, or so he'd said. There was no evidence to suggest the old man was aware of Jake's more valuable talents, although he knew full well that things were seldom how they seemed. Right now he was ideally placed to explore the area undetected, and he would be foolish indeed not to exploit that considerable advantage. Some survival rules transferred easily from the tangible to the more ethereal realms, and a methodical survey of unknown terrain was never time wasted.

Deciding to start outside the building and work his way back in, Jake made for the door. He couldn't help smiling as he stretched out his glowing ghostly non-hands, complete with magically restored little finger. It did feel good to be back in control for a while, although he was not so naive as to believe he was impregnable inside - or maybe that was outside - within this shining replica of the physical plane. His experiences at Section 12 had revealed a new world of hitherto unimagined dangers, all eager to ensnare an inexperienced Projector.

An electric tingling sensation crawled rapidly up his arms as he pushed against the door, moving slowly through the solid barrier and out into the freezing night. After a couple of dark and noisy seconds, Jake found himself looking despondently around the mist-shrouded churchyard outside. If anything, this place was even *more* depressing on the astral plane than it was on the physical. It was a truly dead place, a lonely place, a dark pool of nothingness amid the sagging workshops and cheerless dwellings that dripped and shivered in the chill river fog. The area had been pummelled repeatedly these past years, first by the Blitz and now by the immovable edifice of a grinding bureaucracy. House after house had been hurriedly boarded up, their brick and tile lives extinguished by bomb blasts or fire as the winds of war had howled gleefully through this neighbourhood. Refugees, builders and looters had emptied out those dead dwellings like an army of ants busily stripping the carcass of an already shattered community. Nearly everyone was gone now, leaving Jake to pass silently through the urban wilderness; a lonely spirit stranded between this world and the next, challenged only by stray dogs and meths-addled lunatics.

Hoping to get his bearings within the wider neighbourhood, Jake left those silent, soulless graves behind and drifted along an equally silent street of shattered houses, like a wraith lost in the freezing mist. Mounds of broken rubble glowed feebly in his wake, as though the city itself were dying, battered first by the bombers using the river as a landmark, and now by the Reich's supersonic weapons of indiscriminate death.

Jake was just thinking about retracing his steps when he rounded a corner and stopped dead in his tracks, staring open-mouthed - if he really *had* a mouth - at the unexpected scene of otherworldly devastation laid out before him.

Now reduced to a rotting and soulless corpse of jutting stone, the once proud church had stood strong for centuries until a V2 had descended from the heavens to wrench one whole side off the building, like the visitation of an angry angel. In an instant that beacon of hope in the darkness had been transformed into just another broken piece of a dying history. Just one ruin among the hundreds slowly shifting and collapsing in the freezing fog with no special treatment, no pardon and no sanctuary.

Although he couldn't quite put his finger on why, Jake found the violation of *this* church even more poignant than the one in which his comatose body patiently awaited his return. At least there the dead still dozed fitfully in their brick tombs, whereas here they'd been shaken from the grave by an explosion which had carved a huge water-filled crater right beside the broken building. The supersonic weapon had also scorched a mighty and venerable oak which had stood in silent vigil over the departed since the church's first foundation stone was cut. The twisted limbs exposed to the blast were dead, charred and blackened in that white-hot moment of detonation; and yet the sheltered side still glowed with dormant, defiant life as the injured tree slumbered on in the winter mist.

Jake turned away to retrace his steps, his heart heavy at the sight of the devastated church with its violated tombs, despite the fact he hadn't attended any sort of service in years. He hadn't travelled more than a few yards before his meditations on loneliness and destruction were interrupted by an imposing headstone looming out of the freezing fog. He wasn't so much startled by the time-weathered monument itself as by the tall, slim figure standing casually beside it. Were it not for his previous experience, Jake might've assumed the featureless silhouette he stared at was merely a lost spirit, dislodged from its physical home to wander aimlessly between worlds, a forlorn soul drifting aimlessly through winter's gloom. However, Jake had only once encountered a genuine spirit of the dead, and it had looked *nothing* like the figure he now confronted. This was something else.

The solid black shadow remained as still as a carved angel guarding an ancient tomb, and so Jake froze too. For a moment it seemed that the only movement in the entire world was the languid swirling of the icy mist between them.

Jake tensed, ready to flee as he remembered that he'd had very few out-of-body interactions with other Projectors, and none of them had ended well. He was just gathering his mental faculties to make a run for it - if running was the correct description - when the unknown observer moved first, suddenly darting away from the startled American rather than closing in to attack as he'd feared.

The fleeing figure passed soundlessly over the low wall surrounding the churchyard and vanished into a narrow, cratered street, heading down towards the river.

Jake jumped, puzzled by the unexpected development as it was normally *he* who did the running in such circumstances. He looked down at the ethereal approximation of his physical form, now well-defined and glowing with an inner effervescence he found surprising given his current corporeal state.

This was easily the longest and furthest Projection Jake had performed since the Cedarwood debacle, and it seemed as though his disembodied consciousness had grown significantly stronger of its own accord in the meantime. He guessed that his increased mental presence probably had a lot to do with a crazy doctor and an even crazier Dutchman. Maybe the fleeing shadow saw him as a threat, an insatiable glowing Shade stalking this all-too-real dreamworld, always eager to devour weak Projectors and the nearly-dead.

It felt intoxicating, inspiring and empowering to be feared on this parallel plane rather than being *in* fear, and so Jake followed a time-honoured tradition of misplaced confidence and set off in pursuit.

6

Throughout the months of living hand-to-mouth in a foreign land, Jake had resisted the promise of limitless freedom this hidden dimension appeared to offer the wide-eyed and inexperienced explorer. He was seasoned enough to have tasted some of the bitter lessons the remote viewer's parallel world was eager to serve up to the unwary. This was no egalitarian realm of mystical enlightenment, for the travellers sneaking through reality's back door always brought their own worldly desires, drives and deceptions with them.

Jake was naturally apprehensive, but he knew he couldn't just let the featureless stranger slip away. He'd been spotted by a Projector whose identity was unknown, and that was worrying. Having successfully evaded both the British and American authorities since the summer, he'd just been seen by someone who'd suddenly left in one hell of a hurry. Jake needed to know more for the sake of his own safety.

At first it was hard to gain momentum as he felt his disembodied feet sinking into the glowing ground beneath him. A focus of will and a few determined strides reversed that inertia, and the pliable earth suddenly launched him forward like a giant trampoline. In just a few strides he'd cleared the graveyard wall, while his next step launched him headlong down another steep and ruined street. The sensation of running downhill felt like a continuous controlled fall as the secret luminescent world flashed by in a dizzying blur.

Jake saw the dark shimmering expanse of the Thames rising fast to meet him as he silently sped past an anti-aircraft emplacement, and then a checkpoint guarding the iconic Tower Bridge.

Up ahead, Jake's quarry was already across the river and vanishing into a maze of streets and grandiose buildings that were the arteries and chambers of London's commercial heart.

As Jake reached the far side of the river he pushed still harder against the more solid feeling pavement, his non-feet barely touching down as he flashed past the famous Tower of London. By his reckoning their destination was somewhere in the City itself, or maybe the more glamorous streets of the West End. Jake had gotten to know the major centres of London fairly well, moving unnoticed among the bustle of his countrymen travelling to and from the Continent. As he was undoubtedly listed as a deserter, Jake had quickly realised the truth of the old proverb regarding trees in forests. Despite his unearthly talents he'd still needed money and somewhere to sleep if he was to survive "on the trot" as the Brits called it. With hindsight, his rapid transition from rising star to underworld pariah was entirely predictable. His own experience of men and money should've counselled against falling in with the likes of card sharps and other "businessmen," but the pockets of such unscrupulous souls were always deep and ready cash was what he needed most of all.

Jake quickly realised that he'd lost sight of the fleeing figure as he rounded a corner at a dizzying speed. He took another leap of nearly fifty yards and concentrated on his landing, planting his ethereal feet firmly on the deserted road and pitching himself forward, sliding along mist slicked tarmac before bumping gently to a halt against white-painted kerbstones. It wasn't the most elegant method of stopping quickly but it was the most efficient he'd yet discovered, and he was out of practice.

Jake rapidly stood, thought about dusting himself down and then remembered that such an idea was meaningless in this place. Instead he looked around, trying to get his bearings as he didn't recognise the street in which he'd landed. He cursed his lack of concentration for allowing the faceless Projector to elude him, knowing that by now the shady stranger could be anywhere, or perhaps even nowhere. Jake turned around and quickly retraced his steps to the last place he remembered seeing the elusive traveller. As expected, the painfully shy shadow was long gone.

Knowing it was probably too late but refusing to give up entirely, Jake took a more careful look at his surroundings in case he was back around these parts someday soon. After all, his mysterious fellow traveller might live or "work" just around the corner somewhere.

On closer inspection it was obvious that the area had survived the worst of the Nazi's aerial attacks, nevertheless Jake could see some damaged roofs and boarded windows nearby, the tell-tale fingerprints of explosive blasts.

Jake slowly made his way along the pavement, almost mesmerised by the tiny shards of glass stubbornly lodged between the paving slabs. They seemed to somehow soak up the weak light emitted by the ethereal world and magnify it, throwing it back into the atmosphere in a minute but intricate display of multi-coloured rays which disappointingly faded as he passed out of the blast area.

Finally accepting that he'd lost his astral companion completely, Jake had at least managed to learn he was in a neighbourhood called High Holborn. Now knowing the name of his location but still no wiser as to where he actually *was*, he drifted on, looking for some familiar landmark. He'd been moving for less than a minute before he stopped dead at the mouth of an insignificant side street. Glancing down that narrow alleyway, he could see the tell-tale glow of a living human being.

Curious as to who might be out and about at such a late hour, Jake drifted down the claustrophobic alley like a moth drawn to the glow of a candle. Rounding a corner, he was surprised to see a heated argument taking place in the darkened side street. Invisible and unnoticed he drifted closer, trying to understand the unexpected altercation.

A civilian, who seemed to be in his early thirties, remonstrated furiously with a policeman and two large soldiers who flatly refused to grant him entry to an unremarkable looking steel door.

Jake was struck by a sudden feeling of déjà vu as he noticed that the soldiers looked too muscular and hard-faced to be run-of-the-mill conscripts, and the cop was no flabby night watchman either. He drifted closer, as much to bathe in the warm glow of life itself as to hear the heated and yet oddly distant-sounding conversation.

The rules governing Jake's parallel dimension decreed that physical sounds were always dulled, and all living things produced some kind of aura which spilled out into the surrounding atmosphere. Although this outflowing of energy was invisible on the physical plane, the disembodied deserter could discern every facet of its fluxing and restless beauty. Although the swirling colours were wonderful to behold and intoxicating to imbibe, the unfolding exchange in the alley was also an uncomfortable reminder of other men who'd recently departed the physical plane, never to return. Those darker thoughts ushered in an unexpected tide of hopeless melancholy, and Jake tried hard not to dwell on the memory of such beauteous life dispersing into nothing like smoke in the wind.

Still arguing furiously, the unknown civilian glowed an angry red as he pointed to his identity card, while the policeman, stuttering orange, red and blue, explained wearily that there had been a change and his name was no longer on the list. If the man had a problem he'd have to take it up with his head of section. And no, it made no difference that his head of section was on the other side of that same steel door. And no, neither the policeman nor the soldiers were about to start passing messages from unauthorised persons. And yes, perhaps it *was* just a clerical error, but he wasn't authorised to make such a decision.

As he struggled to follow the muffled argument, Jake suddenly realised it was becoming harder and harder to hear what was actually being said. The already distant debate was slowly being swamped beneath a background hum of new, indistinct and disembodied voices whispering from every conceivable direction, yet offering no clue as to their point of origin.

Although he was a long way from his physical form, Jake felt his heart begin to race as the invisible crowd seemed to close in, becoming ever more impatient as they clustered around him. Jake had heard those impossible sounds before, far away in a now ruined French country house, and that chilling recollection stirred up some very unpleasant mental sediment.

Alarmed by the unexpected turn of events, Jake glanced around in an attempt to identify the invisible crowd. It was only then that he spotted the self-same disembodied shadow he'd been pursuing just minutes before; only now it stood motionless in a dark corner not six feet behind one of the increasingly impatient soldiers. Jake had a hunch that his fellow Projector was doing exactly the same thing as he was by drinking in energy and strength from the living.

The door guard shivered and hunched his shoulders, rolling his arms in their sockets as the solid silhouette abruptly ended its feast and boldly stepped straight *through* him as though it were making a point.

Jake got the message and backed away as the sentient shadow somehow walked and oozed forward like a pool of spilled ink. Although he'd never witnessed that manner of movement before, Jake was intuitive enough to know when he was confronted by a highly advanced Sensitive, or worse. The last time he'd encountered a being so at home in the astral realm it had cost him his life, or so he'd been told.

Jake felt his feet burn and tingle as that projected shadow unexpectedly flattened itself to the pavement and stretched out beneath him. He felt a cold stab of fear as particles from his own ethereal body began breaking away, to be swallowed up by his impossibly lightless adversary. It looked like this astral parasite wasn't fussy either, as the energies of the arguing group also began draining into that otherworldly predator's featureless form.

Having accepted he'd just made a big mistake by chasing down a patently more powerful Projector, Jake had only a moment to consider his options. They were few. Whoever or whatever this thing was, Jake knew he might escape by simply returning to his physical form, but he ran the risk of being followed and revealing his earthly identity; not good if this Sensitive was working with authorities. He could stand and fight, but he'd never once triumphed in any non-physical encounter. So that left only retreat, and a rapid one at that.

Ignoring a sudden wave of drowsy light-headedness, Jake gritted his non-existent teeth and dragged himself towards the open but well protected door, causing the implacable policeman to lose his place mid-sentence as he brushed by.

A galvanised staircase glittered and shifted like oil-covered ice as it swept down in a wide arc, plunging into unknown regions far beneath London's streets. For a moment Jake hesitated. Like every other Yank in London, he'd heard about the purpose-built shelters where scores of civilians hid from Hitler's supersonic rockets and the bitter winter cold. He'd also heard they were very deep underground, and previous experience at Cedarwood House had taught him that underground spaces were also an important layer of defence against ethereal snoopers just like him.

A blistering buzz of a hostile energy climbing rapidly past his knees finally resolved the dilemma, and Jake clumsily set off down the stairs. The steep spiral made it difficult to remain upright and created the strange sensation of both falling and flying simultaneously. After several full revolutions Jake had no idea how deep underground he was, and as he plummeted further into the earth his mind sank also, dredging up long buried memories of another, long-forgotten staircase. This one was stone, leading to an extensive wine cellar, and there was something about a bird. With a sudden mental leap in time Jake recalled a second, much more recent cellar, although this one promised not fine vintage but only death, intrigue and half-truths.

Get a grip, Jake! You never owned any goddam wine cellar. The only cellar you ever saw was that prison block at Cedarwood. You're Sergeant Jacob Small of the Fourth Infantry, from Detroit. Now hunted and in hiding because of what you are, not because of what you've done.

Having herded his misplaced memories back into line, Jake found himself staring down a gloomy cylindrical corridor at the bottom of the staircase. A quick glance behind reminded him that there was no turning back as his pursuer swooped around the final bend, half clinging to the concrete wall like a lizard on a cliff face.

Within a matter of seconds Jake's status had plummeted from Prince of the Night to frightened prey, scurrying underground to escape a pursuer he couldn't even identify as fully human. Trapped far from the refuge of his own physical form, Jake made a mental note not to be so cocky in future, if he *had* any kind of future.

The tunnel's non-descript concrete walls were transformed into polished mirrors of glassy granules as Jake raced towards the gas-proof door at the far end. Knowing that the mysterious shadow was hot on his heels, Jake stretched out his glowing non-arms and dived forward, his fingers tingling as they pushed through that dense metal obstruction. The door was thicker than he'd anticipated, and for a moment he feared he'd be tossed back into the corridor like repelled magnet.

Slowing rapidly as though he were diving into molasses, Jake instinctively kicked his legs like a swimmer, watching the door's steel surface glitter and dance for a moment before pushing through the solid barrier and falling face down into the room beyond.

The plain quarry tiles beneath him revived another unpleasant memory of that converted cellar in Kent, a bona fide memory of his very own, and one which he quickly pushed to the back of his mind as he clambered to his feet.

As Jake observed the strange tubular chamber beyond the door, his first thought was of some hidden Morlock settlement, plucked straight from pages of HG Wells. His second thought was that wherever he'd ended up, it *wouldn't* be featuring on any liaison officer's tour of London's Underground system.

7

Dr Hammond scowled suspiciously as Wilhelm unlocked the door to his cell. "What's this, the last walk or a stay of execution?"

Wilhelm beckoned the prisoner out. "Actually it's neither of those things, Herr Doctor, but I'm afraid I do bring bad news."

The prisoner wheeled himself forward, glancing around nervously as he left the converted alcove. "I don't want to hear bad news at the moment. I'm quite depressed, what with living in damp, squalor and filth." He pointed at the chemical toilet with his good arm.

Wilhelm sat on his own chair and extracted several sheets of paper from the large file he carried. "Please come into the light," he said as he rearranged the papers in his hand.

Hammond rolled towards the younger psychiatrist. "I don't suppose that's my knighthood."

Once Hammond had positioned himself, Wilhelm moved his own chair a little. "It's nothing personal, but you know that physical contact is strictly forbidden, and with good reason."

Hammond's grey-streaked beard twitched as he smiled. "Frightened I might dig up some nasty little secret?"

Now it was Wilhelm's turn to scowl. "Having endured your sordid biography, it is not *I* who should be concerned about secrets." He held out one of the sheets. "Do you recognise this?"

The man in the wheelchair snatched the creased paper from Wilhelm before slumping back and staring morosely at the freehand sketch. "Looks like a highwayman in a gibbet, probably drawn by some over-imaginative schoolboy."

Wilhelm fished his notebook from his pocket. "You don't recognise the artist's work?"

Hammond sighed wearily. "If you wish to investigate my attitude towards death and mortality you have a strange way of going about it. Why don't you just ask me?"

Wilhelm scribbled briefly and replaced the notebook before staring directly at the one-legged prisoner. "Because on any given day, there's no telling whose answer I may hear."

Hammond leaned back and studied the archive's vaulted ceiling. "Isn't it fascinating how everything ends up underground. The remains of our greatest civilisations all crumble and sink beneath the earth sooner or later. I suppose it's fitting that our greatest monuments should rise and flourish, only to wither and fall, just like the men who made them." He meaningfully returned the younger man's gaze. "It's probably that same natural law which makes the idea of being buried alive so terrifying. You see, it's not merely a dark and stifling end, it's a subversion of nature's design, to spend one's final moments within the bowels of the earth; the living trapped among the dead." He thrust the grisly sketch back towards Wilhelm. "You're not experienced enough to deal with me. Nobody is."

The younger man ignored the offered drawing and continued. "When did you say you dreamt of Mr Digby?"

Hammond made no attempt to disguise the exasperation in his voice. "A memory test now? Very well, it was no more than three days ago. One thing I *have* forgotten is how often I've reminded you that it's difficult to keep track of time down here, not that you've seen fit to furnish me with clock or calendar."

"*You* drew this, last night." Said Wilhelm without missing a beat.

Hammond frowned and looked at the sketch once again. "I think perhaps I had a dream about this. It's difficult to remember, more of an impression really." He looked back at Wilhelm. "What is the object of this exercise?"

Wilhelm retrieved his notebook once more. "What do you know of Shades?"

"According to the Greeks, they were the tortured souls of the departed who wandered the underworld." Hammond glanced around the underground archive. "I'm beginning to understand what a hopeless, empty and melancholy existence they represent. Trapped in the darkness and divorced from the natural cycle of days and the seasons." He shook his head sadly.

If Wilhelm was losing patience, his voice betrayed none of it. "Tell me about Projekt Schatten."

A quick hiss of laughter escaped Hammond's lips before he composed himself. "Is this some kind of joke?"

Wilhelm's pitch, timing and delivery did not change one iota. "Tell me about Projekt Schatten."

Hammond's usually dour face broke into a wide smile and he struggled to control his chuckling, his left arm twitching more violently than usual. "Fetch me a medium and a Ouija board and I'll do my best for you. Stryker and the rest are all dead, buried, silent. Trapped underground just like us." He slumped back into a brooding silence.

Wilhelm pointed at the drawing clasped between the doctor's fingers. "Why don't you take your gloves off?"

Hammond shook his head.

"Why not?" Asked Wilhelm patiently. "I give you my word that only you and I have touched that piece of paper." A smile crept across his lips. "Who knows, perhaps you'll learn some of my secrets after all."

The man in the wheelchair gripped the crumpled sheet of paper tightly, rubbing it between his finger and thumb. "My abilities are well documented, and I think we're beyond parlour tricks now."

Wilhelm removed his glasses and polished them on the sleeve of his white coat. "It would help your case greatly if you just cooperated, rather than constantly obfuscating."

Hammond's voice took on a haughty tone. "My *case?* You make it sound as though I'm on trial."

Wilhelm's tone became as grave as Hammond's was self-righteous. "And so you are, although you are surely not so naive as to think you will ever see the inside of a courtroom?"

Hammond dropped the sketch on the damp flagstones and released the brake on his chair. "I'm tired of playing your games, young man. You may have been a keen student, but you're no match for your father. *He* understood loyalty, compassion and the things unseen."

Wilhelm watched Hammond struggling to wheel himself back to his cage. "The things unseen? Honestly, such sentimental nonsense from a supposedly rational scientist. If I didn't know better I'd say that was Peter van Cortlandt talking." The younger man shook his head and tutted. "Metaphysics from the great psychiatrist. Whatever next? Tell me, Herr Dr Hammond, when did you begin to realise that your dry medical studies were only the beginning of your journey?"

Hammond stopped and clumsily turned his chair around. "What are you saying, you young pup?"

Wilhelm rose and recovered the crumpled drawing from the floor. "I'm saying that you seem to have become more...open minded since your time at Section 12. Perhaps van Cortlandt's influence was greater than you thought, especially as you began to learn what he and Stryker were really capable of." He held up the sketch to illustrate his point. "Please help us."

"Help you with what?"

"As far as we know, you're one of the last living Sensitives. The remnants of the great lines are gone, the Brotherhood is defunct and their knowledge has all but vanished with them."

Hammond looked around the vaulted chamber. If I'm so important, as you claim, why am I being held prisoner?"

"Do not make the mistake of thinking I'm a fool just because I'm a younger man." Wilhelm tapped his finger on the paper to emphasise his point. "You said you only met Colonel Stryker twice."

"That's right. Once in the guest house, and then at Marsh Pendleton, where he died."

Wilhelm moved his chair and sat directly opposite Hammond. "I assume you would not have discussed the details of Section 12's work with him."

Hammond bristled. "Just what are you implying? It was van Cortlandt's plan to bring him over, not mine."

"But you cooperated." Countered Wilhelm sharply.

The older man nodded slowly. "As you said, the Brotherhood is scattered if not dead, and Nero just couldn't hold on until I was ready. He'd already suffered a great deal and he'd survived far beyond even *his* expected lifespan. By sheer force of will it seems."

"Yes, I know." Said Wilhelm quietly.

Hammond continued. "It was my duty to help the Old Man, and Stryker was his rightful heir. Besides, the Colonel would not exactly have been himself after the Transition. That's the whole point of it."

Wilhelm glanced down at the macabre drawing and then back at the prisoner. "You still have not grasped the obvious problem, the one which is staring you in the face."

"Now you're starting to sound like Nero," Hammond quipped.

"If only," said Wilhelm with a wry smile. "I know you're afraid. God knows I would be, but you must face the truth. If you don't cooperate I believe there's a good chance that you'll go to sleep one night and never wake up. Dr Thomas Hammond will be lost inside somebody else's memory; you will exist only as an annoyance, an eccentricity within a mind much stronger than your own."

Hammond slowly reached forward and grasped the sheet of paper, his good arm trembling slightly as he pushed his lips together. "Something happened. Something went wrong."

Wilhelm nodded slowly. "We *have* to know the truth, please help us while you still can."

Hammond took a deep shuddering breath and laid the crumpled drawing on his lap before awkwardly placing his right hand in his left. After a little effort he managed to pull his good hand out of its tight leather glove. He looked at his exposed fingers and then at the younger psychiatrist. "In case I never see you again, I just want you to know that you're a very different man to your father, but I think he would not have been disappointed with the doctor you've become."

Wilhelm smiled and nodded slowly. "Thank you, Herr Dr Hammond, but I think you will manage today, although I can't be sure how much time you have left."

Hammond swallowed hard, took a deep breath and grabbed the sheet of paper tightly with his right hand. Almost immediately his breathing changed, becoming rapid and shallow. A sheen of perspiration broke out across his forehead as his face took on a deathly grey pallor.

Wilhelm grabbed his notebook and scribbled furiously as he watched Hammond's head slump onto his chest, accompanied by a strangled groan. For a moment there was silence as the prisoner stopped breathing.

Wilhelm realised he was holding his own breath as he waited for signs of life to return. He jumped as Hammond suddenly snorted loudly as though he'd just woken himself.

At last Hammond slowly raised his head, his features pale, chin jutting forward defiantly as his facial muscles tightened into an unfamiliar pattern.

Wilhelm couldn't suppress a smile of satisfaction as he observed the prisoner's familiar yet subtly altered features. He settled himself back in his chair and turned to a fresh page in his notebook. "Now, tell me about Projekt Schatten."

8

As he tucked his frayed scarf into his shapeless overcoat, Mr Digby's hand instinctively moved to check the Browning pistol strapped tightly against his ribs. He disliked the idea of using it in a friendly country, and especially against fellow Americans, but with every twist of his investigation that became an increasingly likely scenario.

Things had gotten a lot more risky now that the *real* Feds were snooping about, and Digby's instincts told him it was only a matter of time before his deception was discovered. He wasn't concerned about the FBI directly, as he could easily pull rank and tell them to mind their own goddamned business. However, experience had taught him that those clean cut boys just didn't understand politics, a failing which made them dangerous and unpredictable. It only needed one officious G-man to go running back to the Bureau and all hell would break loose.

As he tramped steadily up Haymarket, Digby reflected that the supreme irony of being a ghost in a foreign land was that his real credentials, the ones he could never use in England, were so much more fearsome than the false ones he was obliged to hide behind. Politics again.

He stopped as he entered Piccadilly Circus, still poor, grimy and dim in comparison to Times Square. The partial lifting of the blackout allowed some illumination to spill from the windows of Rainbow Corner, although that did little to spread cheer in the bitter cold.

Even at this late hour, muffled men, women and soldiers gathered near the entrance to the American forces' hostel like moths fluttering around an uncovered bulb. Spivs, shore leavers, call girls and one-man traders huddled and haggled in muted tones. White helmeted military police - Snowdrops as the Brits called them - exuded an air of disdainful tolerance as they looked on. They were short-handed most of the time, so they confined themselves to protecting life and limb. The unspoken truce held as long as nobody got too loud or too obvious.

A young airman sidled up as Digby approached the hostel's famously unlocked doors. "What you need, buddy? I got smokes and I got gum." He grabbed Digby's arm, forcing him to stop. "You need gasoline? I got that too, but not in my pockets." The young man smiled and laughed at his own humour.

"You on leave, son?"

The airman's expression changed as he heard Digby's southern drawl. "Who wants to know?"

Digby produced his fake FBI card. "Special Agent Hardy."

The airman bristled and prodded Digby in the chest. "Back off G-man, I don't answer to no civilians."

Within a split second Digby had twisted the airman's arm into a painful lock and kicked the back of one knee, forcing him into a kneeling position.

A murmur of alarm rippled through the crowd as it rapidly distanced itself from the two men, not wanting to get caught up in whatever trouble was unfolding.

Within seconds two large MPs had forced their way through the rapidly thinning throng, heavy truncheons at the ready.

Digby released the cursing airman and flashed his FBI card. "Would you fellas please help this boy find his papers. He don't seem to like me very much."

One of the Snowdrops, a huge man with a granite face and a Bronx accent to match, yanked the street dealer to his feet. "Okay smartass, make with the ID, and real quick."

Digby smiled and winked at the young man. "I'll leave you to get acquainted with your new pals. Have fun." With that he turned and headed for the entrance doors, scattering nervous onlookers as he went.

A thick fog of blue smoke curled out to greet him as he opened the door and stepped into the hazy hum of Rainbow Corner. Digby quickly cast an eye over the crowd of servicemen and volunteers scattered amongst the tables filling the dance floor. No band at this time of night. Having made a quick survey of the ground floor, Digby made straight for the information desk set back from the door.

The American Red Cross volunteer manning the desk rolled his eyes as the dishevelled civilian made straight for him. "Can I help you, sir?"

Digby turned his back to the crowd and surreptitiously produced his FBI card. "Keep it calm, but I do need your assistance."

The volunteer's eyes widened. "Is there a problem, Agent Hardy?"

"No problem, I just need to talk to someone. See the guy over there playing cards, facing us, table second from the left?"

The nervous Red Cross worker glanced over. "Yeah, I see him. Is he in trouble?"

"No trouble. I just need to speak to him. I'd like you to go over there and tell him that a friend of his mother's is here to see him."

"You want I should call the Snowdrops?"

Digby shook his head and glanced over the nervous man's shoulder. "I'm not here to arrest anyone. Is that your office back there?"

"Not *my* office, but it's empty at this time of night."

Digby tapped the night volunteer on the shoulder. "Now remember what I told you. His buddies don't need to know there's a G-man asking after him."

The young man nodded, took a deep breath, straightened his tunic and plunged into the smoke-filled recreation area.

Digby casually entered the empty office and slumped into the worn but comfortable manager's chair. He'd barely had time to balance his feet on the waste paper basket and extract his cigarettes before a wide-eyed army Sergeant appeared in the doorway.

The fake G-man smiled a little too broadly. "Why Sergeant O'Malley, you do look like a man who's just lost a hundred bucks. Shut the door."

O'Malley gently closed the door and took a seat opposite Digby. "What the hell are you doing here? You said you'd keep contact to a minimum. You know I'm dead if they find out I've been talking to the Feds. No ifs, no buts, no excuses, just plain *dead*. That'll be me."

Digby lit a Lucky Strike and tossed the pack across the desk. "Relax, Sean. None of your crew knows you're here tonight, and nobody here knows that I'm a Fed, unless you slip up."

O'Malley's eyes narrowed. "How did you know I was here?"

Digby shook his head sadly. "We're the FBI, remember?"

"Yeah, right. So, what do you want, Agent Hardy?" O'Malley helped himself to one of Digby's cigarettes.

"Well, it's coming up to Christmas and that's a time for togetherness. You haven't called and you're making me feel all lonely." Digby's tone suddenly hardened. "Where the hell have you been? You should've had this deal buttoned up by now."

O'Malley's hand shook as he took a long drag on his cigarette. "Listen, they've changed my shift at the depot and I've not heard a damned thing from Davis. I think something's wrong."

"You reckon they're onto him?"

"Yeah, maybe. They say the Guvnor's one smart son of a bitch. They say he can find out anything he wants. *Anything*."

Digby half smiled. "Maybe we should fire *your* ass and hire *him*, how about that?"

O'Malley hunched further forward and lowered his voice even more. "Listen, it's no joke. Everyone's scared of him...and I keep hearing things?"

Digby leaned back and rubbed his chin. "What sort of things."

"I dunno, just like weird sort of stuff."

"Like *what* weird sort of stuff?"

Digby's informant licked his lips nervously. "Well, they say he can see stuff. I know that sounds really crazy."

Digby's expression never changed. "Go on."

O'Malley paused for a moment, searching for the right words. "Well, I've never met the guy myself, but the word is he's got special protection, and not from above either."

Digby raised his eyebrows. "You believe that?"

The informant thought for a moment. "I don't know. I've never been much of a churchgoing sort. What I *can* tell you is that those guys are organised, ruthless as hell and their boss always seems to know what's gonna happen next."

Digby crushed out his half-smoked cigarette. "What, you reckon he's got some kinda crystal ball?"

O'Malley's expression was grim. "You tell me, you're supposed to be the smart one. All I can tell you for sure is that none of the other bosses mess with him, and the word is he operates pretty much untouched. Now Davis is missing. You know, the guy you said had watertight cover."

Digby looked up at the yellow stained ceiling. "Then I wonder why none of the other firms makes this guy a sweet offer. I mean if I were them and this guy's as smart as you say, then I'd want him in my outfit. Wouldn't you?"

O'Malley shrugged. "Yeah I guess, but Davis told me that the other bosses hate his guts, said it was something political, old scores, that kind of shit."

Digby thought for a moment before coming to a decision. "So I guess we'd better just sit tight for now. I'm betting that clever Mr Tooley still wants his order, so I reckon you're still in the game."

"What the hell does *that* mean? What happens to *me?*"

Digby's tone was matter of fact. "Nothing, if you're smart and you keep your cool. There's nothing to tie you directly to the shipment, except getting caught with it, so you just keep your head if anyone comes asking. Remember this is a classified operation, which means not every G-Man in London needs to know. Understand?"

O'Malley sucked in his cheeks as he thought. "Yeah, sure, no sweat. There's another problem though."

"There always is," observed Digby.

O'Malley hesitated.

"Well?" Digby prompted patiently.

"I'm on a seventy-two hour pass."

"Lucky you."

"Real funny. My point is that the rest of the crew think I'm arranging payment and delivery right now. If I don't come back with something solid then I'm in line for a nasty accident."

Digby sighed sadly. "Seems like no one trusts you these days. Shame."

O'Malley crushed out his own cigarette. "You gonna help me or not? Right now that shipment's still sitting in a hole and my only contact's vanished."

Digby fished in his pocket and produced a crumpled scrap of paper. "Then you'll have to go see the broker again, won't you? The fact that Davis might've been tumbled doesn't necessarily implicate you, especially if you can still come up with the goods." He held the paper up for O'Malley to read. "You know this address?"

O'Malley reached for the paper.

Digby pulled it further away. "Do you know it?"

The Sergeant shook his head. "Never heard of the place."

Digby produced his lighter and promptly set fire to the evidence. "Well it's south of the river, and that's bandit country in these parts."

"So what?"

Digby dropped the last of the burning paper into the large glass ashtray. "So, that'll be the best place to make the delivery, understand? And don't get too smart either, I know they talk funny but not all these Brits are as dumb as they sound."

O'Malley lit another cigarette. "Me? And just what the hell makes you think *I'll* be delivering anything? That wasn't part of the agreement."

Digby's tone was hard, icy. "Neither was losing Davis, but it looks like he's gone so we'll have to make do and mend. You'll just have to be convincing."

"Why can't you just bust these guys right now?" Asked O'Malley sullenly.

"Politics that's why. That shipment needs to be delivered intact, and that's all you need to know."

O'Malley shook his head. "No way, no goddamn way. I'll take my chances in jail."

Digby's tone softened, as did his expression. "Relax son, Mr Tooley will be very grateful. After all, he's already paid a big deposit, and you know how touchy these gangster types are about honouring deals."

O'Malley rubbed his forehead hard. "Jesus Christ, how did I ever get mixed up in this?"

"You got caught." Digby stood up, adjusted his flaccid collar and made for the door. "Now if I was Tooley, I'd be tearing this city apart looking for my missing merchandise so you'd better get a move on and get it organised."

The Sergeant clambered slowly to his feet. "Okay, I'll speak to the broker. How will I contact you once I've arranged delivery?"

Digby paused in the doorway. "You don't. I'll find *you*. In the meantime, want some advice?"

"Sure, why not?"

"Find another game besides poker. You're a terrible bluffer." With that parting shot, Special Agent Hardy of the FBI was gone.

9

For just a moment Jake thought that he really *was* safe in his bed and simply dreaming as he surveyed the astonishing scene he'd stumbled into. For just a moment he imagined that the plotlines of adventure stories and pulp novels had somehow entwined themselves with his sleeping mind to create a boyish fantasy of secret bases and hidden underground labyrinths.

It took him precious seconds to figure out that he really *had* stumbled into some kind of underground command centre, although it wasn't really surprising when he thought about it. He could easily imagine the bigwigs in Germany and maybe even his own government in Washington making similar plans in case things got too hot up top.

Still mindful of the shadowy threat close behind him, Jake made his way forward as swiftly as he dared, trying to take in as much detail as possible as he passed unnoticed through the smoky, subterranean space. The room itself was in fact a long tunnel which had been sliced up into separate compartments, with a steel exit door at the far end mirroring the one he'd just pushed his way through. The whole bunker was arranged in a similar manner to a railway carriage, with a series of compartments branching off a long corridor. A quick sidestep through a thin partition wall revealed a room dominated by a large trestle table covered by a series of highly detailed maps. With space at a premium, desks were crammed into every available corner with their occupants often having to bend over to seat themselves comfortably. A glance at the paperwork on the desks suggested this room was connected with the ambulance and fire services.

A telephone rang on a crowded desk and a middle-aged man in civilian clothes picked up the receiver. As Jake listened in on a conversation regarding a lack of spare vehicle parts, everything began to make a lot more sense. The madness at Cedarwood House and even the Brotherhood's opaque motives were suddenly a great deal less fanciful. Men like him were highly prized in times of crisis as the invisible superstars of the espionage world, but then, what of tomorrow? What about afterwards, when there was no more war and he'd reverted to being just another security risk? Who would look out for him then? Only when he was stood in the middle of that secret underground installation did Jake fully appreciate what that crazy Dutchman had been trying to tell him. Nero had been right all along, and he'd dismissed the old man as the relic of a dying world, a man whose ideas were foolishly outdated. Jake suddenly understood that if he could penetrate a secure complex such as this with his obvious lack of formal training, what might others be able to achieve? Luckily for these guys he was just a passive observer, a Yank with personal axes to grind but no political motivation; but what of his unknown pursuer?

Dark ideas ran through Jake's mind as he understood the potential not just for passive observation, but for offensive action too. He'd already learned it was possible to reach back into the physical world and deliver death from the outside, and he had no reason to think his unknown pursuer's capabilities were any less than his own. He shuddered as he began to understand the disaster that could befall the Allied armies currently freezing in France should the Nazis manage to field even a halfway competent Sensitive, let alone any kind of psychic superstar.

Well aware that he was still far from safety, Jake quickly threaded his way through the clerks and typists crammed into the tubular room, noting that most of them were civilians with a scattering of army officers here and there. As he made his way towards the far exit, the overall impression Jake felt was one of rushed and breathless administration as opposed to actual command. Having accidentally penetrated this secret world, Jake had half expected to see Churchill himself wandering the corridors, surrounded by an entourage of secretaries as he issued a constant stream of orders. The reality was something of an anti-climax as he realised that the men and women he watched were just clerks, typists and hard-pressed administrators trying to run a damaged infrastructure with few staff, no gasoline and precious little communication.

Jake turned as he reached the steel door at the far end of the room, feeling a chill of dismay as he saw that his tormentor had not abandoned the chase. He watched, almost mesmerised as the silhouette at the far end of the room swivelled its head towards him, somehow sensing his attention.

That next steel door loomed large in Jake's vision as he threw himself towards it, banking on the fact that increased momentum would help him pass through it more easily. For a split second there was only darkness before the corridor beyond was revealed, coloured by the familiar glowing palette of the Projector's astral world.

Hoping desperately that he could find another exit, Jake set off towards a shorter flight of steps at the next corridor's far end. As he flew towards what he hoped was freedom, he sensed the distant hum and rumble of machinery, guessing it was probably generators and air pumps. Not wasting time looking back, he lengthened his stride and found himself almost flying up the stairs.

Jake had surmised that the second staircase would eventually lead to a spiral ascent and street entrance similar to the one he'd just passed through, and he quickened his pace as yet another solid looking door glimmered ahead. Determined not to lose momentum again, Jake threw himself headfirst at the next barrier, fearing that he would be pitched back down the stairs as he felt it stretch like a sheet of rubber before it finally deposited him on the other side.

Jake had been expecting to see perhaps another corridor, another staircase, or maybe a service entrance. His imagination had not prepared him for what he actually *did* see.

There must've been hundreds of them, crammed onto platforms, squeezed between the rails and lining the narrow passageways of the underground station. Men, women and children all staked their claim to a tiny square of the cramped public shelter, with each family's allotted space defined by blankets and beds in a curious echo of those minute gardens Jake had seen throughout England's towns and cities. Many tried to snatch some sleep while others gathered together and talked in hushed tones. Some of the more adventurous ones engaged in quiet games to pass the time, and Jake even recognised a notorious card sharp from his own encounters with London's underworld. Like any other smart GI, Jake knew that the unwary gambler was easy prey for the unscrupulous gangs who worked the shelters and speilers. The sharps probably handed a slice of their scalp to the ARP wardens who supposedly supervised the shelters. It was their job to keep order, but short of a major disturbance they confined themselves to ejecting troublesome drunks and quarrelsome housewives. They had neither the training nor inclination to deal with the professional predators stalking London's night shelters.

Stopping for just a moment to take stock, Jake looked back and found that he'd entered the tube station through an unassuming steel door cut into a non-descript passageway. He wondered how many of those taking shelter in the station were even aware of the secret world beyond that anonymous service entrance.

As Jake expected his featureless pursuer to burst through that door at any moment, he began making his way along the crowded passage, carefully skirting around a mother and child dozing fitfully on a narrow cot. Though huddled beneath a pile of coats and blankets, both emitted the familiar vaporous light of life itself.

He quickly threaded his way along the corridor and headed for the nearest platform, feeling more energised and invigorated with every step he took. With so many live bodies crammed into one confined space the air was thick and heavy with swirls and gusts of glittering energy. The raw ethereal leakage from each and every sleeper gently mingled with that of his neighbours to form a benign and multi-coloured fog throughout the station complex.

As Jake drifted invisibly onto the crowded platform he began to wonder if the faceless phantom had finally given up the chase. His unspoken question was soon answered as he spotted the relentless hunter at the far end of the corridor.

Jake stayed close to the platform's curved wall and moved as smoothly as possible, hoping that he hadn't been spotted through the obscuring clouds of coloured mist. He felt a sudden stab of despair as his nameless nemesis emerged onto the platform all too quickly.

Jake was just about to launch himself headlong down a darkened train tunnel when he noticed that the faceless Projector had stopped dead in his tracks, seemingly confused by the glittering blizzard of intermingled energies. Still ready to flee at a moment's notice, Jake saw the solid shadow's head roll drunkenly on its shoulders, its unusually long fingers curled into claws as it fed on the life leaking silently from London's sheltering population.

As he watched that colourless glutton gorge itself on the invigorating atmosphere, Jake was also beginning to feel an intoxicating mental rush brought on by that thick, omnipresent fog of living colour. Fortunately for him, his combat experience had taught him not to allow a surge of adrenaline to metamorphose into a feeling of invincibility. Such a mistake only ever led to one outcome.

Jake's plan to slip away unnoticed was thwarted when the pursuing shadow suddenly tilted its head towards him, and if he was ever asked in court, he'd have sworn that featureless face was smiling somehow.

Before Jake had time to react, the newly energised shadow flung out its arms and clenched its unnaturally long fingers into fists. Immediately the billowing clouds of twinkling energy were drawn to a single point between those anonymous hands, like smoke caught in the suction of a powerful fan. Within seconds a single, constant point of light winked into existence, growing rapidly in size and intensity as those commandeered particles packed together to form a concentrated mass of stolen energy.

The sleepers closest to that shadowy Projector began to stir and mutter, as though they somehow saw the disturbance through the window of their dreams.

Jake wasn't certain of what his rival was up to, and he sure as hell wasn't sticking around to find out as he set off into London's seemingly endless underground tunnels, rapidly accelerating to the speed of an express train as he flashed through the grimy darkness.

He wasn't sure how long he'd been running – if it could be called that – but Jake figured it couldn't have been more than half a minute before he sensed a change in the atmosphere. The presence, the vibration emanating from the pursuing Projector had faded to nothingness, just like the ethereal glow from the crowded station he'd left far behind.

As he drifted to a disembodied halt in the darkness, Jake realised he was quite alone at last, his pursuer having either given up the chase or maybe taken a wrong turn somewhere.

Reassuring himself that wherever he'd ended up, he'd taken the wisest course of action, Jake opted for a quick exit while he was far away from that colourless Sensitive and his colourful creation, whatever *that* would've ended up as. He mentally reconstructed the heavy sensation in his limbs and the parching thirst which invariably followed his out-of-body excursions. He imagined himself waking up in the place that he'd last seen himself asleep, huddled in an old army cot inside a half ruined church.

Nothing happened.

Jake tried again, imagining the ancient odour of damp stone.

Despite his determined efforts to return to the physical plane, Jake found himself stranded far from home in some unknown part of London's tube system. Maybe *this* was why Projectors were loath to travel underground, perhaps the earth itself was an obstacle even for a talented remote viewer like him; and the thick electric cables hugging the tunnel walls probably didn't help either. However, Jake figured the solution to his problem was simple enough. He'd entered the underground complex the same way as everybody else, so that would be the method of his escape. Back up the stairs just like any regular guy.

Convinced that his reasoning was sound, Jake set off at a more leisurely pace. The astral echo of the train tracks guided him along a silvery white path amid the muted browns and greys of the lightless tunnel. It was a peculiarity of the remote viewer's realm that no object was ever seen as *truly* black, except for fellow Projectors who'd somehow learned to obscure their identities. In this place there was no such thing as an absence of light, unless a living mind willed it so.

Jake kept up a steady pace for what he guessed was about half a mile, all the while keeping one eye on the cables and electrical boxes lining the tunnel walls. Most of the thick rubberised power lines were cold and dark as they were switched off during the night. However one still hummed with life, carrying a strong current that strangely stretched the space surrounding it. Acting like a poorly made lens, the live cable distorted the world a few inches in every direction while a much thinner cable beside it carried a jumble of voices between distant telephone exchanges. Jake tried to pick out any discernible threads of conversation, but he found it impossible. In fact, he wasn't even sure he was really *hearing* that low rumble of background chatter, it seemed more like he was *feeling* the voices as they were translated into minute electrical impulses.

Moving further down the line, Jake came across a large array of junction boxes carrying far more potent electrical currents, strong enough to pull tiny chunks of the ethereal world into themselves in a never ending stream of particles. He gave them a wide berth as he travelled onward.

Jake was beginning to wonder if retracing his route would've been a wiser course when a glimmer of light finally flickered in the tunnel ahead. He quickened his pace towards what he assumed was the next station, but when he finally arrived at what *looked* like a platform he was puzzled. Instead of the light of life and the muffled sound of thousands taking shelter there was only an eerie subterranean silence, punctuated by the quiet whirr and hum of distant machinery. A quick glance up and down the tunnel confirmed he was indeed standing in some sort of station, except it was sealed off by a partition wall running almost the entire length of the platform. Still, a disused station was as good an escape route as any, and the remaining stub of accessible platform must surely lead to some kind of exit.

In one smooth jump, Jake had left the tracks, cleared the platform and landed in a narrow access corridor beyond. The place looked like it was still used for maintenance purposes as a string of service lamps had been hung from the wall, disappearing into what Jake guessed were the remnants of the station itself. He quickly followed the lamps away from the tracks and around a sharp corner.

It was only when confronted by a waiting sentry that Jake realised he'd casually strolled into a very different facility to the one filled with sheltering civilians. The soldier was young and combat fit with a rifle on his shoulder, a revolver at his hip and a large Alsatian by his side.

Jake immediately backed away, but it was already too late as the dog began to snarl and growl at his projected presence. Whatever kind of place he'd stumbled into, it was clear that preparations had been made against unauthorised observers just like him. He had only a moment to realise what was happening as the sentry's free arm never reached for his revolver or moved to unsling his rifle, instead he grabbed a heavy duty switch bolted to the wall beside him.

Jake looked at the thick electric cables doubled back on themselves, designed to strengthen the electrical field waiting to flood the confined space. By the time he'd realised this was no access corridor, but rather a defence perimeter designed to thwart Projectors it was already too late. He turned to run, but there was no chance of escape as the guard threw the switch.

The pain didn't last long, but while it did it was excruciating, and Jake felt as though every last cell in his body was being torn away from its neighbour. The glowing astral world vanished in an instant, replaced by random flashes of jagged colour which somehow corresponded to roaring waves of noise and pain that quickly drowned out the distant sound of the barking Alsatian. It was impossible to measure time, but it couldn't have been more than a few seconds before the roaring and flashing climbed to a jagged peak before levelling out onto an unbroken plateau of noisy, endless red.

10

Somehow, over the course of an uncertain timespan, the darkness of nothing had evolved into a tenuous sense of something; and as that sense of something strengthened, a vague idea of reality returned.

As Jake crossed the no-man's-land between oblivion and awareness, recollections of past times and places settled back into their appointed order, more or less. As consciousness slowly returned, he briefly wondered if he might *really* be dead this time. However, the sensation of a bed beneath his body convinced him that he still walked with the living, at least for now.

As his senses began to settle, Jake became aware of his own eyelids blotting out the light. An atmosphere heavy with paraffin fumes, damp and dust scratched at his red raw lungs and his dry lips stuck to his teeth as the abrasive air left his parched throat feeling like salted sandpaper.

Although Jake's mind was beginning to wake, his muscles remained resolutely asleep. Every inch of his slumbering body felt numb, absent, and he was unable to move so much as a finger. Desperately fighting against his post-projection paralysis, Jake turned his mind to physical things, practical things, corporeal things. As he tried to marshal his thoughts, the projector screen of his memory replayed only the sentry, his drooling dog and a streaking disintegration of the glowing astral world, like a watercolour doused by a fire hose.

He felt drowsy, drugged and distant from himself, as though his consciousness were banished to some isolated antechamber while his soul searched for its rightful home, whether in this world or the next.

At last his deepest sense of self returned, and Jake felt his consciousness flooding back into the cells of his own alien and inert body. His eyelids flickered, allowing flashes of the physical world to enter his mind, bringing a welcome distraction from the never-ending loop of disintegration repeated by his disjointed memory. Without warning, a long-forgotten incident unexpectedly bubbled to the surface as Jake recalled how he'd once blacked out in his father's study. The memory was hazy and incomplete as he must've been very young at the time.

No, wait, that can't be true. Jake also recalled that he'd never actually *had* a father who'd owned a study, or any other kind of father for that matter. That must've been a different person, a different place, a lingering shadow cast by a different life on which the sun had set long ago.

The ascent towards the light continued inexorably, and Jake began to feel the weight of blankets across his body, an alarming revelation when he remembered that the old man must've moved him while he was still unconscious. What if he'd done more than that? What if he'd called the police, or even a doctor? That could mean more hospitals, with more rounds of questions, tests and experiments. More men with shadowy motives, more politics and more bullshit. Jake was already acquainted with some inhabitants of his newly discovered clandestine world, and they were serious players with few scruples.

Knowing that he needed to wake up fast, Jake forced his eyelids open, and then shut them again as the light streaming into his mind somehow amplified the odours of damp wood and coal smoke. Jake steeled himself for a moment then opened his eyes again, squinting as they adjusted to the muted kerosene glow inside the room.

At last some feeling returned to his limbs, enough for his fingers to grasp the rough woollen blanket covering his body. He slowly raised his head and looked around; the stone walls, stuttering hurricane lamps and broken bookcases confirming his fears. Someone had found him, someone secretive and scholarly, someone just like the Brotherhood. It didn't surprise him to see his mysterious benefactor snoring gently in a faded wingback chair. What *did* surprise him was that the grizzled old timer huddled beside the potbellied stove was clearly no gangster, and didn't look much like a doctor either.

As his senses settled, Jake began to recall fragments of their brief exchange in the crypt. The guy had said he was a priest, although Jake could see no shirt or clerical collar beneath the old man's blanket. Even if he really *was* a priest, that fact was of little comfort as Jake already knew that the very darkest motives could hide behind the facade of any respectable profession.

The sleeping man stirred and stretched in his chair, his dog-eared army blanket slipping onto the floor as he blinked and stared at the Sergeant. He leaned forward, groaning as he reached to retrieve the fallen blanket. "Awake at last eh? How are you feeling?"

Jake was surprised to hear the so-called priest's strange Cockney accent. He'd never imagined a man of the cloth - if that's what he really was - speaking in such a way. Although he had no particular reason to think so, it just didn't seem right somehow.

Jake licked his dry lips and pushed against the sheets which suddenly felt like restraining straps. "Water, drink." He gasped.

The old man levered himself out of the armchair and crossed to Jake's narrow cot. He stifled a cough as he produced a round British Army canteen.

The American snatched it gratefully and gulped down large mouthfuls of cool if slightly metallic water, nearly choking himself in the process.

The ageing minder removed the canteen from Jake's grip with surprising strength. "Careful son, you'll drown yourself."

Jake wiped his mouth on the rough blankets and let his head slump back, closing his eyes once again. "Too bright in here. Too bright."

The alleged priest raised his eyebrows. "Really? I can barely see a bloody thing these days, even with my glasses. Still, that gives me an excuse not to read any more theology." Taking the canteen with him, he shuffled across to an overcrowded desk and tutted to himself before returning to Jake's cot. "I really should be better organised. They say cleanliness is next to godliness, but I hope that's not true otherwise I'm well knackered." He smiled broadly, revealing a boxer's grin of interspersed teeth and gaps. "These were in your pocket, along with some other bits and pieces." He handed Jake his dark glasses.

Jake gratefully took the spectacles and hurriedly pushed them onto his face before allowing his head to fall back onto the pillow. "Where am I? And who the hell are you?"

"I'm the Reverend Josiah Piggott; well I'm sort of retired really, but some folk still call me Reverend."

Jake turned his head towards the priest to study him more closely. Piggott's face was kindly, although the pallor of his skin and the deep furrows creasing his brow and mouth made it difficult to judge his true age. Although his hair was thinning it hadn't yet retreated over his scalp, and Jake could see it had once been jet black before age had painted it mostly grey. Piggott's eyes were still middle aged, and yet his face wore the unsurprised weariness of a much older man.

Jake frowned as he looked intently at the collarless priest. "Do I know you?"

Piggott groaned and placed his hands on his knees as he straightened up. "Not likely, I'd have remembered *you*. I hate this bloody damp weather. Plays havoc with my rheumatism. You got a name, son? It's a bit rude to just be calling you Yank when you're sleeping in my house, even if it *has* seen better days; sort of like me I suppose."

"The name's Jimmy Partridge," Jake lied. "Where am I?"

Piggott made his way back to the cluttered desk and opened a drawer. "You're at St John's, Bermondsey, at least what's left of it. You should know that already as you've been camping out down in the vaults. Bloody stupid thing to do in your condition. You should be in a hospital."

"Funny, I was going to say the same thing about you."

Piggott ignored Jake's sassy if weakly delivered remark. "If I hadn't come along you'd have joined the full timers down there by now, and I'm tired of burying folk." Piggott slammed the drawer shut and approached Jake with a slim leather case clasped his hand.

Jake groaned incoherently and rolled away from the advancing priest, flipping the cot onto its side as he attempted to escape.

Piggott shook his head as he pulled the thermometer from its protective case. "Stop mucking about, son. Sorry, *Jimmy*. Beds and blankets are hard to come by and I need to know if you're running a temperature."

Breathing heavily from the exertion of leaving his bed, Jake eyed the thermometer suspiciously. "What for?"

The priest tapped his temple with a finger. "You all right, son? You understand what I'm saying? Last time I met someone who looked like you I was planting him in the ground. I'm no doctor, but you're dripping with sweat and you're shivering too, so let's not kid each other about how tough we both are. I'm too old and you're too sick for that nonsense."

Jake groaned and tried to crawl towards an arched doorway as Piggott advanced with the gleaming glass tube.

Piggott stopped and looked at the sick man scrabbling on the cold flagstones, then he looked at the thermometer in his hand. Shaking his head ruefully he crossed back to the desk, rummaged in the bottom drawer and pulled out a half-finished bottle of French brandy. He quickly sloshed a little into a chipped enamel mug and stirred it with the thermometer's bulbous end. "Quite right too, son. Can't be too careful with germs and such. After all, I don't want to catch something off you, I've got enough trouble as it is." He smiled, stuck the thermometer in his own mouth and leaned back on the desk, folding his arms for a few seconds before removing it from his mouth and nodding sagely. "Well *I'm* still alive, now let's see if you are." He advanced once again, stirring the brandy with the glass tube. "Tell you what; if you're not dead you can help me finish up this Frog grog. Nothing like a tot to help ease a troubled conscience. I should know."

Jake reluctantly opened his mouth and let the older man place the thermometer under his tongue with surprising gentleness.

Piggott quickly straightened out Jake's makeshift bed before retrieving the thermometer and frowning as he looked at the reading. "You're running a heck of a temperature, Jimmy. It's back to bed for you." He bent stiffly and placed a hand under Jake's arm, helping him back into the cot. "Well Jimmy, you're a mystery all right. Get some sleep and we'll talk later. I reckon it's going to be a good long chat."

11

Jake was grateful to feel the sun's warmth on his skin as Special Camp 26A sagged and peeled in a remembered echo of summer's shimmering heat. He could easily tell the difference between a simple dream and a full-blown out-of-body experience as he turned a slow circle in the centre of that long deserted parade ground. This dream-place lacked the cold, frosted sparkle of the so-called astral plane; that parallel dimension invisibly overlapping and somehow intermeshing with the realm of things physical. The reality of being awake inside his own dream was nothing new for Jake, but what he couldn't immediately fathom was why his fever-heated brain had conjured *this* particular fantasy.

Whatever the case, Jake was glad to be dreaming in spite of his misgivings. Nocturnal adventures inside his own mind had been few and far between since his encounters with the nefarious Dr Hammond and the unearthly Peter van Cortlandt. However, when lucid dreams *did* occur, he was eager to embrace such adventures as they were a good deal safer than the uncertain world of the remote viewer. Scotch seemed to solve the problem of spontaneous projection, but it also closed the door to the more benign realm of his own subconscious constructions.

Jake was certain that his uncannily lucid dreams were just another side effect of whatever crap Hammond had pumped him full of, but what the hell. Roaming free as master of his own nocturnal dominion was about the only positive thing he'd experienced since Section 12 had gotten hold of him, so he figured they owed him that much.

He watched the summer breeze send a tiny dust devil spiralling towards the ranks of empty prisoners' huts as they sweated and bleached on their brick supports, their windows dulled by a film of fine dust. Even Cedarwood House had been rebuilt by his sleeping mind, perched back atop its gentle slope despite the fact it was nothing but cold stone and burned timber back in the real world.

As Jake stared up at the house through flaccid coils of rusting barbed wire, he wondered if the dreamer's nocturnal world was in fact a forgotten path to psychic stability. If he could somehow teach himself to dream more then maybe he would project less. Not only that, but his intricately detailed visions were blissfully sealed against the memories of long-dead strangers leaking in to muddy his own story. He figured that the fact he could think clearly while fast asleep was hugely significant, and the more Jake considered it, the more convinced he became that the unspoiled domain of his dreams was the key to taming his own extraordinary yet errant consciousness. He just hoped he was smart enough to figure out the method by himself, as the so-called experts just couldn't be trusted. Experts always concealed their own agendas, even though they always denied it.

Jake allowed himself to hope that perhaps he wouldn't need to cut deals with anyone to save himself. If he could find a way to rescue his vanishing personal history, then maybe he could regain control of his fractured self *without* the intelligence community's conditional protection. Sure, working with those guys gave him a chance to serve and do the right thing, but deep down he sensed that Peter van Cortlandt was right when he'd warned there would inevitably come a time when his extraordinary skills transformed him from asset to liability.

Buoyed up by a renewed feeling of hope if not optimism, Jake continued to stare through the rusting perimeter fence. Cedarwood House was a part of his own past, and the fact he was standing inside a deserted POW camp struck him as significant. Perhaps his psychic departure from this place of incarceration would be his first real step on the road to rehabilitation. He could consider such a conscious act to be his opening salvo in the battle to regain control of both his own past and future.

Even though he was dreaming, Jake's heart still leapt in his chest when he turned away from the house, only to be confronted by ragged ranks of tired looking soldiers suddenly filling the camp's hard-baked parade ground; each one staring expectantly at him. He'd been quite alone a moment ago and now, inexplicably, he was just one among hundreds. Even *more* disturbing was the fact that those hundreds had never passed through Special Camp 26A during his brief stay at Cedarwood. So where had his unconscious mind conjured them from?

Although Jake couldn't read the message, he was certain that the waking and sleeping parts of himself were exchanging signals across the no man's land of night. If he could decode the symbolism then perhaps he might learn how to consciously express something that he already knew deep down, something he was unable to convey with the limited tools of words and speech.

Was this a warning or an opportunity, a shadow of disaster or a portent of triumph? Whatever the truth of it, Jake sensed he was on the cusp of a significant discovery, and he was determined to awaken with at least *some* grasp of what he was trying to tell himself.

He stood still and made a conscious effort to properly observe the uneven formation his mind had created seemingly from nothing, and that forced dispassion was immediately rewarded as Jake noticed there was something unusual about that impromptu parade of the silent dead.

It was a truly international affair.

Among the many pale and dusty Germans stood almost as many pale and dusty Americans too; not to mention Brits, Canucks, Japs and even a few Italians hiding among those ragtag ranks. Jake had only ever seen Japanese and Italian soldiers on the newsreels, so he was perplexed as to why his sleeping mind should bring them here.

Jake became increasingly aware of a quiet, cautionary voice in the back of his mind as he stepped forward to get a better look at his uninvited guests. It was a surreal experience to stare directly at a facet of his own subconscious, while at the same time being pricked by deeply rooted distrust of that hidden part of himself. He felt frustration boiling up as he instinctively sensed he was missing something fundamentally important about the ever more unsettling episode.

Jake almost slapped himself on the head when at last his gaze focused on a face he'd known so very well both in life *and* death. Standing unobtrusively among that sea of silent strangers was none other than the late PFC Fred Ohlson, and just behind him he spotted Private Ribitsch, also deceased for some months now. As Jake's sleeping perception was sharpened by that revelation, more and more familiar faces stood out among those ranks of anonymous, sunken eyed wraiths.

It wasn't long before Jake had spotted them all. Ohlson, Ribitsch, Dillard and the rest of his ill-fated platoon were scattered seemingly at random throughout that silent mass of the nameless departed. Those familiar faces among a sea of strangers had to mean *something*, but what? Jake's dreams had always portrayed his dead comrades as grotesquely malformed casualties of war, so perhaps this change in them meant that he was beginning to forgive himself at last. Perhaps it was a sign that he was finally finding a little peace, at least as far as his dead platoon was concerned.

Jake walked across to the parade of the fallen, nodding to Private Ribitsch in a small acknowledgement of that dead man's humanity and sacrifice. Anything more than that simple gesture felt oddly inappropriate. After all, how *does* one begin to make peace with a ghost?

Whether that single act of recognition was what triggered the change or not, Jake would never know for sure. All he could be certain of was the despair he felt as he watched death's decay suddenly swarm across Ribitsch's already cadaverous features. Within seconds, Ohlson's face had also begun to dissolve and deteriorate like an ice sculpture ravaged by the August sun.

Jake backed away as the grinning face of the grave quickly spread from one ragged wraith to his neighbour, transmitted and multiplied like a contagion of corruption as several months of decomposition was somehow shoehorned into a matter of seconds. That wave of decay rapidly bloomed among the ranks of the dead like the spores of some fetid fungus, transforming Jake's mental landscape from a haven of safety and learning to a place of horror and hostility. It was a sickening feeling to finally understand there was literally *nowhere* he could be in complete control, not even deep within his own mind.

Although Jake hadn't figured out *why* his own subconscious was turning against him, he'd already seen enough to know that it was time to bail out, and fast. He turned to scan the rusting perimeter fence, searching for a way out. He was both surprised and relieved to see that the camp's neglected gates had already been breached by a battered army jeep. At long last it seemed his errant memory had reconstructed a *useful* recollection of this hopeless and lonely place.

Without any conscious effort, Jake suddenly found himself standing beside the mangled vehicle and staring through a curtain of steam hissing from its punctured radiator. He half expected to see a dazed echo of himself slumped behind the wheel, but thankfully the vehicle was empty.

Having done it before back in the real world, Jake wasted no time in wriggling through the gap between the crumpled car and the splintered gate; only this time he was reversing the journey he'd made during the heat of that strange summer which had transformed him forever.

Once safely outside the camp's perimeter, Jake paused to look back through the abandoned coils of rusted wire. He was intrigued, fascinated and appalled by Special Camp 26A's undead occupants, and something deep inside him recoiled as he began to understand that he was watching nature's irrefutable order running in reverse. The more the bodies of the dead were decayed and diminished, the stronger, faster and more certain their movements became.

Fred Ohlson was at the head of the advancing crowd just as he'd always been in Jake's nightmares of old, only this time he didn't seem at all angry. It was difficult to read any humane expression in Ohlson's milky eyes, but Jake sensed there was something different about *this* version of the man who'd so often shuffled through his darker dreams since the summer. He felt a wave of nausea in the pit of his stomach as Ohlson's already shrunken lips ripped and cracked open in an unholy parody of a smile, both hideous, and yet somehow more expressive and more alive than in any of his previous panic filled encounters. Jake quickly supressed the idea that *this* Fred Ohlson might be a great deal more than just a frightening but ultimately harmless shadow trapped inside his sleeping imagination.

There was no real plan in his mind as Jake virtually flew up the long slope leading to Cedarwood House, only to find himself arriving at an altogether different and even more sinister destination.

Confused but not wholly surprised, he backed away from the ornate and chillingly familiar entrance doors to Chateau Dessous. Jake looked up at the mysteriously transformed building, still clinging to the hope of seeing the honey coloured stone of Section 12's erstwhile HQ. A stab of dismay pierced his soul as he instead found himself staring at a house built in the ostentatious style of an ascendant aristocracy, and requisitioned by a madman.

Fearing the worst, Jake glanced back down the valley towards the prison camp, only to discover that the unseen director of his dreams had silently shifted the scenery once more. Special Camp 26A was gone, replaced by Chateau Dessous' once grandiose formal gardens, now defiled by barbed wire and sandbags.

Jake's mind began to reel and spin as he tried to make sense of a metaphysical nightmare which had begun as the benign promise of a revelatory dream. It was bad enough that his sleeping mind had suddenly transplanted him from one ruined house to another, but the fact it had *also* resurrected the Chateau's dead defenders was nothing short of psychological self-flagellation.

Just like the ghosts of the Cedarwood estate, Colonel Stryker's long-dead garrison stared hatefully at the agent of their earthly destruction, adding alarmingly to the grim roll call of vengeful wraiths prowling Jake's increasingly hostile subconscious.

He turned back towards the house, only to find himself facing something far more dangerous than the twisted projections of his personal guilt, if indeed that was *all* they really were. Jake wasn't sure whether he'd resurrected Colonel Kurt Stryker from the tomb of memory, or whether the dead man had somehow managed to take to the stage of his own volition. Whatever the case, the sight of Stryker in his immaculate SS uniform rang an immediate alarm inside Jake's slumbering consciousness. He'd only ever met the man twice in the real world, and on both occasions the tall Sensitive had worn civilian clothes. By the time Jake had figured out that the dead man was more than just a shadow cast by his own memory, it was already too late.

He never actually sensed any movement as the Colonel suddenly vanished from sight, and for a second Jake entertained the foolish hope that this most dangerous of dead men had departed voluntarily. A sudden shove between his shoulder blades demonstrated the dangers of wishful thinking as he suddenly found himself flying towards those ostentatious entrance doors.

Jake *felt* rather than heard the entrance to Stryker's personal kingdom crash open as he fell headlong into an altogether different kind of place.

12

For a while, Sergeant Jacob Small's idea of himself was reduced to a single image among thousands whirling around his mind's eye like leaves cartwheeling in the autumn wind. As he clung tightly to his own identity amid that maelstrom of confusion, Jake sensed that the placid harbour of his own mental creation was far behind him as he was swept into more open, troubled and turbulent waters.

It was a fleeting perception, but Jake had sensed a shift in the mental landscape at the very the moment he'd been hurled into a new and nameless chaos by a dead man; and not just *any* old dead man either, but a dead man whom his dreams had known long before their paths had crossed in the "real" world.

At last the clamour of confusion began to quieten as some surprisingly familiar surroundings swam back into focus. Jake instantly recognised the damp sarcophagi and mouldering walls of St John's crypt, the place where he'd first encountered the peculiar and most likely mad Reverend Piggott. The rational part of his mind reasoned that his own subconscious had naturally linked the dead Colonel with that freezing sepulchre buried beneath the church, although a larger and more instinctive part of him didn't really believe that all-too-tidy explanation.

Whatever the truth of it, he'd already decided that this particular nocturnal adventure had become far too complicated, not to mention downright dangerous. Although Jake was no stranger to lucid dreaming, he was wary of getting lost while wandering the uncharted labyrinths of his own subconscious and far beyond. Labyrinths always harboured monsters, and he was keen to lay them to rest, not reawaken them.

Jake quickly laid flat on the damp flagstones and rolled over, first onto his side and then his stomach as he tried to re-create the process of falling from his bed back in Piggott's makeshift quarters. He'd acquired the bruises to prove that a sharp contact with a hard floor never failed to jolt him back into the real world...except on this occasion. Maybe he was losing his touch, or maybe Hammond's mysterious injections were finally wearing off. Either that or some unknown force was interfering with his more exotic mental abilities.

Frustrated by his failure, Jake stood up and looked around, his fears of outside influence growing by the minute. He was beginning to suspect that even his dreams were somehow less private and personal than he'd always believed, or at least had *wanted* to believe. His thoughts kept returning to the man who'd flung him into this altogether different kind of reality, if such a word had any meaning here. Although Standartenführer Stryker was dead for sure, Jake was beginning to wonder just how much of an inconvenience merely dying might actually *be* for a man such as that.

Accepting that he was trapped, at least for the moment, Jake also accepted that succumbing to fear or panic was a sure way to make any survival situation that much worse. What he needed was information, not speculation, and so he tried to ignore the feeling that he wasn't alone as he set about studying his surroundings more critically.

It was St John's crypt all right, and yet it was oddly altered and re-imagined either by a sleeping part of himself, or more likely by somebody else. Here the heavy stone coffins had somehow been shifted and lined up neatly against the back wall, rather than being more evenly spread around as they were in the "real" version. Those simple, anonymous coffins had also been re-fashioned by some unknown artisan and capped with life-sized figures reposed in prayer, reminiscent of mediaeval knights and kings. However, the thing that *really* worried Jake about those inexplicably upgraded tombs was the way they pulsated, glowed and glittered in the semidarkness of that damp mausoleum. The crumbling caskets looked almost like they'd been dragged straight from the astral world and dropped into whatever realm, or plane of existence, that he'd been so casually cast into by a man who'd been dead for some months now.

Jake gingerly reached out to touch one of those strangely modified sarcophagi, marvelling at the coolness and solidity beneath his fingers as he gazed at each one in turn. Although most of the tombs' occupants were unknown to him, the last two caskets in that luminous parade were uncomfortably familiar. That they both belonged in a darkened vault was beyond doubt, but his witnessing their passing did nothing to stop those lifelike reliefs of Kurt Stryker and Peter van Cortlandt from ratcheting up his already heightened apprehension. He couldn't fathom exactly what danger the two dead men might pose, but he was experienced enough to know when he was out of his depth.

Unable to simply wish himself out of his predicament, Jake crossed to the iron gate guarding the exit to the churchyard above. Well it *would* be locked, wouldn't it? He braced his shoulder against the flaking bars and pushed hard, the rusted chain and padlock refusing to relinquish their hold as he tried to force a gap wide enough to squeeze through.

Jake couldn't be sure whether brute strength had triumphed, or whether his ethereal form had simply passed *between* the solid iron bars as he suddenly found himself standing on the other side of the gate. His curiosity as to exactly how he'd escaped from the crypt was soon forgotten when a quiet yet ominous hissing caught his attention. The sound felt as though it originated inside his very own ears, although he immediately had a strong hunch as to its true source.

Knowing that he'd probably wish he hadn't done, Jake cautiously peered back into the damp and gloomy mausoleum. He didn't need any advanced esoteric knowledge to be troubled by the unearthly darkness which had begun to bubble inexplicably from each of those oddly altered tombs. The strange, lightless substance moved like a heavy, oily smoke as it rolled and stretched across the floor of the crypt, quickly rising to overwhelm the ethereal glow emanating from those newly installed marble reliefs.

Jake turned on his heel, climbed the worn steps in two long strides and abruptly skidded to a halt when it became clear that the same mystery mason who'd re-fashioned the crypt beneath him had been hard at work above stairs too. The reaper's roll call had somehow expanded from mere hundreds in the "real" St Johns, to many thousands in this washed out and almost monochrome copy which was neither astral plane nor physical place. Rank upon uneven rank of leaning, eldritch monuments faded into the distance before finally vanishing behind a veil of sickly grey and unhealthy looking fog. He looked up to see broken silhouette of St John's spire still rearing above the suddenly endless jumble of desolate brick tombs, although it seemed shorter and more badly damaged than he remembered.

A quick glance behind confirmed Jake's fears as the smoke, darkness, or whatever-it-actually-was began to roll up the steps from below and spill out into the strangely colourless churchyard, like an ever-expanding pool of gravity-defying ink.

First it was dead soldiers, then *more* dead soldiers, then a dead Colonel, and now Jake found himself fleeing from some kind of semi-sentient shadow as he set off across St John's inexplicably expanded estate.

The encircling mist made it difficult to judge distances, but Jake figured he'd travelled about a couple of football fields before he finally spotted a definite line of Victorian headstones looming fast out of the fog, probably marking some kind of boundary between the churchyard and...wherever. Eager to escape the cheerless realm of the dead he pressed on, not daring to look back lest he should see only a perfect and endless darkness hard on his heels.

Jake momentarily forgot the formless fear behind him as he burst across the border and passed into the unexplored region beyond the relative safety of St John's, or at least what was a reasonable copy of it. Once again he stopped in his tracks to stare dumbfounded at an impossible place that somehow felt oddly familiar, like the faded echo of a long forgotten dream.

He'd expected to see something strange as he left St John's re-modelled and larger-than-life necropolis behind him, but the endless expanse of emptiness ahead still stunned him into a state of mental paralysis. Motionless and mirror flat, a lake of silent grey *something* stretched away to touch a distant, inky black sky that arched gracefully to meet it at some interminable and forever unreachable point.

Staring across that silent and fathomless expanse of grey, Jake was surprised to feel his heart suddenly filled with an unexpected and overwhelming sense of sadness and isolation. The sheer *deadness* of the place drowned him in a deep hopelessness as he somehow understood that the motionless, colourless barrier was a final, unspoken and irrefutable statement. It was quite literally the end of the line on the road to nowhere, and it was easily the most desolate place Sergeant Jacob Small had ever seen, heard about, dreamt about or had even *tried* to imagine.

As he struggled to regain his composure, Jake glimpsed a slight movement in the corner of his eye. Suddenly the pursuing darkness behind and the vast expanse of emptiness ahead seemed a lot less strange as he stared perplexed at a forlorn figure standing on that loneliest of shores. Although the Reverend Piggott's astral form was weak and faded, his presence in such a strange, nameless non-place proved there was much more to that so-called man of faith than met the eye. He should've known it.

Seemingly unaware of Jake's presence, the old man stared intently across the endless grey abyss, his eyes fixed upon the horizon as though he expected to see the sails of a ship at any moment. The ageing priest wore the look of a man who'd been waiting for something, and waiting for a very long time.

Even though he possessed no physical form, Jake still felt his heart leap into his mouth as Piggott slowly turned to look directly at him, his face an inscrutable blend of suspicion and sadness. For a while both men stood motionless, staring each-other down like a pair of Hollywood gunmen in the most surreal of showdowns.

Eventually it was Piggott who made the first move by cautiously stepping backwards, slowly moving away from both Jake and the shore of that impossible ocean, while an expression of fear and uncertainty rapidly clouded his already melancholy expression.

For a moment Jake thought that Piggott was wary of *him*, before he saw the old man's eyes flicking nervously in the direction of St John's strangely stretched out churchyard. As he reluctantly followed the direction of Piggott's nervous gaze, Jake sensed that something had changed. The two of them were no longer alone in that colourless nowhere at the edge of infinity.

The impenetrable black mist spewed up by St John's crypt hovered and roiled around the damp, gloomy gravestones, as though trapped inside the domain of the dead by laws and methods both invisible and unknowable. Jake was both fascinated and appalled to see misshapen faces briefly forming within that swirling, mindless mass before twisting with rage and frustration as they were torn and scattered by a non-existent wind.

Jake backed away as a rolling tendril of darkness suddenly breached the boundary wall and spiralled towards him, the semblance of a human hand appearing so briefly as to make him wonder if his disembodied eyes had deceived him. Any doubt was quickly dispelled when he watched another phantom dart forward, reaching for the pale priest on the shore before dissolving into a swirling nothingness once again.

Twisting in and out of existence with ever increasing speed, the formless wraiths trapped in the churchyard soon worked themselves into a frenzy as they struggled to reach the still-living souls trapped on the shores of eternity.

It was only when he felt a sudden chill around his non-existent feet that Jake realised he'd inadvertently stepped into the shallows of that unfathomable, colourless expanse of grey. Startled, he immediately tried to escape that smooth, unbroken non-water's embrace as a layer of frozen mud, or something, grabbed ferociously at his ankles.

Within a single breath that colourless nothing had risen to Jake's shins, and then further up to his knees. As he struggled frantically against the immovable grip around his legs, Jake noted that his efforts produced no ripples of any kind to disturb that otherworldly ocean's flawless surface.

As the freezing non-water climbed inexorably to his waist and then up to his chest, Jake caught sight of the old priest running to the shore and desperately reaching out, seemingly wanting to help but also fearful of that silent, soulless expanse of the unknowable.

Jake emitted a final roar of fear and frustration as his shoulders disappeared beneath that freezing liquid glass, and there was no sound at all as the flat glossy silence closed quickly over his head.

13

Jake breathed a long sigh of relief as he opened his eyes and saw the vaulted ceiling above him. The light inside St John's vestry was still dim, but its sooty yellow quality had been displaced by weak winter daylight seeping through the boards covering the window. He closed his eyes again and tried to steady his fluttering heart, the taint of coal smoke and paraffin scratching at his burning throat as he waited for the thudding in his temples to subside. As he stretched and turned over, a sharp stab of pain helped to speed his return to the waking world.

He gingerly lifted the rough army blankets to reveal a heavy chain padlocked tightly around his wrist. Looped through the arch of a cast iron boot scraper protruding from a lump of Victorian doorstep, the heavy weight was a homespun yet effective variation of the classic ball and chain.

Jake knew that the thermometer toting priest and God knows who else might return at any moment, and from then on there was no telling what may happen. Gripping the sides of the cot, he carefully swung his feet onto the freezing stone floor, wincing as the sudden pain in his left knee diverted his attention from a thudding post-projection headache. He quickly felt around the joint and wiggled his toes. Nothing felt alarmingly out of place so he concluded he'd probably bruised it at some point, most likely down in the darkness of the crypt.

The chain around his wrist and the pain in his knee were forgotten when Jake spotted the round canteen of water waiting on the floor beside his cot. Only after he'd grabbed the container and swigged down half its metallic tasting contents did he wonder if the water was safe to drink. He quickly dismissed the idea of interference as he'd been out of it for quite a while, and wholly at the collarless clergyman's mercy. The old man could easily have smothered him, stabbed him or simply called the law. The makeshift shackle suggested the ageing priest didn't exactly trust the stranger he'd found in his basement, but he wasn't that trusting of officialdom either.

With its contents finally drained, Jake let the aluminium canteen clatter to the floor as he rolled onto his back and stared at the ceiling once more. As the all-consuming thirst subsided, he looked back at the empty water bottle. That was the second time there had been water ready and waiting when he woke up. Was it anything more than coincidence? Had the peculiar priest simply left a sick man something to drink out of kindness, or did he know for sure that Jake would want water more than anything else when he finally awoke? Every second that Jake stared at the ceiling, more questions crowded into his mind, and he knew he wouldn't find any answers laid flat on his back.

Gritting his teeth against the pain in his leg, he placed the soles of his feet firmly on the flagstones once more, grunting against the discomfort as he slowly stood up. The chain around his wrist was just a little too short to let him stand straight as he quickly took stock. He was still in the dishevelled civvies he'd been wearing when he'd collapsed in the crypt, and a quick feel of his face revealed a heavy stubble, suggesting he'd been out of it for quite some time.

He heaved up the stone block and shuffled awkwardly across to a door which he assumed led to the interior of the church. Not surprisingly it was locked. Not wanting to waste time, he ignored the obviously locked outer door and turned his attention to the room itself. Crossing to the iron stove, he opened the grated door and let the escaping heat radiate across his aching knee while he studied his surroundings more closely.

It was immediately clear that St John's vestry was a makeshift billet. Furniture was sparse, consisting of his camp bed, the hurriedly rigged stove, a nearly empty bookcase and a battered old bureau. The antique writing desk immediately caught his attention as it had been cleared to make room for the contents of his kitbag.

Jake felt a sense of relief and even a twinge of self-pity as he saw his few material possessions neatly laid out. A quick mental inventory confirmed that nearly everything was present and correct. His high-legged army boots, a couple of pairs of socks and a large wad of banknotes held together with a stout rubber band. His army issue Colt, minus its magazine, was placed on top of his two volumes of Baring-Gould's *Lives of the Saints*. Jake briefly wondered if there was some kind of silent reprimand in the way his collection of forged identity cards were carefully laid out beside those battered books. The Canadian Army uniform he'd bought on the black market was hung neatly over the back of a worn wooden chair, which was a clear mismatch with the sturdy but neglected bureau.

A frisson of alarm ran through his mind as he realised that his single most valuable possession was missing. He instinctively reached for the pistol, his hand hovering above the grip for a few seconds before he left the empty gun where it was and carefully placed his fake uniform on the tired desk

Jake heaved the makeshift weight closer, slumped into the chair and considered his predicament. Whoever this old man really was, he seemed to have no intention of harming or robbing his sick guest, and Jake was only too aware that he desperately needed allies if he was to survive as a wanted man. Besides, there was something familiar about the guy...

The clatter of the vestry's lock and the squeak of hinges interrupted Jake's deliberations before he'd really got started. He watched closely as his host, or captor, stepped into the vaulted stone room and carefully locked the door behind him.

The Reverend Piggott leaned back against the wall and gazed thoughtfully at the battered, leather-bound notebook in his hands, drumming his fingers on the scratched and worn cover. Piggott's pale and pinched features were a fitting accompaniment to Jake's dog-eared and dishevelled journal, both giving the impression of having travelled too many miles and for far too long.

Jake swallowed down a sudden surge of both anger and relief as he saw his battered notebook in a stranger's hands. For a moment he considered trying to retrieve it by force, but immediately realised that even if he overpowered the older man, there was no guarantee he'd ever find the key to his makeshift manacle. Dragging an antique doorstep through the streets wouldn't pass unnoticed for very long, and he couldn't rely on the assistance of the local underworld either. They *might* help him, but then they'd be just as likely to turn him in to the other firms who'd already put the word out. "You shouldn't go reading people's personal stuff," was Jake's eventual and somewhat weak opening line.

The priest gave no reply as he fished in his jacket to retrieve his glasses. Only when the wire arms were safely tucked behind his ears did he speak. "Well, I suppose you could argue that it's wrong. But theft and trespass don't exactly give you the moral high ground here, mate. And a man who walks around here permanently armed clearly fears retribution for his past misdeeds." Piggott stared hard for a moment before continuing. "You want to tell me your real name, son?"

Jake shook his head, clinging to the forlorn hope that Piggott hadn't already learned it from his notebook. "Safer for you if I didn't."

Piggott removed his glasses and rubbed one eye. "All right then, *Jimmy*, have it your own way. Let's try something else. Why don't you tell me where you got all that cash from, why you've got several false identities and where you learned to speak German?" Piggott flicked through Jake's notebook and pointed at a long passage written in the enemy's language. "I picked up a bit myself the last time around, but you write like a native."

"I didn't write that," said Jake quietly.

Piggott sighed. "I'm running out of patience, son. Whoever *didn't* write the German part of this diary obviously *didn't* write the rest of it either. It's all the same handwriting, see. So either you wrote it all, or this is something *else* that don't belong to you." He snapped the notebook shut. "I find a man hiding in my church with a wad of cash, false papers, and documents written in German. Give me one good reason why I shouldn't call a constable, or even the Snowdrops right now."

Jake glanced at the outside door and realised that Piggott was making sense, despite the fact that the old man and his bombed out church didn't exactly seem legit themselves. Once again he considered jumping the weaker man, but if he could make a successful escape it was still a bad idea. At present, certain parties had no firm evidence as to his status, living or dead. If Piggott reported the strange nine fingered American to the police then the men he most feared would surely double their efforts to track him down. The only way to be certain was to shut the old man up forever, but Jake drew the line at rubbing out a priest, even a lapsed one. Instead he asked the obvious question. "Why am I still here and not in jail already?"

Piggott stepped forward, closer to the iron stove. "You might end up there yet, or perhaps I'll just turn you over to Pete Finch. That fat bugger's offering two hundred quid to whoever finds you first. He hates card sharps, unless it's him doing the cheating of course."

"Yeah, I know. Can't trust anyone these days. But I never cheated him; I'm just good at reading people, and cards."

The old priest nodded slowly. "And I suppose Finch is the reason you tried disappearing down here, in George Tooley's manor."

"Who?"

Piggott pinched the bridge of his nose and squeezed his eyes shut. "You may be good at cards but you're a terrible liar, which means you're no gangster."

"So what am I then?" Jake mentally kicked himself for directly challenging the man on whom his future might rest, whether he liked it or not.

Piggott flicked through the notebook once again before turning back towards the door. "Well, you're either a rubbish gangster, an even worse spy...or perhaps you're something else."

Jake squinted at the older man. "You know, I'd swear I've seen you somewhere before."

Piggott's tone suddenly took on a sour note. "Hang around down the soup kitchen, do ya?"

Jake held up his left hand and wiggled his four remaining fingers. "There's plenty of my buddies won't be needing any soup. Y'know, it'd be real nice if you guys would say thanks rather than whining about your women and your stomachs all the time." He angrily shook the chain around his other wrist. "And I'm not your goddamned pet either, so just let me go before you end up in more trouble than you've ever dreamed of."

The priest produced his key and unlocked the door again. "Don't try to kid me you're *giving* us anything; it all comes at a price. Besides, I ain't seen a hungry Yank yet." He gestured around the room. "Anyway, speaking of food, there's a tin of spam knocking around somewhere, and there's a pot by the bed if you need to take a leak. If you've got half a brain you'll stay put and keep schtum. You're a long way from home or help, my Yankee liberator, so don't try anything heroic. I may be a priest but that don't mean I can't shoot straight." With that last warning Piggott stifled a cough and disappeared back through the door, leaving Jake alone with the crackling stove.

After the old man's footfalls had receded, Jake carefully rolled up his grimy trouser leg to examine the throbbing bruise around his knee.

It was completely unmarked.

14

Major Giles Clarke wondered if the dim-out had been extended underground as he reached the bottom of the spiral staircase. The rope handrail clinging to the circular wall felt smooth and greasy in his hand, suggesting that these isolated backstairs had recently been used a great deal more than the rusted entrance above ground suggested.

The neglected stairway opened into a cavernous and damp smelling cellar, littered with slowly swelling furniture. Long forgotten cabinets bulging with long-forgotten files slowly deteriorated in ragged ranks stretching away into the darkness.

Clarke's eyes were instinctively drawn to a pool of light spilling from a doorway some distance ahead, and he was left in no doubt that he had found his destination. As he set off towards it, he noticed that the slick flagstones underfoot had been worn clean by many pairs of shoes tramping to and from this particular room, a room which ordinarily might receive one visitor each year. However, the current circumstances were far from ordinary.

As he wound his way through the bowels of the Victorian prison, Clarke caught sight of several bunk beds, now dismantled and stored below ground following their erstwhile occupiers' summary eviction by an ever-expanding security machine.

Clarke had no idea who'd first thought of it, but requisitioning one of London's most infamous landmarks had been a masterstroke. The building was solid, secure and its new occupants could remain safely anonymous inside. This was not the first time Major Clarke had liaised with MI5 behind those soul destroying walls, although on his first visit he'd been surprised to learn there was a significant counterintelligence presence hidden inside His Majesty's penal system.

Clarke couldn't help smiling as he neared the main switch room of HMP Wormwood Scrubs. At least the location showed that somebody had taken the trouble to read his report regarding the recent debacle in Kent, and that somebody had the imagination to understand that one could never be too careful.

The Major paused as he reached the open doorway, unsure if he should knock or just walk straight in. Usually it was *he* who summoned others to meetings, and those to whom Clarke answered invariably had at least one private secretary to open doors and announce his arrival.

"Do come in, Major Clarke. Come in, please." A soft, well enunciated voice issued from the room, the clear-cut Oxbridge accent not quite obscuring all traces of a northern dialect, possibly Mancunian.

The Major stepped over the threshold and peered into the cramped room. Thick electric cables festooned the walls like a rubberised industrial bindweed, crawling over the large switch panels crammed into the confined space. The gleam of a single table lamp reflected off a pair of thick pebble glasses as the room's occupier beckoned him inside.

Once Clarke had closed the door behind him, a small man waddled awkwardly from behind his borrowed desk to shake the Major's hand effusively, as though he were meeting a movie star or sports champion. "At last, the great Dr Death himself. You know, I've followed your career with keen interest and ever increasing admiration. In my opinion, posterity will one day rediscover you as perhaps the greatest of the men who never were."

Clarke tried to reclaim his hand but the man in the pinstripe suit held it firm, refusing to relinquish his grip with a familiarity that was rapidly descending into rudeness.

The man who'd summoned Clarke to this unusual meeting was small, rapidly balding and rotund. He waddled and puffed and reddened in the manner of one who was morbidly obese rather than merely overweight. The waddler's palm was soft, fleshy and unpleasantly clammy as he continued to pump the

Major's arm whilst overflowing with excited and very one-sided conversation. "It's so rare to meet someone with an open yet disciplined mind such as yours. Most men I meet are fools, rocks, or just plain fantasists. Very difficult to make friends with someone if you know he's a fool, a rock or a fantasist. I'm sure you have the same trouble yourself."

The plump little man finally released the Major's arm and gestured to a damp wooden chair opposite his makeshift desk. "Please make yourself as comfortable as you can. I'm sorry we couldn't meet in more pleasant surroundings, but I don't have to lecture you about taking precautions. Besides, I know you're no stranger to roughing it. To be honest, I find it all rather exciting. Most of the people I work with are used to privilege and comfort. They don't understand the necessity of immersing oneself in the culture within which one operates, not that I'm a field man myself. Lord no. I mean, look at me, I can barely *finish* the hundred yards, and as for my time, well, perhaps a calendar would be more appropriate than a stopwatch."

The short man stopped talking abruptly. Leaning heavily on his desk, he closed his eyes and took a long deep breath through his nostrils, expelling it slowly through his mouth before opening his eyes again. "Please do forgive me, Major. I have an unfortunate habit of babbling uncontrollably when I'm nervous or excited. You know it's a funny thing, the JIC and the Chiefs of Staff don't concern me at all, but I always get excited when I meet a man who works at the sharp end. Please do take a seat and we'll get down to brass tacks. Goodness, there's so much to discuss it's difficult to know where to start."

Clarke sat and idly stroked his beard as he studied the peculiar little man. "Well, we could start with your name, and then move on to why you've asked me here."

The rotund civilian pulled a pressed linen handkerchief from his pocket and dabbed at his forehead before groaning into his own chair. "Quite right, Major, quite right." He looked thoughtfully at the handkerchief for a moment as though studying the patterns left by his own perspiration.

Clarke rummaged in the pocket of his tweed suit and produced his pipe as he waited for the small man to speak again.

As though finishing some inaudible internal conversation, the bespectacled interviewer nodded to himself, pocketed the handkerchief and clasped his hands on the mouldering desk. "My name is Thorndike." He waved his hands at the humming switch panels crowding the room. "I'm sure I don't need to explain what we're about to discuss."

Clarke raised his eyebrows. "I'm surprised anyone took me seriously."

Thorndike smiled, his soft, thick lips parting to reveal a well ordered set of off-white teeth, the reflection from the desk lamp suddenly flaring across his spectacles as he shifted his head. "You have no idea *how* seriously, my dear Major." He suddenly ducked down behind the desk and produced a battered leather briefcase. Throwing back the flap, he rummaged inside and produced two plain brown files of the highly restricted type Clarke was well used to dealing with. "I've no intention of raking over the minutiae of your report regarding the Cedarwood incident as I know you to be a man of good judgement, and anyway, we don't have time to discuss every aspect in detail. However I *would* like to just clear up one or two issues arising from your submission."

Clarke's eyes widened as he stared at the folders. "Those reports are highly secret. Only the members of the Joint Intelligence Committee are authorised to see them."

Thorndike raised his eyebrows. "Really, I'm surprised a man like you is so naive as to think the JIC, Chiefs of Staff or anyone else who may be of interest to history would have anything to do with such hare-brained ideas. Remote viewing, secret societies, shadowy front institutions." Thorndike tapped the files with a pudgy finger. "What made you think that the JIC would do *anything* except drop such fantastic and impossible notions like a hot potato?"

"A hot potato you were waiting to catch," observed Clarke as he shifted in his chair, trying not to think about what havoc the black mildew might wreak on his suit.

"Quite so, my dear Major. I might be described a specialist in the unlikely, which I flatter myself to think makes us kindred spirits in a way."

Clarke sensed that it might take a while to arrive at the true reason for their meeting as he reached into his other pocket for his matches.

"I'd rather you didn't," snapped Thorndike irritably. "I have extremely sensitive sinuses."

Clarke failed to mask the scowl which flashed across his face as he clasped his hands in his lap. "So, I imagine that a specialist in the unlikely would've read both my own and Miss Parsons' reports, and if he'd decided that they were of no use or interest, he wouldn't have gone to the trouble of arranging what I assume is an off-the-record meeting, in the middle of an electrical field, hidden in the cellar of a prison."

Thorndike smiled broadly and rubbed his hands together with glee. "I can see that your reputation for farsightedness is well founded. Now I'm *sure* you're just the man for the job. Naturally suspicious, yet flexible enough to accept the evidence of your own experience."

Clarke shifted in his seat again as the omnipresent hum of the switchgear began to irritate, somehow transferring itself into his body and seeming to resonate through the caverns of his consciousness. "What is it you wanted to discuss?"

Thorndike opened the report submitted by Ellie Parsons and quickly leafed through it. "This Miss Parsons, is she reliable?"

"Absolutely," confirmed Clarke. "I can guarantee she would never have submitted any information she was not completely certain about, and she would always qualify theory or speculation as such."

Thorndike pursed his lips and picked up the second file. "Glad to know we have such able operatives at our disposal. Your own report, naturally, is far more interesting. Now correct me if I'm wrong, but the only two Sensitives, as we call them, to survive the Cedarwood episode were Dr Thomas Hammond and this Sergeant Jacob Small."

Clarke nodded. "That's right."

Thorndike flicked to the last page of the report. "So, you now have Dr Hammond safely contained, both in this world and the next." The specialist in the unusual smirked at his own wit. "However, you have no information as to the whereabouts of this American, this Sergeant Small."

"No, we don't know where he is, but I'll wager my pension he's somewhere here in London."

Thorndike sounded surprised. "Really? Why so?"

"It stands to reason. He's a Yank trapped in England. Where else can he hide? The countryside's no use, he'll stand out like a sore thumb with that accent. His only hope is to blend in, and to do that he needs to be among other Yanks or even Canadians. His chances of survival are far greater in a city, and he knows that London's the place where an American's least likely to draw attention. Added to that, it would be much easier to obtain the necessities of life via the underworld. My guess is he's running with the racketeers and the deserters."

Thorndike shoved a finger behind his thick glasses and rubbed one eye. "How do you suppose he made it to London from Kent? No papers, perhaps injured, and certainly looking a frightful state. How do you suppose he managed that?"

Clarke spread his hands. "I don't know exactly, but by all accounts he's an intelligent and resourceful man. That's probably one of the reasons Section 12, the Brotherhood, OSS and God knows who else are interested in his particular talents."

Thorndike suddenly removed his glasses and stared pointedly at the Major. "How hard have you looked for him here in London?"

"My section hasn't looked for him at all, at least not actively. We can't go kicking down doors and spinning speilers without drawing attention to ourselves. The only members of the regular police we could possibly trust might be Special Branch, but we can't really ask them to take on the search for a supposedly ordinary deserter without a good reason. They're stretched as it is. Besides, Jake Small isn't about to help the British intelligence community, and he'd probably tell Uncle Sam where to get off after what Hammond put him through."

"What about the Yanks, what are they doing?"

Clarke absentmindedly reached for his tobacco before remembering Thorndike's admonition. "They're keeping their eyes and ears open just like us, but they're even more hamstrung than we are. Without local police co-operation of some kind there's not very much they can do, considering the fact they're supposedly guests in this country."

Thorndike leaned back and steepled his fingers. "Well I must say, you read and handled the Cedarwood situation correctly, but your tidying up has been less than exemplary."

Clarke's patience was beginning to wear thin. "Well I'm terribly sorry, Mr Thorndike. Dealing with criminals and those of questionable character necessarily means you can't always guess what they're going to do next. Had I anticipated I'd be interviewed in a maintenance room by a specialist in the unusual I would've tried much harder."

Thorndike seemed not to notice the edge to Clarke's reply. He merely glanced at his watch and laboured to his feet. "Well, Major Clarke, I have a couple of calls to make before we proceed any further. If I were you I'd find a place to have a quiet smoke and perhaps something to eat. I will see you back here in one hour." With that the portly civilian picked up the two brown files, dropped them in his battered briefcase and waddled towards the switch-room's grimy metal door.

15

Jake didn't move as the lock clicked and the vestry door swung open. Huddled beneath his blankets, he waited patiently as he heard the Reverend Piggott call softly to him. The smell of food filled his nostrils as the old man shuffled closer.

It was only when the priest had leaned down to pull the blankets back that Jake finally exploded into action. Even though he was partially restrained, he had no difficulty in grabbing Piggott's wrist with both hands and viciously pulling him off balance.

The priest gave a strangled squawk as Jake's foot connected hard with his stomach.

Pressing home his advantage, Jake sprang into a crouch and pushed the old man down onto his front. The cot creaked, rocked and finally gave way as he forced Piggott's arm behind his back and drove his knee between the priest's shoulder blades.

"Christ!" Was Piggott's gasping response as he twisted his head to avoid breaking his nose on the stone floor.

"All right grandad, make with the keys." Jake rattled the chain around his wrist.

Piggott's reply was not especially coherent. It was just a groan and a few muffled words.

Jake upped the pressure. "Come on old timer, don't make me hurt you."

"Who's making you?" Piggott's voice was distorted with pain.

Jake eased the pressure a little. "Look buddy, just give me the keys and I'll be on my way, no questions asked. Let's face it, I'm hardly gonna call the cops am I?"

"Do you always treat your hosts..." The rest of Piggott's response was lost in a sudden coughing fit.

Confident that he'd knocked the fight out of his opponent, Jake relaxed his grip and quickly helped the old man into a sitting position.

Piggott breathlessly nodded his thanks and gripped Jake's shoulder tightly as another bout of coughing shook his thin body.

Jake looked down at the floor, pretending not to notice the pink spittle which Piggott hurriedly wiped from the corner of his mouth. Once the old man had caught his breath a little, Jake pointed to the chair beside the glowing iron stove. "Just sit yourself there before you go and die on me. I don't want to hurt you, but I won't be played for a sucker either. Just hand me those keys and I'll be out of your hair."

Piggott slowly clambered to his feet and half staggered across the room, leaning heavily on the chair as he twisted himself into it. He produced a small bunch of keys and selected one, pointing at the drawer of his scratched desk. "In there." He pointed with the key.

Jake hefted up his ever present burden. "Now don't get any stupid ideas. I'll just take my stuff and be on my way. It'd be a sin to hurt a sick old man but that won't stop me, understand?"

Piggott nodded and placed the keys on the desk. When he spoke his voice was strained, grey and breathless despite its defiant tone. "Well *you've* recovered bloody quick, sunshine. Last time I looked I thought I was gonna have to bury you."

Jake ignored the observation and shuffled forward, his eyes narrowing when he noticed that his battered journal had reappeared on the desk, along with a steaming bowl of good-smelling stew. "You shouldn't have read that. It's private, and anyway it's nothing but trouble."

Piggott squeezed his eyes shut. "The desk, son." He pointed to the locked wooden drawers.

Carefully placing the iron scraper on the floor and keeping one eye on the old man, Jake grabbed the small key and unlocked the bureau. "You'd better not be joshing with me. I'm not in the mood."

The old priest folded his arms tightly across his chest and leaned forward as Jake slowly pulled the drawer open. "Brandy, that's what I need."

Jake recovered the good quality liquor. "It's a bit early," he observed as he handed it across to the older man.

Piggott grabbed the bottle and slopped a good measure into a chipped china mug before reaching gingerly into his pocket and recovering a small glass phial. He breathed a sigh of relief when he saw it had survived the struggle and quickly poured several drops of milky liquid into the liquor with a shaking hand.

Jake found himself filled with both compassion and alarm as he watched the struggling priest. "You sure that's a good idea? I mean, I'm no doctor and all, but shouldn't you measure that stuff more carefully?"

Piggott drained the mug in two mouthfuls and slumped back into the chair. "What do you care? You nearly broke my arm, you ungrateful little bleeder."

Having emptied the drawer and tried all the other keys in the padlock, Jake closed in on the priest once more, keeping his voice soft as he realised the combination of sickness, alcohol and laudanum might see the old man pass out at any moment. "Reverend, I need to get out of here, you know that." He pointed to the empty gun and papers on the desk to underline his point. "Please Reverend, where's the key for this padlock?"

Piggott squeezed his eyes shut again and shook his head violently as though trying to clear it. "I had a dream about you, son. We were on a beach, or something like that, then we were somewhere else, but I can't remember. It was dark and cold though, I remember that much."

Jake gently shook the old man's shoulders. "What do you *mean*, you had a dream?"

Piggott smiled far too kindly for a man in his condition as he pointed towards Jake's battered notebook. "Looks like you've got some real talent, son. But you're not the only one with eyes."

Jake felt the hairs on his neck stand up. "Eyes? What do you mean, Reverend?"

Piggott was suddenly and inexplicably alert despite the alcohol and opiate he'd just swallowed. "You ain't the first, and you won't be the last bloke who's got himself in trouble with his gifts."

Jake leaned forward, disturbed but not altogether surprised by the sudden turn of events. "What do you know about it?"

Piggott suppressed a cough and poured himself another brandy. "I know not to go writing my whole life story down for any fool to find. Bloody stupid thing to do."

Jake didn't trust the old man enough to reveal the truth, so he tapped his scarred head. "I've got a bad memory, probably always gonna be like that now. Things just come and go. Sometimes when I wake up, I can barely remember my own name, then other days I'm just fine. The shrink told me it was shellshock y'see."

Piggott raised his eyebrows. "Yeah? Did he tell you that all that other stuff you've been writing about was shellshock too?"

"Is that what they told *you?*" Jake countered.

Piggott's eyes narrowed suspiciously. "Who are you? Why are you *really* here?"

"I don't know why I'm here, Reverend. All I can tell you for sure is that I'm done with the army and I'm sure as hell nothing to do with the Brotherhood. I think they're all dead now anyway. Good riddance if you ask me."

The priest frowned. "Do I look like the sort of bloke who's interested in funny handshakes?"

Jake waved his hand dismissively. "It doesn't matter. Forget about it. I'm just trying to keep my head down until I can figure out what to do next."

There was an awkward silence as each man paused to weigh the other up.

Eventually it was Piggott who spoke. "I suppose you made the mistake of letting the army brass in on your little secret; but it didn't work out quite like they said it would, did it?"

"It wasn't my fault." Jake found himself protesting before he realised he'd made any kind of admission.

Piggott smiled a pained smile of triumph. "Don't worry, son. If I was going to call the Snowdrops on you I'd have done it by now."

Jake looked around Piggott's makeshift quarters, suddenly struck by the frightening thought that his own twilight days might mirror those of this sick old priest; alone, hiding and dying slow. "What was it like for *you*, Reverend? What did you see? What did they tell you? Is that why you became a priest, or were you one already?"

Piggott's chin began to sag onto his chest as the pain, brandy and laudanum finally took their toll. "That's a long story, son, a *long* story. But I can tell you for sure that there were things out there, in the fog and the smoke and the gas. I saw them plain as day, sort of. A few blokes like me know it and the top brass knew it too, but they weren't about to let on. Why would they? Didn't want to upset the apple cart you see. They just wanted us all to do all the bleeding so they could keep things exactly the way they were, in this world and maybe even the next as well."

There was another pause while Jake considered his next move. "Listen old-timer, I'd really like to stay and talk with you but we both know I can't. I have to keep moving. Just tell me where the rest of my stuff is and I'll be on my way."

Piggott pointed towards the vestry door, his voice now a little more dreamy, a little less certain. "Just across the way there; the keys are on my bedside, and you'll find some clean clothes in there too. I wouldn't walk around in uniform if I was you."

Jake couldn't prevent a slight smile playing on his lips. "You an expert on evading the cops, huh?"

Piggott smiled back, his eyes suddenly alert again although his head swayed slightly as he pointed towards Jake's notebook and the rapidly cooling plate of stew beside it. "You need to get out of here, sunshine. Get that grub down you and get your stuff together. You're right, you shouldn't stay here."

"Don't you have any family? A place of your own?" Jake asked.

Piggott grimaced. "Family's all gone, house is gone too, long time ago."

Jake's conscience finally got the better of him. He had to speak up, he had to say something. "Listen Reverend, you should be in hospital. I mean it ain't right."

A sudden flicker of fear passed across the old man's slightly glazed eyes. "No! No hospitals. You have to promise me!" Grimacing against the pain, he leaned forward and placed his hand on Jake's dog-eared notebook. "No hospitals and no doctors, understand?"

"Okay, no doctors then." Jake reluctantly agreed. "Don't you have anyone, I mean..."

Piggott interrupted Jake's question. "No time for that now, you need to pick up your stuff and go."

Jake shook his head with exasperation. "Yeah, I wish I knew where to. I always thought I was a pretty smart guy but all I've done is run in circles and get myself in more trouble; and not with the law this time."

"Don't worry, *I'll* tell you where. There's a place you'll be safe."

Jake straightened, a suspicious expression falling across his face. "Someone once told me that before, and it turned out to be bullshit." He glanced across at his journal.

Piggott smiled thinly and shook his head. "It's not like that. I'd never let something like that happen to you. They've done enough damage already."

Jake swallowed down the lump which had unexpectedly risen in his throat. "You *sure* we've never met? I *know* I've seen you somewhere."

The priest shook his head sadly. "Sorry son. Wish I could say the same, but there's no way I'd have forgotten *you*."

The younger man thought for a moment, and then came to a decision. "You're right, I'd better just go. But why the hell did you lock me up in the first place?"

Piggott leaned slowly across and grabbed Jake's notebook. "Hadn't finished the story, see. Didn't bloody well know who you were then, did I? You could've been some volatile lunatic for all I know. This war's driven plenty of blokes over the edge."

"And now?"

Piggott solemnly handed the battered book back to its owner. "Just get yourself changed, son. I'll tell you where you need to go."

16

Major Clarke glanced at his watch again. Thorndike was late, and although he didn't know the man's habits it struck him as a sign that something important was happening. That fact that Thorndike, rather than the JIC or any other official body was handling the meeting was true to form. Indeed, Clarke's own Section C had operated as just such an autonomous and deniable department. If tales of their exploits ever leaked out, they would be nothing more than lurid rumours, pub stories fuelled by beer and wishful thinking.

While providing essential political wriggle room, the perennial problem with such unofficial "consultancies" was their nasty habit of going off the rails in pursuit of conflicting agendas, as in the case of Section 12. They could do terrible damage before anyone at the centre even realised what was happening.

Clarke's contemplations on the moral and practical limits of state power were interrupted as Thorndike puffed back into the switch room. He quickly slumped into his chair and dabbed his forehead with his handkerchief.

"Are you all right?" Clarke asked mischievously.

"I'll survive," Thorndike responded as he pocketed the handkerchief. "We're lucky there are fitter and stronger men than I to do the important work on the front line."

"Surely you regard your work as important," countered Clarke. He was curious to see what the plump little man was made of.

Thorndike fished in his briefcase and produced the two plain files once again. "I was beginning to think my area of expertise was being overlooked until your report landed on my desk. Indeed, if I'm completely honest, I was disappointed to learn that Section 12's work was proceeding without my knowledge."

Clarke stared steadfastly at the plump man with the obviously false name. "Curious, I would've thought you'd be the *first* to know. But at any rate it's of little importance. If you'd been involved with Section 12 you'd have ended up tarred with the same brush, if you'd survived at all. You can thank the Brotherhood for that mess."

Thorndike placed his briefcase on the floor and clasped his hands on the desk. "The Brotherhood aren't really all that opaque. In many ways they're just like the rest of us. After all, I'm sure you want to see you and yours prosper, even if that's at the expense of others."

Clarke leaned forward to mirror Thorndike's posture. "Yes, but me and mine aren't endowed with unnatural abilities, and ambitions to match them."

"Unnatural abilities," echoed Thorndike softly. "That brings us rather neatly back to the subject of Dr Thomas Hammond. I've heard that he can perform extraordinary feats of psychoscopy, as well as being a force to be reckoned with in the fields of psychiatry and medicine."

"In many ways the man's brilliant," Clarke conceded sadly. "That's what makes his questionable loyalties all the more difficult to live with."

"But live with him you do," observed Thorndike. "That is, you keep him stored below ground, in a place much like this I would imagine."

Clarke was too experienced not to notice when somebody was fishing for information. "What is it that you want to know, Mr Thorndike? My report was submitted some time ago, and I must confess I'm surprised to see that it still exists. The fact that it hasn't yet been destroyed can only mean there's some kind of ongoing situation."

Thorndike opened the brown folder once again and flicked to the final page. "Don't you worry, we'll get to the whys soon enough. For the moment I just want to make sure I'm properly briefed on the situation as it stands now. I'll have to make some decisions based on that information, so I need to be sure I understand what's happening."

Clarke leaned back and clasped his hands firmly in his lap once again, trying to ignore the ever more urgent desire to reach for his pipe. "As I'm sure you know, Section C operated as an autonomous body, answerable directly to the Joint Intelligence Committee, and only *then* on the understanding that operational details were withheld for mutual protection. Just *knowing* some things could put a lot of senior staff in some very awkward situations. Bearing all that in mind, why should I tell you anything?"

The light gleamed off Thorndike's glasses as his head shifted slightly. "Because I'm one of the few men alive who can persuade the JIC to my way of thinking. I asked them to delay destruction of your report and to allow this meeting, so why don't we save ourselves a great deal of trouble and you just treat this as though it *were* a JIC meeting."

Clarke considered resisting for a moment, but he knew the smaller man held the stronger hand. "What exactly do you want to know?"

Thorndike matched the Major's gaze for a moment longer before looking back down at the file. "As I understand it from your own and Miss Parsons' reports, there were five of these so-called Sensitives present at Section 12 HQ. They were one Corporal Williams, Peter van Cortlandt, Colonel Kurt Stryker, Sergeant Jacob Small and last but not least, Dr Thomas Hammond himself."

Clarke nodded.

Thorndike continued. "You yourself have confirmed that Stryker, van Cortlandt and Williams are now deceased."

"Absolutely. I identified van Cortlandt personally, Stryker was in a real mess but we were able to identify him from our files at Section C. Poor Corporal Williams was still wearing his identity tags when they dug his body out of the rubble."

Thorndike suddenly changed the subject. "I understand Hammond is being looked after by Dr Werner, the younger."

"That's right. He's proved himself to be no friend of the Nazis, and seeing as how the Werners were extracted along with van Cortlandt, he's one of the few men both qualified and experienced enough to deal with these Sensitives."

Thorndike closed the file and reached for his handkerchief once again. "So that just leaves Sergeant Jacob Small of the Fourth unaccounted for."

Clarke rolled his eyes with exasperation. "It's taken us a bloody long time to get back to where we started. You already know all this, so why are you asking me again? I don't appreciate this amateurish kind of debriefing."

"Just making sure I understood everything before I impart the next piece of information."

Clarke mentally chastised himself as he realised he was leaning forward.

Thorndike cleared his throat. "Having been made aware of the situation regarding these Sensitives, and knowing that the late Colonel Stryker was engaged in some kind of research in France, I did a little digging...well, quite a lot actually. I've finally arrived at the disturbing conclusion that whatever Colonel Stryker was working on, his French HQ was all but empty by the time the Americans arrived."

"I know that," sighed Clarke with exasperation.

The small man continued as though Clarke had never spoken. "Having learned that Stryker's work didn't necessarily die with him, and accounting for the fact that the Germans were willing to risk an air raid on the Kent countryside to prevent his defection, I managed to push through some small security changes at various locations within the capital."

Clarke sensed he was about to learn something important. *"Which* locations?"

"It wasn't easy, but I managed to convince certain members of the JIC to humour me and deploy trained sentries to watch for signs of Sensitive infiltration."

Clarke felt the hairs on the back of his neck stand on end, suddenly acting as miniature antenna to transmit the omnipresent electric hum straight to his spine. "Go on."

Thorndike took a deep breath and looked sombre, as though he were about to break some bad news to a soldier's relatives. "We've been having hits."

"Hits? You mean..."

"That's right. Dogs barking at nothing and impossible to quieten by any method, save for one."

"Which is?" Asked Clarke, trying his best to sound nonchalant.

Thorndike smiled triumphantly. "A little invention of my own. I call it a Blank Trap. We've known for a while that high-voltage electrical fields interfere with the Sensitive's viewing abilities. What do you suppose would happen if one of these disembodied snoopers were suddenly trapped inside a strong electromagnetic field?"

Clarke thought for a second. "I'm not entirely sure, but I think he'd suffer something of a headache, if not worse."

Thorndike nodded enthusiastically. "Quite so. We've not been able to establish the exact effect as we can't actually *see* what's happening. All I can tell you for certain is that once the trap is triggered, the dogs settle. This suggests that the intruder has somehow been neutralised."

"Permanently?" Said Clarke hopefully.

"I doubt it. The hits continue and there can only be a few men, or perhaps women in this world with the ability to project at will and with such accuracy. Even more so when you consider that all the installations in question are below ground, targets which seem especially difficult for Sensitives to penetrate." Thorndike hunched forward and fiddled with the plain wedding band on his finger. "There's someone out there. Someone very talented and very determined, who is attempting to infiltrate some of our most secure sites. Who they are and what they want we don't know, but the only confirmed Sensitive at liberty who even *approaches* that level of sophistication...is Sergeant Jacob Small."

Clarke thought for a moment before he spoke. "You're assuming that such a Sensitive must be based somewhere in this country, physically I mean."

Thorndike tipped his head back, considering Clarke's words. "All the available information suggests there were only two men capable of projecting over such great distances as you suggest. Both were senior members of this so-called Brotherhood, and both are confirmed as deceased."

"You're referring to Stryker and van Cortlandt."

"Quite so," confirmed Thorndike. "I've studied the work of both Dr Werners, and they corroborate that such individuals are exceptionally rare. Those who can project over shorter distances, say within the borders of a host nation are still very unusual, but less so. The balance of probability suggests that whoever's responsible is inside the country, perhaps even somewhere in London."

"So that makes Jake Small our prime suspect," confirmed Clarke.

Thorndike looked hard at the Major. "We need you to find Jake Small for us, regardless of how many people might get upset or what kind of ripples flow through the underworld." He leaned back and gestured with his hand. "Why don't you smoke a pipe, Major Clarke? Our meeting is nearly over and we need to learn to trust one another."

"Thank you, I will," said Clarke as he reached into his jacket and produced his pre-filled pipe. A moment later a box of matches had appeared and the room was filling with noxious blue smoke.

Thorndike smiled, although his eyes were already beginning to water. "If Jacob Small is responsible for these intrusions, then we can neutralise him as a potential threat. If not, then at least we can remove him from the equation. I've spoken at length with various senior parties, and we've decided to take the calculated risk of bringing Dr Hammond back into the game."

Clarke stopped in mid-puff and took his pipe from his mouth. "Hammond? Are you sure about that? His reliability is questionable at best, and Dr Werner has serious doubts about his mental state. In fact, Werner suspects something happened to him at Cedarwood."

Thorndike shrugged. "Hammond is the only Sensitive we can lay our hands on right now, and we can't afford to leave our tools lying idle in the box."

"Tools can hurt you badly if not used correctly," observed Clarke quietly.

"I know, but we're out of options and out of time. These damned rockets continue to fall, the advance has stalled in France and now we've got possible agents prowling around our command and control centres. This war is far from won, and we need to use any methods necessary to contain the situation. In short, we need Dr Death, Section C and its ruthless band of cutthroats, swindlers, thieves and forgers. Add to that your personal experience of these matters and you're uniquely qualified to handle this difficult assignment."

Clarke said nothing while he concentrated on filling the room with tobacco smoke. At last he heard the satisfying sound of Thorndike coughing and saw him reach for his handkerchief. "Assuming I find Jake Small, he's unlikely to cooperate with us after what Section 12 put him through."

Thorndike stood to leave. "Either way, we need him safely tied down, not sliding around the gun deck at a time like this."

Clarke frowned as a thought occurred to him. "How do we know the Yanks haven't tracked him down already? After all he's one of theirs."

Thorndike held his handkerchief over his nose and mouth and hurried to the door, pulling it open and allowing a cloud of smoke to escape into the rest of the cellar. "They'll probably think the place is on fire," he joked before his demeanour became serious once more. "If the Yanks *do* get hold of him before us, can you trust your friend to be candid about it?"

Clarke nodded. "He's a good man, and honest, as far as possible in our line of work. He knows what we're all fighting for so I'd trust him."

"Very well. I'll leave operational details in your capable hands, Major. Needless to say that any records will be eyes only and single copy, to be disposed of at the operation's conclusion."

"Code name?" Asked Clarke.

Thorndike closed his eyes for a moment then smiled. "Operation Dark Spring," he replied with relish. "What will you do first, Major?"

It only took Clarke a second or two to work out his priorities. "Well, the first thing will be to find some engineers. I'll need to re-open the field office, it's been mothballed in the same way I was."

The plump little man finally stepped over the threshold. "No need, Major. I sent some reliable lads down to your old place last week. I'm sure you'll find the new facilities much more agreeable."

17

Pete Finch groaned as he bent to poke at the embers sulking in the grate. He grumbled to himself as he reluctantly selected another lump of coal to prevent the fire from going out altogether. Another expense for the privilege of hearing more customers complaining about less food, and all paid for with little scraps of worthless paper.

He straightened and looked around his dusty grocer's shop, thankful that at least the war had given him an excuse to close his doors whenever he chose, especially when the chance to make some *real* money with the King's head on it came his way. It was a funny old world, and Pete Finch's war hadn't been all bad, in fact far from it. The lengthy conflict had presented rare opportunities for imaginative men, and provided unprecedented expansion into ever more lucrative markets. In many ways the shop was a pain in the arse and a drain on his time, but it did at least provide a legitimate base of operations. The burden he endured in exchange for such convenience was an unending stream of housewives bemoaning a lack of basic commodities that he didn't really give a toss about. After all, Pete never wanted for anything.

He shuffled across to the shop's door and checked the bolts again, just in case. Gently parting the blackout curtains, he peered out into the drizzle soaked street to confirm that nobody was moving outside; it was too bloody cold. Everyone was either sweating in factories or huddling scared at home, but not him. The war would soon be over, and when that day came he'd be leaving all these idiots behind once and for all. It was gonna be the good life on easy street for Pete Finch, with nobody to bend his ear about spam or cheese or anything else. Cards, good scotch and French cigarettes were more to his taste, although the latter had gotten harder to obtain since his regular supplier had suddenly vanished. Still, that was the name of the game.

Finch let the curtain fall back and tramped heavily across the bare, swept floorboards before squeezing himself behind the counter. He stopped at the door to the back parlour, suddenly struck by an unexpected twinge of nostalgia as he surveyed the modest and musty space once more. With its omnipresent scent of paraffin and coal smoke, the dingy converted terrace was the only home he'd ever known; as well as being his late father's legacy to him. For a moment Finch wondered if the old man was looking down disapprovingly from some grocer's paradise up above. He hoped not, but it didn't matter because the street savvy he'd harvested from life's hard lessons was all his own. Dad had been a good man, an honest man, and he'd died alone and with very little money because of it. He'd actually believed the fantasy that hard work, diligence and thrift paved the road to comfort and success, or at least he had done until the Spanish flu came calling in 1919. It was at his dad's funeral that Pete Finch had realised that the world showed only contempt for those who lacked the strength and cunning to stand up and take what was rightfully theirs.

Having settled his unexpected inner dialogue, Finch nodded to himself before opening the door separating the shop front from his living quarters. A new house would take some getting used to, that was for sure, but the way things were shaping up he'd be retiring sooner than he'd expected, and with a lot more capital to cushion the autumn of his life. His greatest regret was that he couldn't sell his lucrative rackets on as a going concern, but once this final and very special order was filled, Pete Finch would be nothing more than a memory in London's folklore. This was the one, the big job, the fancy tickle that spivs and screwsmen dreamed of all their lives. What's more, it had landed straight in his lap, more or less, and he'd never have to lift a latch or break a lock to collect. It was risky though, and Finch knew he'd have to be quick on his toes when the balloon went up, as it surely would. He knew he'd crossed the line between honest racketeering and some far more hazardous and morally murky enterprise. Once again he reminded himself that the world rewarded boldness, not timidity.

Satisfied that the shop was secure, Finch stepped into the back parlour to be greeted by the orange glow of his private and well-stocked fireplace. Crossing to an ancient porcelain sink, he delved into the cupboard beneath and fished a bottle of Bell's whiskey from behind the buckets and detergents. He'd just poured a generous measure of scotch into a grimy glass when a loud knocking almost made him spill his drink.

Swallowing down the fiery liquid, he crossed to the sturdy rear door which opened into the dingy shop's equally dingy back yard. "Who's there, what do you want?"

A muffled voice hissed from the other side of the peeling paintwork. "It's me, you stupid bugger, who do you think? Hurry up and let me in."

"Hold on." Finch waddled to a cracked kitchen cabinet, yanked open the drawer and rummaged inside. He produced a Webley revolver, broke it open, snapped it shut again and puffed back to the door. "Are you alone?"

The muffled voice rose in pitch. "Is this some sort of bloody joke? Of course I'm alone you stupid sod. Now open the door, it's bleedin' brass monkeys out here."

"All right, stand back." Finch slid back the bolts and opened the door a crack. He squinted suspiciously at a tall, stooped man whose face was hidden by a hat and high collar, his arms folded against the December cold.

A jet of steam escaped the visitor's mouth as he became ever more impatient. "For God's sake hurry up before somebody bloody sees me."

At last Finch relented and stepped back. "All right then, and shift yourself."

The taller man quickly slipped through the door and closed it behind him, rapidly sliding the bolts back into place. Whatever he was about to say next stuck in his throat as he turned and saw the revolver clasped in Finch's plump hand.

The portly shopkeeper smiled. "Don't worry, I'm not going to shoot anyone on my own patch; unless I have to."

The visitor unbuttoned his coat and unwound the scarf from around his neck. "What the bloody hell do you think this is, some kind of gangster film?"

Finch crossed back to the cabinet and stowed the pistol again. "Can't be too careful these days, especially with *your* product."

The man in the overcoat remained stooped even in the warmth of Finch's dreary parlour, his shoulders irrevocably rounded by years of hunching over meticulous and detailed work. "I wish I'd never taken on this bloody job in the first place."

Finch replaced the pistol in the drawer and shuffled back to the table, gesturing for his visitor to take a seat. "You need the money just like the rest of us. Do you really think I *enjoy* dealing with that bastard? But let's face it, none of us are getting any younger and we all have to think of our futures."

The stooped man took off his wet coat and draped it over a spare chair before moving it closer to the fire. The bottom of a webbing belt showed beneath the back of his suit jacket as he attended to his now steaming overcoat. "You got the payment, I mean *all* of it?"

Finch flashed his uneven smile and stroked his grey streaked beard. "It's all here, somewhere. So, let's have a look at the goods."

The visitor turned and made his way slowly back to the table. "Just so you know, I've made arrangements for a message to be delivered if I'm not back by a certain time."

Finch frowned and leaned forward. "What time?"

The man with the rounded shoulders smiled and unbuckled the webbing concealed beneath his jacket. "Better hurry up then, hadn't we?"

Finch shook his head sadly. "No need for melodramatics, Ernie. How long have we known each other now?"

Ernie extracted the concealed pouches from his wrinkled suit and sat heavily in the chair opposite Finch, slapping the belt down on the table for effect. "Long enough to know this ain't your usual line of work, Pete. I'm telling you, if I'd have got stopped with this lot I'd have sung like a canary. I can't face another long stretch and I'm not going to cop for that lot, not on my own."

Finch made no attempt to pick up the belt. "Nobody likes a grass, Ernie."

"Bugger that! We're not talking about a couple of stray Yanks or a case of scotch. This is serious, and it won't be some nice safe police cell if we're caught neither. It'll be some damp cellar alone with a bloke who wears a suit, calls himself Smith and hurts people for a living. This is borderline espionage and we both know it."

At last Finch leaned forward, wincing as he grasped the modified money belt. His little finger had never set straight and it still kept him up at night. However, that was a score he knew might never settle before he upped sticks and retired for good. "Risk and reward, me old mate, risk and reward."

Ernie glanced around nervously. "Yeah, well so far I've seen *all* the risk and no reward."

Finch opened Ernie's concealed delivery and extracted several booklets, neatly laying each one out on the table. "Patience my son; patience. Let's have a look at the goods first. After all I *am* paying top dollar."

Ernie's ink-stained fingers tapped nervously on the table. "Nothing wrong with that lot; flawless I tell you. Crafted from genuine blanks and every one leading back the right register. In fact it's probably my best work ever."

Finch picked up an Irish passport and flicked through the worn pages. "Nice. *Very* nice. If I didn't know better I'd say you'd had this sent over from the Emerald Isle herself." He put the Irish passport down and picked up an English one containing the same photograph as its Celtic cousin. "Nice touch with the port stamps. How do you age them to order?"

Ernie smiled for the first time as he leaned back and shook his head. "Trade secrets, me old china, you know all about that."

Finch nodded. "Fair enough." He put down the next passport and picked up a worn and dog-eared merchant seaman's book. "Wonderful work, top notch in fact, and if those silly buggers didn't all talk like Cockneys and Yanks I'd say it was foolproof." He put down the forged identity papers and shrugged. "Still, I'm only the broker so what do I care?" Finch heaved himself out of his chair and crossed back to the kitchen unit. He grunted as he knelt down and pulled out a thick wad of banknotes from underneath before tossing it into

Ernie's eager and nimble hands. "There you are, five hundred quid as agreed."

Ernest quickly counted the money, occasionally holding a banknote up to the dim light.

Finch laughed, a small string of spittle glistening on his unkempt and greying beard. "You don't think I'd try to pass you dodgy dosh? Now that *would* be bloody stupid."

Ernie began repacking his now empty money belt. "I've got to get back, I'm running late as it is."

Finch waddled back across the kitchen and held out his hand. "Well, this is it. I'm off after this job so we probably won't meet again."

Ernie quickly shook Finch's hand before throwing the belt back around his waist. "I'd like to say it's been fun, but if I'm honest I've spent the last six weeks crapping myself and I'm glad it's over."

Finch opened the back door. "You're a true artist, Ernie. You should've done more with your talents."

Ernie paused, pushed the door closed again and lowered his voice. "I know it's not the done thing but I've got to ask. Why him, why Tooley? I thought you blokes didn't exactly see eye to eye, and that's being polite about it."

Finch just pulled a face and shrugged. "I can't stand the bastard, and I hope Special Branch shoot him full of lead before he can pull off whatever hare-brained scheme he's planning, but business is business all the same. He wanted a special order, and he knows that *I* just happen to know the best scribe in London, probably in the whole country."

Ernie looked at the ground for a moment. "Doesn't make much sense to me. I mean the papers are sound but he'll never pull it off. He can't pass for Irish, and I'll bet none of his firm can either."

Finch pulled the door open once again. "Doesn't have to make sense, Ernie. I don't know what he's up to and I don't *want* to know. I'm just a businessman fulfilling an order."

Ernie thought for a moment. "You're right, *I* don't want to know either. Well, I wish you a long and happy retirement."

"You ought to consider retiring yourself," observed Finch as Ernie stepped into the cobbled back yard.

The scribe buttoned his coat. "I can't retire until this bloody war's finished, there's just too much demand for my services. Goodbye, Pete Finch."

With that, Finch closed the back door and Ernie the Scribe was gone forever.

Refusing to slip into melancholic nostalgia, Finch rubbed his hands and surveyed the row of passports and other identity documents spread across the table. This was it. The big score, the final job.

Just one last trip out before Pete Finch could look forward to a long and comfortable retirement.

18

Major Clarke jiggled the light switch and grunted with satisfaction as a string of newly hung lamps sizzled into life, powered by an olive green generator thrumming in the misty courtyard below. "Well at least the engineers have been busy," he muttered as he slid open a heavy door and stepped into the bomb-damaged warehouse.

"No kidding," agreed Digby as he followed Clarke into the damp, echoing space. "Your pals can sure get things done in a hurry." He pointed to the far wall, where an enormous bank of cracked and grimy windows formed a dramatic backdrop for Section C's new offices.

"So it won't be the cold that kills us," was Clarke's dry comment as he regarded the row of pre-fabricated huts squatting inside the larger space. There were five in total; a central rectangle about the size of a large garage was flanked by two smaller boxes each side. Suddenly the oversized generator in the courtyard made a lot more sense when he saw the thick rubberised cables snaking around each insulated hut in turn.

Digby voiced what Clarke was already thinking, although he was unable to suppress the mirth in his voice. "All mod cons *and* snooper-proofed, it's everything the modern man about town needs." He pointed across the warehouse to the far corner, where twisted steel supports and grey December clouds were reflected in the surface of a large puddle. "Looks like Goering's been at the roof again."

Clarke turned up his collar and crossed to a pile of swollen and mouldering tea chests stacked near the entrance. He smiled ruefully as he saw his old office chair secreted behind them. "It's like I've hardly been away. Some simple requisitions and a few pints of paraffin will soon make the place almost bearable." He turned to Digby. "Men of faith say that Providence provides, and I'm beginning to wonder if they're right." He threw out his arms and turned a full circle. "In light of the fact that we're both short of time and manpower, I suggest a gentleman's agreement."

"Go on," said Digby flatly.

"You may consider yourself a non-executive consultant to Operation Dark Spring, and in return I suggest we pool resources regarding our mutual Irish problem. I'd be surprised if there were no overlap between the two."

Digby scuffed at a small puddle. "Dark Spring, hey that's real nice. I know it makes operational sense, but it's political suicide. What if your JIC decides to check in?"

Clarke produced his pipe and matches. "That's why I love intelligence work generally and Section C especially. I can promise you that nobody official will come within a mile of this place. Civil servants can't be seen consorting with common, and some not-so-common criminals. This place has served us well before and it will do so again, now that we have the proper modifications."

Digby joined Clarke beside the pile of boxes and pulled out a dusty paraffin stove. "All the comforts of home. Any idea how you're gonna catch Jake Small? We've both come up empty handed till now."

Clarke waved his hand dismissively. "He'll turn up soon enough, and I've a good idea of which cages to rattle. Rumour has it that he's persona non grata north of the river, so that narrows down the number of holes he can hide in."

"It's a shame my guy's gone missing," observed Digby. "He'd probably have a good idea of where to look."

Clarke chewed on his pipe. "What about your other bloke, the quartermaster, has he heard anything?"

Digby replaced the stove and wiped his hands. "Come to think of it, maybe he's already figured it out for us. He told me a tale about his buyer, some fella called Tooley; he reckons the guy's operating with an unnatural advantage, some crystal ball kind of thing. I tell you he's nervous as hell. It was only my appeal to his sense of self-preservation that kept him from jumping ship altogether. Anyway, what's the betting this Tooley guy's magic mirror is really a nine fingered deserter?"

Clarke smiled ruefully. "I still don't know how you managed to convince him you're a genuine G-man."

"Why *shouldn't* he believe it?" Replied Digby testily. "Anyway, I told him to make delivery within forty-eight hours. I know it's a risk but pressure's building from the outside and we need to get this job finished and cleaned up before something leaks."

Clarke shook his head and looked at the ground. "Tooley. I should've bloody well known it."

"Something you wanna tell me?" Digby asked quietly.

The Major thought for a moment before responding. "I suppose it makes perfect sense really. Tooley's a big noise south of the river generally and in Bermondsey especially. He knows a lot of people down there and he's got God knows how many contacts in the dockyards. I'll bet anything you like he's the link between your pilfering GIs and our Fenian friends."

Digby produced his own pack of crumpled cigarettes. "Well now, you're just a walking filing cabinet ain't ya? Davis, my other guy, was working on this Tooley character as well, before he vanished. What else do you know about him?"

"I know he should've been locked up the day the war broke out. The man's a bloody menace. Ruthless, resourceful and worst of all he's not motivated by profit alone."

"But no friend of Germany either, or you guys would've put him in storage like you said."

Clarke gazed through the hole in the roof. "Tooley's red, not black, and we're all supposed to be friends, remember."

Digby was silent for a few seconds before speaking again. "So I reckon it's a pretty good bet we can find our missing guns and *maybe* our missing guy as well if we paid this Mr Tooley a visit."

Clarke's tone was tired and exasperated. "If we take George Tooley publicly I'll guarantee that lurid tales of rogue Yanks selling guns to Irish Republicans will make all the front pages; he'll see to it. D Notices are only effective if hardly anyone knows what you're trying to supress in the first place. We can't very well lock up every journalist and malcontent pamphleteer we come across, besides there'll be the extra stench of cover-up if we try to keep a lid on it."

Digby lit his cigarette. "Kinda defeats the purpose really. My guy will probably take a couple of days to deliver his shipment, then we can handle this Tooley fella in whatever quiet way suits you. What's good for you is good for us as far as the arms are concerned, but we have to grab Jake Small *now*, today, before he disappears again. That's assuming he's even *with* Tooley in the first place."

Clarke looked straight at his American counterpart. "Even if he *is* running with Tooley's mob and we pick him up, I can't let you take him, not straight away."

Digby rolled his eyes. "Not this again! I've already gone ten rounds with Hammond *and* my own boss over that little prick, and anyway it ain't up to you or me. You've no idea how much pressure's coming down from above on this one, and on top of all that, he's still an American soldier in case you'd forgotten."

Clarke stroked his beard. "Listen, we've known each other for a long time, and we both know what we're doing and why. That's why I need to ask a favour of you now."

Digby lit his cigarette. "Shoot."

"I need you to stall your firm for a while."

The unkempt American chuckled, emitting a stuttering stream of Lucky Strike smoke into the damp atmosphere. "As we've achieved exactly sweet FA so far, I don't really need to stall them, do I?"

"Fair enough, but I agree that this Tooley lead sounds promising. *If* Jake's running with Tooley's firm then I've got a pretty good idea of where to find him. We can probably scoop him up in a sweep, but then I'll need to keep him for a while."

Digby looked down and shook his head. "No way, buddy. My orders are to get him on a plane back Stateside immediately, and that's an absolute priority." He lowered his voice even though they were alone. "They've even authorised me to remove any awkward obstacles, British citizens or not."

Clarke frowned. "Please tell me you're not serious. Please tell me that OSS isn't about to pick a fight with its closest friend."

Digby remained silent.

"Digby, just what the *hell* is going on? Talk to me!"

Digby took another long draw of his cigarette. "There's something going on back home, and before you ask, I don't have a goddamn clue what it is."

Clarke scoffed. "Oh come on, you must have *some* idea. You must have heard *something*."

Now it was the American's turn to stare hard. "Not a clue, not a goddamn whisper. All I know is that it's something big, I mean *really* big. Big enough for me to eliminate friendly civilians if they get in the way. Whatever's going on, they're not leaving anything to chance, and my best guess is they want Jake Small for security duty."

Clarke said nothing for a little while as he sucked thoughtfully on his pipe. "That means somebody on your team has found something out, something that's made them sit up take this Sensitive threat seriously."

"Maybe, but now you know why I can't bullshit the boss on this one. Hell, for all I know they've got somebody watching *me,* just in case."

"That serious?" Said Clarke with genuine surprise.

"That serious," confirmed Digby.

Clarke was silent for a few seconds more before speaking again. "Well, I don't know what's going on in America but I *do* know what's happening here, right now, today."

Digby cocked his head. "Go on."

"I know you're quite sceptical about all this, Mr Digby."

The American shrugged. "This Sensitive stuff is all pretty hard to believe, but after seeing the lengths that some very serious men will go to trying to capture or kill these guys, let's just say I'm open to persuasion."

Clarke nodded. "That's good enough for me." He took a deep breath before speaking again. "I ought to warn you that Jake Small may be more the poisoned chalice than the magic bullet."

"I'm listening."

Clarke frowned with irritation as his pipe went out. "Following the Section 12 incident, there are at least a couple of people who are taking these so-called Sensitives more seriously. I'm told it wasn't an easy sell, but one of my colleagues managed to arrange some special security at a couple of key locations. You can guess the rest."

Digby's expression darkened. "Jesus Christ, don't tell me..."

Clarke nodded. "That's right. We don't know who's poking their nose in, but the list of possible suspects can't be very long, and we can't rule out your golden boy. Do you *really* want to take him back without finding out for sure? And besides, Dr Werner thinks he could be suffering from a serious mental problem."

"Still listening," said Digby quietly.

Clarke tapped out his pipe against a nearby pillar, the hot ash fizzing as it fell on the damp, sagging floorboards. "Come on now, you've seen Hammond for yourself and you know perfectly well that something's wrong. Besides, if you take Jake back with you now, all *I've* got left is Hammond, and I wouldn't trust him to boil an egg without some ulterior motive." He shoved the still warm pipe into his pocket and stepped closer to his counterpart. "We've got a ghost snooping around the few tunnels where we can detect him, and God knows where else. I don't need to remind you that one of those unprotected places is Eisenhower's HQ, and now you're suddenly bogged down in the Ardennes. I'm not suggesting there's a definite connection, but are you willing to take the chance? If we falter in France then you and Jake will have an awful lot more to worry about when you finally get home."

Digby said nothing as he dropped his cigarette on the floor and ground it out with his shabby shoe.

Clarke pressed his point further. "Use your instincts, your experience. You know I'm right, and you know this is a serious problem."

After a few seconds of silence Digby nodded to himself as he reached a decision. "Okay, here's what we're gonna do. I want Jake Small picked up right now."

"We don't know for sure that he's *with* Tooley."

"Then let's find out!" Snapped the American impatiently. "I want him here by nightfall if he's with this Tooley asshole. After that we'll both ask him who he's playing for and what the hell's going on with these goddam freaks."

"Werner will need more time than that."

"Screw Werner, and screw Hammond too! I'm doing you the favour of a lifetime here so let's not start splitting hairs. I can give you a day, maybe two, but after that I'm dragging his sorry ass back to Washington. It might surprise you to know that we've got one or two eggheads of our own. I'm sure they can figure out what's going on even if *your* so-called experts can't. And for Christ's sake can we please get some Goddamn *heat* in here!"

Clarke thought for a few seconds. "Very well then. First things first; we'd best get Ellie in here, I don't want that car sitting around for too long."

Digby nodded and headed back towards the stairwell.

Clarke followed. "You know this is something of a homecoming for her as well. This is the very place I recruited her for Section C."

Digby started down the dark and creaking stairs. "Is that so?" He stopped suddenly, causing the Major to bump into him in the semi-darkness.

Clarke remonstrated. "Save the ambushes for the enemy will you? I've a feeling there'll be more than a couple before this business is finished."

Digby voiced what both men were actually thinking. "You know there's really no telling what the hell's going to happen with this mess."

"Business as usual then." Clarke tapped his companion on the shoulder. "Let's get moving, I don't altogether trust these stairs."

Both men emerged from the warehouse and into the gloom of a greasy cobbled goods yard. The weak winter sun was distant and sullen, hiding far above a veil of churning grey December clouds.

"Christ this place is depressing," observed Digby as he shoved his hands in his pockets and set off towards the wooden gates. "Couldn't you have found somewhere more dilapidated?"

Clarke followed the American across the slick cobblestones. "Don't worry, once we get the stoves working you'll feel right at home."

"Not *my* home," countered Digby as he reached the gates.

"More's the pity," quipped Clarke as he tried to lift the heavy wooden bar securing the deserted yard's sturdy gates. "Give me a hand with this will you, I'm not a bloody weightlifter you know."

Digby and Clarke pushed open the well-oiled but battered gates, quickly beckoning to the Austin staff car idling in the cobbled lane outside. Within seconds the car was inside the compound and the gates were closed once more.

Digby smiled as Ellie climbed out of the driver's seat. "Hey honey, I forgot to tell you how much I love a gal in the service."

Ellie looked down at her WAAF uniform. "You think my Chanel evening dress would attract less attention?"

Digby squinted. "Where did you get a Chanel evening dress? On second thoughts don't answer that, I don't want to know."

"I wasn't going to tell you anyway, Mr Digby. A girl must have some secrets after all."

Digby's tone was suddenly sombre. "Secrets are what get people killed around here. Remember that."

"Then I'm surprised we've all lived so long," was Ellie's quick reply as she opened the Austin's overflowing boot. "This was all I could get without having to start signing forms."

Clarke stepped forward and grabbed a coil of telephone wire. "Well done, Miss Parsons." He turned to Digby. "Be a good chap and give us a hand. The engineers have done a fine job but they're not cleared for this kind of sensitive housekeeping."

Digby grinned. "Not me, buddy. I've gotta get back to my HQ and report, remember I'm still looking for Jake Small too."

Ellie frowned and looked from one man to the other. "Aren't we all?"

Clarke interjected. "Politics, my dear Miss Parsons, politics."

Ellie's frown deepened. "What has politics to do with this, I mean apart from our being on the same side?"

The two men looked at each other for a moment before Digby spoke up. "You see it's like this. You guys want to find Jake Small, and so do we. The trouble is that Uncle Sam's got his own motivations for grabbing the golden boy from Detroit, motivations which don't exactly match with yours. At the moment we're just trying to keep everyone happy and safe, and sometimes the chain of command just grinds too slowly."

"Everyone has motivations," observed Ellie.

Digby continued. *"I'm* motivated by the certainty that prevention is better than cure. I'd much rather deal with this Sensitive problem over here than on Main Street USA."

Ellie's tone was sour. "You make it sound like you're containing an infection. Quarantine."

Digby opened a small gate cut into the larger pair. "Exactly right, but just keep it simple and say we're all pulling in the same direction if anyone asks."

"Like who?"

"Like anyone," said Digby as he disappeared through the gate.

19

Jake stopped abruptly as he caught sight of his reflection in a dusty shop window. He hardly recognised himself in the shabby brown suit Piggott had found for him, and the decidedly worldly priest had even shortened his hair in a couple of places. Although reluctant at first, Jake had to agree that the result was very convincing when the scarring left by the Cedarwood incident was revealed once more. With his Canadian trench coat and British kitbag, Jake looked like just another wounded serviceman trying to gather the threads of a life irretrievably transformed.

The unkempt vagrant reflected in the window not only looked like a stranger, but *felt* like one too as the recollections of Jake's personal past became increasingly blurred, fading like a photograph exposed to the sun for years on end. His fear had grown proportionately as the details of his past had steadily vanished from his mind, transferred to the pages of a crumpled notebook as meaningless words written by a man he knew less and less about. Some quiet, inner part of Jake's consciousness shivered as he finally faced the inescapable truth that he was somehow changing, evolving into something and perhaps even some*one* new. A different man and a stranger even to himself.

What Jake *did* know for sure as he lingered on that freezing street was that of all the possible futures he'd imagined as a child, being trapped inside London's criminal underworld had never played even the smallest part. Fate had somehow left him surrounded by suspicious foreigners who were at best tolerant of his presence, and at worst overtly hostile.

Jake shuddered at the stranger in the window and turned away as a strong yet ill-defined melancholy swirled into his mind like bitter industrial smoke. He angrily reminded himself that he had a hell of a lot to feel sorry about for sure, but that wouldn't help him outwit his lengthening roll call of enemies. He needed to be alert and on his toes, not moping in a corner, and especially at his next destination.

Trying to shake off the feeling that he was no longer on intimate terms with himself, Jake limped on through the winter grey. This part of London, just south of the river, had suffered greatly from the Luftwaffe's attentions. Streets filled with densely packed housing were often interspersed with areas of utter destruction, the surviving structures jutting out like islands of resistance threatened by a rising sea of devastation.

Following Piggott's directions, Jake turned a corner and limped up a shadowy side street as he headed for one such atoll of defiance. He stopped and peered into a darkened yard, almost missing the peeling sign advertising the Dog & Duck public house. It looked like a rough place, a dive, but then Jake reasoned it was no worse than some of the bars he'd known…wherever it was that he'd grown up.

The old priest had assured Jake that he'd be safe here, and that his reputation as a card sharp combined with Piggott's recommendation would open the necessary doors. Jake still didn't know if he could really trust the old man, but he hadn't called the cops when he could have, and he was fast running out of options anyway. Although Jake was a resourceful man, he'd learned that he couldn't survive entirely on his own in a foreign land. What he needed now was safety, protection, family.

Knowing that he actually had very little choice, the American took a deep breath, lifted his chin defiantly and pushed hard at the Dog & Duck's age-blackened and squeaking front door. A strong smell of hops and tobacco smoke rushed up to greet him as he shouldered his way into the pub.

The Dog & Duck's interior was dim, hazy and spartan. A dive, just like he'd thought. A few old men in shabby docker's clothes and flat caps looked up from steaming mugs of tea, or whatever, as Jake made his way to the bar and dropped his kitbag on the floor. Trying to ignore the awkward silence, he tapped gently on the bar's scrubbed wooden top, trying to attract the attention of a large lady who was dispensing thick looking tea from a steaming metal urn. "Pardon me, ma'am, I'm looking for Mabel."

She didn't turn round. "Tell me what you want and I'll leave her a message."

Aware that several pairs of eyes were fixed on him, Jake persisted. "Well, that's kinda private, ma'am."

At last the rotund woman finished her pouring and set an enamel mug of steaming tea on the bar, which was immediately picked up and gulped noisily by an ageing docker who looked like he'd lost a tooth for every decade he'd been on this earth.

She nodded briefly to the tea slurper before folding her fleshy forearms beneath her ample bosom. "Well soldier boy, you can either tell me what you want with Mabel, or you can about-face and march straight back out again. Mabel don't see no-one without an appointment."

Jake raised his eyebrows and hammed up the Kansas farm boy act. "Well gee ma'am, I guess I'll just have to wait right here until Mabel shows up." He rummaged in his pocket and pulled out a ten shilling note. "I'll have a beer and something to eat while I'm waiting, ma'am."

Mabel shook her head and sighed before turning back to the tea urn.

Jake was suddenly aware of a presence close by as someone sat on a creaking stool beside him. A large man with broad, rounded shoulders and a boxer's nose hunched over the bar and stubbed a thin, hand rolled cigarette in the ashtray. "Ain't no beer in here, soldier boy. You see anyone drinking? That's because there's no beer, see."

"It's a strange kind of bar that don't have no beer."

"Rations." Replied the large man, staring straight ahead. "We have to be careful, make do, share things out."

Jake twisted round to check he wasn't about to stumble over his kitbag, and also to let the stranger see the automatic tucked into his waistband. "I get the idea. You have to save up enough pieces of paper, kinda like us back home, except ours have the President on them." He fished in his pocket and smoothed a second note on the bar. "I reckon that should more than cover it."

The nameless bruiser turned and looked the American straight in the eye. "You want some advice, son?"

"Not really."

"Get yourself up West. I'm sure you can find what you're looking for there, much easier than here at any rate. That sidearm don't impress anyone around here, and we've got nothing to spare, no matter *how* much money you've got."

Jake took a deep breath. "Look buddy, I don't want trouble."

"Then you're in the wrong pub, Yank."

The large woman turned and leaned on the bar. "Listen son, just be on your way while you still can. There's nothing for you here."

"That's where you're wrong, ma'am. I was told to come here and ask for Mabel."

"Who told you?"

"The old priest."

The bruiser placed a hand flat on the bar and pushed back a little. "What's your name, son?"

"Who wants to know?"

The docker's expression darkened. *"I* do, and you're in the wrong place to be acting like a cocky little bastard."

Jake stared at the larger man for a moment and weighed his options. He'd probably be able to drop the guy by using his pistol as a club, which would mean it was already in hand in case any of his buddies tried their luck. However, trouble was something he needed a lot *less* of, not more. "The name's Jimmy, but that ain't my professional name."

"Show me your hands," snapped the matriarch behind the bar.

Jake held up his left hand and waggled all his remaining digits, the stump of his little finger clearly visible.

The large woman produced a packet of Craven A cigarettes from behind the bar, along with a slim gold lighter which almost vanished behind her plump fingers. *"I'm* Mabel."

"I figured as much."

Mabel blew smoke into the air and stared at Jake for an uncomfortably long time. "Well then, *Jimmy*, you might just be in luck."

"Oh yeah, how so?" Asked Jake suspiciously.

"I've been told to look out for a nine fingered Yank."

"Told by who?" Jake was acutely aware that he wasn't out of the woods yet.

Mabel finally offered Jake a cigarette. "These are strange times, Yank."

"I'm Canadian."

Mabel smiled. "Whatever you say, mate. Whatever you say. Can't blame us for being careful. I mean you'd think it would be easy to tell friend from foe, but nothing's ever that simple, especially around here."

Jake declined the cigarette. "So what then, am I your friend now that you know how many fingers I've got?"

Mabel smiled. "No Jimmy, a paying guest is what *you* are. Pick up your bag and follow me."

Jake stuffed the notes back in his pocket and smiled at the nameless docker.

Mabel's unofficial bodyguard scowled back. "Just behave yourself while you're here, you understand, Yank?"

Jake ignored the man and stepped round the bar. He followed Mabel through a peeling, yellow stained door and into a long, dim hallway. "You own this place?" He asked.

Mabel put her foot on a flight of sagging stairs barely covered by a length of rucked and threadbare carpet. "Never you mind who owns what. Just pay your board and stay out of trouble. Don't tell anyone you're here, and don't tell anyone *here* anything about yourself."

Jake followed Mabel's voluminous backside up the spongy staircase, running his fingers over the greasy chocolate brown wallpaper. "You don't have to worry ma'am, there's no way I'd ever admit to staying here."

The yellowed bedroom door creaked loudly as Mabel pushed it open. "Here you are. It's not the Ritz, but it's dry and there won't be nobody poking around neither."

Jake looked at the ancient brass bedstead and faded wallpaper before dropping his kitbag and opening the cracked and leaning wardrobe. "This'll be just fine, ma'am."

Mabel folded her arms once more. "Let's get something clear, Jimmy. We look after our own around here, and we won't put up with riffraff making trouble, understand?"

Jake nodded. "Absolutely."

Mabel continued. "I don't know why you're here, but I've been told you're all right and that's good enough for me. Just don't go making a nuisance of yourself. The Guvnor likes to keep things quiet, and he's not a man you'll want to cross."

Jake began unfastening his kitbag. "Guvnor? You mean this Tooley guy?"

Mabel stepped back towards the door. "Rent's five pounds a week, in advance."

"Five pounds? Isn't that kinda steep, ma'am?"

Mabel ignored the question and turned to make her way back down the stairs. "Come down to the back parlour in about half an hour, but don't expect nothing posh."

"Don't worry, I won't."

Mabel called out from the top of the stairs. "Monday is washday, so if you want your sheets doing then put them on the landing before nine."

"I sure will," said Jake as he closed the door.

Once he was certain Mabel was descending the stairs, Jake sat on the bed, massaged his knee and pulled his journal from the top of his kitbag.

20

As he'd expected, the back parlour of the Dog & Duck was dim and dusty, but at least it was quiet and warm which suited Jake just fine. He stretched out his leg and massaged his aching knee as he re-read his personal history for the umpteenth time, his dark glasses no handicap in the curtained winter gloom. Reliving his own past through monochrome prose rather than technicolor memory was a strange sensation, but it gave him some small comfort to reclaim a part of himself when he perused the passages he'd so diligently recorded. Jake had come to think of his precious journal as a mental map, leading out of the past and into the present, although the problem of his forgetting what he'd read within a few hours was a stubborn one. Perhaps his past had finally been reduced to a collection of anecdotes scribbled in a battered notebook, perhaps he really *was* looking at the memoirs of a de facto stranger.

Jake scratched at the scars on the side of his head as he concentrated on the words he'd re-read hundreds of times, despite the fact they stirred little recognition among his increasingly absent recollections. Perhaps he was over-complicating his mental state, and perhaps the only cure he really needed was to re-learn his own past. Loss of memory was not uncommon following head injuries, so maybe his amnesia had a more mundane origin than he'd feared. However, the inexplicable German paragraphs and his scribbled descriptions of places could never have been to were proof positive that he'd suffered more than just a simple bump to the head.

Satisfied that for the moment he could recall where he'd come from, Jake flicked forward to his most recent entries. He quickly scanned the story of his being forced to flee from a disgruntled smuggler, and lastly how the ailing and strangely familiar priest had taken him in. Jake was sure thankful that the old man had showed up when he did, but he was still wary of someone squatting in a burned-out church, who seemed to know far too much about eluding the authorities. However, Jake knew he was a man with few options left and things had worked out okay, at least so far. However hard life on the lam might have become, it was still preferable to the endless tests, injections and "debriefings" he was certain to endure if he were captured once more.

Jake quickly snapped his journal shut and stuffed it behind a thin seat cushion as he heard a swell of distant conversation, a sure sign that the door at the end of the hall had been opened. A few seconds later, Mabel waddled into the empty parlour carrying a large casserole dish.

Her skills as a hostess were unchanged as she unceremoniously clattered the hot dish and an enamel bowl onto the table before extracting some cutlery from her deep apron pocket. "This'll keep you going for a while."

Using his sleeve, Jake lifted the lid off the dish, releasing a plume of steam into the dingy atmosphere. Setting the lid on the battered table, he quickly spooned a pile of thick stew into the chipped bowl. "Smells good, ma'am. What is it?"

Mabel folded her arms and rolled her eyes. "It's meat stew, your Lordship."

Jake grabbed the salt. "Sure it is, ma'am. What *kind* of meat?"

"Mostly rabbit. I think there's some beef in it, and some chicken. And a bit of bacon perhaps."

Jake blew on a spoonful of the steaming brown concoction. "Get many rabbits around here?"

The landlady made no attempt to disguise her impatience. "You should take off those daft glasses, you might see a bit more."

"Can't take 'em off, ma'am; not since I was wounded. The light hurts my eyes, and anyway I see plenty." Jake took a tentative mouthful of stew and chewed slowly. It was thick and the meat was tender, although it tasted a little strange. He tapped his finger on the dark bread roll beside his plate. "Got any butter for this, ma'am?"

"No butter." Mabel leaned casually on the table. "Is it true?"

"Is what true, ma'am?"

"Rumour is you're some kind of fortune teller. I mean a *real* one, not some old lady who reads tea leaves."

"I wouldn't know, ma'am. I don't drink tea." Jake pressed his thumbs into the roll's hard crust, revealing the dense and coarsely milled bread within. "What's for dessert?"

Mabel scowled. "Dessert?"

Jake smiled as he began mopping up the thick gravy with a piece of hard bread. "Yeah dessert, pudding, afters, sweet. Don't tell me you guys have nothing to offer a paying guest, a *well-paying* guest."

"You want pudding, go to a restaurant."

"Can't go to restaurants, ma'am. That's why someone suggested this joint."

Mabel rested part of one thigh and an ample buttock on the table. "Just make sure you don't drag that old man into any trouble. He should be in hospital, but you know how stubborn these old buggers are, especially them who made it back the first time round."

Jake kept his tone casual. "Yeah I know. I kinda figured he was a veteran. What's he *doing* up there in that boarded up church? I mean, couldn't you put him up here?"

Mabel pointed to Jake's hand. "Those aren't the only kinds of injuries you can get in a war."

"You don't need to tell me, ma'am."

"That's where he wants to be. He says he can't stay in a normal house, so all we can do is make sure he's comfortable." She took a deep breath and shuddered. "I just *know* we'll find him up there one day..."

Jake quickly changed the subject. "What about that dessert?"

Mabel levered herself off the table and stamped towards the door. "I think I can find some chocolate."

Jake picked up his spoon again. "That'll be great. I like chocolate."

Mabel smiled for the first time since serving Jake his late lunch. "Well you ought to, it's Yankee ration."

Jake looked up as another brief swell of conversation told him the door from the front bar had been opened again.

Mabel briefly nodded to a well-dressed man in a dark grey suit and wool coat who'd appeared in the doorway. "Hello there, Sam. Haven't seen you down here for a while."

Sam's voice was as cold and thin as his smile. "Yeah, well, had no reason to come down have I? Till now."

Mabel turned and hurried back to the front bar, another brief burst of pub noise confirming the two men were alone in the back parlour.

Jake pretended not to have noticed the smart man lounging in the doorway as he chewed his way through the filling if odd tasting stew. He felt a little vulnerable, and wished he hadn't left his forty-five under the mattress upstairs.

Sam removed his coat and threw it on a nearby stool before taking a seat across the table from the American. Not bothering to remove his hat, he pulled a battered tin ashtray across the table and produced a gold cigarette case. "My name's Sam, what's yours?"

Jake swallowed the last of his stew and grabbed the final chunk of coarse bread, using it to capture as much of the remaining gravy as he could. "The name's Jimmy Partridge, and my guess is you're not recruiting for the Salvation Army." He popped the final piece of bread in his mouth and leaned back, observing the stranger while chewing methodically.

Sam opened the case and offered Jake a cigarette.

Jake shook his head and continued to chew, although he could have swallowed by now. By his reckoning, this Sam didn't look much different to the local hoods back home. Not so well educated but cunning enough, and obsessed with his place in the underworld hierarchy. Jake knew that image and respect were everything to men like Sam. The fine tailored clothes were a firm rejection of the grinding poverty into which he'd almost certainly been born. The thin face, hawkish nose and predatory gleam in his eye were all very familiar. It was the same gleam Jake had seen in some of the Sergeants' eyes at Camp Gordon. Sam liked to hurt people. He liked to hurt them because it furnished him with the respect and authority he believed he deserved, and because he also saw it as a form of sport, a recreation. Sam believed only in the law of the jungle, the law of the strong.

The well-dressed Englishman snapped his cigarette case shut and dropped it back in his pocket. Producing a thin gold lighter, he took a long draw and sent a stream of aromatic blue smoke into the air.

Jake finally swallowed his last mouthful of bread. "Have a smoke, I don't mind."

Sam stared at the American for a few seconds. "So, Jimmy. I suppose you've got an identity card with your name on it."

"Yup."

One side of Sam's mouth struggled upwards, indicating that was about as light-hearted as he was likely get. "Well, I suppose Jimmy Partridge is a lot more believable than Caesar. What the bloody hell kind of name is *that?*"

It was times like this when Jake wished he *did* smoke, it would give him the chance to play for time and look nonchalant while he thought furiously. Instead he wiped an imaginary crumb from the corner of his mouth. "Come again?"

Sam crossed his legs and tapped ash from his cigarette. "You know, that's the bullshit name you gave to Pete Finch, before you trimmed three hundred pounds off his fat arse."

Jake tensed.

Sam held up his palms. "Take it easy, son. I don't care about Finch's dosh. In fact that tickle's made you quite the celebrity in some parts, and quite the villain in others."

Jake rested his fingertips on the edge of the table, ready to throw the entire piece of furniture in Sam's face if things turned ugly. "What about *this* part?"

Sam's half-smile struggled to stay up. "You're safe enough around here. This ain't Finch's manor."

Jake sensed they were coming to the point at last. "Yeah? Then my guess is a guy named Tooley runs things around here."

"Looks like dear old Reverend Piggott's been schooling the heathen again."

Jake raised his eyebrows. "You know Piggott? You don't strike me as the churchgoing type. No offence."

Sam tapped ash again. "Well, let's just say the old bloke's got a bit of a name around here, sort of like yourself."

Jake found himself smiling before he'd realised what he was doing. "If you're looking for autographs, why didn't you say so?"

The weight pressing down on Sam's smile finally became too great and it vanished instantly. "Just watch that smart mouth, Yank. The only reason you're here is that the Guvnor's allowed it. This is *his* pub, see, and he doesn't like flash, bigmouthed out-of-towners bringing too much attention."

Jake looked down at his shabby suit, and then pointedly around the sparse and nicotine stained backroom. "Yeah well, I guess it's not easy to stand out in the middle of all this glamour. Be sure to thank your boss for putting me up in such fine style."

Sam crushed out his cigarette and stood up. "You can thank him yourself. The Guvnor wants to meet you."

"Now? Why?"

Sam wasn't listening. He suddenly jerked his head towards the front bar, listening for a few seconds before leaping from his seat and peering down the hallway.

It took Jake a moment to figure out what had spooked the man in grey, but the approaching rumble of engines soon made it plain enough. For a moment there was a deathly hush before the first police whistle galvanised Jake, Sam and all the Dog & Duck's occupants into action.

Sam voiced Jake's own fears. "Bollocks, it's a sweep!"

"What, *here?*" Jake had heard of hotels, cinemas and even railway stations being sealed off to round up spivs and deserters, but never a rundown pub in the middle of a heavily bombed working-class area.

Sam pulled an American forty-five from his jacket and pointed it at Jake's face. "Never had a sweep in *this* neighbourhood before, that's all taken care of. Who the hell *are* you?"

Jake glanced first towards the parlour door, and then towards the back door. "No time for biographies."

"Smart arse," muttered Sam before he lowered the weapon and quickly tiptoed along the hall towards the front bar. He gingerly opened the door, then rapidly closed it again and slammed home the bolts to gain some time.

Jake jumped to his feet and unbolted the rear door which led into a rundown cobbled yard, but it was too late. He could already hear a truck's engine and raised voices in the back alley. It looked like they were sealing off the whole block, maybe going house-to-house, and it didn't take a genius to figure out that they'd head for the pub first. He quickly re-bolted the back door and turned to see Sam standing in the middle of the room, his American pistol trained at the parlour door. "Whoa there cowboy. I thought *we* were supposed to be the trigger happy ones."

The ghost of a full smile flickered across Sam's face. "Typical bloody Yank. Thinks that a man with a gun in his hand is always gonna start shooting."

Jake was surprised when Sam quickly produced a handkerchief, wiped down the weapon and placed it on the table before turning back towards the gloomy hallway. "That's a Yank gun, nothing to do with me."

"Bastard!" Was the only response Jake could think of as he suddenly heard someone hammering on the door leading to the front bar.

Sam stuck two fingers over his shoulder before making his way back down the narrow hall, shouting above the din. "All right, all right just give us a chance." The hammering stopped as he slid back the bolts and slowly pulled the door open. "Blimey, you blokes..." Sam was cut short as a Redcap with a revolver pushed into the hall and motioned to a white-helmeted American close behind.

The Snowdrop grabbed Sam by the shoulder and pushed him towards the wall. "Just take it easy, buddy. We'll get everything straightened out real fast."

Realising he was completely trapped, Jake quickly stepped away from the table as the bristling officer strode in. Already dressed in dishevelled civvies, Jake stood stooped with his scarred head towards the Redcap, hoping to pass himself off as below average ability.

"Name!"

"James Partridge, sir."

"Identity card!" Clearly this British MP wasn't here to socialise.

Jake made a meal of patting his pockets. "Well gee sir, I can't find it. It must be in my jacket." Jake stepped backwards.

"Stop there!" The indignant officer roared as he finally spotted Sam's automatic on the table.

Jake stopped.

The Redcap called over his shoulder. "Sergeant, in here quickly!"

Within a second, a large Snowdrop with a whistle round his neck and a baton in his hand rushed into the room. He darted forward and grabbed the gun from the table, immediately releasing the magazine and checking the chamber. Handing the weapon to the officer, he tightened his grip on his baton and placed his own face about an inch from Jake's cheek. "What's your name, buddy?"

"Private James Partridge. 31st Combat Engineers, discharged." Jake pointed to his scarred head.

"Bullshit," said the Snowdrop softly. "You smell like a Yank to me. And take off those damned glasses!"

"I'm Canadian, and the glasses are prescription."

The big man smirked and removed Jake's dark glasses with sarcastic gentleness. "I don't give a hoot if they were a present from the King." He waved a hand in front of Jake's eyes. "You blind or something, boy?"

Jake gave a small shake of his head and squinted. "No way, in fact I see *too* good."

The MP turned to the British officer. "Okay Captain, who gets this one?"

The Captain holstered his revolver and folded his arms as he considered Jake's story. At length he turned to the Snowdrop; "you think he's American?"

"I'll bet my next month's pay he is."

The officer crossed to the chair and picked up Jake's threadbare trench coat. After rifling through the pockets he produced a battered Canadian Army card. "Private Partridge."

Jake straightened his stance, although not too much.

The officer continued. "You will consider yourself under close arrest from this time forward. You have no leave pass and you're in possession of at least one item of stolen property." He grabbed Sam's Colt from his American colleague.

"That's not mine, sir."

"Quiet! Cowards like you make me sick! While good men are out fighting and dying, you sit here stuffing your face." He handed the weapon back to the Snowdrop and unfolded a worn sheet of paper attached to Jake's fake ID. He said nothing as he looked from the ID card, to Jake and back again. At last he carefully re-folded Jake's phoney discharge certificate and placed it in his top pocket. "Hold out your hands, Private Partridge."

Jake knew he had no alternative, so he duly complied.

The Redcap nodded slowly, pushing his tongue around inside his mouth as he made a point of looking at Jake's missing finger. "Get something caught in the till, did we?"

"Probably less dangerous than all those sharp pencils."

The Captain's face took on a shade only slightly different to that of his cap as he beckoned to his colleague. "Sergeant, throw him in with our lot for the time being, just until we can learn his real name. I'm quite sure you'll be seeing our nine fingered friend again very soon."

"I can't wait, Captain." The Snowdrop jerked his baton towards the parlour door. "Okay Jimmy. Out front and into the wagon. Now!"

21

This time Jake wasn't a bit surprised when he awoke to find himself still asleep. This time he'd planned it that way, and the sight of his own body snoring gently on a hard wooden bench confirmed that his consciousness had successfully slipped its corporeal cage.

Although he was a deft and experienced Projector, Jake still found the sight of his own sleeping form somehow unsettling, somehow unnatural, somehow just plain *wrong*. However, on this occasion, such uneasiness did not dissuade him from taking a closer look at himself. He was beginning to harbour some dark suspicions regarding his current mental state, and he wondered if he was showing any outward signs of that inner uncertainty.

As with all living things viewed from beyond the physical plane, Jake's sleeping body glowed with the ebb and flow of life's colours as they shifted and changed in a subtle yet clearly discernible aura. Patches of blue, green and yellow painted the air as they gently pulsed with the rhythm of his breath, occasionally swelling outward to release a small puff of ethereal smoke into the surrounding atmosphere.

Although he was extraordinary in many ways, Jake was no trained doctor, and yet it was obvious that he'd recently staged a remarkable recovery. Long nights freezing in makeshift shelters had conspired to fill his lungs with fluid and make each breath a struggle, yet less than twenty four hours later he could see no indication that he'd ever been ill.

The fact that he'd unthinkingly, even miraculously brushed aside a significant bronchial infection as well as the injuries he'd sustained in Kent should've been a source of hope and inspiration, but Jake already knew that everything came at a price. He didn't need a doctor to help him figure out that his enhanced ability to withstand physical stress was somehow related to his ability to roam at will throughout what some mystics called the astral plane. Perhaps he'd brought his infirmities to this softly sparkling facsimile of the real world and somehow left them here. Jake reasoned he was thinking along the right lines, although he wasn't sure why the increasingly sharp pain in his left knee had somehow followed him from the physical dimension and into the astral one.

Satisfied that his body was in reasonable health and safe for the moment, Jake turned away from metaphysical contemplation and focused firmly on more immediate concerns. The first order of business would be to reconnoitre the police station and formulate a plan for escape. The fact he was even *in* civilian custody suggested that the British cops were unsure of his identity, and were trying to figure out what to do with him. On the other hand, maybe they *already* knew who he was and were holding him incognito for collection by...whoever. If his cover story held at all, he might be able to buy himself a day, two at the most before they figured out he was no Canuck. After that he'd be swiftly handed over to the American military police, or Snowdrops as the Brits called them. Once in US custody it wouldn't take long before they figured out who he *really* was. After that it was anyone's guess what might happen, but a choice between an ageing murder charge and further medical examination was a real possibility, and Jake was determined to avoid both.

He approached the cell door and pressed himself hard against the peeling paintwork. Viewed close up, the astral barrier pulsed with countless hues of monochrome grey, as though each metal molecule contained a microscopic light source which glowed in sympathy with his own ethereal form.

Jake took a deep breath - or at least imagined he did - and pushed his arms through the seemingly solid door, feeling the metal's peculiar rubbery resistance as he took a step forward and pressed harder. The glowing astral world suddenly vanished, replaced by darkness and a tearing cacophony as his disembodied consciousness intermingled with the door's atomic structure. After a moment's confusion, all resistance suddenly vanished and Jake stumbled into the narrow corridor beyond. Shaking his non-existent head, he looked around to get his bearings before moving off towards what he guessed would be the administration offices.

As he often did when in this otherworldly state, Jake marvelled at the almost unlimited intelligence potential of rare abilities like his own. Not for the first time, he briefly considered handing himself in to the American authorities. Not for the first time, the idea was dismissed as he recalled the multi-faceted and dangerous world of Section 12 and the Brotherhood. Having been raised by an institution, Jake had found his recent collision with the realities of state power especially troubling. His faith in legitimate authority had been irrevocably undermined, and he could never trust his so-called betters again. Quickly deciding that there was no greater guarantee of safety *inside* the intelligence community than outside it, Jake concentrated on planning his escape from custody.

It took him less than a minute to find a cramped and smoky office containing two tired and world-weary British cops, or *bobbies* as he'd heard them called. Ironically enough, both were smoking Lucky Strikes while discussing a certain Yank who'd been dumped in their cells, which they thought very strange as he was most likely a military prisoner.

Jake concentrated hard and tried not to be distracted by the layers of cigarette smoke pluming around the small office, painting the atmosphere with a thousand shades of blue, purple and grey. The very air seemed thick and slightly glutinous, transforming the office into a translucent palette of perpetually changing colours to transfix any astral observer.

The older policeman, a Sergeant with steel grey hair and a worried expression was seated behind a scratched wooden desk, his hand clamped firmly on the telephone receiver as though reluctant to make a decision. Jake instantly nicknamed the man *477* after his collar number, and felt a surprising surge of empathy for the someone he'd never met before. Jake knew only too well that it was not weakness or indecision, but experience which stayed 477's hand as he mentally weighed one bucket-load of grief against another. 477 already knew that he wouldn't be getting any sleep that night, but he still clung to the hope that he might at least pass a long and tiring shift in relative peace.

477's colleague was far younger, and still clung to the youthful belief that doing the right thing might somehow lead to advancement. Tall and thin with sleek oiled hair, his relative inexperience was reflected by his shoulder number of *868*, and by the way he encouraged his older and wiser colleague to follow standard procedure.

Jake positioned himself between the two desks as he listened to the men discuss what they should do with the Yank from the Dog & Duck.

868 was nervous. It wasn't in his nature to challenge the authority symbols of grey hair and Sergeant's stripes, but his fear of retribution from higher and more remote echelons of the police force trumped loyalty to station colleagues. "Listen Sarge, you know I hate to argue, but Special Branch was very clear and he fits the description right down to his socks, missing finger and all."

477 drummed his fingers on the telephone receiver. "You think he's Canadian?"

"Don't know, Sarge. I can't tell 'em apart, but it won't matter if he's the wrong man anyway. He's got to be either Yank or Canuck, cos he sure ain't no Aussie. Either way, he shouldn't be in *our* nick anyhow. The quicker Special Branch come and get him the better."

477 raised a pair of bushy eyebrows, which had not greyed like the hair on his head. "Ever dealt with Special Branch, son?"

"You know I haven't, Sarge."

The Sergeant leaned back in his chair, the wood creaking as he settled down to impart the wisdom of his experience. "Well don't, if you can help it. They tell bigger porkies than most of the villains we collar around here. If something goes right you can be sure they'll collect all the credit, and if something goes sour you'd better hope your name isn't stapled to any cock-ups, because they'll see to it that any manure rolls downhill. I wouldn't trust them to guard my garage without buggering off with at least a couple of spanners."

"You mean like those extra cans of petrol you've got stashed in there," observed 868.

477 scowled and his tone dropped to match the expression which had darkened his face. "Just watch it, son. You don't know nearly as much as you think, and if you reckon your beat's rough now, trust me when I tell you it's not that bad. There are much worse places to try and keep order."

The younger man shifted uncomfortably at the indirect threat. "What are you going to do?"

The Sergeant leaned forward and drummed his fingers on the receiver again. "Call the Yanks and let *them* argue with Special Branch if they want. We're still bound by the Visiting Forces Act, which means we can let the Americans deal with their own rubbish. That, my son, is the law of the land; regardless of what some spiv with a Special Branch card or a nine fingered Yank who *claims* he's a Canadian might say."

868 hissed through his teeth. "I dunno, Sarge. It's all a bit much for me, but I reckon if we take orders from anyone it should be one of *our* lads, not some flashy Yank. *I* say talk to Special Branch first. They'll know what to do, and if they don't want him I'm sure *they'll* call the Yanks. Besides, the Americans can moan all they want but they can't really bollock us. Special Branch *can*, and I don't want to get on the wrong side of those blokes. They can hold a grudge for years from what I've heard."

868 was less seasoned than his colleague but he was not totally without experience, so he waited a moment before playing his trump card. "Perhaps we should call the Super. He'll know what to do."

"Bugger that," muttered 477. "The last bloke who called the Super out of bed is still babysitting bombsites in case someone tries to pinch some bricks. Anyway, I know what he thinks of the Yanks." His decision made at last, the Sergeant picked up the receiver and dialled. "Hello, Scotland Yard?"

22

As he slowly turned in a full circle, Jake looked curiously at the ragged regiment of cupboards and cabinets skulking in the damp underground cavern. A glance at the ceiling revealed both ancient stone arches and curious patches of what had once been elaborate plaster coving, suggesting a long line of industrious occupants stretching back across the centuries.

He had no memory of travelling to this place, whatever *this place* eventually turned out to be. One moment he was listening to a weary policeman working the night shift, and the next he was here, wherever and whatever *here* actually meant. It *was* possible that he was simply dreaming, having fallen into a natural sleep following an exhausting out-of-body excursion, but Jake figured that was probably too much to hope for in light of the late Colonel Stryker's untimely resurrection.

As he looked around, he soon noticed that angles were a little odd and colours a little dulled, although thankfully not to the same degree as his previous experience. Reality's appearance was only slightly distorted this time around, displaying neither the ethereal life of the astral plane nor the outrageous disregard for scale or continuity which were the hallmark of a more mundane dream experience.

The whole place filled him with the sense of standing inside a three-dimensional painting, some version of a real place rendered entirely from memory, mostly accurate but showing slight distortions and lacking in detail.

Having weighed the available if scant evidence, Jake was finally forced to accept that once again he existed in some nameless state that was neither dream nor projection, neither awake nor unconscious. Just like his recent journey to the shores of nowhere, this was also a place that his own imagination had never conjured before, and his greatest fear was a growing acceptance that it wasn't actually *him* doing the conjuring.

As he tried to get his bearings, Jake noticed an indirect path leading to a series of large arched alcoves cut into the far wall. All were cloaked in darkness save for the furthest one, which spilled dim electric light into the musty smelling cavern.

Hoping to find some explanation for his unexpected departure from the astral plane, Jake cautiously made his way towards that final illuminated alcove. As he passed between a multitude of mysterious cupboards and drawers, he still couldn't figure out whether he was walking through a "real" place or whether he was trapped inside somebody else's mental metaphor. Whatever the case, Jake felt a tremor of excitement as he neared his objective, intuitively believing that, having journeyed through a secret cavern filled with locked drawers, he was about to experience a revelation.

Then something happened. It was an experience shared by dreamers throughout the ages and accepted as just another peculiar non-rule governing that subconscious realm. With one step Jake was making his way towards his goal, and with the next he'd instantly arrived at his destination. There was a time when he would have paid no heed to such a trivial development, but now he found it disturbing as it strongly echoed his recent "dream" of deserted prisons and dead soldiers.

Pushing that trick of time and space to the back of his mind, Jake peered into what was obviously some kind of makeshift holding cell. He didn't know whether to feel anxious or relieved as he realised that everything he saw inside could easily have been lifted from the vast and disordered filing system of his own subconscious mind.

The thick electric cables cocooning the cramped space were no surprise, and neither was the chaotic collage of pencil sketches, scribbled maps and mysterious glyphs covering two walls of those cramped subterranean quarters.

Images of an old man who'd felt the chill of the grave in the heat of summer unexpectedly rushed to the forefront of Jake's mind as he looked at scribbles scattered across those damp stone walls. They all seemed so familiar, and yet he couldn't recall exactly where he'd seen them before.

Jake had been so preoccupied with the disjointed drawings of a dead man that he jumped when he finally noticed a completely *different* dead man snoring gently on his prison cot. He wondered if that sleeping prisoner had suddenly been summoned up by his slumbering subconscious, or whether he'd actually been lying there all along. It was hard to be certain.

Whatever the case, the late Thomas Hammond's hair looked longer than Jake remembered, and his beard was uncharacteristically unkempt. That subtle change in the dead man's appearance somehow made him seem less powerful, diminished, as though his vigour and vitality somehow depended on his outward appearance.

As he stared down at the sleeping psychiatrist, Jake gradually became aware that Hammond's snoring was becoming louder and more strained with every cycle, taking on an asthmatic wheeze as though his every breath was snatched through a rapidly constricting windpipe.

Jake wasn't conscious of having blinked or glanced away, and yet the method and moment of Hammond's silent transformation still eluded him. With one wheezing breath he was staring down at Section 12's erstwhile physician, and with the next the bed was occupied by an altogether different man, an older man, a man who was definitely more dangerous and certainly just as dead as the late Dr Thomas Hammond surely was.

Even though he had nothing to say, Jake was still dumbfounded as he stared at the skeletal frame of Peter van Cortlandt lying fast asleep on Hammond's prison bed. The dead Sensitive's appearance was perfect in every detail, right down to the worn greatcoat, woollen hat and gloves he'd worn to confound the permanent chill permeating his bones. He suspected that Nero's constant struggle for warmth had been a symptom of his unnaturally long absence from the grave's cold embrace.

A mix of emotions ran through Jake's disembodied mind. First there was denial, then fear, followed by anger before finally settling into something akin to acquiescence. Although he couldn't fathom why, he simply accepted the idea that the Brotherhood's most potent Sensitive somehow lived on as an echo inside the fantasies woven by his own, unquiet consciousness.

It was all perfectly understandable, and even rational in a peculiar, intuitive way. At least it *would've* been kind of rational, were it not for the mysterious underground cavern and Hammond's dishevelled appearance, both of which were things he'd certainly not experienced back in the "real" world, or anywhere else. Deep down, Jake knew something was amiss, and he found himself suddenly filled with the same vague, formless sense of trepidation he'd felt down in that oddly altered copy of St John's crypt.

Although he wasn't sure just which of his senses had alerted him to the imminent danger, Jake suddenly spun round to see that the late Dr Hammond had somehow managed to materialise behind him. A moment ago he'd been lying asleep in his sparse underground cell, and now he was rolling out of that locked and darkened archive with the aid of a wheelchair, presumably because his left leg was missing below the knee. He took a step back as Hammond fixed him with an expression somewhere between anger and pleading.

As he racked his brains for some means of escape, Jake suddenly learned that the mysterious dreamscape he'd somehow tumbled into wasn't so much strange as downright hostile.

The shift in the landscape was small, subtle, no more than a few inches, but it was enough to trap Jake *inside* that subterranean cell, suddenly re-casting visitor as captive in the space of a single, wheezing breath. Twice as confused and a good deal more frightened, Jake pressed his back against the paper-plastered wall as the late Peter van Cortlandt sat up, cocked his head quizzically and spoke, or at least *appeared* to speak. The old man's mouth formed a string of words, but uttered only the silence of the grave.

The quiet, rational part of Jake's mind still counselled that he had nothing to fear from either of these dead men, but fear them he did as he was gripped by a grim sense of deep and existential danger. He dashed across to the steel bars, soundlessly screaming for help as he realised all too late that he should've quit and looked for a way home while he'd had the chance. He was out of his league and about to pay a heavy price for his hubris.

Jake was both surprised and immensely relieved when a stranger wearing wire spectacles and a white coat unexpectedly stepped from the shadows and ran towards him. He had only a moment to wonder just *who* the unknown doctor might be before the young man reached between the bars and grabbed him by the shoulder.

When the doctor in the white coat spoke, his voice was an unexpectedly thick cockney growl. "Wake up, mate."

Jake just stared blankly, dearly wanting to comply with the doctor's demand but unable to find a path back to his safe and suddenly very appealing police cell.

The doctor spoke again. "Come on, whoever you really are. Wake up! This ain't a bleedin' hotel you know."

Jake couldn't move. He was paralysed, rooted to the spot as the young man shook him more firmly, his voice growing louder and nearer as the subterranean cell finally began to darken. He just had time to see that both Peter van Cortlandt and the dishevelled Dr Hammond had mysteriously vanished before the young man in the white coat also began fading back into the darkness from whence he'd so suddenly sprung.

As the lightless void of a dreamless slumber mercifully descended around him, Jake at last felt the police cell's blessed wooden bench beneath his sweat-soaked body. He groaned, turned over and opened his eyes, letting them flicker rapidly as they adjusted to the searing electric light of the physical world. He struggled to focus as Sergeant 477 shook his shoulder once again.

The tired policeman jerked a thumb over his shoulder. "Come on, sleeping beauty. You've got visitors."

23

Jake idly spun the tin ashtray on the battered table and rocked back in his chair. He'd quickly stubbed out his cigarette once Sergeant 477 had left the room, but the fact they'd given him a whole pack of smokes was indicative of his rapid rise from cowardly deserter to respected felon. Cigarettes, or *fags,* were as good as currency in this half-starved and frozen country, although Jake wasn't so sure about the tarnished mug of black tea steaming beside the ashtray.

He looked at the two empty chairs at the other side of the table and wondered who would be occupying them. Jake knew the score, and by rights he should already be on his way back to the warm, loving embrace of Uncle Sam. The fact he was still incarcerated in a British police cell could mean only one of two things. Either they didn't know who he really was and were trying to find out, or they *did* know his true identity, and he was about to meet yet another British intelligence officer who fancied a quiet word away from the US Army's oversized ears.

Jake made a conscious effort not to second guess whatever was about to happen, but he knew it would inevitably end with either a direct or indirect attempt to harness his rapidly evolving abilities. Peter van Cortlandt's warning against trusting any agent of the state kept echoing through in his mind.

He wondered if it was a coincidence that he'd only dreamt of the dead man now, when he was once more in the hands of the so-called legitimate authorities. He also wondered why he was suddenly experiencing a new and hitherto unknown kind of lucid dreaming. Perhaps they were a warning, a portent of things to come. In his previous life as a simple Sergeant of the

Fourth, Jake would've dismissed any deeper analysis of his nocturnal activities as ascribing special meaning to rolling a six, when chance demanded that it had to happen sooner or later. Alas that was before his latent talents had placed him on a collision course with the shadowy and driven men who would go to any lengths to study and control Sensitives like him.

Footsteps in the corridor put a swift end to Jake's introspection. He could hear three people approaching the spartan interview room, and one of them was a woman.

Indistinct shapes appeared outside the frosted glass, accompanied by low muttering. A key was quickly twisted in the lock before a man and a woman were ushered into the room, their police escort immediately closing the door behind them and stamping away to other duties.

Jake watched closely as the man smiled coldly and strode straight to one of the waiting chairs, scraping it back loudly before settling into it. He was clearly comfortable with environments such as this, and he was used to being in charge. The tweed jacket and beard gave him the look of a maths teacher who enjoyed intimidating pupils with his exotic equations, while not understanding why their feeble brains could not grasp even the most basic algebraic concepts.

The bearded man's companion clicked forward in her fashionable heeled shoes. Her painted lips parted in a smile of recognition as she flicked a strand of blonde hair from her face. "Hello Jacob. It's good to see you again, even if you *do* need a shave and some decent clothes."

Jake grinned back, genuinely pleased to see one of the best looking and certainly the most dangerous woman he'd ever met. He'd already seen Ellie Parsons dispatch a trained soldier with her bare hands and he was glad that they were on the same side, at least on paper. "Well gee, Eleanor. My tailor's out of town right now and my valet's lottery number came up." He looked deliberately crestfallen and jerked a thumb at Ellie's companion. "Who's your friend? I always figured you for a flyboy kinda gal."

Ellie stared at the scarring on Jake's head. "What on earth happened to *you?* Marsh Pendleton?"

"Yup. I guess even the Nazis hated Stryker in the end, enough to want to bury him there."

Ellie shook her head, frowning. "But how did you get away? I mean we searched that area with a fine-toothed comb and there was no trace of you."

"Yeah, well, I'm tougher than I look."

Ellie persisted. "How did you manage? I mean, you couldn't have stitched those wounds yourself."

Jake remained evasive. "I don't remember much about it, except sleeping under hedges and thanking God it was still summer." He pointed towards the still silent stranger. "Looks like your boyfriend's about to burst."

Ellie pulled back the unoccupied chair and gracefully settled into it, smoothing the creases from her skirt and straightening her fitted jacket. "Jake, this is Major Clarke. He'd like to talk to you."

"I feel like I should know that name," said Jake slowly.

Clarke rummaged in his top pocket with his left hand and extended his right. "I'm very pleased to meet you at last, Jacob, or may I call you Jake?" He produced a pre-filled pipe from his pocket and jammed it in his mouth.

Jake looked down at Clarke's extended hand and shuffled his chair back a few inches. "No offence, Major. But I don't shake hands much these days, sort of an occupational hazard if you like."

Clarke smiled and used both hands to search for his matches. "Yes of course, I do understand. I've gotten quite used to dealing with you chaps lately."

Jake's eyes narrowed. "You chaps?"

Ellie interjected. "Jake, it's all right. The Major knows all about you, Section 12, the Brotherhood. All of it."

"Well, if he knows everything, why the hell is he talking to *me?*"

Clarke produced his matches with a flourish, struck one and began sucking furiously on his pipe.

Ellie scowled sideways as Clarke's infamously strong tobacco smoke filled the room within seconds. "We're here because I think we can help each other."

Jake snorted. "Yeah? The last guy who said he wanted to help me ended up sticking needles in my ass and turning my whole life upside down. So unless you're gonna help by reversing whatever that fruitcake did, there's not much to talk about."

Ellie's eyes twinkled. "Actually, since you've raised the subject, it was *me* who stuck the needles in your ass, Jacob."

"You know, you're right. And the guys back home said I was unlucky." Jake's smile faded abruptly and he stared hard at Ellie. "Last time I saw *you,* you were making a run for it in a pair of dead man's boots and leaving me to rot in that goddamn lunatic asylum. You said you were coming back."

"We *did* come back, Jake. Honestly."

"We?"

Major Clarke extracted the pipe from his mouth and used the end to point at the American. "Now just a moment, my lad. Miss Parsons took a lot of serious risks to find out exactly what was going on down at Cedarwood. None of us had any prior knowledge of your involvement in that affair, which was obviously the way Section 12 wanted it. As soon as Miss Parsons managed to brief us on the situation I can assure you we mobilised significant resources straight away. That, by the way, was a decision for which I'm still being called to committee meetings."

Jake frowned and waved the tobacco smoke away from his face. "Who the hell are you anyway?"

"I told you, I'm Major Clarke."

"Don't get cute with me, you smart limey. I'm not some shit-kicking jar head from the ass end of nowhere."

Clarke adopted a more conciliatory tone. "You're right, I apologise. But in my line of work direct answers are often the most direct route to an early grave. I'm sure you can understand that. My exact role and assignments are classified as secret. However, I *can* tell you that *I* was the one who allocated Miss Parsons to the Cedarwood assignment."

"Why?"

"I had reason to suspect that Dr Hammond and Section 12 were not being entirely forthright with us."

"Go on."

"I can't go into much detail you understand, but I'd gotten wind of the fact that Peter van Cortlandt and Colonel Stryker were trying to broker some kind of deal behind our backs.

Amnesty for the Brotherhood; all completely unauthorised, unacceptable and gross abuse of position and privilege if ever there was one. However, due to the highly, if you'll pardon the pun, *sensitive* nature of Section 12's work, I couldn't just barge in with a list of unsubstantiated allegations. I needed proof. I assure you I was on my way down to Kent within thirty minutes of Miss Parsons' call. Your presence at Cedarwood House was something of a surprise, and a complication."

"Well I'm real goddamn sorry about that, Major."

Clarke suppressed a smile. "That's all right my boy, we're all on the same side after all. I'm just sorry we couldn't get to you in time." He couldn't prevent a chuckle from escaping. "You know, it's terribly naughty of me, but did you know I'm ten pounds richer because of you?"

"Really."

If Clarke noticed the sarcasm in Jake's voice he didn't let it show. "Indeed yes. Many of my colleagues insisted that you must be dead, given the high mortality rate at Marsh Pendleton. However I disagreed. I just *knew* you'd pop up sooner or later, probably falling into our sieve when we sluiced out the drains, as we do from time to time."

Jake rubbed his forehead as the conversation was beginning to tire him. "Well, you really know how to make a guy feel proud of himself."

Ellie leaned forward and touched Jake's arm. "I know you've been through a lot, Jake, but please listen to the Major. We really are trying to help."

Jake moved his arm away. "Okay, if you really want to help, then swing it with the local cops and get me out of here. I reckon you owe me for helping you for the Cedarwood screw up."

Clarke tapped out his pipe in the ashtray and produced a small silver penknife, still talking as he methodically scraped out the bowl. "You did a very useful and valuable job, but don't get any ideas that you did it single-handedly. You're not quite the wild west gunman you think you are."

Jake rubbed his aching knee. "I ain't no glory hunter, and I figure that big French bastard of yours was the one who squealed to the Krauts about Stryker doing a deal. So I guess *he* takes most of the credit."

The Major pocketed his penknife and produced a weathered tobacco pouch. "You have a marvellous brain for intelligence work, Jacob. You really shouldn't put it at risk on the battlefield."

Jake had had enough Major Clarke's conversation. It reminded him of the exchanges he'd shared with Nero and Dr Hammond, who had both displayed an incredible talent for imparting information while leaving him none the wiser. Not for the first time, he wondered if there was a special spy school where you could learn that kind of intelligence doublespeak. He turned to Ellie. "Can we just get to the part where you tell me what the hell you want? Then I can just get on with throwing you both out."

Ellie looked at Clarke, who nodded his approval for her to proceed. "You can ask us to leave, or you can leave *with* us."

"If I don't?"

Ellie's large blue eyes flicked upwards as she thought for a moment. "Then I suppose the Canadians will want to speak you. It may take a day or so for them to check your story, and then it'll be a call to the US Army. That is, if the Major doesn't just call them anyway"

Clarke struck another match and began suffocating his companions once more. "From what I can gather, you'd be no better off than you were down in Kent. I'm certain your superiors are keen to develop a working Sensitive programme as quickly as possible, and I don't think they mind cutting corners or frontal lobes to meet their objectives."

Jake leaned forward. "Why? What's the big hurry? I figure there can't be more than a dozen or so guys like us in the world, and from what I can gather, the most talented of us got buried in that air raid. Why are they so jittery now?"

Ellie spoke up again. "We really don't know, Jacob, honestly. But I promise you that's not why we're here. Obviously I can't speak for the Americans if they get hold of you."

Jake frowned. "So, if you're not interested in my abilities as a Projector, what the hell *do* you want with me?"

Clarke spread his hands apologetically. "We really can't talk about it here. Won't you at least come to a place where we can speak more freely?"

"You can get me out of here?"

Clarke smiled and a dark gleam appeared in his eye. "You'd be amazed at what I can do, Jacob."

Jake leaned back in his chair and pondered his options. Realising they were very limited, it took only a few seconds for him to reach a conclusion. "Okay, but if you're serious you can prove it."

"How?" Ellie asked.

Now it was Jake's turn to smile. "For Christ's sake get me some fresh clothes, I smell like a bum."

24

Jake leaned forward to stare through the windscreen of the cramped Austin staff car. He shook his head ruefully as he watched Ellie drag a red warning sign from the middle of the road, having swapped her smart suit for some US fatigues before leaving the station. She was back in the driver's seat in under a minute.

Major Clarke turned slightly in the front passenger seat as the car bumped forward a few feet. "Just a little window dressing; something to discourage curious adults and adventurous children. In fact, all the unexploded ordnance has been cleared from this area. At least we think so."

Jake watched through the rear window as Ellie jumped from the car once more and rapidly replaced the prohibition notice. Seconds later she was back in the car and they resumed their jolting journey between the mountains of debris which had slipped into the street.

As they continued on their slow, twisting course, Jake wiped condensation from the side window and peered out. A sea of rubble receded into the grey December drizzle, broken here and there by the jagged corpses of dockland buildings which had once kept vigil along the banks of the Thames.

The rapidly gathering dusk darkened still further as they entered a valley of teetering warehouses and collapsed workshops, all bearing warning signs similar to the one blocking the road. The entire area had been declared off-limits as too badly damaged to be salvaged and too unsafe to inhabit.

Ellie twisted the Austin's wheel as the car weaved still further into the deserted labyrinth. It was becoming apparent that, although obscure and tortuous, a trail had been left for vehicles to pick their way through the seemingly impassable destruction. Glass, masonry and splintered wood had been swept away to form a narrow path through the concrete chaos. A secret road winding deep into a dead and deserted corner of the city.

The twisting trail ended at a pair of blast-pocked but solid wooden gates which silently swung open as the car approached, and Jake began to wish he'd stayed with the cops as they passed into what had once been some kind of goods yard. Now empty and silent, it blended in perfectly with the surrounding devastation.

The Austin drew to a smooth halt between what looked like a regular police car and a US Army jeep. Those olive green workhorses seemed to pop up everywhere, and Jake wondered if there were any jeeps left to do any real fighting with.

Major Clarke opened the passenger door. "Here we are, Jacob. I'm afraid it's not as grand as Cedarwood, but you'll find the company's much better. This is a much more honest sort of place. At least my chaps will *tell* you before they scoop your brains out." He winked mischievously as he got out of the car, gesturing for Jake to follow.

The American slowly pulled himself out of his cramped seat and looked around suspiciously. The ruined courtyard stretched away for some considerable distance, with one building at the back corner having all but collapsed, its jagged walls reminiscent of a slighted castle as they jutted rudely into the December mist. Jake turned as he heard the wooden gates clatter shut behind him, noting that the original woodwork had been repaired and strengthened from the inside. The man securing the gate's heavy bolts wore the flat cap, donkey jacket and scarf of an elderly night-watchman, although his movements were the quick and fluid.

"Come along young man," said the Major cheerfully as he clamped his unlit pipe in his mouth. "We have a good deal to discuss and I don't think time is on our side. Although it never is in the middle of a war," he noted sadly as he set off towards a decidedly rickety looking staircase bolted to the least damaged building adjoining the courtyard.

Ellie touched Jake's elbow. "I know you're nervous, but you really don't have to be. You're not in trouble and in fact we really *do* need your help. Besides which, we'll catch our death if we stay out here too long."

"Catch our death," repeated the Jake absentmindedly. He gestured with his arms as he set off for the staircase. "What *is* this place?"

Ellie fell in behind him. "Camouflage; right here in the middle of London. The Germans already know this area's in ruins so they wouldn't waste their time bombing it again. You saw the signs and we have sentries discreetly patrolling day and night, clever isn't it?"

"Genius," repeated Jake with more than a touch of irony. "No, I meant what *was* this place before the Krauts redecorated?"

"Import warehouse," replied Ellie as they reached the spongy stairs and began to climb. "Or was it export? I forget. Goods came in through the entrance gates and down to the docks via a roadway on the other side."

"Come along now, no time to waste." Clarke's voice floated back down the stairs as he vanished through a doorway above.

As he reached the top of the sagging steps Jake paused and looked down into the courtyard, and then further out across an ocean of devastation which was rapidly sinking beneath the winter dusk. Observing the extent of the damage from his vantage point, he wondered if this country could *ever* recover from such a comprehensive pounding. It also made him wonder what some parts of France must look like by now.

Ellie touched Jake's arm again. "Let's get inside. I think we could all do with a hot drink."

Jake grimaced inwardly at the thought of more God-awful British tea, but he kept his opinions to himself as he warily stepped into the large building. He didn't really know what he expected to see, but nevertheless the sight that greeted him was still surprising. He was obviously standing on the upper floor of what had once been a bustling warehouse, its furthest wall dominated by an expanse of glass stretching almost to the ceiling and dropping out of sight below floor level. The large panes were dirty, cracked and taped at numerous points to prevent collapse and further breakage.

Skulking beneath those windows was a parade of hastily constructed offices, if they could be referred to as such. In reality, they were a row of temporary sheds erected inside the larger structure; a cheap and quick way of providing privacy plus added shelter during the winter months. That additional shelter was much needed as Jake immediately saw that one corner of the warehouse's roof was missing, allowing rain to enter and warmth to escape. Crated equipment and provisions lurked in the shadows, shunning scrutiny as they hid beneath protective tarpaulins.

Major Clarke was already halfway across the warehouse and striding towards the central shed, the largest of the group. "Come along my boy," he called jovially before disappearing through the green painted door. "We cannot delay."

Jake stepped forward cautiously and surveyed the tell-tale cables winding around each of the prefabricated rooms. "Exactly what do you people *do* here?"

Ellie smiled. "Like the Major said, I know it's not as grand as Cedarwood but you can see this isn't any kind of medical post, so your head's quite safe. I like to think of it as a field HQ."

"We're not in the field," said Jake suspiciously.

Ellie pointed back to the desolate view through the open door. "You think not?" She replied tersely before hurrying after the Major.

Jake took a deep breath and walked slowly after her, making a mental note of all possible escape routes as he sauntered towards the larger office in the middle of the row. He still didn't know exactly what Ellie's boss wanted, but he was damned sure it was nothing to do with his good looks and jovial company. Major Clarke was seeking an advantage that only a Sensitive could provide, but this time around, Jake was a little older and a lot wiser. This time around, the game would be different.

Jake discovered just *how* different the game would be as he stepped cautiously into the shielded office and spotted the unkempt figure slumped across a battered leather sofa.

Major Clarke raised his hands placatingly. "It's all right, Sergeant. Mr Digby isn't here to arrest you."

"To hell with all of you," said Jake quietly as he turned on his heel and walked rapidly back the way he'd come.

Clarke impatiently jerked his head towards the door.

"Jake wait, it's not what you think." Ellie ran after the retreating American.

Jake spun round as Ellie placed a hand on his shoulder. He twisted her arm downward and pushed her away before making for the exit.

Ellie recovered her balance immediately, and the toe of her boot connected sharply with the back of Jake's right knee. "You can't just walk out." She said firmly as the Yank crumpled to the ground. "Just stop before this gets out of control."

"Control *this*," snarled Jake as he twisted over and lashed out with his leg.

Ellie had seen the kick coming and smartly stepped out of range. "Let's just calm down before someone really gets hurt."

In a second Jake was back on his feet, his eyes searching for signs of a further attack.

Ellie ended the hostilities by adopting a more natural stance. "Really Jake, you don't know what's been happening. The truth is we need your help, and you need ours. Probably more than you know."

Jake thought for a moment before reaching a conclusion. "Yeah, well, the only way you're gonna stop me leaving is either to shoot me or put me in irons."

Ellie rolled her eyes. "Spare me the gung-ho machismo, I see enough of that in the dance halls and it's very unattractive."

Jake turned to continue on his way.

"So, is that it? Are you just going to find some flophouse to rot in, surrounded by people who don't give a damn about you?"

Jake stopped and turned back. "Sounds familiar," he said bitterly.

Ellie took a step forward. "I know it's been hard, and God knows I understand why you find it difficult to trust anyone. I saw what they did to you down at Cedarwood, but don't forget it was Clarke who sent me to investigate Section 12 in the first place. *He* didn't trust them either, and he was right not to. Who knows how you might've ended up if the Major hadn't intervened. That man probably saved your sanity if not your life, and I think you owe him a fair hearing."

Jake said nothing as he pondered Ellie's last statement.

She took another step forward and placed her hand gently on Jake's forearm. "Clarke's explained everything to Mr Digby, and he knows what *really* happened in France, probably. It might surprise you to know that he's taking a big risk just by *being* here." She gestured around the freezing warehouse. "Come on Jake, you've been at Section 12 and you know how these things work. In the end, all we can trust is each-other, and the hope that we're doing the right things for the right reasons. Why don't you just listen to Major Clarke's briefing? It shouldn't take more than about an hour."

Jake stared through the warehouse door and out into the darkening December afternoon. "One condition," he said quietly.

"What's that?" Ellie asked softly.

"I want coffee. *Real* coffee. If I see any more of that goddamn tea then I'm really gonna kick someone in the pants, and where are those clothes you promised me?"

Ellie smiled. "You're in luck. We've all been enjoying some excellent coffee courtesy of Mr Digby, although I wouldn't ask *him* where he gets it from. Come on, I'll make some."

25

"Come on in, Jake. Don't be shy. It's time we all had a good straight talk, as my pop used to say." Mr Digby beckoned from his battered sofa.

Jake remained resolutely outside the door while Ellie squeezed past and crossed to the cast iron stove at the room's centre. The tin chimney stack vanishing through a newly cut hole in the roof sort of reminded him of another, similar stove set up to warm the Reverend Piggott's very different and equally unlikely living space.

Jake quickly surveyed the large wooden shed which served as both office and meeting area. Two desks were shoe-horned into the corners of the room whilst the main area was a cluster of sofas and chairs which looked like they'd been lifted from a bomb site somewhere. The stove took centre stage, with all the furniture radiating out from that single point, as though the fittings themselves were trying to keep warm in the freezing damp. The whole room smelled of fresh paint and tobacco smoke, while the boxes stacked around the walls suggested that the room's occupants were still unpacking.

Digby, still as unkempt has ever, lounged on a cracked leather sofa. Freed from beneath its restraining hat, the American's hair behaved in much the same way as his clothes, refusing to be pressed into any kind of recognisable form. He smiled warmly and beckoned Jake into the room again. "Shut the door, son, you're letting the heat out and the fresh air in."

Major Clarke eased into a second, equally moth-eaten sofa, surrounded by his ever present cloud of noxious fumes as he stared unflinchingly at the Sergeant.

Meanwhile, Ellie had poured a cup of good-smelling coffee into a faded china mug and waited by the stove, as though trying to coax an animal into a pen with food.

Jake began to wonder if his errant mind was beginning to play tricks as a young bespectacled man levered himself out of a sagging armchair and advanced enthusiastically. His drab suit and bowtie gave him the look of a bookish Himmler, and just like the lapsed priest in the scorched church, the stranger seemed somehow familiar.

The young man all but pulled Jake into the room as he grabbed his hand. "Sergeant Jacob Small. This is indeed a real pleasure, sir. I've heard so much about you from my colleagues that I feel I know you already. It would not be melodramatic to say that you are something of a celebrity, at least amongst our select group here."

Jake immediately withdrew his hand and stepped back as he heard the young man's accent. "Another damned German?" He looked pointedly at Ellie. "I thought you guys said you weren't interested in harbouring the enemy."

Clarke removed his pipe from his mouth. "It's all right, Jacob. Wilhelm here is extremely reliable, and he's uniquely qualified to assist with our current situation."

Wilhelm backed away from the American and turned to face the Major. "I am not offended, Major Clarke. I quite understand the Sergeant's suspicions. Most especially when you remember his last encounter with one of my countrymen." He turned back to Jake and bobbed his head. "I am Dr Wilhelm Werner, and I assure you I am *nothing* like Colonel Stryker."

Jake stepped back still further. "What the hell do *you* know about Colonel Stryker?"

Wilhelm glanced at Clarke, who nodded his approval. The German refugee then crossed to a wooden cabinet screwed to the office wall. He quickly opened it and threw the large switch hidden inside before returning to his seat. "I assume you understand the purpose of such a device?" He pointed to the disguised junction box.

Jake looked at the switchbox. "A Blank Space," he confirmed quietly. "That means you're worried about being overheard. And *that* means you know there's another Sensitive somewhere out there."

Wilhelm smiled with genuine warmth. "They said you were bright. Not so well educated, but intelligent nonetheless. That is excellent. It means you will understand things very quickly."

"Gee, you really know how to flatter a guy."

Clarke was becoming impatient. "Would you *please* come in and shut the door. We're trying to keep this bloody colander warm, and standing there gawping on the threshold isn't helping."

Wilhelm nodded in agreement. "You are quite safe here, Jacob. As you seem to know, the Blank Space hides our activities from invisible watchers, and we have the added luxury of shielded rooms, which helps to create a more manageable working space. I for one could never concentrate with my hair always standing on end."

To his dismay, Jake felt a smile creeping across his face. "Yeah, I know what you mean. Old doc Hammond had one of these setups at Cedarwood, although it wasn't as technical. At least my teeth aren't buzzing this time around."

This time it was Digby who spoke. "Jake, we don't have a lot of time so I'd really appreciate it if you'd just sit your ass down and listen. After all, if I was going to arrest you I'd have done it by now."

Ellie pointed to a worn but comfortable looking armchair facing the stove. "Mr Digby's right. We really *do* need your help, and you need ours whether you realise it or not."

Wilhelm continued the charm offensive. "Miss Parsons is quite correct, Jacob. This is an opportunity for us all to help each other. Please do take a seat."

Jake stepped warily into the room, stretching out to accept the steaming mug Ellie offered him.

"Close the door behind you, there's a good chap." Said the Major.

Jake crossed to the waiting chair and leaned over the back of it. "No dice. Gotta let that damned pipe smoke of yours out somehow."

"Very well," grumbled the Major before settling further into his seat. "I think the best place to start is for Dr Werner to introduce himself more fully to our guest. Clearly Jacob is suspicious of him."

Wilhelm cleared his throat. "As you rightly observed, Sergeant, my accent is something of a burden in these difficult times."

"Yeah, I'll bet."

"I am actually only *half* German, as my mother was Dutch."

Still refusing to sit, Jake took a sip of his coffee. "I really don't give a goddamn *where* you come from."

Wilhelm smiled nervously. "But perhaps you should, as my reasons for being here, and how I arrived will be of particular interest to you."

Jake stifled a yawn and sipped his coffee. "I can hardly wait."

The half-German doctor paused for a moment, the silence hanging heavy like the tobacco smoke drifting lazily towards the open door. "My father was the personal physician to someone you once knew. For many years it was his duty to care for one Peter van Cortlandt, whom you also knew under the codename of Nero."

Jake froze in mid-sip.

Major Clarke interjected. "Amid considerable personal and political danger, several members of Section C were able to extricate van Cortlandt, the Werners and a few other folk from the Netherlands. It was *that* operation which vindicated this rather obscure department's existence, and more especially its modus operandi."

Jake looked first at Wilhelm and then back at the Major. "Just full of surprises, aren't you? But what the hell has all this got to do with me?"

Clarke continued. "Because of the often embarrassing nature of our agents, this particular branch of the service operates at arm's length from our various sister agencies. In this case it saved our bacon as we were the only group able to operate successfully in Holland. Most of our other networks had been compromised early on. You won't have read all about it in the papers, but in intelligence terms the Netherlands has been a bloody disaster. However, we managed to get out almost unscathed, and with some very valuable assets."

Jake shook his head sadly. "So you just installed that bloodless bastard down at Cedarwood and let him do whatever the hell he wanted, including using Allied troops like me as guinea pigs."

Wilhelm shook his head. "I can assure you that Herr van Cortlandt was neither bloodless *nor* a bastard. In fact, his family history provides some remarkable reading..."

Major Clarke cleared his throat loudly, cutting off the doctor mid-sentence. "Both Hammond and van Cortlandt convinced us that they could harness and enhance innate abilities like your own astonishing talent for remote viewing, Jacob. And it seems they were at least partially successful."

Jake's reply was bitter. "Yeah, and if you think I'm gonna help any of you bastards now, you're crazy." He turned to Wilhelm. "Nothing personal, doc, but if you ever come near me I swear to God I'll break your damned neck."

Digby crushed out his cigarette in an overflowing ashtray. "Easy son. You'll find you need this little guy more than you know."

Jake's eyes narrowed suspiciously. "And what are you even *doing* here, Mr Digby, or whatever your real name is? Last time I saw *you*, you couldn't wait to bust me, so what's changed?"

Digby smiled and swung his legs off the sofa. "Disobeying orders, Jake. *That's* what I'm doing here. I know it's something you can relate to."

"You're a real funny guy, Digby."

"Yeah, I'm gonna be touring the Midwest after the war." Digby's face fell and his voice hardened. "Listen son. You're a quick learner, I'll give you that, but you're still way behind the rest of us and I don't have time to listen to your bullshit. My orders are to find you, wherever you are and at any cost. I'm then to deliver you back to Uncle Sam forthwith, immediately, without delay...now. Get the picture?"

Jake tensed.

This time it was Ellie who spoke up. "It's all right, Jake. Mr Digby's not going to drag you back to the States in irons. Officially he's not even *here,* and he still doesn't know where you are. He's taking a big risk to help us so I think you really ought to hear him out."

Digby nodded his approval. "Thanks Ellie, it's nice to know *somebody* understands that I've jammed something in the vice by agreeing to this, and it ain't my finger. Now where was I?"

Jake didn't try to contain sarcasm in his voice. "Well, gee Mr Digby. I think you were about to tell me what the huge favour you want from me actually *is.*"

Digby's face darkened and he started to rise.

Major Clarke hurriedly interjected. "Jake, I need to ask you a few questions, and I need you to be completely honest in your answers. You won't be in any trouble I assure you. The only time you *will* be in trouble is if we discover that you've lied. And if you *do* lie, then you can rest assured that we'll find out, sooner or later."

Jake watched Digby sit back again before turning to the Major. "Okay sure, what is it you want to know?"

Clarke tutted as he realised his pipe had gone out and began fumbling in his pocket for his penknife. "Have you been projecting or, remote viewing, since the time you left Section 12?"

Jake drained the last of his coffee and stepped forward to rest his mug on the stove.

"More?" Asked Ellie, who was hovering beside the coffee pot.

Jake nodded. "Yeah, that's real good stuff. Looks like rationing doesn't apply to you guys. Kinda reminds me of Cedarwood."

Digby's voice was calm and level this time. "Quit stalling, Jake. Just answer the man's question. Believe me, it really is important."

The Sergeant sighed and his shoulders slumped for a moment before he raised his head. "Okay then, yeah. I have."

Wilhelm produced a notepad and pencil from inside his jacket and began scribbling. "How often? And how do you know that you're not simply dreaming?"

The American looked quizzically at the doctor. "You can tell the difference. Believe me it's easy."

"Very well. How often do you think you are jumping out, or projecting?"

"Quite often, especially if I go to sleep sober."

Wilhelm scribbled again. "Alcohol interferes with projection?"

Jake nodded.

"That is a classic attempt to supress your natural abilities, and not a very healthy one if I may say so."

"Wow, you quacks really are smart."

Clarke finished scraping out his pipe and tucked it into his top pocket. "Please try to remember as best you can. As I said, you won't be in trouble, but we really need an honest answer to this next question. Don't forget it was *I* who first became suspicious of Hammond and Section 12, so you can trust me."

"If you say so. Okay, shoot."

Clarke leaned forward. "Have you ever been underground, Jacob? Specifically, have you entered the tube system and visited any...other places?"

Jake hesitated.

Digby spoke up. "It's okay, son. You're a pain in the ass but you're no traitor, we just really need to know."

Jake nodded slowly. "What gave me away, was it the dog?"

Clarke beamed and slapped his own knee. "I knew it! Of *course* it was the dog. Did you really think we'd not prepare for such a possibility?"

Jake finally stepped around the chair and sat down. "Makes sense I guess."

Wilhelm stopped scribbling and looked up. "How many times have you projected into the underground system, Jacob? Incidentally, that's quite an achievement. Subterranean spaces are notoriously difficult to infiltrate, especially with all that electrical interference. You know you really are a remarkable Sensitive."

"Just the once."

"Are you sure?"

Jake paused for a moment, then thought better of mentioning his strange non-dreams of church crypts and subterranean cells. "Yeah, just that one time."

Wilhelm's eyes narrowed as he stared at the Sergeant. "And what made you decide to enter the tunnel system on *that* particular night?"

Jake opened his mouth to speak, then hesitated as he realised everyone else in the room had leaned forward.

Eventually it was Ellie who broke the silence by crossing the room and handing Jake his second cup of coffee. "So, you went down there because..."

Jake took a deep breath. "Because I saw something, or someone."

Wilhelm scribbled again. "Another Projector, another Sensitive like you?"

Jake nodded, surprised at how relieved he felt to be sharing his story. "Yeah, I'm pretty sure it was another person, another Projector."

Clarke hissed through his teeth. "It's as we feared, gentlemen. Jacob, I don't suppose you saw anything that might help us *identify* this person, in the real world I mean?"

Jake thought for a moment before answering. "I don't know who it is or where he might be, but I'll tell you one thing. Whoever it is, he means business; and I don't think he's down there just for the excitement."

"Why not?" Asked Wilhelm simply.

"Because, he knows some of the same tricks that bastard Stryker once knew. My guess is that the CO might be dead, but at least *one* of his soldiers is still breathing."

Clarke nodded slowly. "Well Jacob, you've confirmed the existence of a threat I hoped we'd never have to face." He gestured to the open door. "We'll continue this debriefing a little later. In the meantime Dr Werner will sort you out with some hot food and a change of clothes."

26

Jake turned his collar up against the freezing damp as he stepped out of the main office.

"This way, Jacob." Wilhelm beckoned as he bustled ahead, a bulging collection of folders and papers shoved under his short arm. "I am just two doors down, at the end." He pointed to one of the smaller huts huddling in the corner of the warehouse.

Jake glanced at the temporary wooden structures, noting the tin chimneys protruding from each roof. "Looks like you've made yourselves real cosy here."

"Yes, I like to think of it as our little community," said Wilhelm as he reached his office door. "I obviously don't get out very much, so I have come to consider this as my home street."

"Looks like a classy neighbourhood," observed Jake absentmindedly.

Wilhelm pushed open the door and stepped inside his office-cum-dormitory, ushering Jake to follow. "Alone at last," he said with a broad smile as he gestured to another salvaged armchair beside his own glowing stove. Just as in the main office, several boxes and tea chests were stacked against one wall, adding to the impression of a field office under construction.

Jake sat and stretched out his legs, enjoying the warmth radiating across his nagging knee as he watched the doctor bustling around his cramped work space. He wondered if he was getting a little paranoid, as the more he observed Major Clarke's ingeniously hidden HQ, the more he was reminded of Section 12. Wilhelm's crowded desk and overstuffed old bookcase were reminiscent of the late Dr Hammond's office, and the collection of pencil sketches and sigils pinned to the walls further reinforced that impression. Jake pointed to the bunk bed in the corner. "Looks like you got the short straw here. You should've seen Hammond's place down at Cedarwood."

Wilhelm left the pile of papers on his already untidy desk and sat down opposite the Sergeant, notebook and pencil already poised. "Yes, I've heard that Cedarwood was quite a grand place. Such a pity it was destroyed."

"Yeah, well maybe you're the lucky one after all, but that's something I don't get. I mean, why station yourselves here? Why not requisition some nice comfortable country house, somewhere that might not get a rocket dropped on it at any moment?"

"Well, if a rocket *does* drop on us, there will be little evidence left to suggest the true nature of our work." Wilhelm quickly scribbled a note before leaning forward and staring hard at the Sergeant. "I know you are suffering, Jacob, and I can help you."

"Well, you just jump right in don't you? No small talk, no dinner and dancing?"

The young psychiatrist smiled. "I notice you often use humour to deflect potentially difficult questions. That's good; it's a very normal behaviour pattern, but it won't help you now."

"Maybe you're right," Jake conceded.

Wilhelm tapped his pencil on his knee. "Tell me, how do you feel about the way you've been treated since your return to England? Are you angry about what Hammond did? What about the fact that you barely escaped with your life?"

Jake turned his head to the light, the neatly stitched scars still prominent beneath his recently shortened hair. "Well, it's true that I took a hell of a pounding down in jolly old Kent, but I guess that's what happens in war."

Wilhelm scribbled again. "You appear very stoical about your recent experiences, Sergeant. You surely realise that your adventures are not exactly normal, even by the standards of this war."

"Yeah, well, in the end, *I'm* the one who made it out in one piece. A lot of other guys didn't; your pop's old boss for one. Then there was Hammond, and that lunatic Stryker, although

I reckon the world's a lot safer with *him* gone." Jake cocked his head as a thought occurred to him. "Say, now that I've brought it up, where *is* your pop anyway? I mean, it's kinda funny how he's not here."

Wilhelm's expression never changed. "Really? How so?"

"Well, you told me he was Nero's private doctor so I guess he's the main man around here, especially now that Hammond's dead. Or maybe the reason they've got you babysitting *me* is because he's busy chasing whoever's roaming those tunnels. Good luck with that, he's gonna need it."

Wilhelm sighed and let his head fall back onto the chair. "Two wrong assumptions in one sentence betray a fundamental lack of information regarding our current status."

"Can't you just talk like a normal person?"

Jake's unexpected comment prized a smile from Wilhelm's lips, a smile that faded all too quickly. "You are right about one thing though; my father was indeed the real expert on the van Cortlandt family. Although not a Sensitive himself, his devotion to his work and tireless research has given us many valuable insights into men like Peter van Cortlandt, Hammond and more recently your good self."

Jake leaned across and looked at the steel coffee pot sitting on Wilhelm's desk. "That coffee fresh?"

"No, it's about a day old, but do feel free to make some fresh." He pointed to a small wash basin all but hidden in the corner. "The engineers were kind enough to provide some clean water. I believe there's some kind of tank...somewhere."

"Gee, you want a back rub as well?" Asked Jake sarcastically as he rose and crossed to the desk, then to the sink. "I've noticed that you guys are always quick to tell me what *you* want, all in the name of victory against the fascists mind you, but you've got worse memories than *me* when it comes to keeping your own end of the bargain."

Wilhelm scratched at his chin. "I don't quite understand your meaning, Jacob. I was not under the impression that any bargain had been struck."

"I'm talking about clothes. Where the hell are the clothes you promised me? I'm still walking around here like a damned scarecrow."

Wilhelm nodded quickly. "Ah yes, now I understand. I believe Mr Digby is having a new uniform sent over."

Jake placed the coffee pot in the sink and stared hard at the psychiatrist. "Uniform? No one said anything about a *uniform*. Whose dumb idea was that?"

Wilhelm's voice carried just a hint of sarcastic surprise. "You are still in the army, are you not? Although it is not my concern, Mr Digby has decided it would be best to keep you in uniform, with the correct papers of course. He seems to think it would be the most suitable camouflage for you."

Jake turned back and leaned heavily over the sink. "Yeah, well I guess I'll have to take that up with him." Realising that they'd drifted off the subject in hand, he quickly steered the conversation back to its previous heading. "You said your dad *was* the expert on van Cortlandt," he observed casually as he swirled out the dark brown coffee dregs.

Wilhelm nodded slowly. "Indeed he was, and I am now continuing his work. It is a great pity he was never able to meet you. I can only imagine how excited he would've been."

Jake shook the last of the dregs from the pot and filled it with water before crossing back to the stove. "What happened?"

Wilhelm chuckled bitterly. "I sometimes wonder if fate is capable of malice, or humour, or both in equal measure. My father was killed in a German bombing raid not long after we arrived in England."

Jake sidled over to the desk, quickly scanning the papers strewn across it before picking up a tin of what he assumed was coffee. "Wow, sorry buddy, but screw *his* luck! Let's hope yours is better, although I wouldn't fancy your chances if you spend too long around me."

Wilhelm leaned forward again, pencil poised. "Really, and what you mean by that?"

Jake looked inside the tin, smiled when he saw that it was coffee and delved inside for the metal spoon he saw sticking out. "It's just that things, and people, end up getting shot to hell or bombed to bits when I'm around."

"Well, as you say, things like that happen in war."

Jake spooned coffee into the pot and set it on top of the stove before deftly selecting another item from Wilhelm's crowded desk. He turned and tossed his captured copy of *Lives of the Saints* into the doctor's lap. "If there's anything else you want to know, why don't you just *ask* me instead of rifling through my stuff?"

Wilhelm flinched as the book fell on him but quickly recovered his composure. "I'm afraid we don't have time for such niceties as personal privacy, and I don't believe you are so foolish as to think we wouldn't have searched your lodgings. However, it is your more distant history which interests me the most. It would be helpful if you could fill in some details which aren't clear. For example, I forget which American institution raised you."

Jake folded his arms and leaned against the stove's warm chimney. "It was..."

Wilhelm tapped Jake's confiscated book with his finger. "Yes?"

The American frowned. "It was...wait a second."

"You can't remember, can you?" Said Wilhelm softly.

Jake scoffed. "Hey, I'm not going senile *just* yet."

"No Sergeant, I don't believe you are. Senility would perhaps be a simpler and kinder explanation for why you cannot recall the most basic facts regarding your own biography. The sum total of your past self, which is the foundation of your present self, is disappearing before your very eyes. That is what I meant by suffering."

The American swallowed hard and struggled to contain the quiver in his voice. "Some days I can hardly remember anything. It's like there's a screen inside my head and someone keeps changing the movie reel." Suddenly feeling weak at the knees, Jake slumped into the vacant chair.

For a while the two men sat in silence. Eventually it was Wilhelm who spoke. "What do you know about the Brotherhood?"

Jake rubbed his forehead. "I know that they're rich, or they were. And I know that they're crazy, special abilities or not."

Wilhelm smiled and carefully placed Jake's book on the arm of his chair. "You speak more truth than you know, Sergeant." He lowered his voice. "I really don't know how much I'm supposed to tell you. But then Major Clarke and Mr Digby don't know everything themselves."

"And you *do?*"

"I flatter myself that I am the world's leading expert on the Brotherhood of the Shadow, if only by default."

"Stepped right into pa's shoes huh?"

The young psychiatrist nodded. "In a manner of speaking, yes."

Jake rose and examined the coffee pot, knowing full well it was not nearly ready. "What's this all got to do with me, and my forgetting the easy stuff everyone else can remember?"

"I suspect you already know the answer, Jacob. As a psychiatrist I would suggest that you're reluctant to voice those darker thoughts for fear you may confirm that which you constantly struggle to deny."

Jake began to pace the room. "Okay, Mr smart guy. You're the one with all the answers, so lay it on the line."

Wilhelm's voice never altered to reflect the magnitude of his next statement. "Sergeant Jacob Small is in mortal danger, in fact he may be dying already."

Jake's voice took on a defiant tone. "Wouldn't be the first time, according to your old pal Nero."

Wilhelm leaned forward, his eyes suddenly bright and intense. "Tell me, what exactly *did* happen? Why would van Cortlandt say such a thing to you?"

Jake shrugged. "Bread and butter for you guys I guess. I was out wandering one night when I bumped into a certain Colonel Stryker of the SS, and his pet of course."

"A Shade?" Enquired Wilhelm excitedly.

"You got it. Anyway, that...*thing* managed to get a hold of me and I must've blacked out. Nero was there when I woke up and he told me that I'd just died, although he'd managed to pull me back." Jake suddenly stopped. "Jesus, I can't believe I'm even *having* this conversation with you!"

Wilhelm said nothing for a good minute as he scribbled furiously, filling page after page of his small notebook and shaking his head. Eventually he stopped writing and looked up at the Sergeant. "I'm afraid this is much worse than I'd thought, and I'm sorry to say that you may have very little time left."

There were several long seconds of silence before Jake began to chuckle. "Listen buddy, if you think you can scare me into doing whatever you want then you're wasting your time. Doc Hammond already tried that down at Cedarwood, and it turned out he was just feeding me a bunch of bullshit so he could pump me full of Christ knows what. Maybe I didn't go to any of your fancy schools, but that don't make me a fool."

Wilhelm flicked back through his notes. "Yes indeed. Dr Hammond has a great talent for bringing his medical expertise to bear on cases like yours, and van Cortlandt's of course."

"You mean he *had* a talent."

Wilhelm just shrugged. "Obviously he cannot work without the strictest supervision now, but his knowledge may yet be useful. After all, this concerns him too."

"Dr Hammond is dead," said Jake matter-of-factly. "I was there. Surely they briefed you." He rubbed his aching knee again.

Wilhelm raised his eyebrows. "How do you know that?"

"Are you deaf? I just *told* you I was there! Christ, I thought *I* was the forgetful one around here."

Wilhelm gestured to the chair once again. "I think perhaps you should sit."

Jake stared at the doctor but didn't move. "What are you trying to tell me?"

"Well, judging by the reports I've seen, Marsh Pendleton was annihilated by a night raid, so I can understand how you would make such a mistake."

Jake tried to swallow down the lump in his throat. He failed.

Wilhelm saw Jake's reaction and nodded slowly. "I'm surprised no one else has mentioned it, but I assure you that Dr Thomas Hammond is still very much alive."

27

Jake said nothing as he tried to formulate an appropriate response. In the end his reply was simple. "What?"

Wilhelm looked straight at the American. "Oh yes. Despite being seriously injured he has recovered very quickly, although his mental faculties are becoming increasingly muddled, just like yours. Alas he will never be the same again physically…" Wilhelm tailed off and looked pointedly at Jake's legs. "Is there something wrong with your knee?"

Jake stopped abruptly as he realised he'd been unconsciously rubbing his leg. "Yeah, I must've twisted it somehow"

"I see," replied Wilhelm flatly. "Well then, perhaps you'd better sit down and take the weight off, as they say."

Jake sat.

Changing the subject, Wilhelm flicked back through his notebook. "To refresh your memory, you were raised by the St Alphonsus orphanage of Detroit. Parents unknown. Precise date of birth, unknown."

"Yeah, that's it. I just use the date they booked me in, it's as good a day as any when you don't know the truth."

"As you say, Sergeant." The psychiatrist leaned forward. "You know, during his more lucid episodes, Dr Hammond and I have had some absorbing conversations regarding your own astonishing talents and the legends surrounding your adopted patron saint."

Now it was Jake's turn to change the subject. "If Hammond's still alive then where is he?"

"Don't worry, Jacob. Dr Thomas Hammond is safely contained. Having shown just how untrustworthy he really is, we've taken steps to secure him in every possible sense."

Jake nodded thoughtfully. "Then I guess he's in a Blank Space, somewhere underground?"

"*Deep* underground I assure you, surrounded by as much electricity as it's possible to muster. I'm not convinced he's a projection risk in the same way that you are, but one can't be too careful. Besides, he is rather unwell following the Cedarwood episode. He's becoming decidedly paranoid and I believe he could be very dangerous in the wrong circumstances."

Jake wasn't listening. He closed his eyes and let his head fall back as he rubbed his forehead with his fingertips. "He's lost his left leg below the knee and now he uses a wheelchair."

Wilhelm's eyes widened and a broad smile lit up his small face. "You are quite correct, Jacob. However that could be just educated guesswork; after all you *did* witness Amabilis shooting him in the leg, assuming Hammond's own report is accurate."

Jake leaned forward, still rubbing his forehead. "I just don't get you guys at all. You spend half your time spouting off about how you believe in people like me, and the other half questioning everything I say."

Wilhelm's patient tone never wavered. "It is not a case of disbelieving your abilities, but rather of discerning the extraordinary from the mundane. It is a matter of separating projection from imagination, and real clairvoyance from simple coincidence. The existence of your undeniable talent does *not* make you infallible."

"Are you saying I just made it up? Why would I do that? Anyway, I'm not your damned lab rat so you can believe what you want, and at least I've figured out where I've seen you before."

The young psychiatrist took off his glasses and rubbed his eyes before replacing them. "If I am to help you then I must know as much about your experiences as I possibly can. What you have just told me is significant because there are no known Projectors capable of penetrating Hammond's holding cell. Are you claiming that you were able to overcome our defences?"

Jake shook his head and held up his hands. "Steady there, doc. I'm not claiming anything."

"Yet you knew about Hammond's leg and you also claim to have seen *me* before."

Jake waved his hands dismissively. "Look, let's just forget about the whole damned thing. I wish I'd never mentioned it in the first place."

Wilhelm pursed his lips and tapped his notebook with the end of his pencil. "But you *have* mentioned it, and I am duty-bound to report any possible security breaches to my superiors."

Jake knew he'd made a mistake, but still he tried to downplay the whole situation. "Look, it was just a stupid dream, that's all. Like you said, it's all about separating the strange from the ordinary. Hell, I might flip ten heads in a row but that don't mean I've got some kind of mental control over the coin."

Wilhelm's eyes flicked up towards the ceiling. "One of the burdens of studying psychiatry is that one always knows when the patient is lying."

"I ain't your patient. Get that straight, pal."

"Very well, let's discuss something else for a moment." Wilhelm picked up the battered book Jake had thrown to him. "Can you tell me a little about this?"

Jake was more than glad to change the subject. "Yeah, I lifted it from a library in Hackney, I think. Don't reckon anyone had looked at it for years. It was dusty as hell."

For just a moment, Wilhelm's patient smile sharpened at the edges, taking on a slightly devious appearance. "Yes, as hell. Tell me, why would you steal a volume of Baring-Gould's *Lives of the Saints* from a public library?"

"Not gonna report me are you?" Jake smelled coffee brewing and rose from his seat once again.

Wilhelm idly flicked through the volume once again. "Don't you find it fascinating that as well as the accounts of bilocation, St Alphonsus also possessed the gifts of healing and prophecy?" He leaned forward, his expression excited. "Perhaps these dusty old Catholics once knew more than they realised as they prayed for both the living *and* the dead. They seem comfortable with the notion that many things remain undecided long after this physical life ends."

Jake poured coffee into two battered and chipped earthenware cups. "Listen, are you actually gonna *tell* me anything, or just talk in circles like Clarke, Hammond, Nero and all the other so-called educated men I'm forced to put up with?"

"I am merely trying to prepare you for ideas which seem fantastic and yet, deep in your heart, you already know to be true."

Jake sat once again, passing coffee to the doctor. "Such as?"

Wilhelm paused for a moment. "Have you ever seen anyone die?"

"What the hell kind of question is *that?* I'm a soldier and this is a war."

"I don't mean here, I mean over there on the astral plane, the Place Removed."

Jake took a sip of his coffee and grimaced. "The Place Removed, huh? Never heard that one before."

Wilhelm didn't reply.

"Yeah, I've seen it, and I can tell you it's probably the most depressing, tragic and heart-breaking thing I've ever had to watch."

Wilhelm's voice was quiet and deadly serious. "There was no coherent form afterwards? They just...dispersed?"

Jake nodded slowly. "Something like that. Looks like you learned a lot from Nero and your pop."

Wilhelm smiled and leaned back in his chair. "Much more than you can possibly know as of yet." The smile disappeared abruptly. "From what Dr Hammond has told me, you already have some understanding of the Brotherhood's rite of Transition."

"I pretty much got the idea. They somehow think they can transplant themselves from one generation to the next."

Wilhelm took a sip of coffee and also grimaced. "Quite so. Talented Sensitives like van Cortlandt, Stryker and perhaps you yourself already possess the ability to transcend your physical form. Is it *so* difficult to imagine that, with the correct training and preparation, a Sensitive might manage to retain some sense of self-awareness following corporeal death? In fact, the Brotherhood's primary aim is to prepare those with potential to undertake this change, this Transition, to keep at least a shadow of that former self alive."

Jake suddenly felt uncomfortably hot and balanced his coffee on the arm of his chair. "I don't buy it. It's too fantastic, even after everything I've seen."

"You can't deny it, Jacob. Transition of this kind is a very risky affair and many things can go wrong, especially if the process is interrupted."

Jake felt his fists clenching involuntarily. "What happens then?"

Wilhelm shrugged. "Then we are off the map, as they say. However, if you put yourself in van Cortlandt's shoes then it's not difficult to imagine what could've happened at Marsh Pendleton."

Jake tried to ignore the growing ache in his knee. "I don't like where this is going."

"I'm sure you don't, but you need to hear the truth if you're going to survive the Cedarwood episode."

"I *did* survive it! I'm right here!"

Wilhelm raised his eyebrows. "Really? If a man contracts a fatal disease then it's just a question of time until he meets his inevitable destiny."

Jake shuddered. "You're a creepy son of a bitch. Are you *sure* you're a doctor?"

"Probably the only doctor in the world who can help you now."

Jake drained the last of his coffee and clasped the still warm mug tightly in his hands. "What are you getting at, Wilhelm? Are you trying to tell me I'm dying? I don't believe you."

Wilhelm held the Sergeant's gaze. "Not dying exactly; more like fading away, slowly disappearing piece by piece. Your earlier life has already vanished, drowned out by the stronger recollections of the dead, and believe me, they are so very hungry for a second chance of life, or any *semblance* of life."

"How long have I got?" Jake heard himself asking that matter-of-fact question before he'd even realised he was speaking.

The young psychiatrist rose and crossed to his desk, picking up a plain brown file, somewhat bulkier than the others. He opened it and gently, almost reverently began leafing through the mass of papers inside. "My father devoted his life to the care and study of the van Cortlandt family."

"Yeah I know. Must've been a great paying gig," Jake added bitterly.

Wilhelm continued as though he hadn't heard. "The one constant feature throughout the Brotherhood's tangled history has been instability, an interesting irony don't you think?"

"Can we skip to the part where you say how you're gonna help me *not* to go crazy?"

"We are coming to that, please believe me. Although you're no trained psychiatrist, you're obviously a very perceptive man. It will come as no surprise when I explain that trying to preserve one's own sense of self while assimilating the recollections, attitudes and beliefs of those who have gone before puts an enormous psychological strain on any Sensitive. Weaving several diverse strands of consciousness into one coherent mental tapestry is an exceptionally difficult task."

"Really? No shit!"

Wilhelm extracted a battered looking postcard from the file and stared at it thoughtfully. "The problem with Transition is that every few generations, the effort of controlling those competing streams of consciousness becomes too much, even for the most gifted and well educated Sensitive."

Jake frowned, partly through curiosity and partly because he realised he was accepting every insane word the young doctor said. "So, what happens then?"

Wilhelm dropped the creased card face down on the desk. "Suicide, sudden death, insanity, the sorts of things you would expect. The collective wisdom of generations past suddenly dissipates and fragments like a flock of startled birds."

For once Jake found himself ahead of the story, and he did not enjoy suddenly knowing what was coming next. "So the van Cortlandts paid your daddy to come up with a solution."

Wilhelm suddenly smiled broadly. "*Now* I think you begin to understand. My father devoted his life to solving the problem of how to nurture those shadows of the dead inside a healthy living mind, while allowing both to thrive and grow. He called this delicate balance the Cronus Equation, although he was never able to formulate a stable solution."

Jake felt a wave of revulsion sweep through him. "Jesus, that's a sick idea!"

"Really?" Wilhelm sounded genuinely surprised. "The instinct to commune with our ancestors is one of the oldest drives within the human psyche. Can it *really* be just a foolish superstition, derived from nothing but vacuous hope? Imagine the possibilities. Our history books overflow with the same old bloodied mistakes, the same old cycles of progress and destruction. Vast libraries of recorded wisdom seldom help us avoid our own folly, but perhaps if we maintain a *living* memory of horrors past we can prevent their repetition. Perhaps by truly holding onto the past we can truly change the future."

"And I guess the Brotherhood would be in charge of all this," observed Jake flatly.

"Why not?" Asked Wilhelm defiantly. "Wouldn't it be better to trust someone who can draw on not just one but two, three, perhaps even a hundred lifetimes of wisdom and experience?"

Jake couldn't help smirking, despite his serious situation. "Sure, then we could do away with all those messy debates and elections. I can see why the Nazis were so keen on you."

The psychiatrist's face darkened in an instant. "How dare you! How dare you throw me in with those savages! Sitting safe in your greasy diners far across the sea, you know *nothing* of life under their rule!"

Jake held up his hands. "Okay, okay buddy. Look I'm sorry about that. I guess I can see why those bastards would've been so interested in your father's work. That really *would* bring a whole new meaning to the thousand year Reich."

Wilhelm reached into his pocket and extracted a small brass tube, carefully unscrewing the top to reveal the glass capsule inside.

Jake raised his eyebrows. "That what I think it is?"

Wilhelm nodded. "Yes, and I would not hesitate to use it if I thought there was any danger of being captured again. You see, I'm not a very brave man and I know I could not resist any kind of torture. It would be better to die quickly and leave them empty handed."

Jake suddenly felt rather awkward as he realised that he didn't really give much of a damn about Wilhelm's politics or ideology. He was much more interested in his own predicament. "Well listen, *I've* only got one life and I'd really like to enjoy the rest of it while I can still remember my own name."

Wilhelm visibly relaxed and carefully replaced the tube in his pocket. He slid the worn postcard across the desk and stared hard at Jake. "You must understand that there may no cure for your condition, but I think perhaps I could help you gain better control of your somewhat splintered consciousness."

"I guess I've gotta take what I can get right now."

Wilhelm's voice was quiet. "The father of the gods feared his children's future power and devoured them; nonetheless they still escaped out into the world to spawn a whole new dynasty."

Jake could contain himself no longer and leaned forward to flip the battered card over. He wasn't a bit surprised to see Goya's crazed cannibal staring back at him. "Christ, I could do with a drink," were the only words he could think of to relieve the tension.

Wilhelm beamed with delight. "I'm quite sure the Major has some good scotch stashed away. After all this does call for a small celebration."

"Celebration? What the hell for?"

Wilhelm looked confused for a moment. "We're moving into uncharted territory, and you don't seem to understand just how impressive your record *is*. Dr Hammond informed me that you've already demonstrated skills on a par with the fabled Adepts of old. That is something most serious students of hidden things could never achieve, despite their recent boasting in print. *You* did it all by accident and without even trying."

Jake was not at all flattered. "Yeah well, dying is something most people do by accident, and it's hardly ever part of the plan."

Wilhelm's tone was suddenly more sombre. "By now you'll have realised that when you cross the abyss and return to the land of the living, you leave a part of yourself there, in that other place. Those who dwell beyond the veil have sensed you now, and I fear that perhaps you will never be free of them."

"Free of *who?*" Jake asked, hoping desperately for an answer that would contradict what he already suspected.

Wilhelm shook his head with rueful admiration. "You've managed to preserve most of your faculties despite enormous pressure from both sides of the grave, and that's one hell of an achievement, as you Americans would say."

Jake rubbed his forehead. "Yeah? Well I'm getting one hell of a headache, and I don't feel much like celebrating. Can't we just get on with it? Whatever *it* is."

Wilhelm looked a little disappointed but he soon rallied himself. "Very well, I'll make arrangements for some transport."

Jake felt his suspicions rising again. "Transport? Where to?"

"You certainly need a bath and a change of clothes, and then after that I shall brief you on your mission."

"What mission?"

Wilhelm sounded surprised. "Perhaps you've forgotten that you're still a wanted deserter. I can help you, but you'll need to show some commitment to those who labour on your behalf. There's still a highly advanced Projector out there somewhere, and we still need your help to find him before he does some real damage."

28

Jake shone his new torch into the top of his new kitbag, taking care not to crease the US Army uniform packed neatly inside. "Are you sure this is gonna fit?"

Ellie called back through the Austin's front window. "Of course it will. Don't worry, you'll have a chance to get properly cleaned up before you meet your old friend."

He quickly retied the top of the kitbag and laid it in the Austin's boot beside his old one, which had clearly been recovered from the Dog & Duck. Having rifled through both bags, Jake was alarmed to discover that his precious journal was missing, and he hoped its conspicuous absence was simply down to a slapdash search of George Tooley's dingy pub.

Unsure of whether to feel relieved or concerned about his vanished notebook, Jake made his way to the passenger door. "So I guess you just happened to have all that gear just sitting around, waiting for me."

Ellie switched on her own torch, helping to expand the small pool of light in the freezing dark courtyard. "You can thank Mr Digby for your new wardrobe. He thought you might need some things when we eventually found you, and he was only too happy to help."

Jake had just clambered into the back seat of the car when he heard a door slam shut somewhere in the darkness. A moment later, a third torch snapped on and began to waver and wobble its way down the almost invisible steps. "You make it sound like a foregone conclusion that I'm just gonna put on a uniform and be grateful."

"Hurry up, Doctor." Ellie's voice cut across the pool of light in a plume of steam as Wilhelm finally reached terra firma and puffed towards the waiting car.

Jake frowned with irritation as the psychiatrist all but fell backwards into the Austin's rear seat, a large bundle of files almost spilling out of his arms.

Ellie smirked as she looked round from the driver's seat. "Are you boys comfortable?"

"You're a real funny girl, Ellie." Replied Jake as he straightened up the chaotic pile of papers sliding across his lap. "I can see why they're queuing up to take you dancing."

"You know it's true." Ellie winked before revving the engine and easing the car forward, only switching on the hooded headlamps as they neared the yard gates.

Jake leaned across the fumbling physician and pulled the door shut just in time to prevent half his papers spilling onto the slimy cobbles.

Werner smiled and removed his glasses, polishing spots of freezing rain from the lenses with the cuff of his jacket. "Thank you, Jacob. There is so much to do that I often forget the things around me."

Jake was reminded of Dr Hammond's hastily furnished office at Cedarwood House as he flicked through the stack of files he'd briefly inherited. Here was that same peculiar mix of scientific articles, hand written notes and esoteric looking glyphs and symbols. He leaned back casually, trying not to look like he was reading as the night watchman opened the gates. "So, where are we heading to? The Hilton? The Ritz? You know I should really stop off and pick up my dinner jacket."

Ellie smiled at Jake's overplayed English accent. "Not bad, I can tell you've been practising. Sorry old chap, but the Hilton is positively bursting so we'll have to make do with a more modest billet."

Jake turned to watch the gates slam shut with a reverberating clatter. "Seriously though, I need to make a stop and pick something up."

Werner grabbed the front seat as Ellie weaved the car around the piles of rubble spilling onto the road. "I'm sorry, but we have to get you to a more secure location without delay. I'm sure we can collect any personal items for you."

"That's just the point. It's *personal*, private, get the idea?"

Ellie chimed in. "Sorry Jake, but orders are orders. You know that."

"Yeah, sure." He turned to the young German beside him, tapping the folder he'd been flicking through. "If I didn't know better, I'd say this was one of Hammond's old files."

Wilhelm's response was casual. "So it is."

Jake's eyes narrowed in the darkness. "I thought these would've all gone up in smoke, and besides, I thought *you* were the real expert on this stuff. What do you need Hammond's notes for?"

"The fact that I am an expert does not make me omniscient. Dr Hammond's research and expertise will be vital if we are to succeed."

"Oh, hell no!" Jake began shaking his head. "Nobody said anything about *working* with that bearded bastard."

Wilhelm beckoned for Jake to hand the files back. "I can assure you that Hammond has no operational authority, especially after that business in Kent. Unfortunately, the sad truth is that we need Dr Hammond. After all, this concerns him too."

Jake took off his glasses and narrowed his eyes. "What are you getting at?"

Wilhelm's response was simple and clinical. "Hammond was also affected by van Cortlandt's botched Transition, and more seriously than you." He smiled slightly at Jake's stunned silence. "That is correct, my American friend. You are not quite so unique as you thought. Although speaking personally, I find you are much more agreeable company."

Jake let his head slump back on the seat and groaned out loud. "And I thought things couldn't get any worse."

This time it was Ellie who responded. "Don't expect anyone to feel sorry for you. Right now I'm thinking of that nice young Corporal they dug out of the rubble at Cedarwood. Perhaps you should think about how *lucky* you've been, rather than focusing on your misfortunes."

"And you're an expert on misfortune, are you?"

Ellie brought the car to a stop as the warning barrier was illuminated by the car's headlamps. She turned to look over the back of her seat. "No Jake. I've never been posted abroad, I've never seen a battle and I've never been maimed or wounded. What I *do* know is that I have a chance to play my part in ending all this unspeakable cruelty. If we could ask them, I'd bet any one of the millions lost to these murderous years would swap places with you in a heartbeat. Actually, as you're supposed to be the all-powerful seer of things unseen, why don't you ask them yourself? That is, when you're not too busy complaining to those who're trying to help you. Don't you think that Dr Werner's expertise would be valuable in helping God knows how many *other* damaged soldiers? But still that's not enough for you." With that she opened the car door and stamped towards the obstructing barrier.

Jake quickly placed the pile of folders on his seat and followed her. "I'll tell you something, Ellie. If this is your idea of helping, I'd hate to be around when you guys get mad at me."

"I can manage quite well thank you," said Ellie curtly as the Jake grabbed one end of the wooden trestle.

"Just trying to gratefully do my part, ma'am," drawled Jake in his best shit-kicking-dirt-farming voice.

That effort prised a reluctant smile from Ellie's lips as she walked backwards, holding her end of the barrier. "Whoever said you Yanks were just a rabble of loud-mouthed, thoughtless, ungrateful hooligans?"

"I really don't know, but they were probably right," replied Jake as he suddenly shoved at his end of the painted wooden plank, jabbing the opposite end hard into Ellie's sternum.

Ellie emitted a strangled squawk as she stumbled over a pile of debris.

Jake immediately dropped his end of the trestle and leapt forward, grabbing Ellie's wrist and twisting her arm away from her body.

Although caught off guard, Ellie reacted fast and kicked out viciously, aiming for the American's crotch.

Jake grunted against the pain as Ellie's boot missed its target but still connected solidly with the inside of his thigh. Feeling his right leg collapsing under him, he viciously twisted Ellie's arm further still, forcing her onto her stomach and winding her as she broke his fall.

"Sergeant, stop! What is happening?" Wilhelm leapt from the car in a flurry of paper as he saw the pair wrestling in the darkness.

Knowing he had only seconds before the odds became two to one, Jake kept the pressure on Ellie's arm while his other hand reached over her shoulder and felt inside her coat.

Ellie squealed a feline roar of rage and frustration as she kicked up with her heels and sank her teeth into Jake's arm.

Grateful for his thick jacket, Jake quickly searched his adversary, his fingers scrabbling between folds of cloth, jagged rubble and the soft warmth of her breasts. Eventually he found the butt of Ellie's Browning pistol, and with one quick movement he pushed his knee hard into her back and wrenched the weapon from its concealed holster.

Wilhelm skidded to a halt and raised his arms as Jake sprang to his feet and pointed the gun squarely at his face. "Please Jacob, what is this nonsense?"

There was a clatter of masonry as Ellie rolled over and scrambled up.

Jake rapidly sidestepped around the frightened doctor so that he could cover the furious Ellie Parsons. "Just stay there or I swear to God I'll ventilate the pair of you."

Ellie wiped a smear of mud from her face before spitting out a mouthful of grit.

Jake raised his eyebrows and smirked. "That's real classy, Miss Parsons."

"Go to hell, Jake!"

Jake's smirk broadened into a smile. "Boy, you're even prettier when you're mad."

"And you're *insane,* Sergeant Small. Just what the bloody hell do you think you're doing?"

Jake wiggled the pistol barrel, indicating that Wilhelm should walk towards Ellie.

Wilhelm walked.

Jake backed away towards the car. "I'm sorry about roughing you up, Ellie, but I've seen what you can do in a tight spot. I know my face won't ever make me rich, but it's the only one I've got and I've kinda gotten used to it."

"I'll bloody rearrange it for you," snarled Ellie as she took a step forward. She stopped immediately when a bullet kicked up a brief shower of sparks as it ricocheted off the cobbles and whined away into silence.

Jake levelled the gun at her chest. "Don't make me do it, Ellie. The next one'll put you down for good, and the one after *that* will end Dr Werner's very interesting career."

It was Dr Werner who spoke next, lowering his hands to a more comfortable height. "Sergeant Small, Jacob. Just *what* are you doing?"

Jake finally reached the car. "What the hell do you *think* I'm doing? I'm getting out while I still can. I *knew* I shouldn't have trusted you."

Werner took a cautious step forward. "But you said..."

"I *know* what I said!" Snapped Jake, cutting off the psychiatrist mid-sentence. "Guess what...*I* can lie too! They probably taught you all about lying in psychiatry school. If you ever really *went* there."

"But why?"

Jake shook his head ruefully. "You honestly don't get it, do you?"

Ellie's voice was calm, measured. "Jake, you're not well. You're not thinking rationally."

The American ignored her and pulled open the driver's door. "Did *he* tell you that?" He pointed the gun at the psychiatrist.

Now Ellie took a step forward. "Jake, I know you've had a rough time, and I can't even *imagine* what must be going on in your mind, but I think this is your best chance to get the help you need."

Werner nodded in agreement. "Yes Sergeant. We can help you, and perhaps by helping you we might just help many others we don't even know."

Jake snorted and sat in the driver's seat, keeping the pistol levelled through the window as he closed the door with his left hand. "Yeah, someone else told me that not so very long ago. Now he's locked up underground, and I swore I'd never let the likes of him anywhere near me again. Thanks, but I'll take my chances on the outside. You've got Hammond, so you don't need me to help find this mysterious snooper."

Werner lowered his hands and took another step forward. "Hammond has his gifts, but they are not like yours. Please reconsider, Jacob. If you die, or your mind falls apart then the knowledge of generations could be lost forever."

"Maybe the dead should stay where they belong, and anyhow, I only agreed to listen. Well, I've listened all right."

The psychiatrist persisted. "Jacob, both Clarke and Digby will be furious if you leave now. I won't be able to protect you when you're recaptured."

Jake pulled his arm in through the window and tossed the Browning onto the front seat. "Yeah? Well that's *my* problem now," he retorted as he threw the car into gear and stamped down hard. Within seconds the car had vanished into the freezing mist with a squeal of tyres.

29

Major Clarke drummed his fingers while he scribbled an unintelligible note on his pad. Still drumming, he finished writing and tossed his pen onto the desk before leaning back.

Ellie swallowed hard while Wilhelm cleaned an imaginary speck of dirt from his glasses.

When at last the Major stopped drumming and spoke, his voice was calm and cold. "Stop your fiddling, or you'll spend the rest of the war pretending to give a toss about internees' feelings toward their mothers."

Wilhelm hurriedly replaced his glasses and almost shoved his hands in his pockets before wisely mimicking Ellie and clasping them loosely behind his back.

Clarke resumed drumming for an uncomfortably long time, but eventually his fingers slowed and became still once more. "Tell me again, exactly *how* you managed to let our single most important asset drive off in one of our own cars."

Wilhelm cleared his throat nervously. "I would not describe it that way…"

"Shut up!" Clarke's voice all but rattled the office's thin walls. "I honestly don't know why we keep you here, Dr Werner. Let's face it, you're pretty bloody useless when I consider all the facts. You haven't actually *done* anything, except allow probably the best Sensitive we'll ever see to just drive right out of here. And with half your bloody files on the *back seat!* What on earth were you *doing* with that much material in the first place?"

There was a slight tremor when Wilhelm spoke again. "I'm very sorry, Herr Major, truly. But it's not perhaps as bad as you think. I was merely reviewing some of Hammond's old files, at least what's left of them."

Clarke squeezed his eyes shut and opened them again. "Oh well, that's all right then. Nothing to worry about, everything's fine. You have no *idea* how serious this could be! Jake Small is a desperate man, so first he'll read them, then he'll hide them...and then he'll sell them."

"But why would he do that?"

Clarke stared hard at the squirming psychiatrist. "It's exactly what *I* would do if I was on the run and had something of great value in my possession."

Ellie spoke up. "It was my fault as much as his, Major."

Clarke jabbed a finger at his best female operative. "I expected *you* to know better, but I know you've always had a soft spot for those dashing Yanks."

"Now wait a minute..." Ellie clamped her mouth shut and swallowed down the rest of her retort.

Clarke merely raised his eyebrows and lowered his voice. "I thought as much. You're quite happy to kill an Englishman with your bare hands, but if a bloke has Old Glory on his shoulder then you just go to pieces." He shook his head and hissed through his teeth. "Perhaps you're not suited to intelligence work after all, *either* of you."

Ellie took a deep breath then spoke calmly. "He took me by surprise, Major. He took *both* of us by surprise."

Wilhelm chimed in. "He'd led us to believe he would co-operate. I took great pains to explain the situation to him."

"Obviously it wasn't explained clearly enough."

Wilhelm continued. "The man's scared and confused. All his past certainties have been snatched from beneath him and he simply doesn't know who to trust. Right now he'll be heading for whatever he considers his home to be."

Clarke drummed his fingers while he thought, suddenly stopping to yank open a drawer and retrieve his pipe. "Eleanor, you'll liaise with our Redcap friends again. Have them throw up some cordons around Bermondsey, but keep it vague like last time. Just tell them we're helping the Yanks track down some serious offenders."

"Jake Small's no fool," observed Ellie. "If you don't mind my saying so, I think there's little hope of simply scooping him up with a roadblock. Chances are he's either left the area or gone to ground with the local firm. He *did* say something about stopping off to pick something up, so he might be heading to the Dog & Duck."

Clarke raised his eyes to heaven. "For God's sake just *do as you're told* for once. Time is short, Eleanor."

"Right away, Major." Ellie quickly made her escape, leaving Wilhelm marooned in the middle of the office.

"Take a seat," said Clarke as he fished in a drawer and produced a tightly wrapped cloth bundle. Jamming his unfilled pipe in his mouth, he carefully unwrapped it to reveal Jake's copy of *The Lives of the Saints*. "I *would* say well done, but we both know it's sheer blind luck that you decided to keep this."

Wilhelm gratefully pulled a chair towards Clarke's desk, his eyes never leaving the battered book.

Clarke retrieved his worn tobacco pouch from his pocket and began filling his pipe. "So, now it's time for you to start earning your keep. The free ride is over."

"I would hardly describe my experiences here as a free ride, Herr Major."

The Major continued as though Wilhelm hadn't spoken. "The fact that Sergeant Small has gone under the wire puts us in a difficult position, more difficult than you realise."

Wilhelm shrugged. "I'm not sure I understand what you want of me."

Clarke rewrapped the dog-eared book. "First things first. How long will it be before Jake Small is useless to us?"

"Difficult to say with any certainty."

Clarke gave the impatience in his voice free rein. "Well you'd better start saying *something* with *some* degree of certainty, or *you're* bloody useless!"

Wilhelm rubbed one eye beneath his glasses. "Very well, Herr Major. I will give you my honest opinion, guesswork and all."

"If you would, please."

The psychiatrist paused before delivering his opinion. "I must confess that I'm surprised at how well he's coping with the strains on his mental health. When you consider the harrowing accounts of past Transition failures he shows a remarkable resilience, despite the obvious loss of some earlier memories."

Clarke interrupted. "Yes, yes. I understand the general idea, but I want to know how long it'll be before Jake Small forgets who he is, or was."

Wilhelm's tone was apologetic. "I'm afraid it's really impossible to say. As we do not understand how the impossibility of Transition actually occurs, we have no information on which to base any kind of reasonable estimate. The stress of the last twelve hours may produce total amnesia. On the other hand, he clearly has a robust sense of himself, so perhaps he will be able to assimilate the alien memories which are masquerading as his own. Alien to *him* of course, but not to those who actually lived those lives, who are now dead, and yet live on somewhere inside the consciousness we call Jacob Small. Isn't it fascinating? When you consider the concept of the self in light of these revelations, who among us can be certain that we are who we *believe* ourselves to be?"

Clarke rolled his eyes and struck a match to light his pipe, deliberately sending a cloud of blue smoke rolling across the desk. "So after all your education, experience, and the considerable losses incurred by extracting you from the Netherlands, the best you can give me is, *I've no idea*. Which, by the way, is the same answer I could get from the bloke on the bloody *gate!*"

"Nobody took any risks on *my* behalf, Herr Major. We both know I was a mere bonus, not the mission's target."

"Is it any wonder? You never give me a plain answer, you fail to help the one Sensitive we *do* have in custody, and then you lose the other one just as soon as we pick him up for you." Clarke leaned forward, the battered desk creaking beneath his elbows. "I'm now going to ask you a simple question, and I swear to God Almighty that if you don't give me a straight answer, I will personally have you reassigned to the most far flung, flyblown toilet I can possibly think of."

Wilhelm swallowed hard.

Clarke paused before speaking again. "Can we use Dr Hammond to find Jake Small?"

"Probably. Although I'm sure you're aware that whatever Hammond may learn will be fragmented and without context."

Clarke sat back in his chair again. "There, you see, that really wasn't so difficult was it? Now, let's try another. If we *can* capture this slippery bugger, again, can you patch him up at least well enough to help us with our problem, assuming he's not the damned *cause* of it in the first place?"

Wilhelm nodded. "Assuming he's still mentally competent, I'm certain he has the ability to track down this intruder. The more pertinent question is, can he be persuaded?"

Clarke smiled. "I can be very persuasive. Besides, the chance of redemption, a ticket home and a new start should help him to see things as they really are."

Wilhelm smiled weakly. "I don't like to disagree with my superiors, Herr Major, but I think you may underestimate Sergeant Small's resistance to your persuasion. He's an intelligent man who's seen the values he has suffered to uphold blurred, twisted and confused."

"Welcome to Intelligence."

The psychiatrist continued. "Quite so, but I think you may be surprised by Jacob's increasing cynicism and distaste for authority."

Clarke produced another cloud of smoke and drummed his fingers as he weighed the facts. At length he reached his conclusion. "Dr Werner, would you please make immediate arrangements to have Dr Hammond transferred to our base of operations here."

"Are you sure, Herr Major?"

"At the moment we're spread far too thinly, and I want everybody in one place where I can keep an eye on them."

Wilhelm rose from his chair. "As you wish. I will make the arrangements."

Clarke nodded. "Very good. We'll make a success of this cock-up yet."

30

The heavy board bounced and clattered on the cracked floor tiles, shattering the mausoleum silence inside the church. Jake held his breath and waited, listening for movement inside the building's blackened carcass as the echoes of his forced entry quickly faded.

He wriggled through the gap in the boards and dropped into the nave of St John's church. Keeping close to the wall, he slowly stood up, removed his dark glasses and methodically surveyed the damp and gloomy space. His eyes quickly adjusted to the darkness inside the ruined building, revealing a level of detail which, in his heart, Jake knew was far from natural or normal. On the other hand, maybe enhanced night vision was one of the few positive side-effects of his peculiar medical, or perhaps even spiritual condition.

Firebomb Fritz had clearly come calling at St John's, the small device probably lodging in the roof to weaken and collapse a large part of that overhead structure, leaving a cold and bereft space open to the elements as they worked their slow yet determined demolition. All serviceable furniture had been removed while scorched beams and singed pews were stacked haphazardly against the far wall. The aroma of charred wood pervaded the atmosphere in faint mockery of past rites.

The vestry's internal door was shrouded in shadow, while its opposing twin spilled a thin bar of light into the freezing gloom just a few feet from where he stood. Assuming this second door led to Piggott's makeshift living space, Jake quietly placed his ear as close as possible without making contact lest the ageing woodwork should rattle in its frame.

Silence.

Piggott was either out, which was unlikely, or he was in such a laudanum induced stupor that he'd failed to hear Jake's less than clandestine entry. He still wasn't sure whether the old man was on the level, but he figured that since Piggott hadn't reported him to the authorities he was the closest thing to a friend right now. Besides, his options were few, which made figuring out what to do a very simple process.

Jake finally decided on checking the vestry first. He didn't expect to find anyone in there, but he'd feel more at ease if he was certain they would remain undisturbed. Surprise guests were something he could well do without.

He glanced at the altar as he quietly crossed the dark and echoing nave. The elaborate decorations and metalwork had long since been removed, replaced by a simple wooden crucifix more reminiscent of a pauper's grave than a focal point for infinity. It seemed that even the Almighty was on short rations throughout the dark and hungry winter days, with normal service to be resumed after hostilities had ended...maybe.

Jake had experienced enough ritual and symbolism to have long since purged any religious impulse from his system, but still he felt uncomfortable with such a cut-price and cursory nod to the mysteries of life, death and eternity. Such scant regard for the infinite just seemed plain *wrong* somehow, especially in the light of his adventures during the past few months. Jake would never describe himself as born-again, feeling that re-educated was a more appropriate phrase if anyone ever asked, which they hadn't. Whatever the case, he'd certainly been forced to confront the inescapable truth of a universe beyond common human experience. Now there could be no return to the cold comfort of a small and mean-spirited, yet entirely explicable cellular existence.

Jake had just paused to nod a brief acknowledgement to Providence when a slight movement caught his eye. Suddenly alert, he stared hard at the shadows gathered behind the utility altar like a curtain of darkness...a curtain that could be hiding something. He blinked rapidly, stepping forward as he scrutinised the deep darkness beyond the plain wooden cross.

There was nothing. Perhaps he finally *was* coming apart just as the Kraut doctor had warned. Perhaps he was losing his reason as well as his memory, becoming increasingly inept at sorting imagination from reality. Yet still he stared, unable to suppress the intuition that he wasn't alone.

"Who's there?"

The challenge echoed off the damp floor and glistening walls, but there was no response.

Jake stepped forward again, his hand reaching for the butt of his pistol. "I know you're there. Who are you?" He tensed as he perceived a slight movement, a ripple of shadow within darkness. "I see you! Show yourself, you goddamn coward!"

Jake wasn't sure if it was coincidence or whether his challenge had been accepted. Whatever the case, Ellie's Browning was suddenly in his hand as he watched a single shadow somehow detach itself from mundane darkness shrouding the sanctuary.

Jake had little confidence that the pistol would be any help, but he was still reluctant to relinquish the weapon as he advanced a few paces closer.

The shadow walked silently to the front of the altar and stopped, shifting its head as it studied the dishevelled deserter who'd presumed to call it out.

Jake swallowed hard as he realised he hadn't the faintest idea of what to do next. He had no doubt he was facing the same phantom he'd seen down in the tube, and he also realised he had no knowledge of his silent stalker's true intent. The good news was that, hopefully, this nameless and featureless Projector was equally in the dark about *him*.

Sounding far more confident than he actually felt, Jake took a deep breath and made a big show of lowering his weapon. "Hi there, you got a name?" He cringed at his own stupidity.

The silhouette didn't respond in any way.

"Guess we've seen each other before, down in the tunnels. What do you want with me? You part of the Brotherhood?"

Again no response, just a slight shimmer and flicker, like a badly spliced movie reel.

Jake tried again; still unsure if the spectre could respond or even hear him. "Listen buddy, if you're looking for the others then I've got some bad news."

This time the dark spirit bent its head forward as though it were listening. Perhaps it *could* hear after all.

Jake figured that showing some insider knowledge would enhance his credibility in whatever game he'd gotten mixed up in. "Just so you know, I'm not working for anyone, so whatever you're up to just leave me out of it. You hear?"

No response.

"If you're looking for the others; Stryker, van Cortlandt, Hammond, then you're wasting your time."

The shadow moved onto the top altar step, cocking its head and twisting its body in a decidedly non-human way. A definite response.

Jake took a step back. "Sorry buddy. They're gone, dead. Well two of them anyway. I guess that just leaves you and me."

Jake jumped and cursed as the featureless phantom violently arched its back, as though suddenly gripped by an invisible electric current. Within a single breath it had silently stretched upwards, becoming ever more translucent as it rapidly reached towards the charred roof beams, its boneless limbs taking on impossible, almost comic proportions.

Jake backed away as he watched the silent shadow stretch to a height well above ten feet, its transparency increasing with every added inch of growth. Finally size overtook solidity and the faceless intruder was gone. No flash, no wind, no thunderclap...just *gone*.

Jake let out the breath he realised he'd been holding, unsure of whether to be concerned or relieved at what he'd just witnessed. Had he just made his situation better or worse? He looked at the empty altar space for several seconds as he considered his position, finally concluding that whatever else might happen, he was still hiding from just about everyone in London. Featureless wraiths might not need food, money and a place to hide but he *did*. He could worry about his disembodied friend later, assuming he hadn't been captured, killed or lost his marbles in the meantime.

Doing his best to put the visitation behind him, Jake continued across the echoing space and paused at the vestry. He didn't spend too long listening for signs of life inside as the darkness beneath the door suggested the room was empty.

He turned the handle and let the door swing open under its own weight. Not wanting to be mistaken for a looter, he quietly announced his presence and slowly ventured inside. The room was empty as he'd suspected, and a quick examination confirmed that Piggott probably hadn't been inside since their last meeting.

Jake left the empty room and quickly headed for the vestry door's opposite number. Although reason told him it was unnecessary, he still kept a wary eye on the damp and darkened altar as he crossed the no man's land inside the empty church.

He repeated his previous tactic and let the second door swing open while he stood out of sight. This time a flood of warm yellow light spilled into the darkened body of the church. "Hey Reverend, it's me, Jake. I guess you know my real name if you read my diary."

Jake's nostrils were filled with the scents of paraffin, coal smoke and sickness as he peeped cautiously into the room. It was obvious that the Reverend Piggott still had friends in the neighbourhood, and they had made him quite comfortable. Half a dozen hurricane lamps flickered in the confined space, filling the room with a wavering light and throwing restless shadows across Piggott's sturdy and comfortable looking bed.

Jake stepped further into the room, noting the neglect suggested by the half open wardrobe and cluttered dresser. The remnants of a meal slowly congealed in a pair of army mess tins, although there was no cooking equipment to be seen. Jake felt relieved that at least *somebody* was bringing the old man some food and checking in on him.

For a moment he feared the worst as he looked down at Piggott's seemingly lifeless form, but at last the old man moved and took a sharp breath as though he were dreaming.

Jake engaged the Browning's safety and closed the door to keep the place warm. He tucked the pistol in his waistband before checking on the glowing iron stove, which looked like a bigger brother to the one in the vestry. At last he approached the sleeping priest directly. "Hey Reverend, wake up now. Truth is I'm in a jam and I really need your help. There's nobody I can trust in this town any more."

The old man stirred and muttered incoherently.

Jake leaned forward and gently shook the sick man by the shoulder. "Wake up. It's me, Jake."

Again Piggott moved and muttered, but showed no signs of waking.

Jake picked up the half empty laudanum bottle from the bedside table and wondered if he'd be able to rouse the sleeping man at all. Leaning forward once again, he gently pinched Piggott's nose until the old man snorted loudly and his eyelids began to flicker. He followed up by gently tapping the drowsy clergyman's cheek with his fingertips. "Come on old timer, up you get. You seem to know this town pretty good, and that makes you about the only friend I've got right now."

Piggott's eyelids blinked rapidly before settling into a half-open position, and it was a good minute after that before his expression showed any semblance of recognition.

Grunting with the effort, Jake hoisted the old man into a sitting position and grabbed a canteen of water from the bedside. "There you go, buddy; my guess is you'll be thirsty."

The priest gulped down several mouthfuls of water before splashing some in his hand and wiping it across his face. He let his head slump back against the headboard as he finally managed to focus properly. His voice was strained and tired when he spoke. "Thought I sent you to see the Guvnor."

Jake replaced the canteen on the nightstand. "Place got busted pretty much as soon as I got there."

Piggott looked down at his bedclothes. "I heard there was some trouble down there. I did naïvely hope you weren't involved."

"Yeah? How did *you* find out?" Jake asked suspiciously.

Piggott was silent for a while, as though the laudanum had made his mental processes slow and sticky. Eventually he pointed an unsteady finger at the greasy mess tins. "Mabel makes sure I'm fed, and not dead yet."

Jake sat gently on the bed. "You don't act much like a priest, and you keep some pretty strange company for a man of the cloth." He gestured around the room in exasperation. "I mean, what are you *doing* here? Surely the church owes you some medical care or something."

The old priest gestured to the canteen once more.

Jake handed it to him.

Piggott took a long swallow, his eyes brightening, becoming clearer and more alert. "By now you'll know that George

Tooley's the sort of man who understands business, investment and planning. He invests a lot of time and money to keep his places safe. If the Dog & Duck got turned over it means that someone's *really* after you, and it's someone who doesn't mind upsetting a few apple carts along the way." The old man smiled weakly. "He'll be bloody furious you know. I wouldn't want to be in your shoes right now."

Jake sat back, not wanting to push the old man too hard but needing to keep his attention focused. "Listen Reverend, I guess we've both been around the block a few times so let's not bullshit each other."

Piggott's weary smile broadened. "Wouldn't dream of it, son."

Jake smiled back, even though he tried not to. "Yeah I'll bet." He leaned forward a little further. "Who are you? I mean, who are you *really*? It can't just be blind chance that we met."

Piggott's forehead creased with confusion. "Told you that already."

Jake considered before speaking again. "Okay then, let's try this a different way. I know why you're cooped up in this place, and I know why you won't go to a hospital. I sure as hell don't blame you, but I don't really think that matters any more."

Even though the old priest's voice was weak, the sarcasm and impatience was still discernible. "Worked it all out, have you?"

Jake's next statement was quiet but direct. "I've seen your visitor."

Piggott coughed. "Mabel's a treasure, I don't know where I'd be without her."

Jake refused to be put off. "We both know what I'm talking about. You said you had a dream, a dream about me."

The priest's tenuous smile returned. "If you're hoping I'm going to ask you out, don't hold your breath. You're not my type."

Jake silently cursed himself for smirking. "Don't screw around, Reverend. This is real serious, and that sure as hell wasn't Mabel I just saw out there."

Piggott remained silent.

"You got any idea how *dangerous* these people are? Do you know what kind of trouble you might be in?" Jake immediately answered his own question. "I kinda guess you do, otherwise you wouldn't be hiding in a place like this."

Again no response.

The American sighed and pinched the bridge of his nose. "Okay, have it your own way. In the meantime I'll have to bunk in my old room; it's not safe at the pub now." He rose and quietly made his way back to the door.

Piggott's voice suddenly gained some strength. "You don't know half as much as you think, son. You met George Tooley yet?"

Jake stopped and turned back. "Just one of his goons. I reckon this famous Guvnor won't be showing his face for a while. In fact I'm counting on it."

Piggott pushed himself forward so he could lay flat again. "You'd better get yourself back down there sharpish. You don't want to make him come looking."

"Sorry old timer, but I think the medication must be messing with your mind. Why the hell should I make things *easy* for a guy who probably wants my head on a plate? If I had any other choice I'd be miles away and never looking back."

Piggott's voice weakened as he drifted back into sleep. "These are strange times, Jake, and you're strange man. Perhaps you'll find sanctuary in some strange places. I know *I* have."

Jake shook his head. "Listen, I'm gonna heat some water and get cleaned up, and then I've gotta figure out how to get my property back without getting my ass shot on sight. If I'm real lucky then maybe I can just slip in the back door."

Piggott breathed slowly and closed his eyes as he marshalled his waning strength. "You know they'll never stop looking for you, and I'm not talking about Mr Tooley and his friends either."

"I guess not," conceded Jake. "I don't so much care that you've read my journal, what bothers me is that you seem to have *understood* it a little too easy."

The priest ducked the issue. "If you want to stay one step ahead then you'll have to get out, and I mean *out*. For good, and George Tooley's the only man in London who can help you with that." He pointed to the worn bedside dresser. "Open the drawer, I've got something for you."

Curious, Jake opened the drawer and peered inside, his eyes immediately drawn to an envelope with a wax seal securing the flap. "What's this, a love letter?"

"Just take that to Tooley, and for God's sake don't get caught with it."

"So I'm your messenger now. What is it?" Asked Jake suspiciously.

"It's your ticket out of England."

Jake turned the envelope between his fingers. "You and me have barely introduced ourselves, so why should you give a damn about what happens to me?"

Piggott's head rolled sideways as though he'd finally lost the strength to look straight up. "Let's just say I know real talent when I see it. Just take that to George Tooley will you? It'll be all right, I promise."

Jake was saddened by the old man's failing reasoning. "The guy just got his pub raided, and the only reason *I'm* setting foot in that dive again is because I've got no other choice. After that, I'm out of here forever."

Piggott smirked as his eyes closed. "So you reckon."

31

The lookout was still there, muffled in an overcoat and lighting yet another cigarette. To the casual observer he looked like a man having a quiet smoke and gathering his thoughts, although Jake knew better. The bars closed early in this part of the world, and a man standing outside a pub at two in the morning couldn't be anything but a lookout. Clearly the previous day's sweep had made Dog & Duck's clientele even more suspicious than usual, and with good reason.

Jake slipped back around the corner and considered his options yet again. He didn't like them much.

Although he'd managed to stash Wilhelm's files at the church, change clothes and hide the car, his precious journal was still inside the most hostile pub in England. His mental anchor in a stormy psychological sea was now in the possession of thieves, spivs and other assorted lowlifes. Alas, the newly posted lookouts made any surreptitious recovery impossible.

As he shivered in the freezing darkness, Jake fervently hoped that some player with an eye for the main chance hadn't figured out what his battered notebook might be worth to certain parties. For a moment he almost wished that some slag had simply tossed it in the trash, unaware of its potential value. However, Jake quickly dismissed that idea as he considered a further factor, one which both reassured him that his journal was intact and also worried him as much as the opaque machinations of Digby and Clarke. It was obvious that despite his being half delirious and dying for sure, the Reverend Piggott was at least partially cursed with a Sensitive's sight. It was Piggott, the priest with the murky past and the short future, who'd directed him back to this low tavern in the Bermondsey smoke with a message for the man who'd probably put a price on his head already. Jake was counting on the old priest's letter containing something greater than an appeal to the angels of George Tooley's better nature, although it did at least provide him with an invaluable pretext for showing his face again.

As he hid in the gloom, Jake was forced to accept that the more he tried to rationalise the course of recent events, the more unlikely it seemed that mere chance was at work. Although the logical part of his mind tried to deny it, Jake knew in his heart that there were obscure, intangible, yet powerful forces at work around him. For whatever reason, he was *supposed* to be here.

That last thought finally extinguished Jake's indecision and spurred him into action. He had no real strategy, but there wasn't really time to formulate one. He knew the mysterious Dr Werner was right when he said that time was short. If he couldn't figure out a solution soon, then Sergeant Jacob Small might just vanish entirely, to be replaced by...someone else.

Jake pinched the bridge of his nose and closed his eyes against the buzzing pain which had settled around his forehead, while at the same time rubbing his left knee, which was playing up worse than ever in the damp atmosphere. His mind made up, he took a deep breath, stepped around the corner and limped the last fifty yards up the hill towards the Dog & Duck. As he drew nearer, Jake recognised the lookout as the bar room bruiser he'd encountered the previous day, although that felt like a very long time ago.

The watchman shook his head in disbelief as the unwelcome visitor approached. "You've got some bloody nerve showing up here, soldier boy. And don't you look gorgeous too."

Jake was in no mood for small talk, especially hostile and sarcastic small talk. "Just let me in. I need to see the Guvnor, and I guess he'll want to see me."

The flat-nosed sentry stepped forward and shoved his hands inside Jake's new army coat. He grimaced as he yanked the Browning from the visitor's waistband. "You think you're some sort of flash Harry walking around with this?"

Jake figured that was a rhetorical question so he stayed silent as he followed the doorman into the cobbled gloom.

The lookout stuffed the gun in his own waistband and rapped on the battered wooden door. "You must be a bit thick coming back here."

Jake moved out of reach. "At least I had the brains to find my way back."

The watchman frowned and glowered as he searched for the insult in Jake's retort.

The tension was broken when the door creaked open and Mabel stepped into the yard, a rush of thick blue tobacco smoke curling around her like outriders for the goddess of tough landladies. Not surprisingly, she was even *less* welcoming than the doorman. "Piss off you idiot! We'll *all* be for the chop if somebody sees you."

"Better let me in then," said Jake simply.

Mabel said nothing as she resolutely slammed the door shut, the rasp of heavy bolts confirming the conversation was over.

The large doorman stepped forward. "You can go now."

Jake appeared nonchalant. "You've got something of mine."

The bouncer produced Jake's pistol and pointed it squarely at the American's face. "You mean this?"

Jake exploded. He twitched his head to one side and grabbed the bouncer's wrist with both hands, forcing the gun into the air while bringing his knee up squarely into the big man's groin.

The doorman unsuccessfully tried to head-butt his lighter opponent as Jake drove forward relentlessly, pushing the larger man off-balance. The gun went off as both men fell to the ground, the bullet ricocheting off a wall and whining away down the street.

Jake shifted his grip from the man's wrist to the weapon itself, his fingers closing around the weapon's warm barrel. He was beginning to feel his opponent's grip slackening when there was a brief flash of light, accompanied by a loud thud as something hit him square on the temple. A second heavy blow to the back of his skull transformed the world into a quiet and distant place as he hovered somewhere between consciousness and oblivion.

Jake felt the cold cobbles strike his forehead as he slumped to the ground, the world swaying nauseatingly and his eyes stinging as blood poured into them. He struggled to lift himself up but his arm was kicked from under him and he fell heavily for a second time. Despite the assault on his senses, Jake's consciousness doggedly held on as he dimly felt himself being lifted to his feet and dragged towards the bright blur of the pub door.

There was a confusion of movement, noise and a strong smell of tobacco smoke as Jake was dragged bodily into the pub, his toes scrabbling on the bare boards as he struggled feebly to resist.

Something soft hit him in the face as he was manhandled into a chair.

"Use that. Don't be bleeding all over the table."

Jake struggled to identify the deep American voice as he wiped the blood from his eyes and pressed the towel to his forehead in an effort to stop the bleeding.

An unseen hand suddenly grabbed Jake's hair and yanked his head back. He gasped as cold water was poured over his face, rinsing away the blood but also filling his throat, causing him to cough and choke uncontrollably. Memory and reality were momentarily interchanged, and for a second or two Jake believed that he was somewhere else, lying badly beaten on the tiled floor of an empty cellblock.

The hand relaxed its hold and Jake jerked his head forward, quickly wiping the water from his face as the here and now slowly swam back into focus. It was only a little better than the unpleasant memory he'd just relived.

Jake pressed the towel back to his throbbing head and squinted against the light, having lost his dark glasses during the struggle. He quickly surveyed the surly group of men sitting around tables or leaning casually against walls; all staring intently him. Realising he wasn't about to be leaving any time soon, Jake turned his attention to the large, ebony skinned man sitting opposite. "Who the hell are *you?*" He croaked, trying to inject as much defiance and nonchalance into his voice as possible.

Jake's large inquisitor rested one palm on the table while the other hand jammed a large cigar in his mouth, a row of neat white teeth gleaming as he smiled. "Folks around here call me Duke. This here's Yellow." Duke pointed over Jake's shoulder.

Before he could turn around, Jake felt cold muzzle of a pistol barrel jammed firmly into the back of his head. "You stay right there, faggot." The voice hissing from behind was American too.

The chair opposite creaked as Duke settled his large frame more comfortably into it. "So you're the famous Caesar, the guy who took Pete Finch for the shirt off his back. That's the only reason I haven't blown your head off for showing your dumb ass around here again. Any idea how much trouble you've caused?"

Jake swallowed hard, determined not to lose his nerve. "I just want what's mine."

Duke's face fell. "You're not as smart as you think you are, boy. Not nearly."

"And *you* don't know half as much as you think."

Duke's smile returned. "Yeah? Well *I* ain't the one with a cracked head and gun pressed into his skull. Still think you're smarter than us, boy?"

"Stop calling me boy."

Duke nodded to Yellow. "Shoot this dumb cracker. I'm already tired of his bullshit."

Jake yelled out as he heard a metallic click behind him.

A low rumble of laughter rolled around the pub as Jake opened his eyes and realised that he was still alive. His relief was short lived as the empty revolver vanished, to be replaced by the still-warm barrel of his own Browning. His unseen tormentor hissed in his ear again. "That was just to get things going. The next one will be for real, you stupid bastard."

Jake tried to disguise the tremble in his hands as he removed the towel and re-folded it to press a clean patch against his head. He swallowed hard and balled his fists in an effort to keep his voice steady. "Where's the Guvnor? I need to see him."

Another grumble of sour laughter rippled around the pub, further charging the already electrified atmosphere.

Duke removed the cigar from his mouth and grinned. "You got balls, I'll give you that." He jerked his head towards a large, square-headed and broken-nosed man leaning against a nicotine yellowed wall. "Hear that, Frank? The emperor wants to see the Guvnor."

Frank smiled coldly. "Stupid sod."

"Damn straight," agreed Duke. "Still, you'd better go tell him that the boy with the magic eyes is back. You know how the Guvnor likes to be in on things."

Frank nodded. "Okay Duke," was his short response.

Duke reached into his top pocket and produced Piggott's letter, complete with theatrical looking bloodstains following the fight in the street. "Better give him this as well. Looks like our boy here's given up cards and become a runner instead. Kind of a downward career move if you ask me."

Frank stepped forward and took the letter before disappearing through the door behind the bar.

Duke turned his attention back to Jake. "Now why do you think you should get to see the Guvnor?"

Jake stared hard across the table. "He's got something of mine. I want it back, that's all."

Duke's smile disappeared. He cocked his head and narrowed his eyes as he reached forward and waved a hand in front of Jake's face. "You see okay, boy? You been staring at phosphorous or something?"

The corners of Jake's mouth twitched upwards as he deliberately lifted his head to scan the surrounding mob, the dim glow of oil lamps reflecting unusually brightly in his eyes. "Yeah, I see *real* good. Better than any of you guys. Hey, any chance of getting my peepers back? I'm kinda sensitive to light these days."

Duke nodded to someone out of sight and Jake's dark glasses clattered onto the table. "Here you go, and don't take 'em off again while I'm around you creepy-ass son of a bitch."

Jake immediately put them on with his free hand.

Duke frowned and leaned back, pulling the cigar from between his teeth. "How did you get to this stinking city, boy? You jump ship or something?"

"Something like that, it's a long story."

A new murmur of unkind laughter rippled around the pub.

Duke's grin returned once more. "We *all* got long stories around here. You ain't nothin' special here, soldier boy." He reached forward, his large fingers gently tracing the scars on Jake's head. "You seen some action?"

Jake pulled the towel away and looked at it, relieved to see that the flow of blood was diminishing. "Yeah, Utah beach. Well, close anyway."

Duke leaned back in his chair and clasped his fingers behind his head. "Yeah? Well you were smart not to go back once they'd patched you up. I guess by now you've figured out how Uncle Sam likes to tempt fate with the doughboys who love him the most."

Jake couldn't think of a plausible response and the truth was just unbelievable, so he stayed silent.

Duke nodded slowly. "It's okay, boy. Took *me* a while to figure out I wasn't no coward either. I just got smart enough to see that I was risking my ass for someone else's future."

Jake refolded his towel once again. "Yeah? How do you figure?"

"You think they're fighting to build a shining new world for the likes of us, Jimmy? This war ain't about freedom or nothing like that. It's about keeping things the way they were before these Krauts got all uppity and wanted to run things."

Jake smirked. "You reckon Hitler'll give us a pay rise if he wins?"

There was a hint of bitterness in Duke's smile. "*You* maybe, but I ain't reckoning on risking my beautiful black ass to trade one Massa Charlie for another, understand?"

"Yeah, kind of. Like I said, how I got here is one hell of a long story. Let's just say I'm tired of being used by people I can't trust."

Duke looked up as Frank walked heavily back across the pub and nodded.

Duke stood up and gestured to the door behind the bar with a theatrical flourish. "Life and death, Jimmy. In the end that's all there is, and you're about to find out which door *you'll* be walking through tonight."

Jake suppressed a sigh of relief as the pistol was removed from the back of his head. He took the opportunity to stand lest it suddenly reappear again. "Yeah well, I've been through a lot of doors. Like I keep saying, it's a long story." He turned and nodded curtly at Yellow. "It was great to meet you," he said sarcastically before walking towards the back parlour.

Yellow mimicked Jake's tone. "The pleasure was all mine I'm sure."

"Want some advice?" Duke called out.

Jake stopped. "Like what?"

"Don't try to bullshit the Guvnor. He's a lot smarter than you could ever guess."

32

Jake glanced warily up the stairs as he followed big Frank down the rear hall. "Reckon I can get my old room back?"

Frank opened the door to the back parlour. "You trying to be funny?"

"Guess not," muttered Jake as he stepped cautiously into the sparse room he'd left just hours before. He quickly weighed up the two men sitting at the same table where his meal had been so rudely interrupted.

Sam smiled thinly and adjusted the handkerchief in his jacket pocket. "Talk about the bad penny."

Jake ignored the remark and stepped forward to get a better look at the man sat to Sam's right. Dressed in a brown pinstripe suit that looked distinctly dowdy next to Sam's, he didn't seem much like a respected underworld kingpin. "You must be George Tooley."

Frank closed the door to the parlour. "You call him *Guvnor*, get it?"

Tooley stubbed out his cigarette and rested his elbows on the table, all the while concentrating hard on the Reverend Piggott's note.

Jake used the uncomfortable silence to further study the infamous gangster, who reminded him more of a respectable engineer or tradesman than the feared boss of a ruthless firm. His wiry frame, greying hair and swarthy features told the tale of a man who'd risen to his current station by getting his hands dirty. His dark, hooded eyes suggested a quick intelligence and a decisive nature. They were eyes well used to staring unflinchingly at others, and told a tale of real-world experience and hard-learned lessons. Above all, George Tooley exuded the calm self-assurance of a man who was completely comfortable in his own skin and certain of his own mind.

At last Tooley folded the note, placed it in his shirt pocket and looked up at his visitor. "So you're the one who calls himself Caesar. I'm glad you came to see me, son. It saves the lads the bother of going to fetch you, and saves the old man the bother of all those extra feet tramping around. He doesn't need that in his condition." He gestured around the room. "I don't suppose you care about how much grief you've caused. It may not look like it, but you've got no idea how much time, trouble and currency it takes to keep a place like this going."

Jake glanced around. "Yeah, I guess the cleaning bill must be pretty steep for starters."

Sam's mouth twitched as he lifted his lapel to reveal the butt of a new automatic. "You still think you're flash, Yank? How about I blow your head off the next time you get clever?"

Tooley remained motionless, only his mouth moved as he continued staring hard at Jake. "Never had a sweep here before. Always managed to keep the coppers and Redcaps away from the place. You know, toss 'em a slag here and a pound note there. You look like a man who understands these things."

Jake found the mismatch of Tooley's appearance and voice slightly off-putting. The accent was definitely Cockney, but its edges had been rounded off by the standardised diction of the English professional classes. George Tooley was an educated man who seemed both at home and out of place in his underworld environment.

Sam glanced at Tooley, then back at Jake. "What, no smart-Alec remark? You had plenty to say earlier. Maybe you want to start with how you managed to get your sorry backside here at *all*. I suppose the coppers just *let* you out, is that it?"

Jake tensed as he heard big Frank step closer. "Not exactly, but I had the chance to split so I took it, along with one of their cars."

Frank's voice was sceptical. "Oh yeah?"

Jake nodded. "That's right. I can tell you where it is if you want it. It's no good to me."

Tooley glanced up at the larger man shadowing Jake. "Just take a step back, Frankie. Let's give our new friend a little bit of space, for now."

Jake relaxed just a little as he heard big Frank retreat.

Tooley looked at his expensive wristwatch. "I suppose we've known each other personally for about two minutes now."

Jake thought for a moment, but couldn't see what the older man was getting at. "Yeah, so?"

"So why did you offer me a free car? Do you think I *want* one? Do you think I *need* one?"

Jake just shrugged. "Listen, I didn't mean anything by it. I'm not a fool and I know how the world works, which means I know you're right."

A smile appeared at one side of Tooley's mouth. "I'm right most of the time, son. You'll need to be more specific than that. Right about *what?*"

Jake thought for a moment before rephrasing. "Like you said, there must be a lot of hidden overheads when you're running a place like this. I don't know what that car's worth, but it's worth nothing to me."

Tooley asked the obvious question. "Why didn't you just use it to drive out, to get away?"

"I just want my stuff, Mr Tooley. Then I'll be on my way." Jake heard big Frank snigger softly.

Tooley shook his head sadly. "Nothing of yours up there now, son. The Redcaps already looked it over."

Although he knew what was coming next, Jake said it anyway. "I need my notebook, and my money. There was at least three hundred pounds stashed up there, so unless the cops lifted the boards I'm still in the black."

Sam smirked.

Tooley raised his eyebrows. "Actually it was nearer two, and that didn't go very far."

Jake took a step forward and immediately felt big Frank's hand on his shoulder. He grabbed it and swiftly stepped to the side, twisting Frank's arm over and forcing the big man onto his knees.

The appearance of Sam's new pistol swiftly ended the altercation with Jake releasing the larger man, stepping back and raising his hands.

"You're quick," observed Tooley as he stood up and leaned forward. "Quick men are either an asset or a liability. Which are you?"

"We should just drill him now and stop wasting time." Sam hissed as he rose to his feet, his forty-five pointed squarely at the American. "He's a grass, has to be. How else could he have gotten away from the law so fast?"

Big Frank scrambled to his feet. "Yeah, we've had nothing but trouble since he turned up. Maybe the old man was wrong."

"The old man?" Echoed Jake.

Tooley shot Frank a withering look before turning his attention back to the American. "Let's all just settle down a bit. There's been enough excitement for one day and I'd like to get to bed without anyone getting killed. Frank, you go and get yourself something to eat. Sam, I know you're dying to shoot someone, but you won't be doing it here. Go and get yourself a drink, you'll have your chance soon enough."

Big Frank shook his head. "No way, George. I'm not leaving you with this bloke."

Tooley fished in his pocket and handed a key to big Frank. "The back door's locked, so the only way out is through you lads and I *know* he's not that stupid; are you, Jimmy?"

Jake took a deep breath. "Listen Mr Tooley, I just want my stuff before somebody gets hurt."

Tooley turned to Sam. "Go on my son, go and have a drink, and if this slag is foolish enough to lay a finger on me then you have my permission to torture him to death."

Sam's mouth twitched again and a slight sheen of perspiration shone from his forehead. "I hope you're as simple as you look."

Jake made a show of looking Sam up and down. "Yeah, and I hope you're as *rich* as you look, but I know you ain't."

Sam bristled. "You little..."

"That's enough!" Tooley stood up and gently pushed down on the barrel of Sam's pistol. "Listen mate, it's been a bloody long day and I want to get some rest. I've had enough of greasing palms and smiling at slags I can't stand the sight of. You two wait outside while I educate this flashy Yank about the ways of the world."

Both Sam and Frank shot Jake murderous looks as they shuffled reluctantly out of the room.

Once the parlour door had closed, Tooley pointed to a wooden chair near his table. "Have a seat, Jimmy."

Jake stood his ground. "I just want my stuff, Mr Tooley. That's all."

Tooley reached behind his seat cushion and produced a bottle of Bell's whiskey. "Scotch?"

Jake shook his head.

Tooley shrugged, sat and poured out two good measures. "For God's sake sit down. This just might be the luckiest day of your life."

Jake felt his anger growing despite his precarious situation. "I don't call getting ripped off and having guns shoved in my face *lucky!* And what the hell did he mean by the old man being wrong?"

Tooley took a sip of scotch, dragged an American cigarette from the packet on the table and tossed it across to Jake. "Looks like you've got a guardian angel after all. Just remember that the *only* reason you're not at the bottom of the Thames right now is because our mutual friend has put in a good word for you."

"Piggott?" Asked Jake as he tried to shake the feeling that he half-knew what was coming.

"At least you've got a brain between your ears. Have a seat."

Knowing that he wouldn't be leaving without Tooley's say so, Jake reluctantly slid into the empty chair.

Tooley pushed a glass across the table. "Where are you from, son?"

Jake tapped the scars on his head. "Sorry, but my memory's not what it used to be."

Tooley's eyes narrowed. "You must've taken one heck of a bump to forget something like *that.*"

The American just shrugged.

Tooley leaned back in his chair and shook his head sadly. "Doesn't do for a bloke to have no past. I wouldn't fancy it. The way I see it, our past is what makes us who we are. I reckon if I'd been born as the son of a Duke then I'd see the world very differently; but I wasn't, so there it is."

Jake wondered if that was what Wilhelm had really meant when he'd warned of Sergeant Jacob Small suddenly disappearing one day. Perhaps the wily gangster was right, and if he really *did* forget everything about his past then perhaps he would indeed cease to exist in any meaningful way. He decided not to voice such philosophical considerations and remained silent.

Tooley continued exploring the idea. "Yeah, I reckon our pasts are the sum total of our present and maybe even our future selves." He pointed to the parlour door. "Take Sam out there. I know he would've turned out a lot different if his mum hadn't been stark staring bonkers, but then perhaps that's just hereditary." He lit his cigarette with an old-fashioned brass lighter. "See this?" He placed the lighter on the table and produced a well-worn lock knife. "That's all that's left of my old dad now. Just that old lighter, his knife and a collection of stories from the front. And me and Frankie of course."

Jake was relieved that Tooley had changed the subject. "Frank's your brother?"

"That's right, although you wouldn't think it to look at us. So I suppose we're his legacy, his gift to the world if you like."

For once Jake resisted the urge to make a sassy comment, although he was struggling to find any relevance in Tooley's reminiscences.

The Guvnor continued. "You see, by some miracle dad made it back. Piggott always said that he'd been spared in order to tell the world how he'd watched his friends die, mostly from disease and cold, and even a few deaths in battle. Not many folk wanted to hear his story though."

Jake chose his words carefully. "Listen, Mr Tooley. I'm real sorry to hear about your pa, but at least he *survived* the war. I don't want to be unkind but I'm not sure what your family history has to do with me, *or* Piggott."

"It all comes to bear, son. Dad died from consumption in thirty-one. Couldn't afford the doctor's fees you see, not that it would've done him much good most likely."

"I'm sorry."

"Not half as sorry as he was," said Tooley with a grim smile and a bitter tone. "But the old Reverend stayed with him, right to the end. He helped my old man find some sort of peace with himself and this world."

"So I guess you figure you owe him." Jake drummed his fingers for a few seconds as he chose his next remark carefully. "You know, I can't help thinking I've seen him somewhere before."

Tooley smirked. "You spent much time in any monasteries?"

"No, I can't say that I have. That where Piggott's been, since the war I mean?"

Tooley just shrugged and stared at his last remaining heirlooms.

Jake pressed the point as he instinctively knew it was important, although he couldn't quite figure out why. "Let me guess. Shellshock followed by spells in various hospitals and institutions. That's why he won't go near them now, even though he knows he's dying."

Tooley shook himself from his reverie and placed his father's possessions back in his pocket. "If you can find a way of changing his mind then be my guest. You think no one around here has tried? Listen, the old guy's vouched for you and that's good enough for me, for now. But you can't stay here."

"No kidding."

The gangster took another sip of scotch. "You can stay at Piggott's place. You'll be safe there and the old man shouldn't be alone at a time like this anyway."

Jake rubbed his forehead again and squeezed his eyes shut. "I'm gonna level with you now, Mr Tooley. The truth is I'm not really interested in what you guys have done or are doing, and I've got nothing to gain by making waves."

Tooley continued as though he hadn't heard. "Can't let you stay here now. The coppers are onto this place and I can't keep every nosy Tom, Dick and Harry away from you."

Jake persisted. "Mr Tooley, I came here for my stuff, my money and my notebook. Just give me those things back and I'll be out of your hair."

Tooley rested his cigarette in the ashtray and stared hard at Jake once again. "You *know* it doesn't work that way."

Jake wasn't very surprised by that last statement, although it still left a sour taste in his mouth. "So what do you want?"

Tooley leaned back and retrieved his cigarette. "You still owe me a lot of money."

The American's face darkened. "What?"

Tooley's tone was business-like. "You've cost me dear today. Straightening everything out after that sweep was an expensive business and your two hundred was just a deposit. You owe me, big."

Jake stood up. "So take it up with my lawyer."

Tooley's face cracked into a smile. "It's good that a bloke should have some guts, never get anywhere in this world without them." He pointed at the chair again. "Just sit yourself down and you might hear something that could change your life."

Jake reluctantly sat. "You gonna make me an offer I can't refuse?"

Tooley reached behind his seat again, this time producing Jake's journal "It's funny, you didn't have any trouble remembering your dim and distant past when you wrote it all down, although your grammar's shocking in places...*Jacob.*"

Jake hissed quietly and rolled his eyes.

The Londoner smiled cagily. "Don't worry, me old son. Jimmy's what's written on your ID card so Jimmy you are as far as I'm concerned. Do you really think Duke and Yellow are those blokes' real names? Safer for everyone that way."

Jake stared at the notebook. "I guess you're not gonna just give me that back."

Tooley idly flicked through the pages. "If I didn't know better I'd be calling the coppers myself, either that or the men in white coats."

"Yeah funny. Someone else said the same kinda thing not long ago."

Tooley flashed an off-white smile. "Lucky you've got good references, or you'd have been in a lot *more* trouble than you already are."

At last Jake grabbed the whiskey glass and took a large swallow. "Is that why I'm sat here? If you reckon I'd be useful for raiding banks then you've got the wrong guy."

Tooley raised his eyebrows in mock amusement. "You don't exactly strike me as the upstanding law-abiding type, but in any case it doesn't matter. You owe me and I've got a little job for you."

"Forget it. I ain't your errand boy."

The Guvnor's fixed stare returned. "This ain't no errand, and it's man's work."

Jake rapped the empty glass down hard on the table. "Sounds even worse than before."

Tooley stuffed Jake's journal behind the cushion again. "Listen son, you don't seem to realise just how lucky you really are. There's probably only two men in the whole of London who just might take you seriously, and who *aren't* connected to the government. Yanks don't venture into this part of the Smoke, and yet here you are sat alone with me. You know how much graft a bloke has to do before he gets a meeting with me? Like I said, you've got a guardian angel looking over your shoulder."

Jake's answer was simple. "No deal. Whatever it is forget it."

Tooley persisted. "Once you've done this one easy job for me, I'll consider your debt repaid. You can have your sodding scribbles back and bugger off to a monastery yourself as far as I'm concerned...but I know that you won't."

"Yeah?" Jake asked, suddenly curious as to what the gangster was thinking.

Tooley leaned forward and grabbed Jake's left hand. "How much did Uncle Sam reckon your finger was worth?"

Jake snatched his hand back.

Tooley leaned back again. "Here you've got a choice. You can wait until they catch you again and send you out to get killed on *their* terms; or you can take back what the bastards want to keep for themselves, and what they'd happily sacrifice you to hang onto."

Jake thought for a moment. "I'm not gonna rub anyone out, understand?"

Tooley grinned and poured another couple of drinks. "I don't need you to rub anyone out, Jake. I just need you to pick up a parcel."

33

Mr Digby patted his companion on the shoulder as the gas-proof door thumped shut high above them. "Take it easy, pal. You're getting real jumpy these days."

Wilhelm stepped off the steel staircase and headed for the underground archive. "I'm *supposed* to be jumpy, Mr Digby. I'm an enemy citizen hiding in a hostile land, operating within a group which at best circles the outer orbit of the legitimate state. I think that nervousness is a completely rational reaction to such circumstances. Don't you agree?"

Digby removed his battered hat and stooped slightly as they entered a low ceilinged tunnel. "Tell me, do you ever just *do* or feel anything without analysing it to hell and back?"

Wilhelm's voice echoed slightly in the claustrophobic corridor. "Interesting turn of phrase. We do *everything* to hell and back around here, you should know that by now."

Digby replaced his hat as he followed Wilhelm into the spacious underground storeroom. "What are they gonna do with all this stuff, whatever it is?"

"I've no idea but I'll wager it's all destroyed before long."

The American nodded. "Yeah, the whole world's changing, and soon there'll be no time for consulting the experience of ages past."

"Do you think the world will be forever changed once the Nazis are crushed, or do you believe it will revert to type?"

Digby didn't need to think very long. "I know that once you've over-stretched a cotton sheet it never goes back into shape, not completely."

Wilhelm took a sharp right turn and headed off towards Hammond's subterranean cell. "You believe the world is made of cotton?"

Digby chuckled. "I'm from the South, son. I *know* it is."

Wilhelm stopped abruptly and signalled that Digby should stay put. "He's usually asleep at this hour."

The American grunted. "So we'll wake him up. That pompous bastard's cost *me* enough sleep these past weeks."

"He's kept many of us awake," agreed Wilhelm. "But the early hours are one of our most interesting times for observation."

"We're not in your lab now, Herr Doctor. Clarke wants the man out of here and back in action, fast. God knows I agree with him."

Wilhelm nodded his assent. "Come along if you must, but please remain silent and do not enter the cell."

Digby pushed his hat forward, Popeye style. "I think I can cope with a one legged nancy boy."

"You do not understand, Mr Digby."

"Why do you educated European types always think I'm dumb because I'm a Yank?"

Wilhelm's worry-lined face finally cracked into a smile. "I think many things about you, Mr Digby, but being a stupid American is not among them."

Digby couldn't resist the bait. "Oh yeah? So what other things do you think about me? Seeing as we're alone together and all." He deliberately hammed up his southern drawl for the last sentence.

"I believe you are driven by a strong sense of duty. In fact you are a living example of the dangerous paradoxes at the heart of deeply ingrained moral beliefs."

Digby tilted his hat back again and scratched under the brim. "I may regret asking, but what the hell does *that* mean?"

"It's very simple really. For reasons which are unimportant for our current discussion, you firmly believe in the moral rightness of America."

Digby squinted as he thought for a moment. "I know Uncle Sam's not perfect, but he's a hell of a lot better than anything else on the table right now."

Wilhelm nodded. "Quite so. And internalised moral absolutes can be very demanding, often necessitating the dilution or even the destruction of other, shall we say, more expendable standards."

Digby shook his head sadly. "And people actually *pay* you for talking like that?"

"It's not so complicated as it sounds, Mr Digby. Psychiatry is a profession like any other, and thus it develops its own deliberately impenetrable language to discourage non-initiates."

"So you guys can keep your rates comfortably high," observed Digby.

"Exactly. If I were to simply state that you're prepared to violate any established law or custom in the service of what *you* believe is a greater moral good, then my superhuman insights vanish like the morning mist, to be replaced by dull, mundane and inexpensive common sense."

Digby thrust his hands into the pockets of his shapeless trousers. "Well, I'm just an ordinary common sense kinda guy."

"You do yourself a disservice, Mr Digby."

"And I reckon you do the same." Digby pointed to the still darkened alcove. *"He's* no ordinary guy, so it stands to reason that we're way past the normal experience of your average headshrinker."

Wilhelm looked sheepishly at the ground. "I'm an ordinary man too; an ordinary man trying to understand the extraordinary, the uncanny and the seemingly impossible." He reached in his pocket and retrieved his notebook. "Now, unless I'm mistaken this will be your first encounter with, shall we say, a more unusual aspect of this particular Sensitive's nature."

The American's eyes narrowed. "In plain English please, Dr Werner."

The psychiatrist paused for a moment. "I don't know how much I'm supposed to tell you, so I'll simply say that Dr Hammond is not exactly himself these days. Especially in the mornings."

Digby shrugged. "I'm mean as hell until my first cup of coffee."

"Just stay outside the cell and try to be as unobtrusive as possible. You may find this very instructive, and more than a little unsettling." Wilhelm flicked on the lights in Hammond's cell, the low wattage glow accentuating the peaks and troughs in the uneven floor. He beckoned the American to follow as he quietly walked towards the bars.

Digby made a conscious effort not to squint and furrow his forehead against the ever present crackle cocooning the prisoner in a cloak of electromagnetic darkness.

Wilhelm quickly donned a pair of leather gloves, unlocked the cell and stepped inside.

Digby shuffled forward and peered through the bars, watching as the dishevelled Dr Hammond stirred and spluttered on his bunk. He'd spent years interviewing criminals and victims, learning to read every subtle tick of the mouth and shift of the eyes, and yet he had no real explanation as to why he felt apprehensive as he watched the prisoner stirring in his bed. There was something *wrong* him. Perhaps it was the fact that Hammond was more unkempt than usual, or perhaps it was the dim light. Whatever the reason, the simple fact was that Hammond looked...different somehow. It was as though the muscles surrounding the prisoner's eyes and cheekbones were arranged in a subtly different configuration, like a stage actor conveying a metamorphosis of character.

Wilhelm bent close without actually touching the man on the bunk. "Dr Hammond, it's time to wake up. We have urgent business."

At last the prisoner's eyes flickered open and he yawned before awkwardly shuffling to a sitting position. He took a long rasping breath and squinted at Wilhelm, trying to focus. "Who's there? Who *is* that?"

Digby frowned and grasped the steel bars, pushing his face between them as he strained to get a better look at the man he'd gotten to know quite well over the past few weeks. He found it impossible to shake the irrational idea that was staring at a stranger.

Wilhelm checked his watch and scribbled in his notebook. "It's me, Wilhelm. Who else?"

Hammond looked down with a start as his left arm twitched spasmodically, as though his errant flesh was somehow unfamiliar. Then he squinted back at Wilhelm before trying to focus on the watching American. "These lights give me a headache. Who are you?"

"It's Mr Digby. How you feeling today?"

Hammond leaned forward and rubbed his eyes with his good arm. "You look familiar, but I can't see you properly over there."

Wilhelm shook his head sadly.

Hammond sighed heavily. "My sight has grown very dim of late, and this world grows increasingly dark. Both my eyes and my very soul sense it."

Digby tried to fathom the unusual quality in Hammond's voice. Something subtle had happened to the precise Oxbridge pronunciation he'd heard at their previous meetings. It was as though the sharp edges of Hammond's diction had been chipped away, somehow softened and rounded by a new, unknown element. Dr Thomas Hammond's voice sounded the same way his face looked, familiar yet undoubtedly different.

Meanwhile, Wilhelm had finished taking notes and moved slightly to attract Hammond's attention. "We have to go, Herr Doctor. We have urgent business."

Hammond's face brightened at the news, then fell a moment later as his twisted left arm struggled ineffectually with the blankets. "Damn it all! I used to be fit. I can't cope with this life."

Wilhelm glanced at his watch as Hammond freed himself from the bedsheets. "We must hurry, the train will be here very soon." He quickly dragged Hammond's wheelchair across to the bed and held it steady while the prisoner awkwardly seated himself. Once settled, Wilhelm draped an old greatcoat over Hammond's shoulders and threw a blanket over his knees.

Digby pulled the cell door open as Wilhelm pushed the wheelchair towards it.

"Wait!" Hammond's voice was unexpectedly firm as he drew level with the American. The prisoner squinted for a moment, his left arm twitching with irritation like a cat's tail. "Digby," he said quietly. "I might've known *you'd* have something to do with this charade. Well let me tell you I won't help, and there's nothing you can do to make me comply."

"We must hurry," Wilhelm pointed towards a steel door set into the far wall.

Mindful that Hammond's normal diction was mysteriously restored, Digby kept pace with the wheelchair. "You're being reactivated. I thought that was what you wanted."

The prisoner suddenly grabbed one wheel with his good hand, causing the chair to spin on the spot and forcing Digby to jump out of the way. "I don't believe you."

Digby ignored him and walked the last few yards to the security door. "Through here?" He asked Wilhelm.

"Don't touch that door!"

Digby was startled by the sudden vehemence in the quiet German's voice.

Wilhelm quickly crossed to a cabinet bolted to the nearby wall. Delving in his pocket, he produced a set of keys and unlocked the metal box to reveal a series of heavy duty switches. He quickly pushed one upwards to the *off* position, before moving a second to the *on* position. "If you would be so kind, Mr Digby."

Digby slid back the heavy steel bolts, noting that the door was exceptionally well-made and possessed no locking mechanism. Without serious explosives or some serious tools, the door could only be opened from the inside. The smell of ozone and a rush of warm air barged into the archive as the lockless door swung silently on well-oiled hinges.

The American poked his head through the doorway and was surprised to see a miniature train platform extending about twenty yards either side of the exit. The smell of burned dust and the dim lights strung along the tunnel wall confirmed this was not a public place. "How about that, our own private station. Hey, I'll bet not even the King's got himself one of these."

"Some kind of maintenance siding, so I'm told. Probably from when the tunnels were dug. The main line runs a few yards beyond that wall." Wilhelm pointed across the tracks.

"He okay?" Digby nodded towards Hammond.

Hammond's lip had begun to tremble and tears welled in his eyes. "I never thought it would be like this, I never thought I'd be taking the train."

Wilhelm stepped in front of the prisoner and leaned down. "Please concentrate, Dr Hammond. I know it's difficult but there's really nothing to be afraid of. This is the way we brought you in, if you remember."

Digby stepped forward as he heard an approaching rumble. "We're taking you to a new place, above ground. This is your big chance to show Uncle Sam what you can really do. Isn't that what you wanted?"

Wilhelm shot Digby a dark look as Hammond finally broke down and sobbed uncontrollably, his good hand covering his face.

Digby pointed at the blubbering psychiatrist. "What the hell's wrong with him *now?*" He mouthed as the roar and clatter of the approaching train grew ever louder.

Wilhelm leaned across and cupped his hands next to the American's ear. "He's developed a great fear of trains, well sometimes anyway."

Digby thought he heard Wilhelm say something about deportations before the squeal and clatter of metal drowned everything out and the lead engine of a blacked-out train slid past the platform.

Ignoring his sobbing patient, Wilhelm pushed the wheelchair forward and beckoned for Digby to follow. The train had barely come to a halt before the doors opened and a Royal Marine officer stepped out. Without a word he scrutinised the three men and then consulted his clipboard. He glanced at his watch and made a note on his checklist before stepping aside. "Please take a seat quickly, gentlemen. We have to re-join the main line without blowing a hole in the maintenance schedule."

While Digby, Wilhelm and Hammond boarded the train, the officer rapped on the reinforced door to the driver's compartment before sitting down and returning to his notes.

As the train began to move, Digby suddenly realised he had no idea of their next destination.

34

Jake glanced up as the powerful Railton rolled smoothly to a halt. He wiped mist from the window and peered out at a darkened terrace of dead houses.

Sam switched off the ignition while big Frank Tooley leaned forward from the back, making his presence felt by resting his considerable weight on the front passenger seat.

Jake felt a chill run through his body as he began to think that George Tooley's "little job" might involve seeing how well he could survive a bullet through the head. His anxiety heightened as Sam drew his American forty-five and motioned with the barrel. "All right soldier boy, out you get."

Jake weighed up the odds of survival and rapidly decided they were slightly better outside the confines of the car. He opened the door and quickly stepped into the freezing night, but not so quickly as to beat big Frank onto the painted curb.

Although he tried not to, Jake still jumped as Frank clapped him on the shoulder and pointed towards the far end of the darkened street. "Off you go. Fetch boy."

Jake quickly recovered and threw off the big man's grip. "What the hell are you talking about? Where are we anyway?"

Sam climbed out of the car and nonchalantly walked around the front, making no attempt to conceal the pistol in his hand. "Why do you care where it is? Planning on holding some tours for your ignorant, pissed up Yankee mates?"

Jake ignored the insult and removed his glasses to give his night vision free rein. At first glance the gloomy terrace looked like it had been spared the worst of Goering's attentions, despite the pockets of heavy damage they'd passed on the journey to wherever it was they'd arrived at. However, as his eyes adjusted, he began to notice deep fissures and cracks climbing the grimy brickwork from pavement to sagging, twisted roof. Natural subsidence and explosive shockwaves had conspired to evacuate this particular street, and they were quite alone.

Trying to contain his growing sense of unease, Jake turned to Sam. "Tooley said we were going to a railway junction."

The end of Jake's sentence was jolted from his mouth as big Frank cuffed him roughly around the back of the head. "You call him *Guvnor!* I *told* you that."

Outnumbered two to one and in unknown territory, Jake chose not to argue the point. "Okay then. The *Guvnor* said something about a railway junction, and this ain't no railway junction."

Sam's voice hissed in the darkness. "And they said you lads were thick. You don't miss a trick do you, soldier boy?"

"Stop calling me that, you goddamn spiv! You've never risked your ass for *anything* in your whole miserable life."

Sam smiled his thin, wicked smile. "You've got a lot to learn, and you're living in the *real* world now. No more meal tickets from Uncle Sam or King George from here on in. All you've got now is your wits and your new found mates." He pointed to himself and big Frank. "You're just a sucker like the rest of 'em, riding out bravely for king and country, only to find out that king and country don't love you no more when you come home all twisted and useless. You've been jilted, me old china; spun round by a lover who's all talk and loose buttons, but in the end she never delivers. Yank or Brit, we're all just cannon fodder in the end."

Jake stifled a sigh of relief as Sam pocketed the gun and produced a plain brown packet, along with a banknote. "What's this?"

"That, my old son, is a tenner. Fair payment for a risky pickup."

Jake pocketed the money, knowing that he had no other source of income for the foreseeable future. "So, what have I gotta do for this king's ransom?"

Big Frank chuckled. "You're a funny bloke, Jimmy."

Sam pointed down the street to where the houses vanished behind a wall of mist. "Take a stroll down one of England's fine inland waterways. They say the canals are lovely this time of year."

Big Frank sniggered again.

"And?" Asked Jake, sensing that the punchline was fast approaching.

"Wait under the railway bridge and just remember that your watch is broken. You'll know what to do." Sam handed Jake the tightly wrapped packet. "I don't need to tell you they'll be expecting exactly that much. No more and no less. Any funny business about the price then you just come straight back and tell me, understand?"

Jake looked down the darkened street once again. "That it? What happens if some cop or a watchman stops me?"

Sam merely shrugged. "Improvise, soldier boy. Fob him off or shut him up, I don't care either way. Just make sure you're back here in three quarters of an hour."

"With my broken watch," quipped the Sergeant.

This time big Frank didn't laugh.

"What's to stop me just heading for the hills with the payment, *and* your tenner?"

Sam fished in his pocket for his cigarettes, jamming one in his mouth and replacing the packet without offering them round. "Like I told you, and like the Guvnor told you; we're all you've got now, so if you want to make it out there on your own then go ahead. Just remember that word gets around, and from what I hear there's plenty of other firms on the lookout for you. If you mess up, who knows what the future might hold for you or your new friend the Reverend Piggott. These are hard times and a sick man doesn't need too much upset at his time of life."

Realising there was nothing more to be said, Jake pulled his collar tight, hunched his shoulders and began walking up the evacuated street, his boots crunching on scraps of masonry and glass which had escaped the clean-up. As he neared the curtain of freezing fog he heard the Railton's doors slam shut, followed by the loud cough and roar of an engine. He glanced back just in time to see the car's tail lights vanish into the swirling night smog.

As the sound of the Railton faded, Jake felt a sudden and unexpected melancholy chilling his very bones and leaking down into the darker recesses of his mind. The silence, the mist and the sense of loss exuded by those mourning homes suddenly reminded him of another place of silence, cold and darkness; a place not of this world. For just a moment, he felt as though the veil between the planes had parted and the two had merged together, making both this life and the afterlife equally cold, cruel and empty.

Jake shuddered as a droplet of freezing water trickled down the inside of his collar to break the spell and shatter that otherworldly illusion. He quickly stamped his feet, both to feel his own physical presence and to make a sound, *any* sound in the eerie and freezing desolation.

Taking a moment to find his bearings, Jake set off once again, his eyes flicking constantly between the ground and the mist-veiled world surrounding him. The blackout had been partially lifted some weeks ago, but that concession only had meaning in those places where the living gathered. Out here, amid the darkened docks, canals and warehouses such cheery news meant nothing, and Jake wondered again if some parts of London would ever recover from the onslaught visited upon them.

Even though he was concentrating hard, he still stumbled over a low wall which seemed to just spring up beneath him. Cursing silently, he skirted round a deep-looking puddle before following a short muddy track which joined the towpath of a stagnant, stinking canal.

He stopped and turned a slow circle once again, taking in the dim shapes of ruined and abandoned warehouses lining the canal's far bank. He couldn't see a single light from where he stood, and a sense of futility and isolation unexpectedly bubbled up to envelop him as he finally understood that he was completely alone in a city of millions. Jake had seen close action in France and impossible things in the hereafter. He'd battled men with the powers of demigods and explored tunnels of deceit undermining the very foundations of what were once self-evident truths. How could it be that the gods of life, death and beyond had seen fit to leave him washed up on the banks of this debris choked canal on a such a miserable, damp December night?

In a cruel reprise of a recent dream, Jake once again found himself trudging through a place abandoned, forgotten, removed from the sight of men and demigods alike. A place left to the stragglers, the unwanted, the deserters and those predators who preyed upon the weak and the lost.

Something in that broken, silent atmosphere urged Jake's mind to turn inward, providing an unexpected clarity he'd not experienced in several weeks. Suddenly he not only knew but also *felt* the truth of Wilhelm's preposterous theory as the young man's grim prediction replayed itself in his mind. Some deeply buried part of himself cried out as the memories and experience of those long dead adepts remorselessly wrapped themselves around the central pillar of his very soul. Like a metaphysical parasite slowly choking its host, the recollections of the dead grew stronger at the expense of the living, and suddenly Jake Small knew that in time he might well vanish altogether, lost in the grey ocean of a false past, his self-awareness slipping beneath that glassy surface forever. Drowned in silence.

That last thought chilled Jake to the core of his being, as though his very soul was frozen by a cold blast of winter air. Dying at home or in battle, or even in the gutter was one thing; but to be slowly suffocated inside his own mind was a fate he couldn't properly comprehend. It was a fate which he sensed was fast approaching unless he could figure out how to quieten the whispering dead.

A shape suddenly loomed high in the winter mist, jolting Jake's mind from its wandering reverie as he stopped to study the outline of a Victorian railway bridge more carefully. He figured this was the place Sam had talked about and so he hurried into the shadows beneath the rusted ironwork and waited, not knowing what to do next.

He'd only been stood in the dripping darkness beneath the bridge for a few minutes before he heard footsteps, followed swiftly by two silhouettes materialising through the freezing mist. One of the men was slim and wore a standard overcoat and trilby while the other was squat and powerful looking, wearing a workman's cap.

A thick and deep cockney voice called out softly. "Anyone here?"

Jake stepped forward. "Looking for someone?"

The slim man caught his breath and put his hand to his chest. "Bloody hell mate, you scared the bejesus out of me. Have you got the right time?"

Sam's peculiar statement immediately made sense, and Jake realised he'd already been given the prearranged response. "Sorry buddy, my watch is busted."

The larger man grunted. "Thank God for that. Feels like we've walked for bloody miles."

The slim man with the hat moved closer. "Got something for us?"

Jake glanced around. "Yeah, sure." He fished in his inside pocket and produced the small parcel Sam had given him.

The slim man grabbed the packet and stuffed it in his overcoat before producing an envelope of his own, only this one was larger and secured with string.

"You ain't gonna count it?" Asked Jake as he completed the exchange.

"Bugger that! It's bloody freezing out here and I can't see a thing, unless I get me torch out. Anyway, I've been told to say that your boss can kiss goodbye to the main order if he tries to short change us."

Jake shrugged and nodded to the silent man in the cloth cap, who was obviously the muscle in the partnership. "Suit yourself, I'll tell the man." He flipped the envelope over in his hands. "What the hell *is* this anyway? A bunch of love letters?"

"Don't know what it is, don't *want* to know either. Better that way." The slim man cocked his head as he watched Jake stuff the manila package inside his coat. "Have we met before?"

Jake squinted through the darkness, even though he could see perfectly well. "Don't think so."

"What's your name?"

The spiv's bodyguard took a step closer.

Jake's face fell as he sensed the situation was deteriorating. "I ain't giving you my name. What if you get busted?"

The courier smiled thinly. "Yeah, I *do* know you. I never forget a face, me. Not seen you for a while...Caesar. You've made quite a name for yourself, getting all pally with red turncoats like George Tooley."

Jake swallowed and tensed. "Sorry buddy, but you must have the wrong guy. We've never met before, and anyway I'm not interested in politics."

The courier's smile broadened to a threatening leer. "I was working the door on the night you cleaned out Pete Finch, remember?"

Jake still tried to bluff as he tapped the scars on his head. "The memory's not what it used to be."

The hired muscle moved closer still.

The man in the trilby continued to leer. "Well *I* remember it just fine. You had a smart mouth back then too. Yeah, you took poor old Pete for a pretty penny that night."

Jake finally abandoned his pretence. "Listen buddy; he lost fair and square, and I don't have to listen to him whining through his errand boys if he can't take his medicine like a man."

The man reached inside his coat and produced a large flick-knife, the blade catching what little light there was as it sprang open. "The name's Jack, and I ain't your buddy."

Jake backed away, keeping his eyes on the blade. "I can't help it if your Guvnor's a lousy card player. Besides, *you* didn't lose anything."

The man in the flat cap spoke at last; his voice thick and solid like his body. "Might've known you'd take up with the likes of George Tooley. Just as bad as the bloody Krauts if you ask me."

Jake tried to make a joke. "The man's a bastard for sure. Anyway, what happened at that card table is between me and your boss. It's nothing to do with you guys."

The knifeman advanced. "Yeah, you had *really* good luck that night, and when the Guvnor started asking around, you'd had *really* good luck everywhere. For weeks on end."

Jake backed up against a dripping brick wall. "Yeah, well, my winning streak's come to an end and now I'm running errands just like you guys." He cursed inwardly as he realised he'd said the wrong thing.

The courier's face fell and his eyes hardened. "The Guvnor don't like being cheated, Caesar. He wants his money back."

Jake's eyes darted left and right as both men advanced. "Don't got it, buddy."

The courier paused for effect. "Well, it's either the dosh or your bollocks. Nothing personal, *buddy*."

Realising that a confrontation was inevitable, Jake chose to strike first. He stepped inside the knifeman's reach and punched him hard on the nose, making him stagger backwards.

As he'd had anticipated, the large minder responded by swinging hard and fast at his face. He deftly ducked under the big man's arm and allowed his attacker's fist to connect solidly with the brick wall behind. A scream of pain and anger echoed along the deserted canal as Finch's foot soldier collapsed in a heap, nursing his broken fingers.

Jack the Knife quickly recovered his footing, spat blood and advanced, holding the blade low. "You're dead now, you little wanker!"

The American sidestepped and let the attack pass him by, quickly reaching out to grab Jack's wrist as the blade missed his stomach. Stepping in close, Jake grabbed his attacker's left shoulder and drove his knee hard into the man's groin, following up with a swift head-butt to the bridge of his already bleeding nose. Keeping up the momentum, Jake hooked his leg behind his stunned assailant and pushed hard. That final shove sent the gangster toppling backwards, a loud splash in the darkness confirming that Jack was out of the action.

Jake turned and was surprised to see the squat workman stumbling towards him, still nursing his shattered hand. By this time it was almost too easy as he stepped aside once more and grabbed the heavy man's collar, speeding his progress towards the icy canal. A second splash confirmed that the hired bruiser had joined his companion in the freezing, filthy water.

Jake quickly jogged away from the botched exchange, only slowing to look back after he'd counted a full minute. The lonely bridge had already vanished into the mist, although he could still hear some faint shouts and curses as his would-be assailants struggled to reach the bank.

Confident that he'd secured his objective, Jake hurried back towards the relative safety of the waiting car.

35

Jake's footsteps echoed as he returned to the dead street. His eventful expedition had taken less than fifteen minutes, and he wondered how long he'd have to wait before his less-than-sociable companions returned to collect him. He was confident that they would, for it made no sense for them to just abandon him with his important cargo, whatever it was.

He'd barely reached the spot where he'd been dropped off before he heard footsteps from behind and spun round, instinctively taking a step back. "Jesus Christ! You scared the crap out of me!"

Big Frank grinned. "Not so smart are you, soldier boy? Walked straight past me you did."

Jake's tone hardened. "I don't like being followed, it makes me nervous."

Frank shrugged and made a non-specific noise before fishing in his pocket and producing a small battery torch. "Had to make sure no one was following *you*. Have to be extra careful these days."

"Oh yeah, why?"

Frank flashed the torch quickly down the street, two stabs of white in the icy mist. "You ask a lot of questions, Yank."

Jake looked down the street as he heard the Railton splutter in the darkness. "Yeah well, I like to know what I'm putting my ass on the line for."

Frank grunted again and pocketed his torch. "Not up to me. You can ask the Guvnor when you get back, but if you want my advice then just keep on the way you're going and don't try to guess about things that aren't your business."

Jake watched as headlamps pierced the winter mist. "Maybe I'll ask him when he's gonna give me my property back, now that I'm done playing paper boy."

"Suit yourself," was Frank's only response as he stepped into the road, allowing the car to glide to a halt between them. "Okay Yank, in the back, and keep a tight hold of that package. It's your responsibility if anything happens."

"Happens? Like what?" Asked Jake as he opened the rear door and tossed the bulky envelope into the car.

Sam stamped on the accelerator the moment Frank slammed the door, forcing Jake to dive onto the rear seat as the powerful car slithered on the oily cobbles.

"God dammit!" Jake cursed as he was pitched into the rear footwell, the car's swaying motion slamming the door shut behind him. Sam's cackle was just audible above the squeal of tyres as Jake righted himself and angrily jammed his parcel under the driver's seat.

"You'll have to move faster than that, soldier boy!" Sam shouted gleefully as he slid the car around a tight corner and onto a tarmac road.

"If you don't slow the hell down we'll get pulled over for sure. We look suspicious enough anyway," retorted Jake as he wedged himself into a corner.

Frank twisted round as the car slowed to a more sedate speed. "Not far to go, but we'll be for it if we get caught. Lucky we don't have to cross the river." He tossed something towards the American.

Jake instinctively shielded his face, and felt very foolish when a piece of soft fabric draped itself over his head. He grabbed it and quickly realised he was holding a drawstring bag. "Please tell me this is for my shoes."

There was a flare of light from the front seat as Sam lit a cigarette. "Don't talk soft, soldier boy. You think you can just walk up to any old gaff and ring the bell? You ain't earned no stripes here yet, least not so far as *I'm* concerned."

Jake shook his head. "Listen pal, there's no way." He tapped the manila envelope with his foot. "Your boss wanted me to pick up this gear, which makes me a courier, and couriers know where they're going."

"*We're* your boss right now," growled Frank. "And *we* make the rules. You put the hood on, and we deliver you *and* the package back to the Guvnor. Or I can put it on *for* you."

Jake's fingertips searched for the door handle, while his other hand slowly reached for the mysterious envelope. "You think you're the first tough guy who's tried to push me around?"

Frank began to shift in his seat, but Sam grabbed his shoulder tightly. "Sit down," was all he had time to say before he stood hard on the brakes.

Jake instinctively braced himself against the back of Sam's seat as the car slid to a juddering halt. For a moment he was confused by the lights and movement outside.

Sam hissed a single word through gritted teeth. "Bollocks!"

Big Frank grabbed the sides of his seat and pushed back hard with his legs. "Hold tight, Yank."

Jake felt time slow down as he saw the ghostly silhouettes gathered around the checkpoint barring the road ahead. A dim lamp bobbed in the mist as a constable walked towards the driver's door.

Taking Frank's advice, Jake pushed himself harder into the corner and waited breathlessly as the policeman tapped on the driver's window. For a moment he feared that Sam might fire a shot straight into the unsuspecting man's face; but Sam was mean, not stupid.

The startled policeman had no time to react as Sam suddenly threw the car into reverse. Within a moment the freezing night was filled with the screeching whine of tortured gears as Sam pushed the accelerator flat to the floor, reversing the car faster than its designers had ever envisaged.

Jake watched the astonished policeman vanish back into the mist as Sam spun the car on the damp road. He dimly heard shouts of alarm above the Railton's engine as the car lurched forward and took a wide, screaming left turn.

"Christ, where did *they* come from?" Yelled Frank as the car fish-tailed down a quiet side street.

"Damned if I know," replied Sam above the squealing tyres and screaming gears. "Jimmy, you're our eyes at the back!"

Jake leaned over the back seat and used his sleeve to wipe condensation from the rear window. His heart leapt in his chest as a pair of headlamps swung into view behind them, accompanied by the distant ring of warning bells. "There's one car on us. I guess you've got a plan."

Sam threw the car into another screeching turn. "Frankie, give Jimmy your shooter."

Frank hesitated. "You sure, Sam?"

"I've got to stay behind the wheel, and Jimmy's a trained soldier. Ain't that right, Yankee boy?"

Jake glanced at the man in the driver's seat and then back at the pursuing headlamps. "Forget it! There's *no way* I'm shooting any cops."

Sam's voice dropped to a menacing growl. "If we get caught with this lot the Guvnor's gonna shoot *us.*"

Jake glanced down at the innocuous looking package. "Just what the *hell* have you got me involved in?"

Frank fished in his pocket and held out a US Army Colt. "Too late to cry off now, soldier boy. Time to earn your keep."

Jake hissed with anger as the car jolted and he cracked his head against the side window. "You're supposed to be the tough guy around here. *You* do it."

Sam laughed out loud despite the serious situation. "You'd better tell him, Frankie."

"Truth is I'm not a very good shot. Guns make me nervous."

Jake grabbed the pistol. "You're kidding me!"

Frank scowled. "It's not like I don't have the guts."

Jake glanced back through the rear window to see the pursuing car still some distance behind. "If you put your foot down you could lose 'em."

"I could crash the car too," observed Sam sarcastically. "Just get on the left side and open your window."

Knowing he couldn't argue his way out, Jake hurriedly positioned himself behind the passenger seat and rolled down the window. Immediately a blast of freezing December air hit him square in the face, making his eyes water.

"Here we go!" Yelled Sam as he took a left turn very wide, wrenched on the wheel and jammed on the brakes, sliding the car to a halt and blocking the road.

Jake wiped his eyes with his cuffs and flicked off the safety.

The roar of the pursuing car's engine and the clamouring bell grew ever louder as the unsuspecting officers struggled to catch up with the faster Railton. A glow illuminated the mist shrouding the junction just seconds before the police car swung into view.

Jake squinted down the pistol's sights and waited as the pursuing car swerved from one side of the road to the other, the driver struggling to control the heavy vehicle.

"For Christ's sake shoot!"

Jake ignored Frank's call to action and waited until the police car was on a straight course before pulling the trigger. The crack of pistol shots was muffled by the revving of engines and the jangling of bells as Jake unloaded into the approaching car's front grille. Immediately a plume of steam and smoke exploded from under the bonnet, forcing the driver to stamp on the brakes as his already foggy world vanished behind a curtain of greasy smelling steam.

"Good enough," muttered Sam as he slammed the Railton into gear and mounted the white painted curb in a wide arc before accelerating rapidly down the street.

Jake ejected the empty magazine and just caught a glimpse of the police car's occupants staggering from their stricken vehicle. The blood froze in his veins as he saw their featureless silhouettes staring hard after him, before they vanished into the freezing mist.

36

At last the suffocating hood was removed and Jake blinked as he looked around the cluttered office. Shafts of watery dawn light pierced paper-covered windows like miniature searchlights, picking out the dust and tobacco smoke swirling through the stuffy atmosphere.

He surreptitiously tried to figure out where he was, while at the same time resolving to exploit the advantage of remote viewing should he ever be blindfolded again. Upon arrival, he'd been guided up a metal staircase to gain entry to this grimy, dusty room; a room that had a distinct exhaust-fume odour about it. Having also heard the sound of gates closing just after they'd arrived, Jake was willing to bet he'd been brought to some kind of commercial yard quite similar to Major Clarke's London hideout. The most significant difference between the two locations were a faint smell of petrol and a lack of serious bomb damage.

George Tooley sat behind a battered desk, the yellow light from a hurricane lamp reflecting off his glasses as he painstakingly reassembled his forty-five pistol. Now dressed in a brown warehouse coat, he looked even more like a reliable tradesman rather than a hardened and respected gangster.

Conscious that Sam and big Frank had taken up position behind him, Jake stepped forward and dropped the mysterious packet on Tooley's desk.

Tooley slammed a magazine into the weapon, chambered a round and stuffed the gun in his coat pocket before looking up at his visitors. "I've been wanting to fire that fucker for ages, just haven't had the chance yet." He glanced at the mud spattered parcel on his desk and then back up at the three men. "You lads look like you've had a busy night. What the bloody hell happened?"

Frank was the first to reply. "We ran into a spot of bother."

Tooley held up his hand. "It's all right, Frankie. I'm sure wonder boy here can explain well enough." He fished in another pocket and produced his well-worn lock knife. Snapping it open, he leaned forward and grabbed the package before carefully cutting through the securing string. "Seems that wherever you go the coppers are sure to follow. Perhaps you're just bad luck, boy. Doesn't do to carry unlucky things around." He brandished the knife. "I only carry lucky things. Things you've travelled the road with, things that you know you can trust. Tried and tested."

Jake felt his patience stretching. "Listen George; I don't care if you call me Yank but don't call me *boy*. I've seen more death and blood than *you* ever will."

"I told you already. You call him Guvnor," hissed Frank Tooley from behind.

Tooley stopped his unwrapping and looked up. "You're lucky you're alive to hear *anyone* calling you *anything*...boy. I'm hearing all kinds of stories about how you completely buggered a simple collection."

Despite the chill in the dusty office, Jake felt a trickle of perspiration roll down his temple. "News travels fast around here."

Tooley looked back down at his precious envelope. "It bloody does when my competitor's left with a mush of soggy banknotes and two of his blokes injured. He reckons I've clipped his delivery, so just what in the name of bloody hell am I supposed to *tell* him?"

Jake thought for a moment. "Tell him his guys should be more professional, and they should stay out of trouble if they can't handle themselves."

Tooley's face cracked into a wide smile. "Hear that lads? We've got ourselves a real scrapper here, bloody *loves* it he does."

"You've got me all wrong, Mr Tooley."

"No I ain't. Anyway, how come this ended up being such a bloody mess? It was supposed to be simple enough." Without warning Tooley plunged the knife into the desktop, leaving it standing upright.

Jake decided that the truth was his best option. "Look, I'm sorry things got screwed up. I really am. I just wanted to get the job done and get my stuff back. That *was* our deal after all."

Tooley's eyelids were unblinking, welded open. "I think you were about to explain what the hell happened last night."

Jake continued. "One of the guys recognised me. You must know there's a price on my head."

Tooley took a deep breath, leaned back in his chair and clasped his fingers. "Yeah I heard, and with everything you've cost me so far, maybe I should just cut my losses and turn you in myself. Pete Finch thinks you're a card cheat, and he's not the only one."

"I'm no cheat, just good with cards."

Tooley opened a drawer and produced Jake's battered notebook. Placing it on the desk, he drummed his fingers on the worn cover. "Yeah, you bloody *should* be. So, what happened then?"

"We got back to the car and then we hit a roadblock, and after that all hell broke loose."

Tooley prised the knife from the desk, folded it and dropped it back in his pocket. "Details my son, details. Don't try to smooth things over with phrases like, *all hell broke loose.* What actually happened?"

Jake rubbed his hands on his arms and stamped his feet. "Christ it's cold in here, like a refrigerator. Anyway like I was saying, we were all having a great time until we happened up on that checkpoint. I guess Sam didn't want anyone snooping around the car so he threw it into reverse and hightailed it."

Tooley looked at Sam. "That how it happened?"

Sam nodded. "Pretty much, Guvnor."

"You managed to lose them though."

Sam's half smile appeared. "The Yank knows how to shoot all right, and under pressure too. Left 'em behind in a cloud of steam and shredded rubber."

Tooley nodded approvingly. "Good lad. It's not wise to ventilate a copper unless you're forced to. That's something we could do without right now."

Jake rubbed his arms and stamped again. "Oh yeah, why's that?"

Sam stepped closer. "You're pretty bloody nosy for a slag deserter."

Still stamping, Jake turned to Sam. "You ain't gonna be on my Christmas card list this year, just so you know. I mean, I wouldn't want you to get *me* something and..."

"That's enough!" Tooley sent the meandering dust motes into a frenzy as he rose from his chair. "I swear to God if you two don't pack it in I'll cancel *both* your contracts, savvy?"

For a few tense seconds the room was still as each man waited for the others to speak or act. Eventually it was Tooley who broke the impasse by sitting back down with a heavy sigh. "All right then. It sounds like everyone's had a busy night so why don't you lads go and get yourselves some breakfast; I need to have a chat with Mr Partridge here."

Sam's face darkened. "Another cosy chat eh? You know, some of the lads starting to worry."

Tooley's response was calm. "Worry? About what?"

Sam shifted uncomfortably but said nothing.

Tooley's face darkened rapidly. "Don't you bloody dare start with *that!* Don't tell me there's a story and then clam up on me."

Sam's voice was a little quieter. "I'd rather not say, Guvnor."

"Well that's just too bad! You thought it was important enough to mention a few seconds ago, so bloody well get on and *mention* it! Just to remind everyone, *I'm* in charge around here and I won't tolerate little whispering groups behind my back. So whatever it is, *say* it."

Sam's jaw jutted forward. "All right then, it's just that me and the lads were wondering why you've given this flashy Yank carte blanche and just let him breeze straight in. What makes *him* so special?"

Tooley leaned back in his chair. "You just leave the planning to me, and that includes staff."

Jake interjected. "Listen, if you guys want to be alone for your heart to heart then that's fine with me. The sooner I'm out of here the better."

Sam turned and squared up to the American. "You ain't going nowhere, soldier boy. Who are you?"

Jake took a step back. "Screw this bullshit, and screw you too! Mr Tooley, if you'll just return my property as we agreed then I'll be on my way. Looks like I've worn out my welcome anyhow." He moved towards the door but big Frank sidestepped, barring his way.

Tooley interjected. "Everyone had better just calm down before I really lose my temper. I'm still in charge and we've got to have some discipline around here if we're to succeed."

Sam turned back to the Guvnor; his voice more pleading than angry. "Come on, think about it. This Yank just *happens* to turn up now. Not last week, not next week but *now*." He turned back to Jake and stared him straight in the eye. "I reckon he's a plant."

"Planted by who?" Asked Tooley patiently.

"Dunno. Maybe the US army, or maybe he's one of those G-men we keep hearing about. After all he wouldn't be the first, would he?"

Jake interrupted. "Do you guys mind not talking about me like I wasn't here?"

"Shut up! Shut your slag mouth!" Sam stepped forward.

Jake tensed.

The sound of Tooley's heavy Colt slamming onto the desk made everyone jump.

Tooley's voice was quiet, low and menacing. "I don't like having to repeat myself, so for the last time will everyone just calm the hell down. This is no time for anyone to be risking an injury, or worse. I need every man in this room able-bodied and ready for action."

Big Frank chimed in. "Maybe Sam's right. I mean, it's one heck of a coincidence, this bloke turning up just now."

Tooley's attention focused on Sam. "We've known each other a long time; most of our lives in fact." He picked up the pistol and released the safety, pointing the weapon straight at Jake. "Sam, you probably know me better than anyone. Do you think I would hesitate to shoot this bloke on the spot if I suspected he wasn't playing straight?"

Sam thought for a moment. "It's not like you don't have the guts, so why take the chance at this late stage?"

Jake spoke up again. "You guys just carry on, don't mind me will you."

Tooley ignored the sassy comment. "Have I ever steered us wrong, Sam?"

"No Guvnor; you've always been dead right, about everything."

Tooley continued. "Then you need to trust me now. I know this Yank's on the level for the same reason I knew Davis was a snitch."

Sam's eyes widened. "You mean..."

Tooley nodded. "Yeah that's right. I'm reading from the same book that *you're* not supposed to know about, but I know that you do because you're such a nosy bugger."

Sam's eyes flickered between Jake and his trusted boss, his usual cold clarity usurped by uncertainty. "You sure about this, Guvnor? I mean, that old man's not long for this world now; perhaps his judgement's not what it used to be."

Tooley let the weapon drop and placed it back on the desk. "It was good enough for my old man, and it's good enough for me because he's never been wrong for either of us."

Big Frank backed his older brother up. "Come on, Sam. Tell you what, if this bloody Yank turns out to be some kind of slag informer then I'll help you bury him myself."

"Well, that's real big of you," remarked Jake.

If Tooley was annoyed by Jake's sarcastic comments he didn't let it show. "Frankie, you and Sam go get yourselves some breakfast. There's something I need to discuss with our new mate here, something to do with the old man."

Sam hesitated.

Tooley pressed his point. "Go on, go and get some grub. The old man was right about the last Yank we had in this firm and he's right now, just like he's always been."

At last Sam relented. "All right, but I still don't like it."

Big Frank slapped his colleague on the shoulder. "Come on, I'm bloody starving."

"I'll be watching you, real close," Sam hissed in Jake's ear as he followed Frank out of the office.

Jake waited until he'd heard the door click shut before speaking again. "I guess I should thank you for convincing that paranoid psycho that I'm no snitch."

Tooley pointed to the dusty chair beside his desk. "Sit down son. You ain't in the clear yet."

37

Jake refused to sit. "Just what the hell do you want from me? If you think I'm gonna hang around here at your beck and call then you can just shove that idea up your stupid limey ass. I'm trying to keep my head down and I don't need this crap."

Tooley opened his drawer once again, this time producing a bottle of good French cognac and two cheap glasses. "You know, I'm starting to get a feeling of déjà vu. That's twice my blokes have wanted to sort you out for good, and twice I've had to face down *my own men* to save your sorry backside." He pushed Jake's battered notebook across the desk. "Here, a bargain's a bargain, even if you *are* an ungrateful little toerag."

Jake scoffed as he snatched up the journal and stuffed it inside his coat. "Yeah, I'm *real* grateful for everything you've done, like sending me off to get skewered by Pete Finch's firm, chased by the cops and singled out for your pet lizard's special attention. You know he's crazy, right?"

Tooley poured two good measures of illicit booze and pushed one across the desk. "From what I've read, crazy seems like a holiday compared to what *you've* been through. Besides that, I thought you'd have been more pragmatic about your situation."

"You seem pretty keen to believe some rambling old man who's high on laudanum half the time. How do you know I'm not just some lunatic with shellshock?" Jake tapped his scarred head to make his point.

A smile spread over Tooley's face, quickly evolving into a gleeful grin as he gently emptied the thick manila envelope. "Now that's the kind of craftsmanship you just don't see these days."

Jake leaned forward, his curiosity gaining the upper hand. "You're kidding me! This is nuts."

"Is it really?" Tooley selected a battered looking Irish passport from the parcel and slowly flicked through the pages, shaking his head with admiration. "Beautiful, beautiful work. Creased and aged just right. Ain't that just the business?"

Jake picked up a worn merchant seaman's card. "You guys planning a vacation?"

Tooley closed the forged passport and placed it back on the desk. "Not exactly, but you're a man of the world so I don't suppose I need to spell it out."

Jake backed away. "Listen, I don't know what you're planning and I don't *want* to know either. I'm just getting out of here while I still can. Personally, I think you're all a bunch of crackbrained lunatics and I'll be happier when I'm on my way."

Tooley held Jake's gaze. "There's still time to have one more of these cooked up, if you're willing to pay the going rate."

Jake rubbed his forehead and looked at the dusty floor. "Listen, I hate to break this news to a respected criminal mastermind, but I don't think I'm gonna pass for Irish, and neither is the rest of your firm."

The gangster leaned back in his chair and rolled his eyes. "Well bejesus now, aren't we lucky to have such high-powered intellect sent from across the sea to show us foolish Brits the error of our ways?" Tooley dropped his hammed up Irish accent. "Do you need to *sound* like a Yank to hold a Yank passport?"

Jake didn't respond.

Tooley continued. "These aren't just good quality bits of paper; these are whole new identities, each with a checkable history guaranteed against nearly every line of enquiry. I'm holding a new name and a new life here in my hand, and if anything *does* go wrong then a neutral country is a much better place to do stir."

"Listen Tooley, if you think you're gonna co-opt me into your cosy little club then forget it. I did what you wanted, I've got what I came for and now I'm out of here, and I swear to God I'll drill anyone who tries to stop me."

"You'll find it difficult without this." Tooley opened his drawer again and produced Jake's confiscated Browning, placing it neatly on the desk. "I believe you, Jake, I really do. That's why it'd be such a shame to let those bastards in Whitehall get hold of you again, and they *will* you know. Now I'll admit you're a bright bloke, and tough too. You might stay on the trot for a while but this war will be over before next Christmas, so what then? Do you honestly think you can just keep your head down when all those other Yanks start buggering off home? I know you're not that daft."

"I'll survive."

Tooley shook his head wistfully. "I used to think I was the toughest bloke in the world as well. I used to believe I didn't need anybody." He pushed the pistol across the desk.

Jake quickly picked up the gun, checked it and stuffed it out of sight in his waistband. "Listen buddy, I'm not in the mood for some kind of Road to Damascus lecture from the likes of you."

Tooley smiled. "There's that Catholic education of yours again, and I'm not sure what you mean by *the likes of you*. You mean a criminal?"

"You ever tried earning an honest living?" Jake enquired sarcastically.

Tooley chuckled and shook his head sadly. "You young lads are so naïve. Ever heard of Merton Place, son?"

"Should I have?"

Tooley took a sip of brandy. "I suppose not. It just happens to be the ancestral seat of one Lord Horatio Nelson. Want to know how he built it?"

"Am I supposed to be interested?"

Tooley nodded. "Well you should be. Merton Place was built with prize-money. That's loot plundered from all them Yank and Froggy ships he captured while he was a pillar of the Establishment. You see, when it comes right down to it, the only real difference between a pirate and a hero is whether or not he's got the right piece of paper. Both assert authority by force, whether it's in the service of some greater cause or just to serve themselves, and usually it's both at the same time."

Jake finally sat and picked up his own drink. "Yeah, well you're probably right. So what?"

"If I let you pitch in with us you'll at least have a *chance* of getting out of this country in one piece, with a new name and some real money in your pocket. Think of me and Piggott as patrons if you want."

Jake smiled and nodded. "So there it is. I *knew* it was just a matter of time before you said it."

"Said what?"

"You can dress it up however you want, but in the end you're only interested in me because I've got something you want. How can I trust you to pay me for it when a bullet in the head's a hell of lot cheaper?"

"Cheapest is hardly ever the best solution, Jake."

Jake checked both the gun and the journal were secure beneath his jacket "What's your point?"

"The point is that I've had the privilege of having my eyes opened, just like you."

Jake suddenly found himself growling angrily at the underworld boss. "Don't you dare tell me that! You've probably done a lot in your life but I guarantee you've *never* seen the world through these eyes. You don't know a damn thing about it!"

Tooley feigned a hurt expression. "Oh that's so sad. I didn't realise you were the only one who's had a hard time around here. You reckon Sam's mum brought him up proper? That boy's been stealing to eat for as long as he can remember because she was too busy with gin and navvies. And what about Duke, or don't them darkies count where you come from? Listen son, you're really special, but that don't put you above anyone else in these parts, including me. Everyone's got a story and none of them are pretty, believe me. Now if you want to sulk off all hurt because nobody understands your pain, then you can just piss off to some slag bar or opium den. Truth is that a lot of folk around here are tired of being stamped on, first by our own bleedin' toffs and now the sodding Krauts. You can run away and drink yourself to death if you want, but some of us are making a stand."

Jake had heard enough. "No way. If you've got some hare-brained scheme about using me to stake out banks then forget it. I'm not interested, and I doubt it would work anyway."

"Suit yourself, Mr high and mighty morality. For your information it *does* work and it *has* worked; but that's not what I'm offering you. I've got something much bigger in mind."

"Like I said, I'm in enough trouble already, without having half a dozen larceny charges dumped on my plate as well."

Tooley let out a long, deflating breath before he spoke again. "Do you know what leadership is, Jake?"

"What the hell are you talking about *now?*"

Tooley continued, oblivious to Jake's less than wholehearted response. "Leadership's all about looking forward, planning ahead. It's about seeing the world as it really is, not how you've been *taught* it is or even how you *want* it to be. Your journey's brought you here, to the truth, just as mine has. Although the things we can see might be different, we've actually got a lot in common."

Jake shook his head. "We've got nothing in common, Mr Tooley."

"You don't think so? I can offer you the one thing you really want in life."

Jake pulled a sarcastic face. "So you reckon you know what I want out of life, do you?"

Tooley nodded, his expression deadly earnest. "Of course I do; it's not so complicated really. You want out. You want out of London, out of England and so far away that those bastards who want to use you up will never find you."

"Wow, you figured all that out by yourself?"

Tooley's expression darkened. "I've already caused mutterings in the ranks by bringing you in, so the least you could do would be a lot less bloody rude. My patience has its limits."

Jake said nothing as he stared hard at the man behind the desk.

Tooley relaxed a little. "As I was saying, you must know that you can't stay out of trouble with just with a dodgy passport and a pound note slipped in a ration book. The kind of people who'll be looking for you are very clever, and they'll never stop. You'll run out of luck sooner or later."

Jake's tone was weary. "Let me guess. You want my help, just this once, just for that last big job, the final score. Then it's a lifelong vacation in some place with palm trees and sandy beaches, some place you saw in a picture book when you were a scrawny, starving, snot-nosed kid. Jesus! If you really think that's a proper plan then *you're* the one who needs his head checking. How many big scores have you ever read about in the papers? They never happen, and even if they *do,* the stupid bastards always end up shooting each other later on. It's a fool's game and it always plays out the same way."

A wide smile cracked across Tooley's face. "I knew it! I *knew* you were brighter than the average bloke, *much* brighter. You've seen enough of the world to know how it really works, and I've seen enough of gifts like yours to know just how valuable they can be, if the price is right."

Jake sighed. "Right now I doubt there's *any* price that would be enough."

Tooley produced Piggott's letter from his pocket and rubbed it between his finger and thumb. "I can offer you what nobody else can. I can't just get you out of London, but out of this whole bloody country. Not only that but you'd have enough dosh under your mattress to set you up for life, if you stay away from booze and birds and keep your mouth shut. I can help make Sergeant Jacob Small vanish forever, *without* fitting him with concrete boots."

Jake shook his head sadly. "Oh yeah? And what would I have to do, case the Bank of England for you?"

Tooley held Jake's gaze. "I don't want you to case *anything,* not for a while. All I want from you is one night's work. I need men who can handle guns and use them properly."

"Who would I be shooting?"

"Hopefully nobody, but you can never be sure. I don't need to give you lessons about how people can act under stress."

Jake thought for a few seconds, then shook his head. "No, it's bullshit. If you don't want me for my viewing skills then I'm just another hired gun; a hired gun you don't know so well, and you're way too smart to let a stranger breeze into your tight little band just like that."

"That's a very fair point, son." Tooley produced his father's lighter and casually set fire to one corner of Piggott's letter. "Firstly, I know you ain't no grass because Piggott told me so, and I reckon you of all people should know he's got a real talent for that sort of thing."

Jake did his best to sound nonchalant, despite realising he might never learn what Piggott had written in his mysterious letter. "So I guess that's what he used to do back in the old days. I guess that's why *they* wanted him."

If Tooley saw the bait he didn't bite as he dropped the flaming paper into the large ashtray. "Trouble is, your timely arrival has caused a bit of friction around the place. I mean I can't exactly spell out your *real* credentials to the blokes downstairs." He pointed to Piggott's note as it finally disintegrated.

"How dreadful for you, old chap."

Tooley ignored the sarcasm. "Everything you've said is true, Jake. I *could* do this job without you, but I still want you on board."

"Why?"

"Back to leadership again." Tooley leaned forward on the desk, his face brightening. "You see, I'm thinking about the future, afterwards. It's one thing to pinch a fortune but it's another to *keep* it, and it's another thing still to use it properly. You see, that's what those bastards up in Mayfair and Whitehall have learned over the centuries. They don't just *have* money, they understand what it really means."

Jake frowned. "I still don't get it. What exactly do you *want* from me?"

"We'll be moving into a whole new world after this job, one that's just as dangerous and deceptive as this one, probably more so. Right now I'm looking for a first class security officer, and you've got qualifications that no amount of money can buy."

Jake frowned. "So you want me to sniff out snitches for you, and what would I get in return, assuming I even agree to this?"

Tooley leaned back and delivered the punchline. "You'll get a new name, a new passport and a new nationality, although you'll have to keep your head down till the papers are ready. We'd best stick to Irish naturalised and Canadian born what with your accent. The world's changing around us, Jake, and we need to be ready to shape that change and even up the score a bit. In the end I suppose it all boils down to one simple question. Do you still want to be at the bottom of the heap when the dust settles?"

Jake watched the cigarette smoke swirling through the grey winter dawn. "You're starting to sound like a politician."

"Yeah well, it's politicians who decide what a crime is in the first place. But besides all that, you don't have any real choice in the end."

"Oh yeah? How do you figure?"

Tooley gazed intently across his desk. "I know all about settling scores, and I'm telling you that unless you deal with these people, and I mean really *deal* with them, you'll always be looking over your shoulder. You need some brains and muscle behind you if you're going to take them on."

Jake took off his glasses and squinted as his eyes adjusted to the dim light inside the room. "You're putting a lot of faith in me, Mr Tooley. I appreciate it but I'm not sure it's really justified."

"How so?"

Jake looked down at the floor. "If you believe what I've written in this here journal, then you must also know that I could seriously lose it at any moment. The truth is that you think I'm an asset now, but what about tomorrow?"

The Guvnor's face never changed. "Sometimes you just have to take chances, and I'm willing to do that considering the huge advantage you could give us. Anyway, there are always methods for dealing with liabilities."

Jake pulled his coat tighter against the cold. "Sorry Mr Tooley, but I guess you'll just have to execute your master plan without me. Right now I don't know a damn thing about what you're up to and that suits me just fine. I did what you wanted so I guess we can call it quits."

Tooley stood up and leaned on the desk. "That's a real shame, son. Still, a man's got to make his own choices I reckon."

Jake mirrored Tooley and stood also. "So what happens now?"

"Our business is concluded, and if I were you I'd get myself back to St John's and get some sleep. You don't look all that clever."

Jake turned and made for the door. "I don't know the way back."

Tooley returned his attention to the documents on his desk. "The lads will make sure you get back to your digs. We're civilised people here."

38

Dr Hammond's face began to harden as he observed the prefabricated huts sulking in the damp warehouse. Something moved in the shadowy depths behind the twitching psychiatrist's eyes as a change in the swirling tides of his inner self was reflected by a subtle yet observable shift in his expression. Suddenly the gifted yet petulant intellectual was gone, swept aside by a fearsome intelligence and bolstered by an unshakable sense of certainty. Hammond's voice echoed his altered expression as it overflowed with a haughty aristocratic disdain. "First it was a filthy prison, then a lunatic asylum, followed by a dungeon, and *now* I'm expected to live in a glorified kennel. Do these petty humiliations amuse you?" Once again he grabbed the wheel of his chair, making it pivot on the spot.

Wilhelm winced as the wheelchair ran over his foot. "Dr Hammond, I'm growing weary of your constant vacillation. We have important work ahead so please concentrate."

Hammond gave a snort of derision. "Important work? You? You're just a clerk, an office boy, so be a good lad and tell your father I'm here. We have grown up matters to discuss."

Wilhelm whipped out his notebook and bent low, scrutinising Hammond's subtly altered features. "My father was killed in a raid. I told you that before, Herr Dr Hammond."

Hammond's face fell for a moment before clouding with something akin to annoyance, although it was difficult to be certain as he wore an expression somehow foreign to his own features. "Really, this is entirely unsatisfactory! Wolfgang Werner was a most able and imaginative physician;

irreplaceable in many respects. I'm sure Peter misses him terribly."

Wilhelm made a quick note. "You mean Peter van Cortlandt?"

Hammond's twisted arm twitched. "Your father was always too indulgent, a common weakness among intellectuals."

Wilhelm continued to scribble.

Hammond fixed the younger doctor with a steely expression. "You lack your father's gifts, although that's no personal criticism. He'd have been kinder to find you a position at a bank or some other business house instead of expecting you to perform above the limits prescribed by your nature. Very few are born to lead, and it's unfair to impose such a burden on those so clearly unable to bear it."

Wilhelm spoke quietly. "Van Cortlandt's dead too. You know that, you were there."

Hammond's brow creased and his head dropped to his chest as though Wilhelm's last statement had stung him physically. His voice was weaker and more familiar when he spoke again. "Yes, yes of course. A terrible tragedy, just terrible. Things will never be the same without him."

Wilhelm straightened the wheelchair and continued slowly across the warehouse.

Hammond squinted at the olive green packing crates lurking beneath their tarpaulins. "What is this place?"

"Your new home, at least for the moment. You will find it's more comfortable than your last billet. The walls are insulated, which makes the electrical field somewhat less intrusive."

Hammond rubbed his chin with his good hand. "Van Cortlandt's gone, Stryker's gone and yet *still* you fear the Brotherhood."

"It's just standard procedure, Herr Doctor. Although there are very few men like you, we can't account for all of them at this time."

A smile spread across Hammond's lips. "Now I'm beginning to understand."

Wilhelm stopped a few yards from the prefabricated block, the hum and crackle of high-voltage already beginning to fill the air. "Good, that should make the briefing a great deal easier. Easier than getting you here at least."

"I don't follow you."

"All that nonsense on the train, honestly."

"Train?"

Wilhelm opened his notebook once more. "Remember, in the dining car? You were most annoyed when they had no French cigarettes."

Hammond paused for a second before answering. "Yes of course. Well, I've grown used to them, and I think I'm entitled to some small comforts after all I've been through."

Wilhelm scribbled for a moment then snapped his notebook shut. "There *was* no dining car, Dr Hammond. You don't remember the journey at all, do you?"

"Of course I remember."

"Describe it to me."

Hammond's arm twitched. "I think we're wasting time with trivialities, surely there's more important business at hand."

Wilhelm bent close and whispered in the doctor's ear. "I can't help you if you continue to resist me. We both know exactly what ails you, and it's getting worse. You're not coping."

"Coping with *what?*" Hammond scoffed.

Wilhelm straightened quickly as the prefab door opened and Mr Digby stepped out.

Hammond brightened immediately. "Well, things are looking up after all. It seems that Uncle Sam has finally decided what's in his own best interests."

Digby pointed at the man in the wheelchair while addressing Wilhelm. "He okay now?"

"He is sat right here, Mr Digby. Please don't speak as though I were absent."

Digby stared hard at Hammond. "I'm starting to wonder if you are."

"I don't follow you, Mr Digby."

"You had a funny turn on the train. A *very* funny turn."

Hammond shrugged dismissively. "Yes well, unusual reactions are quite common after periods of confinement, especially in isolation. So in fact it was *not* a funny turn at all, just normal and predictable behaviour."

"Yeah sure," was Digby's sardonic response.

Wilhelm interjected. "Gentlemen, I believe we have urgent business."

Digby retreated back into the office while Wilhelm and his patient followed.

Hammond's face fell again as he observed the cluttered coffee tables and sheets of paper pinned to the walls. "Somehow I expected the strongest nation on Earth to be better organised."

"The butler's out of town, preparing the hunting lodge," retorted Digby as he flopped into a battered and cracked leather sofa.

Wilhelm engaged the brakes on Hammond's chair and seated himself close by.

Hammond drummed on the wheelchair's arm with his good hand. "So, what is it you want from me?"

Digby smiled and grabbed a pair of leather gloves from the coffee table. After quickly pulling them on he retrieved a cloth bundle from beneath his sofa and carefully unwrapped it. He pointed to the battered book inside. "I'm told you have a talent for this kind of thing."

"What kind of thing?"

Digby's tone hardened. "Cut the crap, Doctor! We don't have time. Just do your thing and find this guy."

Hammond raised his eyebrows. "Really? I'm impressed. I always had you tagged as an ardent sceptic."

"Yeah? Well, I'm starting to find a little faith and right now I'm willing to try anything."

The man in the wheelchair stretched out his good arm, beckoning Digby to pass him the artefact. "I'm assuming this will help my case for emigration."

"Well that's not my decision, but it certainly won't do any harm." The American shrugged. "Sorry, but that's the best I can do and I don't want to bullshit you." He leaned across and handed the musty-smelling book to Hammond.

Hammond turned the book over in his hands before laying it flat in his lap. "The Lives of the Saints. Now this *is* an intriguing artefact, and well-travelled too judging by its condition."

"There's some notes scribbled inside, you want to read them?" Asked Digby.

"No. I don't want to lead myself astray. The less I know at the beginning the better." Hammond turned to Wilhelm. "I won't speak during the session but I'll probably have much to say afterwards, so please be ready."

The younger man rose and put two pencils and a sheaf of paper within easy reach before crossing to the junction box mounted on the wall.

Digby interjected. "Wait a second; no one said anything about *this*."

Wilhelm opened the cabinet. "It stands to reason, Mr Digby. The electrical field prevents any disembodied consciousness from invading our space, but of course it will also prevent Dr Hammond from following the trail left by the artefact."

The American pursed his lips and shook his head. "Sounds damned risky. We know there's at *least* one other Sensitive snooping around this city."

Wilhelm readied himself. "There simply is no other method, and I think you'll agree that we need to take risks to make progress."

Digby relented reluctantly. "Okay."

Wilhelm turned to Hammond. "Ready?"

Hammond pulled the leather glove from his left hand and then awkwardly freed his right. He took a deep breath and clasped the aged book firmly between his exposed fingers. "Ready."

Wilhelm threw the switch, immediately plunging the small office into an unfamiliar silence as the faint but constant background hum suddenly vanished.

As a world-class token-object reader, Hammond already knew what to expect. The process started predictably enough with an itching warmth rapidly flowing into his fingertips and up his arms. He fully expected it to creep smoothly across his body and gradually smother all sense of time, place and self. However, *this* time the reaction was far more violent and immediate than anything he'd ever experienced. With a startling crack like an ice shelf breaking, the room around him suddenly vanished before he'd even had time to draw breath. Hammond felt as though every cell in his body was pulled out of shape as some unknown yet overpowering force dragged his consciousness to another time and place. Through a blinding, directionless chaos of colour and sound, some distant part of himself urged him to drop the book and return to the safety of the office, but it was too late for that.

Although he had entered an incorporeal state, Hammond still felt as though he was physically drowning as his consciousness was mercilessly dragged backwards against the natural flow of time.

Gradually the flashing, racing and streaking colours began to converge while the omnipresent roaring slowly faded. The chaos of dissolution reluctantly surrendered to the order of awareness, although it was an awareness of another life and a time not long past...and a face Hammond had never expected to see again.

Though the vision of his mind's eye was rippled and distorted, Hammond immediately recognised the tall yet stooped figure of the Reverend Josiah Piggott.

If he'd had one in his disembodied state, Hammond's jaw would've dropped open as he gazed out through the eyes of whoever had last held that dusty old book in the ageing priest's presence.

Hammond quickly took stock of his location, noting that he was inside some kind of old building, probably a church if his erstwhile subject's vocation was anything to go by.

Knowing it was unwise to linger inside the shadows of past events - especially when observed through the recollections of strangers - Hammond tried to identify exactly *whose* memories he was hiding inside. He looked down at himself to see the shabby shoes and creased trousers of a civilian, and one who was down on his luck by the look of things.

Hammond noticed nothing further about his surroundings as his attention was transfixed by the sight of that unknown stranger's left hand. Dumbstruck and at a loss for any kind of explanation, Hammond looked first at Piggott, and then back down at Sergeant Jacob Small's missing finger.

It was incredible, amazing and portentous to learn that not just one, but *two* men Hammond had believed dead were both very much alive and had somehow been drawn into a single, shared orbit. The disembodied doctor immediately understood that the revelation was not simply a record of the recent past, but it was also of vital importance for his own future, although he couldn't quite discern how and why.

Hammond's intuition screamed caution as he realised he'd unwittingly invaded the memory of an exceptionally gifted Sensitive, which meant he was effectively blundering through a metaphysical minefield. Although he could sense no specific threat, he knew better than to dally in such a dangerous non-place.

Only too aware of the potential risks to his safety, Hammond immediately focused his attention on an empty corner of the room, imagining it dissolving into darkness as a catalyst for his consciousness to leave Jake Small's past and return to his own present. Unusually, he felt the pulling and tugging sensation of travel *before* the corner of the room had started to fade from view.

By the time the doctor realised that something was wrong it was already too late. He felt a sense of panic as the normal pull of disembodied motion quickly evolved into the indescribable stinging agony of a thousand tiny pins piercing his non-existent flesh. He vainly visualised himself waking up in his wheelchair as he watched that spreading darkness begin to change and swell of its own accord, rapidly metamorphosing into the featureless shadow he'd heard his former patients describing countless times.

Hammond screamed soundlessly as the unknown intruder silently beckoned to him with long fingers; its controlled, mocking movements leaving no doubt as to who was master of *this* domain.

Jake Small's memories began to streak and dissolve around him as Hammond desperately clung to a mental picture of the office in which his physical form slumbered, patiently awaiting his return.

The roaring pain inside Hammond's captured consciousness reached a screaming crescendo as the laws of gravity were suddenly repealed and he found himself falling uncontrollably towards that impossible intruder.

39

The smell of flour filled Jake's nostrils as he felt the world swaying and bumping around him. He heard a muffled voice somewhere in the distance, although it was all but drowned out by the post-projection whine buzzing in his ears. Although he felt very vulnerable as he struggled to reconnect with his physical form, Jake had managed to learn the location of George Tooley's secret HQ while leaving his escorts none the wiser, and he already had a feeling he might need that information.

Jake was dimly aware of being thrown forward as the GPO van pitched down an unusually deep pothole, and for once he was glad that big Frank Tooley was at hand to save him from injury. He heard the distant voice of their nameless driver as he joked about something or other, although he couldn't make out what anyone was saying as his consciousness slowly settled back into its customary vessel.

The physical world suddenly detonated with a painful, buzzing brightness as the flour sack was yanked from his head, and big Frank's voice was suddenly much closer as he squeezed his burning eyes shut and scrabbled for his smoked glasses. What was the man saying?

"Bloody hell! You look like you need a doctor."

His glasses safely in place, Jake gingerly opened his eyes a fraction. The little green van's interior slowly swam into focus as his senses re-adjusted to the physical plane, and he briefly wondered if the transition between disembodiment and "reality" would ever get any easier. It never seemed to.

Big Frank leaned forward and shook the American by the shoulder. "Come on, hurry it up. We can't hang around for too long."

With his senses rapidly settling, Jake leaned his cheek against the cold metalwork of the van's interior. "Where are we?" He asked, even though he knew very well.

"Home sweet home, my son." Frank's voice contained more than a hint of sarcasm.

Jake shook his head to clear it, feeling as though he'd had a heavy night on the scotch as he reached for the rear doors. "Well, I've had a great time, fellas. You really must look me up next time you're in Beverly Hills." He opened the rear door and shuddered as the chill and rank river fog swirled eagerly into the van.

Big Frank suddenly leaned forward and grabbed Jake by the arm. "Listen Yank, do us a favour and tell the old bloke..."

Jake stopped. "Tell him what, Frank?"

The big man shuffled uncomfortably. "Just tell him I'm sorry he's ill, and I'm sorry he can't come with us."

Jake did his best to sound nonchalant. "Didn't know he was supposed to be going anywhere, except a damned hospital. Stupid old fool."

Big Frank tightened his grip, preventing Jake from leaving the vehicle. "He ain't no fool, not by a long way. He's at *least* as clever as you or the Guvnor."

Jake adopted a more conciliatory tone. "Yeah, it's a real shame. Hey, maybe *you* could talk him into doing the right thing. He'd be more comfortable in a hospital until...you know."

Frank's tone softened as well. "I know, Jimmy. It just don't seem right. I mean, this is as much his job as the Guvnor's, maybe even more."

It suddenly dawned on Jake that Frank Tooley was assuming knowledge that he didn't actually possess, and he did nothing to correct the big man. "Yeah, he'll be a real loss. Maybe you guys should set up a memorial, build a church or something."

Frank smiled sadly. "That would be nice. After all, without him we'd never have found this big chance."

Jake nodded. "Yeah, well, I gotta go. I'll tell him you said hi."

"Tell him it's going ahead, tonight."

Jake couldn't resist a smile. "Sure, I'll tell him, and maybe I'll tell the cops too."

Frank shook his head, clearly pleased at his own superior insight. "No you won't. If you were a grass we'd have found out ages ago."

Jake gestured towards the church with his head. "I guess you found that out the same way the Guvnor finds the jobs where nobody's gonna rush to call the law."

The anonymous driver suddenly piped up. "Will you two stop flirting back there, the last thing we need is some bored copper sticking his nose in."

Big Frank sounded genuinely sad. "Well, this is it. I wish you'd come with us, Jimmy. My brother's right you know, there's nothing for you here. You'll run from one place to the next until some firm rubs you out or the law catches up with you again."

Jake stepped out of the van. "Goodbye Frank," were the only words he could think of as he slammed the door shut.

He pulled up his collar and thrust his hands deep into his pockets as the small green van trundled away, finally disappearing around a corner as it headed back down the hill.

Suddenly Jake was alone again, with only the mournful groan of steam whistles echoing from the river for company. Although he could hear the sounds of life nearby, he suddenly noticed that the area surrounding St John's was as deserted as a school on Saturday. The firebombed church was absent not so much from sight as it was from mind; always present but never noticeable, and Jake began to wonder if the invisible veil between St John's and the surrounding city was more than just a product of his imagination. The more he focused his attention on the ravaged building, the more the place seemed to whisper of forbidden things, urging all those who drew near not to dally in this dark and unwholesome place.

Jake rubbed his knee as he pushed through that vague idea of a veil and into the churchyard itself, stopping beside a leaning Victorian headstone as he peered up at the shattered roof and broken spire. He had to concede that although Frank Tooley's wasn't the sharpest mind in the firm, he'd been right about one thing. This was no way for anyone, especially a lapsed priest and respected Sensitive to end his days, skulking like some homeless hermit as he waited for the inevitable. That last thought made him shudder as he quickly scanned the large headstone, complete with a poignant yet clichéd epitaph to some beloved wife called Moira Partridge.

Partridge! Jake snatched the journal from inside his coat, quickly flicking through the dog-eared pages as he hunted for that elusive name, a name he felt sure had once meant something to him. He became ever more frantic when he couldn't even remember which pages he should be scanning, and he began to feel physically sick as a terrible truth dawned on him at last. His lack of reliable recollections prior to arriving in England meant that, in a sense, he'd *always* been at war. His life before the conflict, Section 12 and the Brotherhood no longer felt as though it were truly his own now that it existed only in those dull, dead pages clasped between his shaking fingers.

He reached out and traced the headstone's soot-blackened lettering, as though his touch might reveal some hidden truth or awaken some lost memory. There was nothing. The stone was just as cold and lifeless and dead as Moira herself had been for the better part of a century.

Panic and haste conspired to loosen the book from his grip and Jake stifled a cry of anguish as it fell onto the damp and puddled flagstones. He hurriedly bent to recover it, reflexively grabbing Moira's monument as his knee gave way in a searing stab of eye-watering agony.

He'd been fighting it for so long, but at last a sob of fear and self-pity escaped his lips as he awkwardly twisted into a sitting position and quickly wiped the damp notebook against his clothes.

As Jake flicked back and forth through the scribbled and pasted pages, the ghost of an idea stirred somewhere in the deepest recesses of his mind, filling him with a sense of familiarity more definite than déjà vu but less certain than memory. A lump tightened his chest as the pieces fell into place and he suddenly recalled that he'd seen just this kind of chaotic memory collection before; not spread among the pages of a battered book but rather writ large in the sketches and photographs pinned to the walls of his cramped and chaotic quarters.

His breathing shallow and rapid, Jake flicked to the first few pages of his precious memory book and scanned his own largely forgotten story. No, not *his* quarters. Not *his* quarters or *his* house, but rather a room remembered by another mind, a mind far older and more devious than his could ever be. A mind whose recollections were now irretrievably blended with his own, like an artist's oils mixing to produce a new and novel shade.

Nero!

With a sudden and sickening realisation, Jake finally understood why the old man had covered his home with that seemingly disjointed collection of notes and images. Although Peter van Cortlandt was a gifted perceiver of hidden things, he was also a man who'd long been struggling to keep his own self in plain sight. Just as Jake clung desperately to the lifeboat of his journal, van Cortlandt had also tried to control those conflicting currents consciousness as they'd swirled and eddied through his own self-awareness.

Jake slammed the book shut, unwilling to face the revelation that he was treading the very same path that sick, insane and now dead Sensitive had travelled before him. He took a deep breath and stood up, resolutely stuffing the journal back in his jacket and clenching his fists. He was *not* Nero, Stryker or any other goddam dead man. He was Sergeant Jacob Small of the Fourth, and he was going to stay that way.

Silently repeating the mantra of his own name, Jake glanced around to make sure his stumble hadn't drawn any unwanted attention. He was in luck for there was nobody in sight, and he was struck by the uncomfortable idea that he had in fact *become* one of those forbidden things inside that unconscious exclusion zone surrounding St John's.

Jake quickly made his way to the vestry door and found it firmly locked. It took only a few seconds to walk around the building and reach the high window he'd clambered through during the previous night. He was quickly between the boards and once again crouching inside the darkened, smoke-smelling building.

Satisfied that the church was empty, he made straight for the old priest's bedroom. He'd check on the old guy, pick up his gear and be on his way before nightfall. Hell, he might even call someone in spite of Piggott's admonitions. After all, how could anyone possibly hurt a dying priest?

Jake heard Piggott cough and murmur as he stepped quietly into the bedroom. It was only after he'd closed the door and glanced around that he noticed an all too familiar figure standing stock-still in a darkened corner. He froze as he came face to face with his increasingly bold stalker once again, and he tried to swallow down the unwelcome idea that the faceless phantom had been patiently awaiting his return.

40

Although his every instinct clamoured for escape, Jake clenched his fists and dug his toes into the soles of his shoes as he fought the conflicting urges to both retreat and pull his gun. He knew that neither course would help him.

The solid silhouette swivelled its head to acknowledge Jake's presence before returning its attention to the sick man bundled beneath the bedclothes. Gliding silently closer to the sleeping priest, its already slim body stretched taller still as it leaned forward at an impossible angle, its blank non-face hovering just inches above Piggott's sweat-beaded and furrowed features.

Jake edged closer, instinctively protective of the old man's safety yet afraid for his own. He froze as the hovering shadow's gaze snapped back towards him in an unmistakable unspoken challenge. Could this mysterious spirit really be goading him?

Somehow exuding an air of haughty disdain for the hesitant American, the disembodied visitor returned its attention to the dying priest, gently caressing Piggott's pale and pain wracked face with its unnaturally long fingers.

Piggott's knotted features softened in response to the phantom's touch as he relaxed into a deeper and more profound sleep, his breathing rapidly changing from short shallow gasps to a slow and steady rhythm.

Jake warily shuffled a little closer, his every instinct confirming that he was facing the same Projector he'd encountered beside the altar the previous night. He already knew just how dangerous that silent shadow could be in the twilight of the astral plane, a hard lesson which forced him to wonder just what this advanced Sensitive might be capable of here in the physical.

At last compassion trumped caution and Jake took another step, gingerly reaching towards the completely colourless visitor. He was afraid to touch the apparition, but unsure of what else to do.

If the ethereal intruder was aware of Jake's proximity, it gave no indication as it continued to caress Piggott's face, seemingly bringing some respite to the dying man. The silent stalker made no attempt to evade Jake's hovering hand, although it did turn to look at him once more to confirm an awareness of what was about to happen.

"Who are you?" Jake whispered as at last he made physical contact with the eerie phantom's featureless form. A warm, static-like feeling immediately enveloped his hand, crawling rapidly under the sleeve of his coat and bringing the hairs on his arm to attention as it marched swiftly up towards his shoulder.

Realising that he'd just made a terrible mistake, Jake tried to pull his hand back only to find it pulled *forward* by a stronger and wholly invisible force. As he was dragged remorselessly towards the bed, Jake had just a moment to worry that he might fall on the sleeping priest before he was suddenly enveloped in a perfect and infinite darkness.

Jake braced himself for the directionless falling sensation that was a hallmark of forced astral travel, so he was surprised when instead he found himself utterly immobile, hanging stranded in an endless sky of nothingness.

That nothingness was gradually bent and distorted into something-ness, as a writhing and boiling mass of grey silently swam into focus far below - if a concept like *below* held any meaning in such a non-place. Jake immediately thought of that dead, grey, otherworldly realm he'd recently encountered, and he felt a tremor of fear as he watched the billowing mass twist and dissipate like those nebulous ghosts prowling the shores of that forbidden corner of nowhere.

As he fell further, or perhaps as the grey mass just moved nearer, Jake felt a surge of relief as he realised he was suddenly surrounded by clouds. Good old-fashioned, mundane, non-supernatural clouds. Clouds that paid him no heed as they hurried on by, tossed in the air by a dark and callous winter wind.

Rather than worry about the fact he was Projecting at the behest of another, Jake instead found himself wondering just *how* he knew the wind was cold when he clearly possessed no corporeal form. Perhaps it was merely an impression stamped upon his kidnapped consciousness as it surveyed that dismal December sky. Whatever the case, Jake's mind was drawn to more immediate problems as the sullen broiling mist suddenly parted beneath him to reveal something altogether colder and darker.

As he studied the windswept landscape far below, Jake's first impression was of a large munitions plant, with row upon row of buildings reaching towards a desolate horizon while an orderly pattern of roads and railway sidings added weight to the idea of an extensive industrial operation. However, the dense and multi-coloured fog of human energy hanging over the sprawling complex suggested this place produced something far more sinister than mere bullets and bombs.

A sudden movement near that bleak, hopeless horizon caught his attention, and Jake watched in stunned awe as a huge bloom of shining ethereal smoke billowed high into the air before fading to nothing. The last cry of countless stolen lives was dissipated by the mournful wind as they twisted and vanished into the grey emptiness of an indifferent winter sky.

Jake's very soul shuddered as he realised just what he was witnessing, or more ominously, what he was *permitted* to witness. He'd heard stories and rumours about the camps just like everyone else, but his imagination simply couldn't prepare him for the organised and industrialised brutality his disembodied mind had just observed.

Although he was no stranger to pain and death, something deep within Jake's psyche railed against this bureaucratic and systematic human cull. Such orderly and callous destruction betrayed a depth of intent far beyond anything a simple soldier like him could ever conceive. This was nothing short of humanity reinventing itself from the ground up.

As he watched the twinkling plume of dying life finally vanish, Jake tried not to think of how many souls must have breathed their last to produce such a spectacular display of human hopelessness and despair.

Jake couldn't be sure of where he'd been taken or why he was confronted by such automated misery, but it was obviously some kind of message, or perhaps even a metaphysical calling card. Whoever that featureless stalker really was, it was becoming clear that his advanced abilities had not been bestowed by any sparkling wellsprings of spiritual truth.

It was as though that last idea had triggered some silent command as Jake suddenly found himself on the move again. He tried not to think about the angels of Old Testament lore as he passed over that dark citadel of death with its grim and bright harvest blooming from countless brick buildings as he sped by high above.

He'd been travelling for less than a minute before he found himself swooping towards a bristling hedge of coiled wire marking the outer boundary of Death's private domain. He cried out and instinctively shielded his face as he was pulled painlessly through that tangle of sharpened steel and out into a landscape that was every bit as grey and hopeless as the camp he'd just passed over. It was as though the soil itself was somehow tainted by the depravity slowly seeping out of the compound behind him.

Jake needed no cues to confirm that he'd finally reached his destination as he found himself in front of a plain, cheerless construction of grey concrete, surrounded by its own ring of rusting barbed wire. Although he couldn't quite figure out why, there was something about the isolation of this place which sent a renewed chill through his disembodied consciousness. There was no doubt that the tomb-like construction had been poured by the same hands who'd fashioned the larger compound, and yet it seemed that even *those* engineers of genocide couldn't bring themselves to construct this single small building inside the perimeter. Instead it crouched beside its much larger brother like a snubbed sibling, exuding both a sense of dark exclusivity and also a bubbling, churning resentment. It was obviously connected to the camp, and yet somehow not *of* the camp.

Jake wondered just what sort of depravity demanded such separation as the squat building's rusted door eagerly rushed forward to greet him. When it came, the collision filled his ears with a deafening roar as he passed into what he already knew was his shadowy stalker's real home, although the word *lair* came more readily to mind.

Jake braced himself for a revelation as that extraordinary Sensitive's true form was revealed at last; although in the end, his dark nemesis didn't look the slightest bit like he'd imagined. With such dazzling displays of arcane knowledge and raw mental power, Jake had always pictured his faceless foe as an older man like the late Colonel Stryker. In reality though, the Projector casually slumped in an ostentatiously carved chair looked to be somewhere in his late thirties, although Jake knew that advanced Sensitives were often much older than they appeared.

Although the oiled hair, well-groomed moustache and German uniform left a lasting impression on him, Jake found it difficult to stay focused on the man in the chair with so many wretched, dead and dying prisoners scattered about the floor.

They were everywhere, writhing around the sinister Projector's feet like the striped and skeletal worshippers of some dark and twisted demigod. Some still crawled like exhausted insects in jars while the Sensitive at the centre extracted a steady stream of precious, glowing life from those who hadn't yet passed beyond all pain.

Jake backed away as a tendril of glowing energy broke away from that twisted mass of misery and flowed towards him, like a snake tasting the air for its prey.

The young man in the chair smiled and gestured as though offering his guest an aperitif, while the swaying energy tentacle mirrored his movements like a sinister shining marionette.

Jake sank to his non-existent knees as the surging stream of stolen lives suddenly engulfed him and swamped his sense of self in a blinding eruption of images and emotions. The harrowing cry of each desperate and dying soul rang out inside the already confusing labyrinth of Jake's consciousness, as though those broken and starved slaves hoped to cheat the abyss by finding somewhere dark to hide inside their unexpected saviour's disembodied mind.

Jake clung vainly to the lifebelt of his own name as the cries of the dead were suddenly cut short and he was overwhelmed by a sudden, bright and silent stillness.

41

After a few seconds - or perhaps years - the howling darkness began to quieten and Dr Thomas Hammond became aware of himself once again. Scrabbling panic and blind incomprehension were his first reactions as he tumbled helplessly through the recollections of an alien mind, swamped and subsumed like a tributary stream vanishing into a larger river. The feeling of another, stronger consciousness tugging at his own mind was overwhelming as his self-awareness retreated to its redoubt in a darkened corner of his soul.

As nothingness solidified into the distorted shadows of a stranger's past, Hammond tried once again to retrace his steps to the chilly warehouse from whence his wandering consciousness was so callously kidnapped. Once again he failed, and he tasted a fresh, new flavour of fear as he wondered if his mind might remain forever separated from his weak but still breathing body. That dry academic idea was suddenly redefined as fresh, real and immediate as Hammond recalled the tight-lipped spies and criminals he'd once subjected to his own radical procedures. Despite his best efforts, some of those prisoners had remained locked in deep and unresponsive comas, neither living nor dead. Perhaps *they* were lost in the same way that Hammond was suddenly lost. Perhaps those unresponsive sleepers were killing time on the banks of the Styx, waiting for the ferryman who never came.

As darkness finally surrendered to form and Hammond glimpsed a large, taped window through somebody else's eyes, he realised just how mistaken he might have been. He'd always assumed that the endless slumber of his former subjects was caused by chemical damage and his own inexperience. It had never occurred to him that the injuries he'd unwittingly inflicted might in fact be spiritual.

The disembodied Sensitive struggled to maintain his sense of what it meant to live as Dr Thomas Hammond as he gazed out at the murky recollections of a mind that seemed somehow familiar. He began silently repeating his own name as a charm against the half-formed ideas of a hungry intellect that gnawed relentlessly at his sense of self, ever eager to consume the dead just like the ghouls of rustic folklore.

Strangely separated from his own identity, Hammond heard the repetition of his own name grow distant and fade into silence as that alien consciousness finally prevailed in bringing that beautifully crafted window more sharply into focus.

Stranded somewhere in the distance and isolated high in the last stronghold of his own self, Hammond shuddered as he finally realised that he'd somehow become entangled inside the recollections of the dead. As he surveyed that fortified chateau's gardens far below, the disembodied doctor was left in no doubt that he was somehow re-living the last days of one Colonel Kurt Stryker, deceased.

Impossible! Yet it was happening, and Hammond was powerless to prevent that dead Sensitive's memories from permeating every root and branch of his own mental life, like a delicate plant taking up tainted water.

At last Hammond's confused consciousness was completely pushed aside as Standartenführer Stryker clawed his way up from the darkness of nothing and into a state *almost* reminiscent of self-awareness; and for a dead man, he had a lot on his mind.

The late Colonel made no effort to suppress a smile as he gazed through the windows of his headquarters. It was very confusing and yet reassuring to remember something...*anything* once again. He'd been trapped inside that nondescript nothingness of no-self for far too long. For all he knew, centuries could have passed since his untimely demise, although some deep intuition told him that he'd only been lost for a short time.

Stryker immediately knew that even he shouldn't *be* stranded in this non-place at a past time. Something must have gone terribly wrong with his Transition, although a cloud of uncertainty obscured his mind's eye as he strained to recall his last living moments.

As he tried to make sense of his new and strange state of being, Stryker began to sense that he was not alone. He could feel another consciousness close by, an energy very different to those blurred shadows beyond his half-remembered window. Although the Colonel couldn't identify who the intruder might be, he wondered if perhaps this other, living mind was the method by which he'd recovered something of himself, a lifebelt cast into that endless ocean of oblivion.

It was hard to remain focused in such an unnatural state, even for a formidable Sensitive like Stryker. Both being dead *and* still thinking clearly was almost impossible, a truth confirmed by the fact that his mind had immediately sought out the comforting memory of the last time he'd been in complete control.

Stryker turned away from the window and strode across his impressive, if sparsely furnished office. There was so much to do, and those damned Americans would be arriving sooner than expected.

Sullen wraiths of dust and tobacco smoke shifted grudgingly as Stryker quickly made his way down the wide marble staircase, through the bare entrance hall and into the empty banqueting room. Skulking shadows and half-remembered ideas were the only guests in this barren, empty and soulless space that existed only within the mind of a dead man.

Passing quickly through the bowels of the house and across the large, dusty cavern of the main kitchen, Stryker made determinedly for the cellar. He knew this place was important, although he couldn't remember exactly why. He grasped the handle and pulled the door wide, instinctively stepping back as a blast of impossibly cold air rushed up the steps to greet him. He shivered and tensed as a jolt of electricity passed through his consciousness, causing the nowhere-realm of his dead memory to ripple like a desert road in the summer heat.

The unexpected disturbance vanished as quickly as it had appeared, but it had not gone unnoticed. Something had changed, something was different, something was wrong.

Stryker made a determined effort to marshal his undisciplined thoughts, and his struggle was rewarded with a growing realisation that he was not simply *recalling* times past, but was instead acting freely and consciously within the landscape of his own history; a feat that even *he* had believed was impossible. Surely the past was fixed, immovable and unchangeable.

Knowing that he was exploring uncharted territory, the dead Colonel pressed on down the steps, fully expecting to see a young Gestapo agent slumped in the interrogation chair just the way he remembered it, just the way it really had *been*.

Sure enough, the cavernous stone cellar's black and red ceiling looked just the same as the day Stryker had commissioned it. The large, solid looking table was still there, as were the two chairs, along with a heavy brass incense burner. However, the man occupying one of those chairs and the emaciated bodies strewn about his feet were definitely *not* any aspect of Stryker's own memory, and he was glad that his sense of smell was non-existent in this place, wherever it really was.

Naturally the Colonel knew of the camps based far to the east, established to finally prune the more diseased branches of human evolution. Although he'd never been to such a place, he had no doubt that this approximation had been expertly spliced into the movie of his memory by a powerful and dangerous director who really had *been* there.

Mindful of what strange powers the nearly dead might command in this twilight place, Stryker stepped forward to confront the man holding court over his ragged subjects.

The self-styled Duke of the Dead's shimmering suit, trimmed moustache and cigarette holder gave him something of a Hollywood air, although Stryker knew that no one would ever make a film about *this* man.

The self-appointed monarch of nowhere rose from his makeshift throne, spreading his arms wide in a gesture of welcome as his emaciated subjects cowered and cringed.

Stryker tried to back away but found himself rooted as he wondered how the well-dressed intruder had managed to hone his talents to such a fine pitch, and with such seemingly superhuman speed.

As though to answer Stryker's silent question, the misplaced movie star threw back his head and curled his fingers while the nearly dead shrank and grovelled about his feet.

It was a matter of mere seconds before a thin, weak and somehow sickly looking stream of ethereal energy was wrenched from the emaciated men scattered about the floor. In less than a minute it was all over as the Duke of the Dead consumed what little remained of his unfortunate victims' pasts and futures, his smile broadening to a maniacal grin as he watched them slump and twitch their last on the concrete cellar floor.

Stryker watched his erstwhile pupil sway and almost lose his balance, no doubt drunk on the surge of stolen life coursing through his consciousness.

Despite the uniquely perilous position that Stryker found himself in, he was still puzzled as to exactly *how* his protégé had gained the mental strength and deep esoteric knowledge to retrieve a dead man from the infinite ocean of oblivion, at least after a fashion. How was this possible?

Stryker didn't have to wait long for an answer as the ethereal thief steadied himself, tightened his grip and furrowed his brow as he demanded still more from those who'd already surrendered everything.

For the first time in many decades, the late Kurt Stryker felt real fear as he watched an extraordinary, unforeseen and hitherto undocumented event unfolding. Slowly at first, but then in an increasingly strengthening stream, some new and impossible energy was ruthlessly wrenched from those who clearly had none left to give. Those exotic unearthly particles behaved exactly like the more familiar flows of coloured astral energy...except for the fact that they were perfectly and uniformly black.

Stryker soon understood his mistake when he looked more closely. Those rapidly thickening ribbons of inactive non-life were not merely *coloured* black, they were in fact tiny absences of *anything*, minute grains of nothingness that clustered eagerly around their master, crawling over his body like a swarm of tamed insects.

As he was already dead, Stryker could feel nothing, neither hot not cold nor pain nor pleasure, so he wasn't sure exactly *which* sense had warned him to look down. He still felt nothing as he saw that his own legs had mysteriously vanished below the knee, silently swallowed by a rising tide of that same dark nothingness.

The Colonel looked back up at the man he'd entrusted to continue Projekt Schatten far from the Allies' reach, but there was nothing and nobody left to see. His protégé had silently vanished, replaced instead by the endless, cold and soundless oblivion of the nowhere from which he'd so recently escaped. Stryker cried out silently as he felt the sum of his self-awareness fading away, becoming an indivisible part of that unthinking emptiness once more.

By the time his torso had begun to vanish, there wasn't enough of Stryker's consciousness left to fear the timeless, lightless grave that eagerly rushed forward to embrace him once more.

42

Jake's first reassurance that he even still *existed* was the sound of laboured breathing, a distant asthmatic wheeze which rapidly made the transition from being nowhere to coming from somewhere. As his mind tuned into reality's ongoing transmission, he became increasingly aware that the irritating snorer was somewhere very close by. When his consciousness finally flowed back into to its corporeal container, Jake felt a fleeting moment of mirth as he realised that *he* was one making all the noise.

After a further but unknowable period of time, Jake finally felt his physical senses returning to their proper places. Their first report warned him that he was slumped over something and lying prone at an unnatural angle, which at least explained the sudden ache in his neck. He groaned with the effort as he tried, and failed, to lift his head off the rough woollen blanket beneath his face.

At last Jake's memory clicked back into gear and he began to struggle and convulse, suddenly swamped by a deluge of fear as he recalled exactly where he was and how he'd come to be there. His twisted neck protested violently as he rolled off the Reverend Piggott's prone body and half-slid, half-fell off the bed.

Jake took several breaths as he lay on the floor, rubbing his tender neck and enjoying a bug's eye view of the threadbare rug that kept the flagstones' chill at bay.

When at last he felt strong enough, the American rested one shaking arm on the bed and levered himself up, doggedly resisting the urge to lay down again and sleep. For a moment he thought his knees might fold as he grabbed the footboard and rested his weight against it.

Jake shivered as his meeting with the astral stalker replayed itself in his memory. He'd already guessed that the old priest must surely know *something* about his incorporeal rival, but intuition told him that the man in the German uniform hadn't been entirely honest with the ailing cleric. There was no clue as to what his nameless nemesis might be planning, but judging by what he'd seen so far Jake figured it wouldn't be anything wholesome or virtuous.

Still unsteady on his feet, Jake limped to Piggott's bedside and drained half the old man's canteen to quench his post-projection thirst, although he had to fight hard against the urge to finish every drop.

Replacing the canteen on the bedside, he leaned over to recover the Browning pistol which had fallen from his waistband while he was unconscious. Placing the gun close at hand on Piggott's night table, he checked the sickly cleric's pulse. His shoulders slumped and his heart sank when he realised that the ageing priest's weakened body had finally surrendered to the inevitable.

Jake was surprised to feel a lump rising in his throat. It wasn't like the old geezer was family, or even an old friend, and the odd circumstances surrounding the strangely streetwise man of God suggested he was no saint either. Nevertheless he'd been an ally of sorts, and more importantly, the late Reverend Piggott had been a Sensitive. Not nearly as gifted, or cursed, as Jake himself was, but nonetheless one of very few who understood the challenges of living a multi-layered life.

He sat gently on the bed, clenching his fists and clamping his mouth shut, determined not to break down for the second time that day. Some inner instinct warned that a surrender to despair would be his end either by capture or worse still, by his sense of himself finally drowning beneath encroaching tide of the impatient dead.

Jake leaned forward and gently put his hand on Piggott's grey and furrowed forehead. "Well Reverend, at least you had it your own way. No doctors or hospitals, just like you wanted; and I really hope you made it across that lake." He pulled the bedsheets over the dead man's face and pondered his next move as he looked around Piggott's makeshift bedchamber. As he surveyed the sparsely furnished space, Jake recalled seeing the same neglect, decay and squalor in Peter van Cortlandt's filthy quarters, despite the fact he had no memory of ever actually *visiting* them. Was this how all their kind ended their days, hiding from the world and waiting for that final jump out from which there could be no return?

He shuddered at that idea and shook himself from his reverie, quickly forming a plan of action. First he'd search the dead man's effects for anything useful, either in a practical or perhaps a less tangible sense. That wouldn't take very long as the elderly priest didn't have much stuff. After that, Jake knew he'd have to make himself scarce. Mabel would find the body soon enough and no doubt make the necessary arrangements.

Jake had just opened Piggott's bedside drawer when a shuddering sigh from beneath the bedsheets froze him to the spot. He'd heard ghoulish tales of the dead sighing, belching and even moving around, although he'd never seen any of those things actually happen.

Even though he was listening for signs of life, Jake still jumped when the old man moved his head and mumbled incoherently. Within a second he'd snatched the cover away from Piggott's face and was chiding himself for not checking on the old guy more carefully. He couldn't suppress a smile as he watched the indomitable old priest swallow and lick his dry lips, his eyelids flickering as he struggled to hold them open.

Jake watched with a sense of wonder and relief as Piggott struggled to sit up within a minute of being unofficially declared dead. He quickly helped the old man to get comfortable, arranging the pillows behind him and grabbing the canteen from the bedside. "Here, try to drink some of this."

Piggott swallowed, coughed and groaned, his head falling forward and water dribbling down the front of his dishevelled nightshirt.

Jake waited patiently as the old man's breathing became a little more steady and regular.

Seemingly with some effort, the priest raised his head and squinted at Jake. "It's very dim in here. I can't see a bloody thing."

Jake said nothing while he wondered if Providence couldn't have been more merciful and just let the old man slip quietly away.

Piggott suddenly screwed his eyes tight shut. "Jesus Christ, it hurts!"

Jake glanced at the half empty laudanum bottle on the dresser and tried to dismiss dark thoughts about a merciful release. "Hey buddy, you had me worried for a minute there."

Piggott said nothing as he drew in a series of deep breaths through his nose. At last he gingerly opened his eyes and squinted at the American again. "Who is that? I can't see properly."

"It's me, Jake. Listen, I know you said you didn't want any hospitals but I really *should* call someone. I mean, it's not like..." Jake tailed off, unsure of how to finish that sentence.

The old man furrowed his brow as he tried to focus. "Jake. Jake, Jake...Jake. That name just doesn't suit you; I'd choose another if I were you." He crossed his hands across his chest. "Oh my God! I never thought it would hurt *this* much. I just don't know how anyone endures it."

Jake tried his best to be reassuring. "You just need some medicine, that's all." He reached for the bottle on the dresser. "A little of this and you'll be right as rain," he lied.

Piggott wasn't listening, instead he tilted his head as he stared at the younger man. "Why are you here, Jake?"

The American forced a smile even though he was wondering if the old man had completely lost touch with reality, and whether that was such a bad thing anyway. "Well that's a long story, kinda like yours I guess."

Piggott closed his eyes and let his head fall back. "I suppose you once thought you were some sort of god, only to be bitterly disappointed, just as your handlers must've been disappointed."

Jake rolled his eyes. "Don't *you* start! I've heard enough exploitation crap to last me a lifetime. Anyway I'm no god, no more than you are."

The old man's eyes cracked open again to reveal a cat-like gleam. "You've crossed the abyss and returned, more than once. You haven't just *cheated* the boatman, you constantly mock him and escape his greedy grasp every time. You really don't know what you're capable of, do you? Although I must concede that your ignorance is actually the fault of others as you were never schooled properly. After all, why bother to educate something that was never meant to be? But then if you were never meant to be, perhaps you're something new, shiny and exciting; perhaps even dangerous. Are you dangerous, Jake?"

Jake picked up the nearest hurricane lamp and moved it closer to Piggott's face. Although he couldn't quite put his finger on it, something intangible had changed in the old man's expression. Maybe it was the tilt of his head or the new intensity of his stare, or the unfamiliar words in his mouth. Whatever the case, it was clear that the Reverend Piggott wasn't quite himself...perhaps literally. Six months ago Jake would've dismissed such a notion as superstitious bunkum, but now he was a little more learned and a little less dependent on his old certainties.

As though sensing Jake's inner dialogue, Piggott nodded and closed his eyes again. "It's fitting that we should meet at last, *almost* face-to-face. There are so very few of us left now."

Jake's face fell and he snatched up his pistol. "Who the hell are you? What's happened to Piggott?"

The old man's eyes opened briefly before fluttering closed again. "What do you *think* has happened? The same thing that happens to us all eventually, even to the likes of you and I."

"Why are you following me?"

"Following you?"

"Cut the bullshit! I've seen you skulking around here *and* down in those tunnels. You should've stayed there, where I couldn't have blown your goddamned head off."

The man in the bed and opened his eyes again and leaned forward, placing his forehead directly in front of the Browning's muzzle. "You don't even know my name and yet you wish to kill me. You must be very sure of everything."

Jake's finger tensed on the trigger for a few seconds before relaxing. "What do you want?"

The man peering out from behind Piggott's eyes twisted awkwardly in the bed, his movements clumsy as though he were controlling an unfamiliar machine. "I wanted to meet the man I've dreamed about so very often."

"So now you've met me. Best skedaddle while you still can."

"How did they die?"

"How did *who* die?" Asked Jake suspiciously.

Not-Piggott screwed his eyes up against a sudden surge of pain before opening them again. "You know damned well who. You told me yourself inside this very church, if it can still be thought of as such."

Jake lowered the pistol, although he kept it in his hand as he backed away. Bottles, ornaments and mess tins chattered their complaints as he leaned on the crowded dresser. "Why don't you figure it out for yourself if you're so smart?"

Irritation flashed across not-Piggott's half closed eyes. Although his voice was weak, the retort was unmistakably peevish. "If I *knew* everything I wouldn't damned well be asking! You owe me an explanation as to how Stryker and the others met their ends."

Jake chuckled. "I don't owe you a goddamned *thing*. I don't even know who you *are,* except someone who's got one hell of a nerve. You know, I'd put a slug through your head right now if I thought it would finish you off for good."

A wicked smirk appeared on the old man's face. "You said yourself that you don't even know me, so why on earth would you harm your brother?"

"You're no brother of mine. I've seen what you are and I've seen what you've done, and now you can't even let a decent man rest in peace."

The man in the bed chuckled weakly. "Decent? You really don't have the first idea, do you?"

"Just shut the hell up and be gone."

Not-Piggott flopped onto his side and shuffled painfully towards the edge of the bed. "That saintly priest of yours has been aiding a gang of notorious criminals for some time now."

Jake shrugged. "Yeah, I figured that. But what do I care?"

Not-Piggott smiled. "You're an interesting man, Jacob. We really should be friends."

The American snorted with impatience. "The only reason I don't ventilate you right now is that I don't want to damage what's left of this old guy's reputation."

Not-Piggott continued. "I can understand your fear, after all, this must be a very confusing time for you. Still, I'm magnanimous enough to call *you* my friend, even though you insist on calling *me* your enemy without even knowing why."

Jake's voice lowered. "I've seen you, out there, feeding on the weak, the hopeless and the broken. *That's* what makes you my enemy."

The man in the bed tried to roar with laughter but instead ended up clutching at his sides and rocking in agony.

Jake was impassive. "Good! I hope it goddamn-well hurts."

After a short while not-Piggott managed to compose himself, although a sheen of sweat had broken out across his grey and pallid face. "You believe you are so superior to us, don't you?"

"Us?"

Not-Piggott steadied himself before continuing. "I saw you there, down in that shelter beneath the ground. You loved it; you gloried in it. You drank in those helpless, cowering fools without a moment's thought for the consequences, and yet you have the barefaced audacity to judge *me.*"

"That was different, it's not the same thing."

"Really? Do you have *any* idea how many sweating, screaming nightmares you father as you pass by in the night? Have you ever stopped to wonder why everyone around you gets killed, arrested or dies? I don't suppose you've thought about any of those things as you only feel sorrow for yourself. Just accept the fact that you're a predator just like the rest of us. We take what we need from those whose paths we cross, whether they know it or not, whether *we* know it or not."

Jake shuffled uncomfortably. "Bullshit! And even if it's true that still doesn't make me like you."

The man on the bed shook his head sadly. "Why fight against your true self? You'll only end up dead, or miserable, and in your case probably both at the same time."

"What do you want with me?"

Not-Piggott smiled an unfamiliar smile. "I want to help you."

"Well you can start by staying the hell out of my life."

The old man's smile broadened, seeming somehow younger, alert and even a little charismatic. "If that is your wish I will comply, although I don't think that Major Clarke and Mr Digby will be quite so accommodating. If you really believe they'll just let you walk away and retire then you're even more naive than I thought."

"You're starting to sound just like van Cortlandt, and he's dead by the way," countered Jake testily. "And I'm not impressed by the name-dropping either."

For a moment not-Piggott looked wistful. "Yes, that's a real tragedy. Peter van Cortlandt was a remarkable man in spite of his foolishness. You were very lucky to have met him. Speaking of name dropping, if I were you I'd take Mr Tooley's very generous offer while you still can. You'll not see its like again, and perhaps I won't be forced to eat your soul if you leave now."

Jake thought for a moment. "Crap. I don't believe you."

The old man pulled a face. "Suit yourself then, but I'd advise you to be on your way quickly. It's only a matter of time before Clarke tracks you down and then it's back to the farm, and you know what happens to geese that don't lay golden eggs."

"What do you know about it?"

"A hell of a lot more than *you* do." Not-Piggott patted himself on the chest. "And this poor old fool - for all his strange and misguided ideas - he knew about it too. That's why he's been trying to get you and this Tooley fellow into bed together. He didn't want to see you suffer in the same way he did, as I have. That's why I helped him, and that's why I want to help *you,* despite our many differences."

Jake homed in on not-Piggott's last statement. "Helped him how exactly? The guy's *dead* for Christ's sake!"

The squatter occupying Piggott's body groaned and hugged his stomach. "Best thing for him, don't you agree?"

Jake said nothing.

Not-Piggott continued. "If you want to honour his memory you can continue his work."

"Thanks, but I already told Tooley I'm not scouting any banks for him."

Another pained, gasping chuckle. "Why do you fear defying the same law that's persecuting you? *My* outlook is that if you're being hounded by the law, you might as well have the money too."

Jake shook his head with exasperation. "I'm trying to stay *out* of trouble, and not having every cop in the country on my ass seems like a pretty good way to start."

The man in the bed shuffled into an awkward sitting position. "Fine then. I've offered you the chance to start afresh, but if you don't want to take it you might as well hand yourself in. You're just delaying the inevitable."

"I can take care of myself," retorted Jake.

"You can barely even *feed* yourself without somebody else's help, and for someone with such supposedly high moral standards you're not all that picky about the company you keep. First it was Section 12, and now you're running with known criminals. It's a pity though."

"Why?" Jake found himself asking before he'd realised what he'd said.

Not-Piggott's smile reappeared. "If you won't cash yourself out when you've been dealt a winning hand it means that you want to stay in the game, no matter what the risks."

"I'm not in any *game*. Why won't anyone just take my word for it?"

Not-Piggott continued as though Jake had said nothing. "If you're still in the game then I'll have no choice but to deal you out the next time we meet, and don't think for a moment that I'd regret it. In fact I'm looking forward to it already."

Jake raised the pistol again.

The squatter in the bed smirked condescendingly. "Go ahead. I know I'm not the first man you've killed."

Jake tensed, then relaxed and lowered his weapon. "You know what the best part about meeting you is?"

"So you can see what a real, pedigree Sensitive can do?"

Jake placed the pistol on the dresser and picked up the half empty laudanum bottle. "No, the best part is that I get to send you to hell more than once." With that he darted forward and grabbed the old man's face, pinching his nose and jamming the bottle deep inside his mouth.

Not-Piggott gurgled and squirmed, biting down hard and shattering the flimsy glass container.

Jake stood back and watched as the intruder coughed blood in a vain attempt to expel the broken glass from his mouth. "It won't hurt for long; more's the pity."

Not-Piggott emitted one last bubbling sigh before he stopped moving and his eyes glazed.

Jake couldn't be sure if the intruder had already departed, or whether he was still trapped behind those sightless eyes for a little while longer. He hoped it was the latter as he picked up his weapon and made for the door.

43

"My God!" Major Clarke wrinkled his face as he looked over Wilhelm's shoulder. "Come and look at this." He beckoned to Digby, who was still lounging on his sofa.

The American shrugged and crossed the room, his nonchalant expression quickly changing to mirror Clarke's as he looked down at the man slumped in the wheelchair. "Jeez, now there's something you don't see every day. Is he even *alive* still?"

Wilhelm removed the stethoscope from his ears and straightened up, draping it around his neck. "Well, his heart's beating and he seems to be breathing normally."

Clarke cocked his head. "But..."

Wilhelm leaned forward and lifted one of Hammond's eyelids. Only the whites showed and there was no response from the unconscious Sensitive. "But as you can see, there is no trace of any mental life, conscious or otherwise."

Digby returned to his sofa and perched on the arm, hands in pockets. "This what usually happens?"

Wilhelm shot him an irritated look. "Of course not. Usually an advanced Sensitive like Dr Hammond will wake unaided, hopefully bringing back the information he's been looking for."

"So, what's wrong with the guy?"

The young psychiatrist adopted an apologetic tone. "I'm afraid I don't know exactly."

"Really?" Clarke chimed in sarcastically.

Wilhelm continued quickly. "It's obvious that something has happened out there in the ether."

Digby raised his eyebrows. "The ether?"

Wilhelm paused as he marshalled the correct English words. "It is a term we have borrowed to describe those places which are elsewhere, not of this physical domain; although you should bear in mind that the ether is not just a single place. It is…complex."

Clarke sat down in a battered armchair. "Well wherever he is, he's no good to us there. We need him back here right away."

The psychiatrist shoved his hands in his pockets and gazed down thoughtfully at his catatonic patient. "It could be very dangerous. The conscious part of his mind is unwilling or perhaps even *unable* to return."

Digby snorted. "Yeah, I get the same thing when I'm questioning hoods, but I always persuade 'em in the end."

Wilhelm continued to stare down at Hammond. "This is a little more complex than persuading drunken thieves to do your bidding."

Digby took his hands out of his pockets and leaned forward. "You're getting real sassy these days, Herr Doctor. But I don't really mind because guys like *you* always end up working for guys like *me*. Wanna know why?"

"Why, Mr Digby?"

Digby smiled and stared unblinkingly at the German-born physician. "Because guys like you always *underestimate* guys like me. You think the fact that I never went to medical school automatically makes you smarter than I am." He pointed to Major Clarke. "It's funny how you've ended up working for this guy here rather than running your own private clinic. You'll wanna think about that."

Clarke interjected. "When you two have quite finished, I'll remind you both that we're pressed for time. Can't you wake him up, bring him back, resurrect him or whatever-the-hell you call it?"

Wilhelm looked up at Clarke. "Perhaps, but I should warn you that we currently have no knowledge regarding Hammond's current state of mind, or even if he still *has* one."

Clarke scratched at his beard for a moment. "So, he could possibly wake up as a gibbering wreck?"

Wilhelm nodded. "Quite so."

Clarke glanced at Digby.

The American agent thought for a few seconds. "All we're doing right now is burning time and getting nowhere. We need to quarantine Jake Small right now, and just waiting to dredge him up with the rest of the garbage is taking too long. That little bastard's no fool and he'll bury himself deep. *I* say let's take the chance and wake him up. It's not like we'd be losing an indispensable patriot now would it?"

Clarke nodded to Wilhelm. "Over to you, Herr Doctor. Work your magic."

The young psychiatrist nodded and gently slid the battered book from under Hammond's hand. "Psychometry is one of Dr Hammond's particular specialities, indeed it is his most potent ability. We all know that he must keep his hands covered to avoid being swamped by the memories and experiences of others. It would be impossible for him to function as a sentient being if he did not restrict the flow of outside information merging with the inner stream of his mental life."

Digby rolled his eyes and retrieved his crumpled pack of cigarettes. "Is it any wonder you don't have a girlfriend?"

Wilhelm continued. "Wherever or indeed *when*ever his consciousness may now be, I'm hoping that my contact with him will now act in reverse, effectively pulling him back towards his physical form."

Digby shook his head and lit a cigarette. "I don't buy this. Are you seriously trying to tell me that Hammond's soul is just floating around somewhere out there?"

Wilhelm nodded in agreement. "A simplistic explanation but essentially correct, although I'm not sure that *soul* and *out there* are accurate descriptions."

Clarke sighed with exasperation. "For heaven's sake get on with it man!"

"Very well. But don't say I didn't warn you." Wilhelm took a deep breath and grasped Hammond's grey fingers with both hands. For a moment there was silence in the room.

"There! Did you see it?" Wilhelm asked excitedly.

"See *what?*" Replied Clarke irritably.

The young doctor stared at his patient's face intently. "I'm certain there was a slight twitch around the right eye."

Both Digby and Clarke leaned forward.

"I see nothing." Said the American flatly.

Wilhelm shook his head slowly. "It was there, I *know* it was!"

Clarke leaned back again and folded his arms. "I think we'll need a bit more than an indiscernible twitch. If we don't get somewhere very soon then I'll use the old-fashioned method."

"I'm afraid to ask," said Wilhelm quietly.

The Major smiled wickedly. "If *you* can't wake him up, then I'll stick his head in a bucket of ice cold water. I've never seen anyone sleep through *that.*"

Wilhelm smiled unexpectedly. "An interesting idea, although I would describe it as a last resort. I'm hoping to use something a little less drastic."

"Such as?"

Wilhelm rose and pointed to the cigarette clutched between Digby's fingers. "May I?"

"Knock yourself out," was Digby's response as he handed over the smouldering Lucky Strike. "What kind of medical school did you go to again?" He asked as he watched Wilhelm crouch beside the unconscious man once more.

"My training is almost unique," replied Wilhelm cryptically as he pushed the red hot cigarette into the back of Hammond's good hand.

Hammond's eyelids flickered briefly, but that was the only response.

Both Digby and Clarke wrinkled their noses as the smell of sizzling flesh permeated the tobacco haze.

Having created a sufficiently unpleasant burn, Wilhelm reached across and stubbed out the cigarette. Using his thumb to apply pressure to the wound, he placed his lips next to Hammond's ear. "Dr Thomas Hammond, you must listen and concentrate only on my voice. No matter where you are now and wherever you've been to, just follow the sound of my voice. Follow me home."

The unconscious man's lips twitched slightly and his twisted arm jumped a little.

Wilhelm continued. "Hurry up, Herr Doctor. The Brotherhood awaits your report."

Seemingly still asleep, Hammond croaked and licked his lips.

Wilhelm grabbed Hammond's earlobe and pinched it tightly between his forefinger and thumb.

A quiet, stuttering sigh escaped from somewhere deep in the slumbering man's throat, while his left arm twitched ever more violently as it struggled to reach his injured right hand.

Wilhelm glanced at the two observers. "He's coming back, or at least something is coming back."

Digby frowned. "What do you mean by *something?*"

Wilhelm suddenly slapped the doctor across the cheek before answering the American's question. "As I said, it looks like he's returning from wherever he's been, but a man can be seriously hurt while exploring dangerous territory."

Without warning, Hammond's eyes snapped wide open and he drew in a long, shuddering breath.

The psychiatrist was momentarily startled but quickly recovered his composure, squeezing Hammond's burned hand once more and grabbing the prone man's hair and forcing him to meet his gaze. "Very good. You're home now. Just look at my face, focus and remember." He let go of Hammond's hand and gestured to the onlookers. "Water please."

Clarke grabbed an army canteen from the table and handed it to the young doctor, watching closely as Wilhelm unscrewed the cap and splashed a little cold liquid into Hammond's face.

At last the confused Sensitive groaned in agony and instinctively thrust his burned hand beneath his left arm to protect it.

Still Wilhelm persisted, raising the canteen to Hammond's lips and pouring some water down his throat. The results were predictable enough as Hammond choked and promptly spat it down the front of his shirt.

At last Hammond spoke, although his voice was dry, weak and somehow distant. "My hand hurts." He twisted his head and squinted around the room, trying to focus before his gaze finally settled on the canteen in Wilhelm's hand. "Water," he croaked.

"Not yet!" Snapped Clarke as he stepped forward and pushed Wilhelm aside before resting his hands on the arms of Hammond's wheelchair. "No more bloody games! We've gambled a lot on you these past years and now it's time to start paying back, otherwise I might just cut my losses. They say you can see things, and by Christ you'd better have seen *something* I can actually *check up* on. If not, you'll be going straight back into that hole I've just dragged you out of, and I promise you'll never surface again."

Hammond gingerly pulled his hand from his armpit and stared at it. "You bastards burnt me!" Although parched and dry, the strength was rapidly returning to his voice as he recovered his equilibrium. "I'm so very thirsty."

Digby spoke up from his perch on the sofa. "Like we give a damn. Just start talking, pronto."

Hammond looked across at the book Wilhelm had taken from him, nodding slowly as though he were remembering something long forgotten.

That tell-tale sign was not lost on Major Clarke, and he leaned in closer to the doctor's face. "You saw him didn't you? You know where Jake Small is, don't you?"

The colour was rapidly returning to Hammond's face as he stared defiantly back at his captor. "I've seen him, although I don't know where he was at the time."

Clarke narrowed his eyes suspiciously. "You're certain?"

Hammond didn't respond and instead stared at the canteen in Wilhelm's hands.

Clarke stepped back and the younger doctor sprang forward, tipping cool water into Hammond's dry mouth.

With the canteen drained, the crippled psychiatrist wiped his lips with his good hand and looked again at the blistering cigarette burn. "Bloody damned savages all of you!"

Clarke leaned in again. "Jake Small, where? What did you see? We have to find him."

Hammond closed his eyes as though chasing a hazy memory from his distant past. At length he opened his eyes again and smiled, his voice quiet and composed. "He's not far away, but you're wasting your time."

Digby stood up and stepped forward. "What do you mean?"

Hammond shifted his attention to the American. "I'd pick him up soon if I were you. You're going to need all the help you can get."

"How do you know *that?*" Asked Digby suspiciously.

A smile of quiet satisfaction settled on Hammond's face. "I know who it is. I know who's been systematically testing your defences."

Clarke interrupted impatiently. "I don't suppose there's any danger of actually giving us a *name?*"

Hammond never took his eyes off the American. "I can help you, but like so much in this world there's a price to be paid, and you already know what I want."

Digby scoffed. "You know you've already flogged that horse to death."

Hammond let his head fall back and closed his eyes. "You're assuming that dead means forever, Mr Digby."

44

Sam brought the car to a bumping halt and looked across at the Guvnor. "Are you sure this is a good idea? I never did trust that fat bastard."

Tooley squinted through the misted windscreen as he scrutinised a darkened railway arch up ahead. "You're right, this is a really bad idea but we've got no choice. We need this delivery and I doubt we can find a new supplier at *any* price. Not this late in the day."

Sam drummed his fingers on the steering wheel. "The man only cares about money and that makes him dangerous in my book; he's got no loyalty. Plus everyone's looking for that bloody Yank of yours and Finch must've figured out he's with us by now. How do you know he hasn't cut his losses and called in the rozzers anyway?"

Tooley pushed the car door open and winked at his bodyguard. "Because it's like you said, the fat git only cares about the dosh and we've got a lot more to spend than the coppers. Finch may be a bastard but he isn't stupid, and in the end he knows which side his bread's buttered."

"You should let me come with you," warned Sam.

"This is between me and him. Just wait here till you see me light a fag and then roll up slowly." With that Tooley slammed the door, turned up the collar of his coat and trudged into the winter darkness beneath the railway bridge.

Tooley's footsteps echoed in the freezing, dripping gloom as he made his way towards the unmistakable outline of his underworld rival. He hoped Finch was in a good mood, although that was unlikely given Jake's performance during the previous night's botched exchange.

As the smaller man approached, Finch made a show of looking past him. "All on your own?"

"Like you wanted," confirmed Tooley as he stood right in front of his disgruntled supplier.

"I thought you'd have brought that Yank with you, just as a goodwill gesture. We've got unfinished business him and me."

Tooley's tone remained flat. "You just let *me* worry about the Yank from now on."

Finch shook his head sadly. "Doesn't take much to show you up for what you really are."

"Oh yeah, and what might that be?"

Finch smirked, the greying whiskers on his unshaven chin catching what little light filtered into the freezing gloom. "You're just a poser, plain and simple. You put all this big talk around town about looking after your own but in the end you're all about the money, just like me. I bet that's not what your old man had in mind when you were scrapping down Cable Street. I wonder what he'd have to say about you harbouring a common cardsharp; I thought you were bigger than that."

Tooley sighed and glanced around. "You don't know nothing about politics, and I didn't see *you* down there, *or* any of your firm. That's the trouble with your sort, you'll take money from anyone."

"Yeah, I'm a businessman for sure. I'll even take money from Reds like you."

Tooley ignored the jibe and glanced around the overweight racketeer. "Your bloke got the stuff with him?"

Finch glanced back at his own car waiting at the other end of the short tunnel. "It's all there, if you've got the cash, and that *includes* last night's payment as well. I take proper banknotes, not soggy mush; and I want three hundred extra."

Tooley's eyes narrowed. "What for?"

"The way I see it, the Yank's in with your firm now which means he's under your protection, which means you're comfortable with his cheating me at cards."

Now it was Tooley's turn to smirk. "You always were a bad loser, Pete."

Finch scoffed. "You telling me he's just *lucky?* Listen mate, why don't you do yourself a favour and cut him loose, I'll even give you a discount. After all, business is business."

"Can't cut him loose. I need him, and for what it's worth nobody cheated you."

The portly racketeer shook his head ruefully. "Looks like he's even done a number on *you,* and I used to think you were clever. What do you need *him* for? You've got plenty of blokes who know how to shoot."

Tooley just shrugged. "Let's just say he's got talent, a talent that I need."

"What talent might that be?"

"He's got a nose."

Finch's eyes narrowed. "Yeah? You know, for an intelligent man you're a silly superstitious bugger. Most blokes with your kind of cash keep booze or birds on tap, but you've got a priest. That's not natural, even if he *was* a bit of a bruiser in his day. How is the old bugger anyway? I heard he was ill."

"Not ill, dying." Said Tooley flatly.

Finch's eyes flickered downward. "Well I'm sorry to hear that, really I am. I know him and your dad went back a long way, what with them making it out of all that mud and wire." He paused for a moment before continuing. "I want to ask you something, just as one professional to another."

Tooley took a deep breath. "Ain't really got time to swap stories, I've got a lot to do."

"Yeah I'll bet," murmured Finch quietly. "Judging by all the gear you've ordered you could be taking on the Crown Jewels for all I know."

"No one's hitting the Crown Jewels; that *would* be bloody stupid."

Finch nodded slowly. "Better bloody not be either."

"What's it got to do with *you* anyway? *You're* the broker and *I'm* the buyer. The end."

"Point is, a job like this must be a tough one. I mean with all that hardware it's obvious you're not just turning over some post office or sorting out a speiler."

Tooley maintained his position. "Like I said, what's that to you?"

Finch glanced around even though the two of them were quite alone. "Listen, we both know how the world works, and I can tell that if this job goes tits up you won't be just be staring at some porridge, it'll be the noose if you're *lucky.*"

"And if I'm not?"

"Then a bullet in the head before you vanish forever."

A smile slowly spread across Tooley's face. "You're worried about somebody squealing if this thing turns bad. You're worried someone's going to kick *your* door in if we get collared."

"Damn right I am," confirmed Finch grimly. "And from what I've heard they'll *make* you talk before they bury you."

Tooley looked quizzically at the larger man. "Just what *have* you been hearing?"

Finch dropped his voice unnecessarily. "My contact's in a right old panic. He's had in the bloody FBI snooping around. The *FBI, here,* in London for Christ's sake."

"I'd heard stories the G-men were about, but I thought they were just a load of tall talk."

Tooley's supplier shook his head. "No way, they're real enough, and I think my bloke's going to sing any day now just to save his own backside."

Tooley shrugged dismissively. "Can't blame him really. Them Yanks are a lot more eager with the rope than us, especially as your bloke's in uniform." He sighed heavily and stamped his feet against the cold. "It's bloody freezing out here so we might as well just get to the point. I know we're not just chatting out of courtesy, so what *else* do you want?"

"I want you to sort out that loose end I just mentioned."

"He's *your* problem, not mine," was Tooley's assessment.

"Can't take the chance. I've got the fuzz and the Yanks breathing down my neck from both ends of this almighty balls up. If you can sort this problem out for me then I'll forget about those soggy banknotes."

"*If* I take care of your wobbly quartermaster."

Finch nodded. "I can't very well do it myself before he delivers, and God knows where he'll vanish to after that. I can do my own dirty work but you know it makes sense this time around. Besides, think of all the money you'll save by just paying my commission. Plus there's the added security."

Tooley reached into his pocket. "We have a deal, but I want my Yank for *free* if I'm going to start cleaning up your mess. That means you lift the contract *today.*"

Finch thought for a few seconds. "Done."

Tooley produced a small velvet bag and tossed it across to his overweight competitor. "You know, I'll miss our friendly fireside chats."

Finch caught the bag. "Well, you always did talk a load of cobblers." He let out a low whistle as he delved inside and extracted a gold sovereign with his fleshy fingers. "Just what the hell have you gotten into, George Tooley?"

A smirk passed across Tooley's face. "Just lucky I suppose."

The portly grocer dropped the coin back in the bag and thrust it inside his coat. "Come on now, we both know we'll never meet again, and there's something I've always wanted to ask you."

Tooley folded his arms. "Oh yeah, what's that?"

Finch thought for a moment before speaking again. "Well, you've always had this reputation for being a lucky bugger, but we both know you don't prevail in our line of work by luck alone."

"So?"

"So, you must be getting bloody good information from *somewhere.*"

Tooley smiled but stayed silent.

Finch took a more direct approach. "Well, are the stories true? I mean about your old vicar."

Tooley sighed and looked downcast. "Yeah they're true all right. Poor old bugger's on his last legs, if he hasn't passed away already."

Finch's tone conveyed his irritation. "Don't be such a bloody smart alec! I mean, seeing as the old bloke's dying, I'm leaving and you're probably going to be dead very soon...is it true?"

"Is *what* true?"

Finch produced a packet of American cigarettes and offered one to his rival. "Can that old priest really sniff out hidden treasure? I've heard he has dreams."

Tooley took the cigarette and sparked up his old-fashioned lighter. Immediately the cars at either end of the tunnel spluttered into life and began rolling forward. "Well let's put it this way; *my* superstition has just made *you* a rich man."

Finch waved his arm to indicate where his own driver should pull up. "Yeah well, maybe you'll make a believer of me yet."

Tooley gestured for Sam to stop beside him. "I'll tell you one thing for sure, this world's a lot stranger than most people reckon."

The large grocer grunted as he stepped forward and opened the boot of his car. "You know what, I reckon you're right." He pulled back a paint spattered dust sheet to reveal a cloth bundle and an ammunition box. "Here's your sample then, and you can collect the full order this afternoon."

"I'm pushed for time today, Pete. Can't your bloke deliver close by? How about the railway yard?"

Finch was implacable. "If you think my quartermaster's going to risk his neck by driving that lot into London then you *are* bloody barmy. Just getting it to the drop-off was pricey enough, and besides, I know he'll run if there's any last-minute changes. I tell you this whole country's going down the pan now that every docker, railwayman and squaddie fancies himself as some sort of entrepreneur."

"People have to eat." Tooley quickly unwrapped the bundle to reveal a brand-new U.S. Army submachine gun. He quickly checked the weapon's mechanism, the metallic clicking amplified under the gloomy railway arch. "Nice; very nice." He turned back to Finch. "What's the bloke's name?"

"What bloke?"

"*Your* bloke, the quartermaster."

Finch smirked. "It's O'Malley."

Tooley hissed and shook his head as he opened the Railton's boot. "I should've known it, a bloody Paddy."

Finch smiled darkly. "Well he's a Yank by birth, but he was pleased as punch to strike a blow for the great struggle, you know how they are over there."

Tooley re-wrapped the Thompson and stowed it in the boot of his own car before turning his attention to Finch's ammunition box. Flipping open the lid he extracted an olive green canister.

Finch's face wore an expression of satisfaction. "It's all there, smoke, pineapples and enough ammo to open up another front."

Tooley quickly closed the box and transferred it to the Railton. "Perfect. So where's the main shipment?"

Finch handed Tooley a book of matches. "Tell your blokes to be at that location *with* the outstanding balance before nightfall. They'll need a map and a lorry big enough to shift everything in one go. What happens after *that* is not my concern."

Tooley flipped the book open and grunted. "All right then, but if I start getting the run around then I won't need a map to find *you*."

"Don't worry, he's itching to unload the stuff." Finch stepped forward and hesitantly offered his hand. "I suppose this is it then."

Tooley grasped Finch's fleshy palm and shook his hand firmly. "Yup, this is it. Listen, for what it's worth, there's going to be one almighty row when this job's done, and the blokes who'll come looking aren't much bothered by Queensbury rules. If you've got any kind of retirement plan then now's the time." He quickly stepped away and opened his car door.

Finch crossed to his own vehicle. "I'll look out for you in the papers."

Tooley sat in his car, closed the door and wound down his window. "If you see me in the papers then someone really *has* dropped a bollock." With that he tapped Sam on the shoulder and the Railton was out of sight within seconds.

45

Major Clarke paused as he opened the office door. "I'm going out for five minutes, and you'd better pray that my colleague has something useful to tell me when I return. Otherwise I'll have no hesitation in getting what I need the old-fashioned way."

Digby briefly stood, stretched and then settled himself back into the sagging sofa. He drummed his fingers on the worn leather for a while before eventually breaking the silence. "This is a waste of time. We've had this conversation before and nothing's changed as far as I'm concerned. You know I don't have the inclination *or* the authority to give you what you want."

Hammond held the American's gaze, his chin lifting slightly as a faint smile played across his lips. "I have new information. Information you can't afford to be without."

Digby exaggerated a yawn. "Yeah? Well let me tell you what *I* think you've got. Nothing. Zero. All I'm hearing from you is the same bullshit you've been peddling for months now. I ain't buying, and neither is my employer."

Hammond pointed to the switchbox on the wall before pulling his glove back onto his twisted hand. "Would you mind? This should really be a private conversation."

Digby glanced around but didn't move. "You seriously think there's someone here right now?"

"I don't sense anything, but I've been noticed now. A certain person knows for sure that I'm still alive, and I promise you he'll not rest until he's tracked me down."

Still Digby didn't move. "And this person's the same one who's been sneaking around the subway?"

Hammond remained silent.

"Have it your own way, although I don't know why I shouldn't just beat it out of you." Digby sighed before levering himself back out of his seat and crossing to the box mounted on the wall. He threw the large switch and groaned as the distant hum of electricity filled the air once more. "I hate this crap. It just gives me a headache, even *with* the new shielding."

"It gives us all a headache, but at least *you* can escape from it," Hammond responded as he methodically worked a glove onto his good hand. "In the tradition of Cassandra, extraordinary gifts always come at a disproportionately high price. In my case it's having to live with that constant buzzing. It's enough to drive a man insane, eventually."

Digby fell onto the sofa once more. "Nobody believed in Cassandra, so I'd say you're doing a little better than her at least."

Hammond raised his eyebrows.

Digby smiled. "Yeah we had books an' writin' pens an' even a lil' ol' schoolhouse out there in the swamps."

"You're very insecure about your level of education," observed Hammond.

"And *you're* about a minute away from Clarke and his toolbox unless you start singing."

Hammond nodded thoughtfully. "Very well, I can tell you how to find Jake Small, but I'm the *only* one who can help you with this security problem."

"But I guess you want something in return."

The man in the wheelchair smiled triumphantly. "You already know the price. I want written confirmation, from somebody meaningful, that I'll be granted asylum in the United States."

Digby tried to suppress a laugh. "You really *are* crazy. I can't even *count* the reasons why that won't happen."

Hammond shrugged. "Then we have nothing further to discuss."

Digby stood once more and smoothed down his irretrievably creased trousers. "Oh I think we do. How about a *different* kind of deal?" He returned to the switchbox and turned off the power once more. "How about, we just put you back in an ordinary cell and let you fend for yourself? Jake

Small might just turn up without your help, plus we have Wilhelm and his pa's research, not to mention our own eggheads back Stateside."

Hammond glanced around nervously. "Stop messing about, man! Your intruder knows I'm alive now, he's *seen* me."

"How do you know that?" Digby asked calmly.

"Because *I've* seen *him*. He probably thought we were all dead after the Cedarwood incident, but now he knows that I'm not, and he'll probably hold *me* responsible for that mess."

The American smiled wickedly. "So, send him a message. Explain that the he'll see his pals again real soon if he keeps on the way he's going."

"Mr Digby, with all due respect you just don't understand. It's never quite so straightforward with us. Surely you must've realised that by now."

Both men turned as Major Clarke entered the room once more, his wearisome cloud of pipe smoke following in his wake. "So, has our guest said anything of real use, apart from his ludicrous asylum fantasy?"

Digby rolled his eyes. "The usual bullshit, although he seems pretty paranoid about our mysterious ghost."

Clarke perched on the arm of another chair and stared unflinchingly at Hammond. "Oh?"

Digby continued as though the man in the wheelchair were absent. "Yeah, some yarn about a kind of super-Sensitive no one's ever heard of before. Funny how it's only just come up now that he wants something."

Clarke removed his pipe from his mouth and leaned forward to address Hammond directly. "I'm only going to ask you this question once, so think carefully before you answer. Where is Sergeant Jacob Small?"

Hammond's left arm twitched. "I don't know exactly, but I can describe the place and I can tell you who he's with, or at least who he's *been* with."

Clarke's tone never altered. "Well, do feel free to share any further information with us...and quickly!"

Hammond took a deep breath. "The man you need to find is called Josiah Piggott. He's a priest, or at least he was. The last I heard of him, he'd withdrawn to a monastery in the north, but seeing as Jake Small's been in contact with him very recently I'd guess that he's back in London, probably in the Bermondsey area."

The Major emitted another cloud of sticky blue smoke. "I've studied all the Section 12 reports and the late Dr Werner's work exhaustively, so be very careful before you answer my next question. Why has this man's name never come up before?"

Digby also leaned forward.

Hammond's eyes flicked down to his lap. "I came across him during my early research, but that was a different life, so to speak."

Clarke cocked his head. "Another Sensitive?"

"No, not really. More like a gifted layman."

Digby interjected. "Gifted, how?"

Hammond waved his good hand to disperse a rolling cloud of pipe smoke. "He was a clairvoyant."

"Was?" Repeated Clarke sharply.

"Still is, I suppose. He would often dream of places he could never possibly have visited, and very accurately."

Digby frowned. "You're not making sense, Doctor. If this guy was so talented, why wasn't he with you down in Kent?"

Hammond turned his attention to the American. "A sensible question, Mr Digby. The truth is that Piggott's abilities were rather erratic. He lacked either the motivation or the ability to develop them for use at will. His talents remained at the level of finding hidden objects and basic projection, but he seldom produced results on demand. Besides which, his political affiliations were far too...red, which made him a potential security risk. We parted company before the war began, and long before Section 12 was formed."

Digby shook his head. "I don't buy it. Are you seriously trying to tell me that of all the people Jake Small could be hanging out with, he just *happens* to stumble across maybe the one guy in all of London who's most like himself? Jesus, you must think we're *really* dumb."

Hammond straightened in his chair. "I've no idea how *or* why Sergeant Small has ended up in the company of the Reverend Piggott, if he even *uses* that name now. I suggest you ask him yourself."

Clarke reached for an already full ashtray. "Don't worry, we will. Perhaps this Piggott's gifts are more potent than you gave him credit for."

The psychiatrist shook his head sadly. "You're barking up the wrong tree, Major. Jacob Small isn't the man you're looking for, and neither is Piggott."

Clarke stood up and stepped forward, leaning both his hands on Hammond's wheelchair again. "I've been in this game too long not to know when someone's being evasive. If you're so certain that neither of those men is behind our security breaches, then you must have some idea of who *is*."

Digby chimed in. "Told me he'd seen him, this guy, whoever he is."

The Major smiled far too warmly. "Come along then, out with it. You know I wouldn't hesitate to put the thumbscrews on."

Hammond's response was barely audible. "The man you're looking for is probably dead, in the same way that Dr Theodore Burton is dead."

Clarke nodded. "I understand. But dead *or* alive, he must still have a name."

After a pensive silence Hammond spoke again. "I believe the person who's infiltrating your installations goes by the name of Morgan Jones, or at least he once did."

"Your installations?" Echoed Digby.

Clarke's tone was sceptical. "Never heard of him. You wouldn't fib to me now would you, Dr Hammond? You couldn't blame me for thinking that, could you?"

Hammond leaned back in his chair, a flicker of his old certainty and arrogance beginning to return. "I would suggest that you consult Mr Thorndike, although he's as likely to have you arrested as he is to hand over any files if you mention *that* name."

Clarke snorted. *"That* little tub of lard? He's a bigger liar than any of us! He'll never spill anything useful."

Hammond smiled mischievously, calling out as he watched both men retreat out of earshot. "You're an imaginative man, Major Clarke. I'm sure you can help him to see the greater good."

The Major waited until Digby had stepped out of the office and closed the door behind him. "What do you think?"

Digby shook his head slowly. "He knows *something,* that's for sure, but how much of it's bullshit is anyone's guess."

Clarke leaned against the office wall and let his head fall back. "I don't like being taken for a fool, especially by someone who's supposed to be on my side."

"You know what my daddy used to say?"

The Major took a deep breath and responded flatly. "No, Mr Digby, I don't know what your daddy used to say."

"He said that you can chase those wild geese all around the county if you've got time for the sport, but if you're real hungry then just head on down to the river where you know the fish are gonna be at."

"You think Hammond's sending me on a wild goose chase?"

Digby shrugged. "Who the hell knows, but *I'm* heading down to the river."

46

"God dammit!" Duke cursed as the Chevrolet plunged into an especially deep rut, sending a spray of freezing mud high into the air. "You sure this is the right place?"

Yellow braced himself in the passenger seat as the ambulance lurched sideways. "Gotta be. There ain't another road for half a mile each way."

The heavy Chevrolet's engine roared and whined as it slithered and struggled to the top of a sharp ridge.

Duke kept the truck in a low gear to control its descent down the steep embankment on the other side. "This is no good. I'm telling you, if we get stuck or bust an axle it won't be just *us* who's screwed."

"No kidding," agreed Yellow quietly as the ambulance leaned dangerously round a sharp bend in the neglected farm track.

Skeletal branches reached out to grab and scratch at the Chevrolet's sides as they pushed deeper into the secluded dell, although there was nothing magical about *this* place. The weak afternoon sun soon vanished beneath the rim of the large natural depression, shrouding the hidden hollow in a freezing semidarkness.

Duke breathed a sigh of relief and squinted through the windscreen as the ground finally began to level out. "Well I'll be damned, how about that."

The outline of a covered army jeep materialised in the winter gloom, with the bright glow of a cigarette confirming that their contact was ready and waiting, just like Guvnor had said.

Duke brought the ambulance to a halt and glanced at his companion. "All right, let's just stick to the plan and get the hell out of here, we're running late as it is."

"You got it," replied Yellow as both men opened their doors and clambered out, their boots squelching in the frozen leaf mould as they jumped from the ambulance's high cab.

O'Malley flicked his cigarette end into a puddle and jumped out of the jeep, hugging himself inside his heavy greatcoat. "About goddamn time too! I've been freezing my nuts off in the middle of nowhere waiting for you guys. These machines ain't exactly built for sitting around in."

Yellow scowled. "Real nice place to meet, couldn't you have found somewhere *harder* to drive into?"

O'Malley turned to Duke. "Your pal always this funny, or is he just making the effort for today?"

Duke ignored the question and scanned the rim of the deep crater. "We're fish in a barrel down here; it's the perfect place to set us up for the G-men."

O'Malley just rolled his eyes. "Oh Christ, not this again."

Duke opened his jacket to reveal the butt of an automatic. "I guess you know where the first shot's headed if anything goes wrong."

"Relax will ya. The Feds think the drop's happening in London, and by the time they realise it's a dud location we'll both be long gone." O'Malley frowned and tilted his head as a thought occurred to him. "Say, there's something I gotta ask you."

"We ain't here to swap personal stories, buddy."

The quartermaster was undeterred. "No I'm serious. I mean I'm a pretty smart guy but there's one thing I can't figure out, and I just gotta know or it'll drive me nuts."

Yellow's response was deadpan. "Wouldn't that be a shame."

Still O'Malley persisted. "This is the thing I don't get. We both know that the Feds are onto my buddies in supply, and that's how they found *me.*"

Duke glanced at his watch. "This is all history, and we're wasting time we don't have."

The quartermaster pressed on. "I guess by now you'll have heard that I had to cut a deal with this guy called Hardy to save my own skin. You know that feeding him the ass end of a fish was the only way I could make this last delivery, right? Oh man, I wish I could see his face right now."

Yellow stamped his feet in the freezing damp. "Is there a point to any of this?"

O'Malley paused for effect. "My point is, how can you trust me now? I mean, how do you know there aren't a hundred G-men just waiting at the end of the road? You know I'm hip deep in shit right now so I gotta sell *someone* out, no choice, but how can you be sure I'm stiffing the Feds and not *you* guys?"

Duke's smile was enigmatic. "Two reasons. First, you ain't in this just for the money. You want your Celtic cousins free of the Brits, and that kind of commitment just can't be bought."

"And second?"

Duke's smile broadened into his trademark grin. "And second, we've been watching your sorry ass for ages now. If you were crooked you'd have wound up in the river a long time ago."

O'Malley shook his head. "No way, there's just no way. I'm careful, I mean *real* careful, and if I'd been wearing any kind of tail I'd have spotted it by now."

Duke shrugged. "Well let's just say the Guvnor's got a real nose for this stuff and leave it there."

The quartermaster shrugged. "Sure, whatever you say, but I still don't buy it."

Duke looked pointedly around the deserted hollow. "You're not buying, *we* are, so where's the stuff?"

"So where's the payment?"

Duke turned to Yellow. "I guess we'd better get started. Why don't we show our friend here what we've brought him?"

Yellow nodded and both men disappeared around the back of the ambulance, returning a few seconds later with a heavy ammunition box and setting it down on the damp ground.

O'Malley glanced down at the box. "So open it," was his unimpressed response.

Duke's response was equally unimpressed. "I ain't your goddamn butler, open it yourself."

O'Malley huffed noisily as he bent down and released the ammunition can's tight lid. He prodded at the thirty calibre belt stored inside. "Hey that's real nice touch, I like attention to detail." He quickly removed the shortened belt to reveal a series of small packages tightly wrapped in oilcloth.

"Won't be waterproof if you open it," cautioned Yellow as O'Malley retrieved one of the packets and produced a switchblade.

"You let *me* worry about that," countered the quartermaster as he carefully cut open one end of the parcel and extracted a single gold sovereign. "Real nice. You know, I'm gonna miss you guys after the war. I doubt I'll ever make this kind of dough back on civvy street, if I ever see it again."

Duke gestured around the gloomy hollow. "So where the hell is it?"

O'Malley grinned and winked as he resealed the ammunition box, grunting at the weight as he dragged it across to his vehicle. "That's the best thing about hanging out with a bunch of engineers, it's amazing what those guys can cook up." He freed the shovel strapped to the side of his jeep and began pacing across the sodden ground. "Over here."

Duke and Yellow exchanged glances as they followed their supplier to a shadowy spot in the darkened clearing.

The quartermaster kicked some mud and leaf mould aside to reveal one edge of a wooden plank. "See, what did I tell you?" A few strokes with the shovel and O'Malley had exposed the top of a painstakingly camouflaged hole dug into the damp earth. "Neat huh?"

The alarm was evident in Yellow's voice. "Neat? It better not be flooded, that's all."

O'Malley pointed over his shoulder. "Relax. There's a culvert over there to drain the water out."

Duke lifted one of his mud caked boots. "Sure there is."

"Give me a hand and we can all get the hell out of here." O'Malley jammed his shovel under the first board and levered it up, quickly tossing it aside before repeating the operation.

Duke made no effort to help, instead motioning for Yellow to back the ambulance up for loading.

With the top boards removed, the quartermaster tugged hard at a large, greasy tarpaulin to reveal a stack of US Army crates and ammunition boxes. "There you go, just like your boss ordered. Thompsons, ammo, smoke, and enough comp B to level Buckingham Palace. All bone dry and guaranteed in good order."

Duke leaned down and dragged the top crate from the hole before producing a screwdriver to prise open the lid. He grinned as he freed a brand-new Thompson submachine gun from its waterproof wrapping. "I always wanted one of these babies."

The air was suddenly filled with the rumble of a large engine as Yellow started the ambulance and backed it up.

The quartermaster clambered out of the hidden arms cache. "Well, I'll be on my way. It was a pleasure doing business with you." If O'Malley planned on saying more, he never got the chance as a single shot from Duke's forty-five hit him square in the chest and knocked him back into the hole. The sound of the quartermaster's sudden passing was neutralised by the Chevrolet's engine and the dell's steep sides.

Yellow shut off the ignition and jumped from the cab, his expression mirroring the look of surprise on the dead man's face. "Hey, I thought we were paying him off."

Duke stuffed the weapon back in his jacket. "Change of plan. The Guvnor doesn't want any loose ends around the place."

"I thought he was cool."

"He was, at least for today, but double agents ain't got no loyalty and the Feds are gonna be spitting mad that he lied to them. I don't know what his plan was, but I *do* know for a fact those G-men don't like to be made fools of. They take it personal when they offer a deal and some snitch gives them the finger. If he ran, they'd find him and make him sing, never mind whatever immunity they'd promised him before."

Yellow looked into the crate of tightly wrapped machine guns and grinned. "Looks like we've hit the jackpot."

Duke quickly replaced the lid and helped Yellow load the first crate into the ambulance. "Let's get this lot stowed away and tidy up. You can drive the jeep back to the warehouse and take care of business, I'm heading straight to the run-in with this lot."

Yellow's eyes narrowed. "That wasn't part of the plan."

Duke grabbed one end of a second crate. "We're behind schedule and the Feds are soon gonna realise they've been hoodwinked, if they haven't already. The Guvnor can't risk driving this lot back into London with that kind of heat building up."

Yellow reluctantly grabbed hold of the next crate. "How come the Guvnor didn't tell *me* that?"

Duke shrugged. "You can take it up with him if you've got a problem, but let's get loaded up and get the hell out of here."

Yellow grumbled something incoherent as he helped lift the second crate into the ambulance.

Duke shook his head ruefully. "I don't why you're bitching. You're gonna have all the fun and we don't even need to dig a hole."

47

Mr Thorndike nodded to the guards flanking the War Office's discreet side entrance. Pulling his overcoat tight around his neck, he waddled across Whitehall Place to a waiting staff car, all but ignoring the driver who held the rear door open.

The rotund civil servant groaned as he squashed himself into the cramped rear seat, clutching his briefcase on his knees.

Within a moment the driver had settled into her own seat and started the engine. "Where to, sir?"

"Where's Michael?" Asked Thorndike irritably.

"I don't know where Michael is today. Perhaps he's off sick."

Thorndike shook his head and huffed heavily. "This really is intolerable. I've enough to do without guiding you to places you've no business knowing about in the first place."

"I'm fully vetted, Mr Thorndike," the driver reassured him. "Why don't you just tell me the address and I'll get you there as soon as possible. I'm London born and I have a map, so all should be well."

"Shouldn't leave maps lying around," observed Thorndike haughtily. "You never know who might pick them up."

The driver's pleasant tone never changed when she observed that the German High Command must be desperate if they were dropping spies to steal London street maps. "So where to?"

"Just head for Richmond and I'll direct you from there," snapped Thorndike. "And try not to find every pothole along the way, I have some important reading to do."

Thorndike's driver shifted into gear and promptly stalled the car, causing it to hop away from the curb. "Sorry about that," she said jovially as she restarted the engine and swerved suddenly to join the trickle of authorised vehicles on the streets of Whitehall.

Thorndike ground his teeth. "Please do be careful! I don't enjoy travelling by car and I must concentrate for an upcoming meeting."

The reserve driver didn't reply as she hummed softly to herself.

Satisfied there would be no further interruptions, Thorndike extracted a file from his briefcase and began reading. Within minutes the rear windows had misted over, somehow bringing grey winter gloom inside the vehicle.

Hunched over his papers, Thorndike failed to notice as the eclectic architecture of central London was replaced by smart residential neighbourhoods, which in turn became more densely packed and down at heel the as they headed further east.

At last Thorndike shoved the file back into his briefcase, only then realising that his new driver had parked along a deserted terrace of condemned housing. "Dammit woman, this isn't..." He tailed off as the driver placed a large automatic on the car's dashboard before turning to face him.

The reserve chauffer smiled and winked mischievously. "Don't worry, sir. This is just to ensure everyone's safety."

Thorndike was so preoccupied by the good-looking driver with the masculine firearm that he failed to notice a dark shape rapidly approaching the car. He yelped as the rear door opened and he was shoved across the back seat by a drizzle-soaked intruder, with collar turned high and hat pulled low.

The civil servant's first reaction was to tighten his grip on the briefcase. "You damned fools! There's nothing here for you, and they'll start searching five minutes after I fail to arrive."

"I doubt they'll think to look here. Not for a good while anyway."

The portly mandarin closed his eyes and let out a long sigh of relief. "Clarke! I assume you have a good explanation for this outrageous behaviour!"

The Major unwound his muffling scarf with some difficulty in the cramped car. "We need a quiet chat, and I couldn't very well wait until you contacted me. You know it's funny, but I couldn't find *anyone* who knows your name or phone number." Clarke nodded to Ellie in the front seat. "Could you open the window please, Miss Parsons? It's going to get rather warm in here."

Ellie nodded and twisted to face the front.

Thorndike reached into his pocket and pulled out a clean handkerchief, lifting his hat to dab his damp forehead. "Yes, well, discretion is our first commandment as you know." An excited gleam appeared in his eyes as he nodded to the driver. "So *you're* Miss Parsons. You know I read your report on Section 12 and it was excellent work. I'm pleased to meet you at last, and I must say I'm *very* pleased that you're on *our* side."

Ellie said nothing.

Thorndike shoved his briefcase down in front of his knees and awkwardly unbuttoned his coat. "You're right, Major, it's becoming uncomfortable already."

Clarke's voice was quiet and measured. "Who is Morgan Jones, and why is our only tame Sensitive suddenly so frightened?"

Thorndike's lips twitched. "I can't talk about that, with you or anyone, and *especially* not with our present company."

Clarke's tone hardened. "Miss Parsons has taken on both Section 12 *and* the Brotherhood. I think that's qualification enough, don't you?"

Thorndike took a deep breath. "Very well then. Morgan Jones is a name, that's all."

"A name that's scared the dickens out of a man for whom this world and the next hold few surprises. You gave me this assignment because you know full well I have a talent for finding things out. Surely you must've realised I'd learn that name sooner or later; please tell me you're not so short-sighted."

Thorndike thought for a moment before nodding slowly. "Very well. But first you must tell me *exactly* how you learned that name, and I'll see if I can help."

"It was Dr Thomas Hammond who first mentioned this Jones to me, after one of his...less than conventional sessions."

Thorndike removed his thick spectacles and wiped them with the lapel of his coat. "It must be fascinating to see a man like Hammond in action, to witness him recover information which is somehow hidden in the very air around us. We live in astonishing times and I envy your part in them."

Clarke would not be deterred. "I'm still waiting for some sort of explanation."

Thorndike replaced his glasses. "I am aware of only one written reference to Morgan Jones, and that was found in the late Wolfgang Werner's papers."

Clarke narrowed his eyes. "I've read all the late Dr Werner's papers and I've never heard of this Jones before."

Thorndike shrugged apologetically. "Then it stands to reason that you haven't seen all the material."

Clarke rubbed his forehead. "I'm trying to remain calm here, Mr Thorndike."

"Well I certainly appreciate it."

"Don't get clever with me!" Clarke's outburst was deafening in the confined space. "You expect me to run this operation from an outside toilet so that smell can't reach your office, *and* you expect me to do it in the dark as well? I was assured I'd been shown *all* documents relating to these bloody Sensitives. Where are the rest?"

Thorndike's expression hardened to match Clarke's. "It was good of your section to recover so much material when you extricated van Cortlandt, but that doesn't mean you rescued all of it."

Clarke rubbed his chin thoughtfully as he gazed out through the misted windscreen. "Are you telling me there's more?"

"Quite so," Thorndike confirmed. "Werner the elder amassed a huge body of research as he studied the medical and, if you like, metaphysical conditions of the van Cortlandt clan. There were diaries and interview transcripts, not to mention a unique collection of rare volumes and manuscripts collected by the family itself. While you were able to deliver both doctor and patient, the bulk of what we now call the van Cortlandt Collection had already been obtained by other means, although I'm not at liberty to discuss the details."

Clarke raised his eyebrows. "I'd imagine there's a lot of potentially dangerous material in such a collection, if someone had bothered to mention it existed before now."

Thorndike's tone took on an unexpected steely edge. "One thing you can be certain of is that *none* of us will ever gain access to the full archive. I've only seen a small part of the collection myself, but I'm informed that its contents are a signpost to realms of impossibility more wondrous and dangerous than anything we've ever imagined."

Clarke sighed heavily. "Miss Parsons, would you be so kind as to shoot Mr Thorndike if the next words he speaks are not directly related to this mysterious Morgan Jones."

Within a second Ellie was facing Thorndike again, and the automatic was no longer on the dashboard.

Thorndike took a deep breath once more. "We actually know very little about him, other than the fact that Morgan Jones is related to Peter van Cortlandt in some way. Alas the old man never disclosed any details, not even to his most loyal and trusted physician."

The Major closed his eyes and pinched the bridge of his nose. "Christ Almighty."

"As I said, Jones' exact ancestry is unknown and I'll eat my hat if that's his real name. Whatever the case, the unconfirmed story is that Jones was the protégé of one Colonel Kurt Stryker. Naturally this was long before the war, Projekt Schatten, Section 12 or any of it. According to the somewhat lurid tale that van Cortlandt told, both Jones *and* Stryker specialised in necromancy; that is to say, manipulating the latent energies of the dead to achieve their ends."

Clarke puffed out his cheeks as he thought. "Jake Small reported something similar after that business in France."

"Quite so. Reliable intelligence is very thin on the ground, but that doesn't mean it's entirely absent." Thorndike continued without waiting for anyone to respond. "Even though we can't be sure of his real name, we *do* know that Jones is an exceptional Sensitive. We know that he sided with the Germans during *both* wars, and we also know he's the beneficiary of at least fifty years' teaching and mentoring by one of the most gifted Sensitives ever recorded."

"Stryker," confirmed Clarke quietly.

Thorndike nodded grimly.

For a while nobody spoke, but it was Ellie who eventually voiced the problem.

"This just doesn't ring true. We know the Nazis don't trust the Brotherhood any more than *we* do, at least not these days. I can't believe they'd just let this Jones character wander around doing whatever he wants, so perhaps they've got him locked up in an electric cage of his own."

"I wish it were so," said Thorndike grimly. "But the incidents over recent weeks suggest that he's still at large, although I've no idea how he's managed to evade capture. At any rate, I'd be doubling my efforts to find Jacob Small if I were you."

Clarke's tone was more resigned than angry. "So you knew all along that it wasn't Jake Small roaming those tunnels."

"I suspected, but even if it *were* him I wouldn't be very concerned about it. Sergeant Small is probably the most talented Sensitive we still have, but he's not politically minded. There's little danger of his trying to use anything he sees for his own ends."

Clarke rolled his cramped shoulders. "So we can't just put a bullet through this Morgan Jones' head, but if we're lucky the Krauts will do it for us anyway."

Thorndike removed his glasses again. "We already have people working on *that* end of the problem, but if we can't neutralise him there's no telling *what* damage he may cause. While Jones is unaccounted for, Jacob Small is undoubtedly our best defence."

Clarke's response was sour. "Seems like we've been chasing the wrong man."

"On the contrary, we still need Sergeant Small come what may, and I must say I'm rather disappointed at your slow progress. Indeed I've had to explain the delay to various interested parties, and I think I should warn you that questions are being asked about your commitment to this mission."

An uncomfortable silence settled over the group, and it was a good thirty seconds before Major Clarke spoke calmly to Ellie. "Miss Parsons, I think Mr Thorndike is late for a meeting, and I need to stop off at the office."

Ellie started the engine. "Anything else?"

Clarke smiled and let his head fall back onto the seat. "Have you been to church lately, Eleanor?"

48

"Bugger off, I'm closed!"

Digby knocked again, this time making the wooden closed sign chatter against the door. "Come on buddy, open up will ya. I got money to burn and I need some supplies."

The muffled voice behind the blackout curtain sounded unimpressed. "So get yourself off down Loot Alley. I reckon you know where that is."

Digby sounded hurt and disappointed. "Aw come on, I'm taking two broads up West tonight and I need some gear. You know what I mean?"

The voice from inside the shop switched from unimpressed to mocking. "Up West eh? Well ain't you a right old cockney sparra, cor blimey guvnor ain't that the God's honest truth. Now piss off before I get my gun out." The muffled sound of receding footsteps and an internal door slamming confirmed that the conversation was over.

Digby cursed under his breath and looked around, trying to quell a growing dislike for jolly old England in general and London in particular. Although in this case the miserable climate was his ally as the darkening streets were already deserted. He made his way around the corner and soon found a narrow alleyway running behind the row of down at heel shops. Within seconds he was over the wall and crouching in the shadows of Pete Finch's back yard. He wrinkled his nose at the smell of vegetable peelings and kerosene as he considered his next move.

He quickly dismissed the idea of simply kicking in the back door and introducing himself. A man like Pete Finch would probably fortify his premises against forced entry, by both official *and* unofficial parties. The best solution would be to persuade him to open the door, but that was a problem as the target had already indicated his reluctance.

Digby smiled in the darkness as the answer finally came to him, and it was so obvious that he'd almost overlooked it. Standing up, he quickly removed his coat and slipped off his shoulder holster before stashing the pistol in the shadows behind a rusting dustbin. Shrugging his coat back on, he walked straight up to Finch's back door and hammered hard. "Listen pal, I gotta talk to you, it's real important."

Silence.

Digby knocked again. "I've got a message."

"Send a telegram."

"I've got a message from O'Malley."

There was a long pause, followed by the clicking of several locks and bolts. Eventually the door opened a couple of inches and Pete Finch's grizzled face squinted through the small gap. "Who are you? What do you want?"

Digby glanced around and lowered his voice. "Listen, we can't talk out here."

"Just a minute." The door slammed shut.

Digby tried to interpret the sounds coming from within as he waited for the next development. It wasn't long in coming as the door finally creaked open under its own weight.

Finch's voice floated out from somewhere inside the darkened building. "You'd better come in then. Have a seat, whoever you are."

Digby cautiously mounted the back step and peered inside. A single stuttering hurricane lamp illuminated a small table, but struggled to reveal the rest of the room. From what little he could make out, he was looking at some kind of back parlour and kitchen, probably connected to the shop via a door concealed somewhere in the shadows.

"Hurry up, you're letting the heat out," Finch complained from a darkened corner of the room.

Digby glanced at the feeble embers in the fireplace but decided against cracking wise about making the room any colder. He knew he was taking one hell of a chance by going directly to Finch but he was out of time, out of clues and out of options. He stepped through the door and quickly crossed to the worn and scratched kitchen table. "Gee, you limeys sure know how to make a guy feel welcome."

The back door slammed shut and a torch beam pierced the darkness, at last revealing Finch's portly silhouette. "Just stop there, turn round and face me. Keep your hands in sight."

Digby followed Finch's instructions.

"Take off that coat, very carefully."

Again Digby complied, letting the shapeless garment fall to the floor. "My tailor's gonna be awful mad at me."

"He can bill your undertaker." Two orbs of orange reflected off Finch's spectacles as he shifted his head. "Now the jacket."

"You gonna freeze me to death?" Digby grumbled as he shed his jacket too.

"Have a seat."

Again Digby followed Finch's instructions, pointing to a half-eaten can of corned beef on the table. "You really shouldn't have gone to all this trouble."

At last Finch stepped forward with his trusty Webley clutched in his soft, clammy hand. "You Yanks think you're so bloody clever, don't you?"

"Well I wouldn't know about that. What I *do* know is that *we're* not the ones shivering in the dark and living on half a potato every week." Digby made a point of looking Finch up and down, "although *you* seem to be doing okay."

Finch smirked at the insult. "Just who the bloody hell *are* you?"

"Doesn't matter who I am."

Finch shook his head and waggled the gun. "Oh but it does, it matters a *lot*. Now you just put those hands flat on the table and keep them there. I may be a fat bugger but I know how to shoot."

Digby placed his hands on the table's tacky surface. "Had lots of practice, have you?"

Finch stepped a little closer. "You must think we're all daft or something. Stop trying to change the subject and tell me your name right now."

Digby sighed heavily. "You want this message or not?"

Finch didn't respond as he crossed to Digby's discarded clothes and kicked them away from the table.

Digby said nothing more either, his eyes methodically scanning the room as Finch retreated back into the shadows.

Suddenly a match flared, quickly growing into a larger flame as the grocer lit a second hurricane lamp to illuminate a grimy looking sink in the corner beneath a blacked-out window. He kept the weapon trained on his visitor as he searched through Digby's shapeless jacket, a small smile flickering across his face as the inside pocket relinquished a slim leather wallet. "So, let's have a look and see if the cobblers in here is the same as the cobblers coming out of your mouth."

Digby just shrugged. "Hurry up. I ain't got the time for all these goddamn theatrics. Jeez, anyone would think we're in some sort of spy movie."

Finch's eyes widened as he scrutinised Digby's FBI card.

Digby seized his chance while Finch was distracted. In one fluid movement he scooped the lamp from the table and hurled it towards the perplexed racketeer. He heard a cry and a clatter as he dived off his chair and rolled into the shadows. The room was smaller than he'd thought and his feet collided with some hitherto hidden shelves.

There was a deafening roar and bright muzzle flash as Finch howled and fired a shot at the table, the bullet kicking up dust and wood splinters in its wake.

Digby was back on his feet and closing in as Finch reeled away, his own jacket and one trouser leg already well alight. The American quickly swept Finch's feet from beneath him, the revolver going off a second, deafening time as the screaming grocer fell heavily to the floor.

The fake G-man stamped hard on Finch's hand, the Webley roaring and flashing a third time before falling from the prone man's grasp. Digby wasted no time in sweeping it into the shadows with his foot before grabbing his discarded coat and quickly smothering the flames.

Finch groaned and clutched his face, the skin already beginning to blister beneath his trembling fingers as the smell of burnt cloth and burnt flesh filled the room.

Digby stood up and shook smouldering ash from his battered coat before stooping to recover his equally battered jacket. "That looks pretty bad, you're gonna need a doctor I reckon."

"Bastard!" Was Finch's only response as he rolled first one way, then the other in his agony.

Digby pursed his lips and shook his head sadly. "Goddamn! Looks like you've lost half your hair! Well let's be honest, it was thinning anyway. Hey, this could be the start of a whole new look for you."

"Just get me an ambulance you Yank bastard!"

The American searched around and found Finch's revolver in the shadows. Picking it up, he checked the cylinder and crossed to the peeling grocer. "I'll help you, buddy, but I need you to help *me* first."

"Go to hell." Finch's voice was weak and breathless.

Digby reached down and tapped the Webley's butt smartly on Finch's blistered head. He winced as the smouldering smuggler howled and clutched his singed scalp. "Careful now. Don't want to upset the neighbours, do we?"

"Oh God it's agony. I need a *doctor* for pity's sake."

The American straightened and continued as though Finch were in perfect health. "You see I've got a problem, and because *I've* got a problem that means *you've* got a problem too."

"Just tell me what you want!"

Digby crossed to the inner door and pushed it wide, letting some smoke escape into the shop. "You see, I really *do* know O'Malley. I know just what kind of treacherous, two timing no good little shit he really is. I mean, how can you respect a man who'd sell out his brothers in arms just to save his own sorry ass?"

Finch groaned and rolled onto his back, his arms falling limp on the floor.

Digby reached down and patted Finch firmly on one reddened and blistered cheek. "Don't doze off now, I'm just getting to the part where you come in."

Finch's eyes flickered open reluctantly.

"That's the spirit! Now where was I? Oh yeah, I was explaining what a no good two faced little runt your friend is."

Finch's swollen lips struggled to form his words. "Not friend, just business."

"Like I care about *that*. Anyhow, because I know that a man who'd sell American guns to Irish insurgents has no sense of honour, I couldn't be sure he wasn't playing *me* for a fool either, so I've had a tail on him these past two weeks."

The burned man groaned again.

"That's right, *me old china.* How do you think I knew where to find *you?*"

"Please God, just get on with it."

The American tutted reprovingly. "You're never going to make new friends unless you work on your conversation skills, and I've a feeling we're gonna get to know each other pretty well, you and me. Anyhow, the truth is kind of embarrassing really, but I gotta fess up and admit that your supplier's given us the slip. It's a shame because we had a real nice arrangement too. O'Malley was gonna lead us to his buyer in exchange for getting out of jail some time *before* he makes pine-box parole. We had it all worked out; time, place and inventory. So what am I supposed to tell the guys who've spent the last twelve hours freezing their butts off, and waiting to drop the net on a fish that never showed up?"

"What are you talking about?" Finch's voice was little more than a whisper by now.

Digby feigned disappointment. "Now let's not start screwing each other around, it's too late for that now. You might not believe this, but I was hoping that we'd never have to meet face-to-face. I mean it could be a real political mess what with you being a Brit and all; but you see that little cockroach has left me with no other option. He's made the big mistake of taking me for a fool and not making the rendezvous where we'd arranged, so that means he must be delivering somewhere *else.*"

A pained and bitter chuckle gurgled up from Finch's swollen throat.

"Now you're getting it." Digby leaned down and whispered in Finch's crisped and soot-blackened ear. "I need to know where that exchange is *really* going down, and I need to know *right now.* Just so there's no misunderstanding between us, I want you to know that I'm quite willing to torture you if it's necessary to complete my mission. So, where's the delivery?"

"You'll get me a doctor?"

"Sure, we're not savages here."

"You swear?"

"I'm losing patience, Mr Finch."

Finch took a deep shuddering breath as he fought against approaching unconsciousness. "Look, I'm just a middleman, a broker. I'm not interested in that kind of thing."

Digby straightened up and half sat on the table. "Maybe, but you'll still take a nice fat commission. So how does it work, who pays who for what?"

The overweight grocer groaned and mumbled something.

The American prodded the prone man with the toe of his scuffed shoe. "Speak up!"

Finch's words were thick and quivering like his puffed up lips. "I take my cut and the customer pays the supplier directly once I've given him the pickup details."

"Nice and safe, at least in theory." Digby shoved his hands in his pockets. "So, where's this exchange taking place?"

Finch didn't respond.

Digby jabbed again with his foot. "You've already been paid, so if you help me now you might even get to keep some of it."

Finch's eyes flickered and he grimaced against the pain, but not so much that the ghost of a smile didn't show on his swollen and distorted features. "Too late, you stupid Yank bastard. The delivery's already happened."

Digby placed his foot on Finch's blistered features and pushed down, raising his voice above the shriek of agony echoing around the room. "I'm gonna get a medal for beating the crap out of you. I just thought you'd like to know that."

Finch whimpered and tried to speak, although the only sounds he made were gurgling whines.

The American grimaced. "Looks like you pissed your pants there; still that don't mean nothing, and I ain't gonna hold it against you. Now listen, you're in the middle of something really serious, and this is your last chance to get out more or less in one piece, so think carefully before you bullshit me again."

Finch finally relented. "Okay, all right, anything. Just get me a doctor, please God."

Digby's voice was quiet but insistent. "What does a man like George Tooley want with all that hardware?"

Finch began to sob. "Don't know, I swear. Would never tell me."

"I believe you, I really do. Okay let's try another. How the hell does he expect to bring all that gear into the city without getting caught? From what I've heard there's plenty of other mobs who'd be happy to tip us the wink and see him put away for good."

Finch forced the words from his wheezing throat. "O'Malley refused to deliver in London, too risky. Tooley said that was better, at least at first he did. Maybe the job's somewhere else."

Digby nodded. "Yeah maybe, but he's outside his own territory with a truck full of gear that he needs to keep hidden. I mean it's not like he's walking around with a revolver tucked into his pants."

"Tooley's got a place in the sticks, out of the way, an old farm or something. I reckon that's where he'll store the shipment."

"A place in the country? Now we're getting somewhere." Digby prodded Finch with the Webley's muzzle. "Where?"

"Don't know."

"Where?"

Finch took another shuddering, wheezing breath.

"Come on, big fella, you're almost home free."

The roasted racketeer was beginning to sound sleepy. "Don't know exactly, honest. Some place out near Amersham I think, up in the hills."

Digby nodded approvingly. "Oh that's great, Pete. In case you hadn't guessed it, I'm not from around here so you're gonna have to be more specific. That could be up in Scotland for all *I* know."

The shadow of a rueful smile appeared on Finch's blistered lips. "Not that far. Not far at all, just look at a tube map and it's the last stop. Just head for Wembley and Harrow, you'll find it."

"Good job, you're doing great. Now all I need is an address."

"Don't know any address, the commie git would never tell me something like that."

Digby thought for a moment, then nodded. "All right then. You just hang in there and I'll get you some help."

Finch mumbled something incoherent as his head sagged sideways.

Digby paused at the back door before turning back to the permanently scarred smuggler. "You'd better not be bullshitting me. If you are then you can expect a hospital visit, and I won't be bringing flowers."

49

Major Clarke checked his watch again. "Do you think that Hammond's having some fun at our expense?"

Ellie looked at the shattered spire of St John's church as it faded into the early winter dusk. "He knows you wouldn't hesitate to throw him back underground, and there's somebody in there for sure."

Clarke drummed his fingers as he thought. "Could be anyone. Probably some poor homeless bloke with nowhere to go."

"Perhaps, but there were whispers about a hermit priest among the Dog & Duck's clientele too, and it would explain why Jake Small hasn't turned up in a speiler or nightclub as yet."

Clarke flexed his cramped shoulders and nodded thoughtfully. "Maybe, but I just can't shake the feeling that something's wrong. Have you noticed something strange about this place?"

"After Cedarwood I don't think *anything* will ever seem strange again."

Clarke reached for his pipe, then changed his mind. "We've been here for a nearly an hour and nobody's come close or even cut through the churchyard. I know the place has been bombed to death but this is still a busy city. There should be more people around, or at least there should be *some* people around. I never thought I'd say something like this, but the place just gives me the creeps as Mr Digby would put it."

Ellie folded her hands under her armpits to keep them warm. "Major Clarke, you're chewing your nails. That's a revolting habit and a sign of nervousness. I didn't think you even *understood* what nervousness meant. What's gotten into you?"

Clarke clasped his fingers together and smiled ruefully. "Sorry Eleanor, you're right. Perhaps I've been thinking about these bloody Sensitives too much. I don't know why, but I just feel a sense of foreboding, as though we're being sucked into something we don't understand."

"Really Major Clarke, I'm surprised at you. We're looking for Jake Small, that's simple enough."

"You know that's not what I mean. I'm wondering how to calculate the odds against one of Hammond's old subjects being involved in this business."

Ellie frowned. "I've already seen proof positive that there's much more to the world than we can see around us, but I promised myself I'd never let that knowledge keep me awake at night, looking for signs of destiny in chance and coincidence."

Clarke said nothing as he reached forward and wiped the condensation from the windscreen.

Ellie glanced across. "Do you actually *believe* this mysterious Brotherhood is a real threat? After all, we don't know who they are or even what they really stand for."

Clarke stared into the middle distance. "Serious enough to lead us a merry dance and put our necks on the block, here in our own country. I used to trust in the power of coincidence too, but now I'm beginning to wonder." He suddenly changed the subject and returned Ellie's gaze. "Would you *really* have shot Mr Thorndike if I'd told you to?"

Ellie thought for a moment. "I honestly don't know. Probably."

Clarke shook his head and stared at the scorched church once again. "You're a frightening woman, Ellie."

"I should be. I was trained by some very frightening men."

The Major smiled. "Well, it's time we saw some of that terrifying training in action. I think we'll go in the back door."

"Churches don't have back doors, Major Clarke."

"Did those frightening men teach you sass along with close combat?"

"No. I learned *that* skill from a procession of wildly overconfident young men. Although I doubt that any of *them* are feeling invincible these days."

Clarke nodded and opened the passenger door. "All right then, we'll go in the side door as quietly as we can. I know we're on the side of the angels, but the last thing we need is some local copper clomping around. Half of them are probably in Tooley's pocket anyway."

Ellie slipped out of the driver's door and pushed it closed as quietly as possible.

Clarke did the same and caught up with her, linking arms before they strolled nonchalantly into the soulless churchyard.

Clarke leaned casually in the vestry's doorway, hiding Ellie as she overcame the simple lock within seconds and drew her replacement pistol.

Once inside, they quickly looked around the dim and sparsely furnished room. Clarke pointed to Jake's new army kitbag. "See? Our boy might be here right now, and that's one heck of a coincidence by anybody's reckoning."

Ellie immediately homed in on Jake's battered autobiography among the books and papers cluttering the desk. "We might just be one step behind for once." She crossed to the inner door and placed her ear close to the woodwork.

Clarke hissed through his teeth as he rapidly flicked through Jake's journal. Although much of it was unintelligible, he still felt as though he were glancing through a forgotten window and into a painstakingly hidden world. He had no doubt that such a world was best left unexplored, but it was too late for that now. He gently closed the battered book and joined Ellie beside the door. "Hear anything?"

She shook her head.

"All right then, let's keep it slow and discreet. There's no telling *who* we may find, or how many of the bastards there might be."

Ellie nodded and pushed the door open, wincing as the clank and squeak of iron hinges echoed through the damp and gloomy church.

Clarke shivered as he followed Ellie into the main body of the building, where the freezing fog and descending dusk conspired to create an atmosphere of forbidden desolation. He pointed to a small door across the nave and beckoned Ellie to follow. "Looks like we've come in the wrong way."

The Major drew his own pistol as he neared the door and briefly wondered why he hadn't done it sooner. He was getting complacent. Technically Jake Small was not an enemy, although he could hardly be described as a friend. In reality he was a desperate man on the run, a fact that made him just as dangerous as any foreign agent or hardened criminal.

Clarke took up position beside the door. If Small or anyone else wanted to come out shooting, well that would just be too bad for them.

Ellie mirrored Clarke's position.

Clarke shouted his challenge. "Police! We know you're in there, so open the door and step out slowly."

No response.

Clarke repeated his instructions, impressing upon anyone inside the room that no further chances would be offered.

Again silence.

Motioning for Ellie to stay put, Clarke reached for the door handle and gave it a sharp twist before quickly withdrawing his hand.

A shaft of warm yellow light spilled across the nave's damp floor as the door creaked open under its own weight.

Clarke glanced at Ellie, who shook her head to indicate she could see nobody.

The Major took a deep breath and stepped over the threshold, quickly pushing the door back against the wall as the pip of his gun sight traversed the room. Within a second it had settled on the man propped up in the bed. He pulled a face at the sour smell of sickness and stale food infusing the atmosphere before barking his next order. "Show me your hands, now!"

The old man remained motionless, his head resting on his own shoulder. Only his bloodied lips and chin moved, quivering slightly as though reciting a silent prayer.

Clarke shuffled forward slowly and used his left hand to twitch the bedclothes away. Satisfied that the stranger was unarmed he let out a low whistle, signalling Ellie to join him.

She was there in an instant. Her face fell as she looked at the once strong but now ravaged old man leaning against the headboard. She looked questioningly at Clarke, who nodded that she should take a closer look.

While Clarke stepped back, Ellie holstered her weapon and leaned forward. "Hello there. We're sorry to barge in on you like this but we're looking for someone...someone who I think you know."

If the old man had heard her he gave no indication. In fact he showed no sign that he was even aware of their presence.

Having quickly assessed the situation, Clarke's own Browning disappeared and he quickly straightened the old man's blankets. "Sorry about that, old chap, but we just had to check. Don't want you to get cold now do we?" He glanced across at Ellie, who was holding up a broken laudanum bottle.

The Major pursed his lips and scowled momentarily before finding his smile again. "I suppose you must be Josiah."

No response. The man in the bed shifted his head slightly but his eyes remained blank, seeing nothing.

Ellie tried again, leaning forward and grasping the old man gently by the shoulder. "Hello Reverend. My name's Ellie and I'm a friend of Jake's. Do you know where he is?"

The old man's lips twitched briefly while an indistinct gurgling sound issued from somewhere in his throat.

Ellie gently pulled a shard of glass from between Piggott's lips and pressed on. "We have to find him as soon as we can. He's sick and he needs our help. It's very important." She looked up at Clarke and shook her head.

The Major returned to the doorway and jerked his head for Ellie to join him. "You think he can tell us anything?"

Ellie glanced back at the old man. "I don't know, but Hammond was spot on. Jake *was* here, and by the look of things he should be coming back."

Clarke glanced around the church. "All right, then this is what we'll do. I'll stay with our drugged up friend while you stash the car somewhere out of sight, and get back here as soon as you can."

"He should be in a hospital," Ellie objected.

"And he will be, I promise, but we can't run the risk of moving him now. If Small sees anything suspicious he'll bolt."

"Shouldn't we call for some help?"

Clarke thought for a moment then shook his head. "No time. I've a feeling that little bastard isn't far away and we can't miss our chance. Just get back fast."

Ellie quickly vanished into the rapidly thickening shadows while Clarke slowly paced along St John's central aisle. He wasn't entirely sure of what he was looking for, but he was certain there was something wrong with the place. From the back alleys of Amsterdam and Paris to the freezing wet streets of London; if Clarke had learned *anything* it was that life was untidy, people were untidy, events were untidy. Neither people nor events wove themselves into an ordered tapestry of occurrences, with conclusions neatly wrapped up in the actions leading up to them. Life was no scripted stage play and the recent convergence of events was just too...tidy.

Clarke knew too much of the ways of men to be especially pious, but as he stared at the water streaked altar he became ever more certain that forces greater than mere chance and human action were at work. The dead church testified to the truth that without human desire even Providence could become cold, silent and obscure. The fact that no living soul had tended to the altar in some while did not negate its existence, but it reflected the fact that, if left to their own devices, the forces of fate were not nearly so bright and beneficent as the human condition often wished them to be.

Clarke shuddered at the sheer spiritual *deadness* of the place, and was about to make his way back to the old man's bedside when something caught his eye. His hand instinctively reached into his coat, hovering above the butt of his pistol as he stared into an impenetrable blackness which had once glowed with soft, warm candlelight. He took a step closer, his eyes straining to discern one patch of darkness from another as he was left with a vague impression of having perceived something, although in reality his eyes had seen only shadows.

"Freeze right there!"

Clarke froze, instantly recognising the voice in the darkness. "Just take it easy, Sergeant. Nobody needs to get hurt here."

"Pull out that pistol, finger and thumb. Drop it on the altar."

"Jacob..."

"Do it!"

Clarke realised he had no choice as he couldn't actually see any target. Besides, his orders were to capture Jake Small alive, not go shooting holes in the bloke. He gently pulled his Browning from its holster and placed it on the altar, stepping back and raising his hands. "Jake, you're not well."

There was a clink of broken glass as Sergeant Jacob Small stepped into the dim dusk light, his own pistol shaking slightly in his grasp. "Still fit enough to get the drop on *your* dumb ass."

Clarke's eyes widened as he watched Jake reach forward and pick up the Browning. He seemed to have lost weight, and his already pale skin had taken on an unhealthy grey hue that was accentuated by his dark glasses. Unshaven and furtive, he looked like a man who was rapidly coming apart at the seams. "Bloody hell Jacob, you're a real mess."

A short bark of bitter laughter escaped his lips. "Hell? You might be nearer the truth than you think."

"Listen son, you can't carry on like this. Believe it or not we really *do* want to help you. Trouble is, we're trying to fight a war at the same time."

"*Help* me?" Jake's tone was sneering. "Sure, the way you helped me by trying to hand me back to that other bearded bastard? Pierre should've shot *him* in the head and done us all a favour."

Clarke nodded. "I often wonder why he didn't, but that's old news now."

The Sergeant snorted. "Maybe for *you,* but I have to live with it every day. That is, when I can remember who the hell I *am* in the first place."

Clarke glanced at the vestry door. "Jake, you must realise you're ill. God knows I understand why you hate Hammond, but the plain unvarnished truth is that we're desperately short of experts and we need *all* of you. You know full well there's someone else out there, someone extremely dangerous."

Jake pointed to Piggott's room. "Yeah I know. I saw you two getting acquainted just now, but if you want anything from *him* you'd better hurry up."

Clarke narrowed his eyes as he tried to fathom the Sergeant's cryptic comment. "Jake, you can't just keep running and hiding like this. You know that we'll find you wherever you go. If you keep this nonsense up then sooner or later some pen pusher's going to decide you're more of a risk than an asset, and you know what'll happen then."

Jake slowly made his way around the rain-soaked altar, motioning for Clarke to step away. "What do you want me for anyway? Hell, Hitler's squashed in a vice right now and the war'll be over in six months, a year, tops."

"It's not that simple."

The Sergeant smiled ruefully. "Maybe not for you, but *I've* got enough on my plate just trying to remember my own *name* when I wake up. That's how simple *my* life's become lately." He began to sidestep towards the vestry. "Goodbye Major Clarke. It's been a real hoot but I'm out of here for good."

Clarke took a step forward. "You can't run forever, Jacob."

Jake pulled open the vestry door. "We'll just see about that. Now I know I don't need to give you all the not following me bullshit. You're not that dumb." He stepped over the threshold. "You're a bastard for sure but I reckon you're also very good at what you do, so don't make me deprive king and country of your talents by being heroic. Oh and say hi to Ellie for me." With that he slammed the door shut.

Clarke ran forward as he heard a banging and scraping sound suggestive of Jake wedging a chair beneath the handle. His fears were confirmed as he tested the door and found it jammed shut. Audibly cursing his own stupidity he glanced around the church's rapidly darkening interior, his eyes fixing on the watery dusk still dribbling through a gap in one of the boarded windows.

Sprinting across the freezing nave, Clarke launched himself at the high opening and scrambled between the boards. The little wind that was left in him was completely expelled as he fell headfirst onto the wet pavement outside.

He staggered to his feet and dashed towards the corner of the building, his heart leaping into his mouth as he heard the crack of pistol shots close by. Sliding to a halt, he peeped cautiously around the corner, taking a deep breath and clenching his fists as he saw the very thing he'd desperately hoped *not* to see.

Knowing that Jake was already long gone, Clarke rushed towards the prone body of Ellie Parsons, partly hidden behind one of the churchyard's dour monuments. He quickly removed his coat and placed it under her head, ignoring the sticky mess of blood which had replaced the right hand side of her face. He felt a sense of relief as she moaned quietly, her arms and legs moving slowly and without purpose.

The Major glanced around, quickly weighing his options as he heard the Austin's engine splutter to life close by. After a short deliberation he gently rolled Ellie onto her side and propped her against a tall Victorian gravestone dedicated to the memory of someone called Partridge. "You just keep still my girl. It's going to be all right."

Ellie emitted a weak and incoherent groan, suggesting that at least some part of her had heard Clarke's reassurance.

Major Clarke suddenly wished he didn't smoke so much as he set off towards the desolate sound of horns moaning on the mist-wreathed river.

50

Jake cursed London's greasy backstreets as the Austin slid determinedly forward like a wilful horse. He pushed back in his seat as the screeching tyres began to grip at last, although too late to avoid the gates of Walker & Sons removals yard. The car came to an abrupt halt with a solid thump, the tinkling of headlight glass lost beneath roaring engine and screaming rubber.

Jake opened his eyes, although there was no time to feel any relief as jumped from the car and stared at the peeling wooden gates, which suddenly seemed reminiscent of a strangely similar accident not so very long ago. He swallowed hard and folded his arms in an attempt to stop his sweat-soaked hands from shaking. Everything had happened so fast, and his nerves and training had conspired against him before he'd realised who he was shooting at. By the time he'd recognised Ellie Parsons she'd already dropped like a stone and vanished behind one of St John's larger Victorian monuments.

He felt sick, then angry and then sick again. *Damn it!* Why couldn't she have shouted or something? He could've aimed wide and just sent her diving for cover, but it was too late for that now. It was too late for *everything*.

Jake knew that he'd crossed the Rubicon as he hammered on the aged but sturdy gates of Tooley's underworld fortress. This time there could be no going back, and this time there was a *real* case to answer, not just some smart-ass lawyer's take on the chaos of mortal combat.

"Hey, anyone there?" Jake knocked again on the faded and grime encrusted gates before squinting through the gap between them. The place had been a bustling if furtive hive of activity just that morning, yet now it looked all but deserted in the descending winter dusk. Tooley had certainly talked about shipping out for good, but Jake hadn't really expected the whole base of operations to have shut up shop quite so suddenly. The only sign of life was the faint glow of a hurricane lamp somewhere inside a tightly closed warehouse.

Mindful of his stolen car and the noise he was making, Jake turned back to check the grey street of mournful houses rapidly fading into the freezing gloom. If anybody was at home they were hiding behind their blackout curtains, making sure they could see and hear as little as possible.

Clearly the gates were no use, so Jake jumped back in the car and restarted the engine. A narrow alley followed the yard's perimeter off to the right, so Jake eased the Austin into that confined space. He hadn't travelled more than twenty yards before a large stone bollard loomed out of the shadows, presumably designed to stop drivers using the lane as a shortcut.

Frustrated once more, Jake got back out of the car and considered his next move. Every cop in London would be on his case now as well as most of the underworld, so if he wanted to keep both his life *and* his liberty then there really was no other option. He figured that the warehouse may well be empty, but he still hoped against hope that he might find someone who was able to get a message to George Tooley. If he was *really* lucky then the offer of employment in the Emerald Isle might still be open, *if* the wily gangster was in a forgiving kind of mood.

Having quickly reached the only feasible decision, it was less than a minute before Jake was standing on the Austin's roof and looping his spare bootlaces around the kitbag he'd rescued while fleeing from the church. His preparations complete, Jake reached up and slung the bag across the top of the wall to create a cushion against the broken glass and barbed wire Tooley had deployed to deter intruders.

Not for the first time was Jake grateful for his army training as he quickly overcame the obstacle and dropped into Tooley's hideout. Trying to ignore his throbbing left knee, he tugged hard on the string loop and deftly caught his worldly possessions in his arms.

Stowing his kitbag safely in the shadows, Jake quickly skirted around the empty yard and crept towards the warehouse entrance. Although he couldn't see inside, the muffled sound of humming and the occasional clank of metal confirmed that someone was home.

Jake paused in the darkness as the thought occurred that he might be walking into a greater danger than the one he'd just fled from. Whatever Tooley's mob had planned, it was something big, and Jake had made it quite clear that he wanted nothing to do with it. Now the bad penny was returning with news that Piggott's refuge had been raided and the old man was dead. Whatever else might happen, Jake had already decided to leave out the part about the priest being rudely evicted from his own body. Who the hell would believe a story like *that* anyway?

In the end, Jake's inner dilemma on how to proceed was resolved when a short, chirping whistle from behind rooted him to the spot.

"Well now, looks like I got myself a surprise visitor. How 'bout that?"

Jake instantly recognised Yellow's voice, even though his countryman was hidden by the shadows. "Jesus, you scared the crap out of me!"

Yellow chuckled and stepped into the dim pool of light leaking from the warehouse. "You're lucky I just didn't blow your dumb-ass head clean off."

Jake looked pointedly at the brand-new submachine gun in Yellow's hands. "I reckon the neighbours might hear your new toy."

Yellow's face fell, and his voice fell with it. "Just turn around and hug that door."

Jake did as he was told and immediately felt the cold weight of the Thompson's muzzle against his neck, while Yellow's free hand quickly removed the Browning from his waistband. "Okay smart boy, just open that door and step through slowly."

Knowing that for the moment he had no choice, Jake gingerly pushed the sliding doors apart to let a thick shaft of orange light lance across the darkened courtyard. He really had no idea what to expect, although what he actually *did* see was still very surprising, and very disturbing. For all Tooley's tall talk and obvious organisation, Jake had found it difficult to take some of his claims seriously. However, as he looked into the dimly lit warehouse, Jake began to understand just how serious these men were.

"Move! Hurry up."

Jake shuffled slowly into the building, his nostrils filling with the scents of kerosene and exhaust fumes as he looked around the largely empty space. Once over the threshold, he quickly sidestepped behind the left hand door. He was counting on Yellow instinctively trying to catch up in an effort to get his prisoner back in his sights.

Jake's gamble paid off and for a second he was hidden from Yellow's view, with only the Thompson's barrel and his captor's hands visible behind the door. Jake seized the opportunity by turning and grabbing the weapon, pulling the surprised deserter into the warehouse and sending him off balance.

Although Yellow had been ambushed, he had no intention of relinquishing his grip on the gun as he tumbled forward. Instead he used his own momentum to pull his attacker onto the ground with him.

Not wanting to end up entangled with an armed adversary, Jake let go of the Thompson and converted his fall into an untidy shoulder roll. Within a second he was back on his feet and bearing down on Yellow, who was trying to take aim and scramble to his knees at the same time.

Jake quickly dodged out of the line of fire and grabbed the Thompson's barrel once more, this time forcing it straight up and using it as a lever to push his opponent back onto the ground.

The back of Yellow's head hit the concrete floor with a jaw jarring thump, followed a split second later by the Thompson's steel barrel connecting solidly with his forehead.

Jake wrenched the weapon from the stunned man's grasp, only to see it slip between his own hands and clatter across the oil stained floor.

Yellow was quickly on his knees again, shaking his head to clear it as blood flowed freely from a vertical wound on his forehead. He lunged for the discarded gun, although the fog of concussion had made his movements slower and more ungainly.

Taking advantage of his opponent's weakness, Jake closed in behind Yellow to clamp him in a classic stranglehold. His arm ached and burned as he doggedly pushed his adversary onto the floor to avoid being thrown over the heavier man's shoulder.

Jake tucked in and held on grimly as Yellow's arms and elbows railed painfully but ineffectively against his ribs and torso. Pressing home the advantage, he waited until momentum was in his favour and rolled onto his back, pulling Yellow over in the process. With the larger man's weight pressing directly on top of him, Jake consolidated his hold by hooking his legs around Yellow's torso to tighten his grip.

Jake groaned and gritted his teeth against the pain in his arms as he grimly held on, his final position denying his opponent any further chance of landing a meaningful blow.

After what seemed like a very long time, Jake finally felt his opponent go slack, although he kept the pressure on for a few seconds more just to be certain.

Jake cautiously loosened his grip a little at a time lest his opponent was faking unconsciousness. Yellow didn't move as he finally let go of the man's neck and awkwardly rolled him over to one side, supporting his head to prevent it sustaining further injuries.

He bent over, gasping for air as he secured the discarded Thompson and fought the wobble in his legs. "Jesus Christ," were the only words he could think of as he raised his head and took his first proper look around George Tooley's London lair.

51

Jake wiped the last of the soap from his face and peered into a dusty full-length mirror. Although he disliked shaving in cold water, he had to admit that the warehouse was a good deal more comfortable than the open field. In fact the soap, razors and towels set out on a large workbench suggested that appearance was crucial to whatever scheme Tooley and his mob were about to pull off. He knew he was lucky to have stumbled upon Yellow while he was preparing to leave the place for good, as it was clear that nobody would be coming back.

Washed, shaved and wearing the fresh uniform Digby had so thoughtfully supplied, Jake felt a little more confident that he might be able to slip through the net which had undoubtedly been spread across London to re-capture him. He just hoped the darkness would hide the worst of the creases. For a finishing touch he pulled a glove onto his left hand and nodded with satisfaction. With a piece of linen rolled up to fill the little finger, the illusion was quite convincing, especially at night.

He turned away from the oil-stained workbench and crossed the largely empty warehouse to inspect four high explosive artillery shells clustered around a central pillar. Surrounded by half a dozen loosely capped drums of gasoline, the arrangement formed a simple yet effective demolition charge. Jake was no engineer or explosives expert, but he knew that whatever survived the initial blast would be consumed in a ravenous conflagration that would spread to yet more brimming barrels scattered throughout the building.

The mechanism to trigger that unstoppable chain reaction rested casually on top of a gasoline drum. Inert and seemingly harmless for the moment, Jake knew that appearances could be very deceptive.

He was relieved when at last he heard a groan from the direction of a solitary jeep parked in the shadowy, echoing space. Time was ticking away, and the sooner they could hit the road the better. He picked up a canteen of water and grabbed a blanket from the workbench before crossing to the last vehicle left in Tooley's London base. His tone was upbeat as he dropped the blanket on the jeep's fabric roof and sloshed the canteen. "Jeez, you look like crap. Here, drink some of this and use the rest to clean yourself up."

Yellow groaned, mumbled something and rubbed his bruised throat. It took a few seconds for him to realise that his ankles were tied tightly to the jeep's passenger seat, but once he did, his reaction was predictable enough. "Go screw your sister, you dumb hick!"

Jake smiled and raised his eyebrows as he reached into his top pocket for his glasses. "Yep, that's what *I'd* be saying if I was in your seat; but this is your lucky day, soldier."

"Up yours." Yellow grimaced and held his head in his hands.

Jake dropped the canteen just a little too hard into Yellow's lap before feeling in his other pocket for his aspirin bottle. He quickly swallowed two tablets without water before tossing them after the canteen. "Here, take a couple of these, you'll feel better once we're in the fresh air."

"Fuck you."

Jake took a deep breath and crossed his arms. "You know I could've killed you, right?"

Yellow sulkily picked up the aspirins. "So why the hell *didn't* you? What are you doing back here in the first place?"

"Your boss invited me and I need a guide."

"So take a tour."

This time Jake only half smiled. "See, that's nearly funny. I never had you pegged as a funny kinda guy."

Yellow opened the aspirin bottle, sniffed it suspiciously and tossed a couple of pills into his mouth before taking a long swallow of freezing, aluminium tasting water.

Jake handed Yellow the blanket. "You're pretty trusting for a guy who's all tied up."

"Like you said, you could've killed me already so why bother to poison me now?"

Jake nodded sagely. "See, I *knew* you were smarter than you look. Now tidy yourself up, you look like some kind of brothel brawler."

Yellow made no attempt to follow Jake's instructions. "You look more KIA than A1 yourself, even *with* those dumb peepers."

"Just get on with it, we've got to get moving."

Yellow looked sideways at his captor. "And just *where* might we be going?"

Jake's response was simple and undramatic. "To our forward base of course, and you're gonna show me where it is."

Yellow spat a mouthful of water down his chest. "The way I see it, one good turn deserves another so I guess I won't kill you when you untie me, but that's all you get."

Jake walked back to the cluttered workbench and picked up his Browning. "Have it your own way. I guess I'll just have to get by without the great George Tooley's protection; but that's okay, I've done it before."

Yellow replaced the cap on the canteen. "You really *are* a crazy man. Even if I *do* take you there, he'll probably drill you on the spot, and then me."

"That's *my* problem."

"Kinda seems like mine as well," observed Yellow.

Jake tucked the pistol into his waistband and returned to the vehicle. "You wanna know what I've learned lately?"

"Not really."

Jake ignored the remark. "Life's a road, a journey into the unknown, and on that journey you just *know* you're gonna wind up in a real crappy diner sooner or later. You might not like it, but you've gotta eat off their menu or just go hungry."

Yellow let his head fall back. "Jesus, you really *are* insane."

Jake pressed on. "Here's today's special, my friend; I can shoot you on the spot *or* you can take me to George Tooley and *maybe* not get shot. No guarantees mind you."

At last Yellow relented. "Sure, I can show you how to get there if we can make it through the city okay. Our chances are pretty good as the cops are gonna be real busy around here."

He pointed to the mass of explosive material in the centre of the empty floor.

"Maybe you're not as dumb as people say." Jake crossed back to the workbench and returned to toss a folded poncho into Yellow's lap. "Get that on. It'll keep the wind off and hide the worst of the crap on you."

Yellow grumbled as he complied.

Jake returned to the cluster of gasoline drums and retrieved the butterfly bomb that would kick-start the planned destruction. Once back at the jeep, he climbed halfway into the driver's seat and waited patiently while Yellow wrestled the poncho over his head and smoothed it down as best he could.

When at last Yellow had finished fidgeting, Jake hefted the diminutive but deadly device in his hand. "I guess this must be the detonator, but why the hell should Tooley go to all this trouble? I mean it's not like this is a military retreat."

Yellow grinned. "Misdirection and diversion. The cops and fire brigade are gonna have a busy night."

"But I guess *we'll* be heading in the other direction."

"You got it," confirmed Yellow enthusiastically.

Jake looked at the lethal device in his hand. "Jesus Christ, just what the hell are you guys *planning?*"

Yellow stayed silent.

Jake stared hard at his captive as it dawned on him that he was suddenly at a disadvantage. He knew he could beat an answer out of the man, but he needed his navigator in reasonable shape to avoid suspicion. "Please tell me you've got papers."

Yellow sounded almost proud. "Good enough to get me where I need to go. How about you?"

"Yeah I'm fine, I think." Jake pointed to the silver cylinder with its trailing metal fins, designed to slow the small but deadly bomb's descent to earth. "So I reckon this is a timed fuse."

"You got it."

"How long?"

"Ten minutes, more or less."

Jake turned the device over in his hands for a few seconds before speaking again. "Okay, how do I arm it?"

"Just twist the spindle all the way out and you'll hear the clock start, if you want to put it beside your head."

Jake followed Yellow's instructions, nodding with satisfaction as he heard a clockwork whirr emanating from inside the casing. "Clock's running."

"Then let's just get the hell out of here, right now." Yellow's voice had suddenly become a little higher pitched and more strained.

Jake ran to the cluster of shells and gently placed the whirring device on top of a gasoline barrel before fully removing the cap. He swiftly repeated the operation on the other barrels, allowing the flammable fumes to fill the atmosphere. He then donned his own poncho before running to the warehouse door and sliding it open. The freezing fresh air in his nostrils was a profound relief after the stifling stench of gasoline.

Having gulped down as much clean air as possible, Jake ran back to the jeep and jumped into the driver's seat before turning to his reluctant navigator. "Now you be a good boy and keep those hands in your lap. Don't ever forget that we're now dependent on each other. I don't know your story, but I'm sure you'll be doing hard time *at least* if we get caught, and I'm your best hope of making it out of here right now."

"Talk about a crappy deal," muttered Yellow.

"Yeah, life's just so goddamned unfair sometimes."

Both men winced as Jake stamped on the starter, aware that any stray spark might ignite the fumes quickly filling the enclosed space. There was no premature explosion as Jake quickly drove the jeep into the yard before jumping out to close the warehouse doors behind them, and then open the main gate in front.

Yellow looked back as they bumped gently out of the cobbled yard. "It's gonna be one hell of a bang; it's a pity to miss it."

Jake stopped the car. "Which way?"

"Straight across the river and head north. We'll take the smaller roads and hope we don't get stopped too often."

"Amen to that," was Jake's heartfelt response as they set off into the freezing December night.

52

Digby bent down to check that the old priest was still firmly strapped to his trolley. "I still say this is a waste of time."

Major Clarke seemed to be lost in thought as the cargo lift juddered erratically towards the upper floor.

The American snapped his fingers in front of Clarke's face. "Wake up, buddy. Listen, I'm as upset about Ellie as you are, but we've still got a job to do."

The Major absent-mindedly fiddled with Reverend Piggott's drip tube. "I intend to bring this whole shambolic affair to a swift and certain conclusion."

Digby's tone was flat and sombre. "Don't be getting any crazy ideas, Major. My orders still stand, even if I *was* dumb enough to try and help you out along the way."

The Major's response was less than cordial. "Jacob Small is still at large and we're really no closer to solving the problem of our night-time prowler. Your alleged assistance has not exactly been spectacular."

Digby looked back down at the grey man beneath the blankets. "You sure this isn't personal, a little payback for Ellie? Anyhow I'm now convinced that Jake Small's hiding behind George Tooley's skirts, and I chased *that* lead down the old-fashioned way."

"And yet still we have nothing to show for all our efforts," was Clarke's simple and blunt response. "All you have for certain is the word of a notorious smuggler and racketeer. So if you want to go chasing off into the hills on Pete Finch's say-so then be my guest. Besides, I'm becoming ever more doubtful as to which team your precious Sergeant Small is actually playing for."

"Oh Christ, not again. I thought we had this settled."

Clarke clamped his pipe between his teeth. "So did I until that nine fingered bastard decided to shoot the only person in this world he might conceivably call a friend. Personally, I think you're putting a lot of faith in one of the last survivors from Chateau Dessous, which was, by the way, the HQ of an infamous and hostile Sensitive."

Digby reacted angrily. "Now wait just a goddamn minute!"

Clarke's voice changed to match Digby's. "No, *you* wait! Dessous lies in ruins, as does Cedarwood House. Both leading centres for Sensitive research have gone up in smoke within the last five months, and the common factor linking them is a man you're willing to risk any asset or embarrassment to recover intact." He fixed the American with an unblinking stare. "I know you're a decent man, and I understand your motivations. You believe in the rightness of your cause and that makes you vulnerable to manipulation."

The cargo lift rattled to a halt but neither man made any attempt to open the doors.

At last it was Digby who broke the silence. "You sound like a guy who needs to get something off his chest."

Clarke looked down at the man strapped to the stretcher. "I'm beginning to wonder if your superiors are playing a very dangerous game."

"What *kind* of game?"

Clarke lowered his voice despite the fact they were alone. "I'm beginning to wonder if Washington hasn't decided to make itself the leading centre for Sensitive development after the war."

Digby thought for a moment before nodding slowly. "Yeah, maybe; but even if you're right I'm the *last* person they'd tell."

"That's true enough," agreed Clarke as he reached for the doors.

"I still think this is a waste of time," observed Digby.

Clarke pulled the heavy doors open to reveal a nervous Wilhelm Werner, clutching his black doctor's bag. "Perhaps, but this man's been harbouring Jake Small and so *I* want to know what *he* knows."

Digby helped manoeuvre the trolley out of the lift. "If I was in the States I'd go pick up Jake Small and then get back to this guy once I'd got them *both* in custody."

A smile flickered across Clarke's face. "Then it's a pity you're in England, Mr Digby"

Wilhelm stepped forward and pressed at Piggott's neck. "I must assume this is the man Dr Hammond described during his psychometry session."

Digby glanced around ostentatiously. "Ain't nobody else around here."

If Wilhelm understood the joke he gave no indication. "This man is gravely ill and I cannot in good conscience allow this session to proceed."

Clarke's face darkened.

Digby hurriedly stepped between them. "Let's just get on with it before this guy checks out and Jake Small gives us the slip again."

"You *saw* him?" Wilhelm raised his eyebrows.

The calmness of Clarke's voice did not reflect the expression on his face. "Stop wasting time, Wilhelm. I don't want this man wandering off into the hereafter and taking his secrets with him."

"Still I must protest."

"We'll be sure to put it in our memoirs," said Digby without a hint of humour. "Now let's just get the hell on with it before this friend of the Almighty leaves us with just the undertaker's bill."

Wilhelm sighed unhappily and began pushing Piggott's trolley towards the cluster of converted sheds. "I really don't know what Dr Hammond will make of all this."

"He'll make what he's bloody well *told* to make of it," was Clarke's heated response as he strode ahead.

"As you say," was Wilhelm's rueful reply as he pushed the comatose priest towards the prefabricated huts.

Dr Thomas Hammond seemed not to notice as Major Clarke stepped into the main office. He appeared lost, deep in thought with his chin resting between thumb and forefinger.

"Dr Hammond, you have a visitor."

Hammond barely responded to Clarke's opening statement.

Wilhelm said nothing as he scurried through the door after the Major.

Clarke closed in and grasped Hammond's shoulder firmly. "Still with us I assume."

Hammond started and looked up. "I'm sorry; I didn't hear you come in. I was thinking."

"The time for thinking is past. The time for *action* has arrived," said Clarke simply.

The man in the wheelchair blinked as though trying to focus. "What action?"

Clarke strode across to the switchbox and promptly shut off the electromagnetic cocoon surrounding the glorified wooden hut.

The sudden, amplified silence was immediately broken by Hammond's protestations. "What you doing, man?"

Clarke closed his eyes as a serene expression settled across his face. "Well I don't know about *you,* but that feels a lot better." He opened his eyes and crossed back to Hammond, grasping the wheelchair's handles and pushing him steadily towards the exit. "You have a visitor, a very rare and important sort of visitor."

Hammond immediately grasped one wheel with his good hand, causing the chair to spin on the spot. "You don't understand what's happening; you must switch that field back on immediately. We're all vulnerable here."

Clarke leaned down and whispered patiently in Hammond's ear. "If you interfere with this chair one more bloody time, I swear to God you'll never do it again." With that he bumped the uneasy psychiatrist out through the door and into the freezing warehouse.

"Oh my God!" Was Hammond's initial assessment as he was finally reunited with one of his early research subjects.

Digby lit a cigarette and thrust his hands in his pockets. "You look like you've seen a ghost, doc. Well you shouldn't be so surprised as you're the one who told us where to find him, more or less. Who would've thought it, another Sensitive hiding pretty much out in the open all this time."

Clarke began filling his pipe. "You know it's the strangest thing. It's almost as though nobody really *wanted* to find him. Once we'd decided to look squarely at that church then there he was, in plain view for all to see."

Wilhelm pressed his stethoscope to Piggott's chest. "I fear this man may expire at any moment."

"Better hurry it up then," observed Digby.

"Better hurry *what* up?" Asked Hammond suspiciously.

Clarke struck a match to begin building his usual cloud of noxious blue smoke. "One of my best operatives has just been shot by a man known to be consorting with organised criminals. Don't insult our intelligence by suddenly feigning ignorance, just get on with it."

"I will not. The strain of such an interrogation would undoubtedly be fatal."

Digby's tone was incredulous. "So you guys have suddenly found your morals, huh? It's a pity you weren't so discerning when you screwed this guy's head up in the first place."

Wilhelm straightened up and sighed heavily. "Major Clarke, you must understand that this man already has a very erratic heartbeat and is showing signs of respiratory failure. He's unlikely survive the stress of Dr Hammond's...direct technique."

Clarke chewed on his pipe for a moment. "It's my responsibility, and you have your instructions."

Hammond protested again. "This is a mistake. Although a lesser talent, this man is still a Sensitive nonetheless. He's been in direct contact with *at least* one other extremely talented individual that we know of, which means there's no telling *what* may happen if I intervene directly."

"I guess you'll just have to take your chances," was Digby's next contribution.

Clarke nodded in agreement. "If you're really serious about mending your ways then it's time to start taking some risks, just like those other poor buggers out there in the field."

If Hammond had any kind of retort in mind he kept it to himself as he edged forward and leaned down, clumsily using his teeth to remove the glove from his good hand.

Wilhelm gently lifted Piggott's limp arm and placed it in Hammond's grasp. "Now we must wait."

It wasn't a long wait. Within a few seconds Hammond's eyelids had flickered and closed, his breathing becoming dangerously shallow and strained as his chin fell into his chest.

Digby was about to flick his cigarette into the shadows when he stopped and leaned forward for a closer look at Piggott. "You guys see that?"

Wilhelm also leaned forward with his stethoscope. "Probably a nervous twitch. I would not pay much attention as it is unlikely that..." He tailed off as Piggott's eyelids flickered, opened momentarily, then closed again.

Now Clarke leaned in too. "What's happening?"

Wilhelm shook his head. "This is quite extraordinary," he said to nobody in particular.

"The whole bloody *thing's* extraordinary," Clarke reminded him.

Wilhelm seemed not to have heard the Major's comment as he abandoned his stethoscope and gently tapped the ageing Sensitive on his deathly grey cheek. "Reverend Piggott, can you hear me? Just move toward the sound of my voice. You are quite safe but time is short, you must surely know that now."

"Well I'll be damned. Back from the dead, huh?" Whispered Digby as Piggott's eyes flickered again and his bloodied lips began to move.

Wilhelm turned and listened intently to Hammond's heartbeat. "Yes, and that is worrying. I think we should be extremely cautious when dealing with this man."

Despite Wilhelm's warning, Clarke leaned still closer to Piggott's frail body. "You said he wouldn't wake up again."

Wilhelm tugged at the Major's sleeve. "He won't. I believe that we are about to meet somebody else, most likely your phantom of the tunnels."

"No shit! And you managed to figure all that out with just a stethoscope?" Digby's sarcastic salvo cleared the way for the coming attack. "Forgive my cynicism, Herr Dr Werner, but how the *hell* would you know that unless you've been holding something back?"

Clarke struck a match to relight his pipe. "That's a very good question, and one that Dr Werner and I will have many pleasant hours to discuss once we've concluded our more urgent business."

Wilhelm said nothing as he stared at the gradually strengthening Reverend Piggott.

At length the old man's eyes opened fully, swivelling this way and that as they tried to focus and make sense of what they saw. The old man licked his dry lips and spoke in a weak, dry yet discernible voice. "It's very dark. Why is it always so bloody dark?"

All three men surrounding the linked Sensitives looked at each other.

It was Wilhelm who finally broke the silence. "Are you in pain?"

Piggott's eyes narrowed as they finally locked onto the German psychiatrist. "No matter how far I travel in this world or beyond, I can never escape the shadow of your family's disloyalty. I suppose it's fitting that you are forever bound by the burden of that same treachery."

Digby and Clarke exchanged puzzled glances.

Wilhelm checked on Hammond's heartbeat before addressing the stranger on the stretcher. "I assume that the old man is already gone, yes?"

Clarke's question was simple. "Wilhelm, what exactly is going on?"

Wilhelm's response was not so simple. "I'm afraid you've been taken for a fool, Major. Although I must confess I fail to see the point of our visitor's rather childish act of bravado."

Clarke sucked at his pipe and frowned with irritation when he realised it had gone out again. "I've just recently warned you about your cryptic conversation style. I don't care for it and I shan't warn you again."

"Very well then, I shall be direct. The old priest is dead and gone, passed over. The man you see here is an imposter, or perhaps thief would be a better description. He's most likely the same Sensitive you've been seeking all along."

"Bullshit!" Was Digby's one word analysis.

"Just a moment." Clarke held up his hand and stared hard at the man on the hospital trolley. "If what Dr Werner says is true then I assume I'm addressing Mr Morgan Jones, if you're still *using* that name."

Not-Piggott squinted upwards. "It's still too dark in here. We should introduce ourselves properly as I doubt this will be our only encounter."

Digby interjected. "Well Mr Jones, I gotta tell you that's a real neat trick. Honest, I'm very impressed. You've used all that divine power and arcane knowledge to squeeze yourself into a body that can't even stand up by itself. That's a real tactical triumph."

Not-Piggott just emitted a wheezing, spittle spraying chuckle.

Wilhelm's eyes suddenly widened and he grabbed the unconscious Dr Hammond's wrist, feeling for a pulse. "Help me, quickly!"

Clarke's expression darkened. "What are you saying, Wilhelm?"

"We must separate them immediately! Hurry!"

Digby stooped to slacken Hammond's grip while Wilhelm yanked the wheelchair out of reach, only just managing to prevent the unconscious psychiatrist falling forward onto the damp concrete floor.

Not-Piggott didn't resist as he laughed again, this time a little more loudly and heartily.

Wilhelm slapped Hammond hard across the cheek. "Wake up, Herr Doctor!"

No response.

"Oh Lord, don't tell me." Clarke looked back down at the man on the stretcher. "Just what the bloody hell do you *want?*"

"I have everything I need, thank you," was not-Piggott's ominous response.

"I'm afraid it's already too late." Wilhelm's voice was grim as he lifted one of Hammond's eyelids.

"Is he dead?" Asked Digby.

"Not dead, merely absent," explained Wilhelm.

Not-Piggott's voice was weak, strained and yet the note of triumph was unmistakable. "That arrogant boy-fiddler never did have any sense of direction. One day he's for this, and the next for that. You should never trust a man without principles or commitment, except to himself and his own cock."

Clarke reached out to grab the man on the stretcher, and then changed his mind. "What have you done with Hammond, where is he?"

Not-Piggott's eyelids began to flutter again, his head falling to one side.

"Not so fast!" Hissed Wilhelm as he darted forward and grabbed the dying man's head, forcing it back before breathing hard into his mouth. "You're not getting away so easily," Wilhelm gasped between breaths.

After a minute of unsuccessful resuscitation Clarke gave the order. "It's all right, Dr Werner. You did your best."

Red-faced and panting with the exertion, Wilhelm leaned over the Reverend Josiah Piggott's lifeless body. "It's my fault. I should've realised, I should've known."

Digby sighed as he looked at the dead man. "Ever get the feeling you've been played for a sucker?"

Clarke looked across at the comatose form of Dr Thomas Hammond. "Yes I do, and I don't like it at all. He warned us that he was in danger but I just thought he was being melodramatic."

Wilhelm wiped his brow. "You mustn't blame yourself, Herr Major. There was no way you could have known."

Clarke ground his teeth. "That's no excuse for being fooled like a selection school amateur. *Dammit!* We've just lost our one reliable asset and got nothing in return."

Digby fished in his pockets for his Lucky Strikes. "Not quite nothing."

"How do you mean?"

The unkempt American lit a cigarette as he gathered his thoughts for a moment. "You're right about one thing. We still don't really know who the hell this Jones guy is or what he wants, but that don't mean we know *nothing* about him."

Clarke rubbed his forehead. "Perhaps I need some more sleep. What are you getting at, Mr Digby?"

Digby flicked ash at not-Piggott's still-warm corpse. "You know I'm still having trouble believing all this stuff. Even though I'm seeing it with my own eyes it still seems unreal to me. Anyhow, I'm no expert like Dr Werner here but it stands to reason that what we've just witnessed is no small deal. I mean what's just happened here is astonishing, even by *these* guys' standards. Am I right?"

Wilhelm nodded in agreement. "Indeed. To invade or, if you like, possess the physical form of another Sensitive is an extraordinary feat."

"Yeah, that's what I thought. An extraordinary feat which takes extraordinary skill, demands an extraordinary commitment and an extraordinary amount of energy. Meaning..."

Clarke finished Digby's sentence. "Meaning that whatever else he may be, this Morgan Jones character must be highly motivated."

Digby pointed at the ground to emphasise his agreement. "Right! If Hammond wasn't a threat then this Jones guy wouldn't have gone to all that trouble and exposed himself in the first place."

Clarke nodded slowly. "Jones must know that other Sensitives are a danger to him, even if they can only help track his position."

"Bingo!" Digby took a long draw on his cigarette. "What we need, more than ever, is a walking, talking, top of the bill Sensitive to keep up the pressure on our will-o'-the-wisp pal here; and I've got us a red hot lead on where to find the very best."

53

"It's just coming up on the left, slow down for Christ's sake or you'll miss it."

"It better be," Jake muttered as he took his frozen foot off the gas and let the jeep coast gently down the darkened country lane. At last the hooded headlamps picked out a gap in the thick hedge bordering the single track road.

Although he hadn't seen much of it in the freezing fog, this rural district felt much more like the England of Jake's imagination. Each village they passed through was supported by the twin pillars of church and pub, reflecting an agrarian life which had changed reluctantly as the centuries passed.

Yellow nudged his captor. "It's tight; you'll have to swing out to get through."

Jake brought the jeep to a halt in middle of the lane and studied the stout wooden gate guarding a shadowy farm track. "You sure about this? How often have you been here?"

"Often enough to know the route by heart. Here, you'll need this."

"Hold it!" Jake reached across and grabbed Yellow's wrist.

Yellow was indignant. "Relax, you'll need the key to unlock the gate, and it's in my top pocket"

"Left hand only," ordered Jake.

Yellow muttered some inaudible profanity as he struggled to follow Jake's instructions, at last producing a small key and handing it to his captor. "For Christ's sake don't drop it or we'll really be screwed."

Jake swung his legs over the jeep's safety belt and dropped onto the freezing wet lane. After a little searching, his torch beam picked out a heavy chain secured by a stout padlock, which Yellow's key fitted perfectly. Within seconds the gate was wide open and Jake was back in the driver's seat, gently manoeuvring the jeep between the two gateposts.

"Better lock it behind us," counselled Yellow.

Jake ignored him as he steered the jeep through the darkened and freezing countryside. Nobody would be coming this way by accident tonight, and if they were coming here deliberately then a simple chain and padlock wouldn't be enough to put them off. However, he did stop the car once they were clear of the road. "Okay, what's the setup?"

Yellow rubbed his torso with his arms. "Jesus, I think I'm freezing to death. One barn and a farmhouse, just give the signal and you can drive straight in."

"What's the signal?"

"Just stop at the fork in the drive and flash your lights twice, wait five seconds and then twice more."

"You sure?" Asked Jake suspiciously.

Yellow rubbed his body again. "Hey, I got you this far didn't I? Let's just get the hell inside. I don't know about you, but I think my feet have dropped off."

Jake tried to ignore the cold as he thought for a moment, still unsure of whether to trust his reluctant companion. He quickly concluded that despite the fact that Yellow was his prisoner, he'd had little choice but to follow the man's directions on faith during the past two hours. However, that realisation didn't stop him from drawing his pistol beneath his poncho as he bounced the jeep forward again.

They couldn't have been travelling for more than half a minute before the headlamps picked out both the barn and the farmhouse Yellow had described. The muddy access road split off to the right in a large loop, sweeping past the rundown house before rejoining the main track just a few yards from the large barn's entrance. Although the darkness hid many details, Jake's excellent night vision told him that although this might have once been a freehold of some good standing, its glory days were far behind it.

Yellow was more than happy to have arrived. "This is it, just flash four times like I said and we can get out of this damned weather before we both die of exposure. Man I hate this country, and I hate these goddam jeeps too. Might as well drive around with the roof down for what good it does."

Jake took a deep breath and flashed his lights as instructed. The barn doors swung open immediately and a cloud of steam, cigarette smoke and yellow kerosene light rolled out to mingle with the omnipresent winter mist. It was hard to make out any details, but Jake thought he spotted at least two vehicles inside the wooden shelter as Duke's unmistakable silhouette hurriedly beckoned them into the building.

Jake slowly let the jeep roll into the barn and parked neatly in what was clearly the last available space. He'd barely had time to shut off the engine and put on his sunglasses before he felt the cold metal of a pistol barrel behind his left ear.

Big Frank Tooley's voice was instantly recognisable as it issued instructions. "Just keep your hands right there on the wheel."

Yellow grinned. "Better do what he says."

"You son of a bitch," were the only words Jake could think of as Yellow reached over to lift his poncho.

Yellow grabbed Jake's Browning and pressed the muzzle into his head, this time from the right. "Now that ain't exactly fair. If I'd told you to flash *three* times you'd be dead by now, so just think yourself lucky."

"I hope your feet have got frostbite," said Jake quietly as Duke appeared at the jeep's passenger side. His customary smile widened to a broad grin as he noticed Yellow's predicament. "You're late. I guess you got kinda tied up, huh?"

Yellow was not so amused. "Real funny, Duke. Everybody's a comedian tonight."

Duke's smile suddenly vanished. "Brought a friend along? You know this party's by invitation only, right?"

Jake tried to ignore the pistols pressing into his skull as he spoke. "It's not his fault, just take me to the Guvnor."

Duke shook his head sadly. "You made a real bad mistake coming here tonight, boy, a *real* bad mistake."

"Yeah maybe, but I've got information for the Guvnor, information he'll want to hear."

Yellow smiled a little too helpfully. "But you can just give that to *us,* we'll be sure to pass the message along."

Duke produced a switchblade and sawed through the ropes binding Yellow's ankles to the seat.

Jake's prisoner groaned and winced as he slowly flexed his cramped and frozen legs.

Duke stood back from the vehicle. "You look like you need some exercise. Why don't you go and tell the Guvnor what we've got here?"

"My pleasure," was Yellow's sour response as he slowly clambered out of the car, his legs wobbling slightly. After thanking Jake for the ride, he quickly disappeared behind Duke's already parked ambulance.

The smell of straw, tobacco and gasoline filled Jake's nostrils as he tried to take in as much of the large and dilapidated barn as he could. "The Guvnor must be a regular tycoon, just how many places has he got?"

Duke's tone was disdainful. "You think this is some kind of ladies' club you can just walk in and out of as you please? We're playing for keeps here, Jimmy boy. If it was up to *me* I'd just erase your sorry ass right now and save us all a whole heap of trouble. That's what you are, trouble. You'd better just pray the Guvnor still thinks you're worth a damn after all the bullshit you've put us through."

Jake said nothing as he tried to ignore the gun barrel behind his ear and fathom some notion of what was about to happen. It was clear that, if anything, Tooley had played *down* the size and scope of whatever job his firm was about to embark on. The secluded barn looked more like a military command post than a gangster's hideout, with men and equipment crowded along the walls and four vehicles taking up most of the floor space. It was hard to make an accurate count of personnel without being too obvious, although he reckoned it was around a dozen men. He recognised some from the Dog & Duck or Tooley's now demolished warehouse, while others were complete strangers.

Jake was just wondering what a British GPO van and an American ambulance might be needed for when Yellow reappeared between those two vehicles. He gave a thumbs up and at last the pistol barrel vanished as big Frank Tooley stepped back.

Duke smiled and shook his head. "Looks like you've got a guardian angel after all." He jerked his head for Jake to follow as he set off across the crowded space.

Jake didn't want to consider the full ramifications of Duke's last statement as he clambered out of the jeep and limped after the larger man, the freezing damp having taken quite a toll on his already aching knee. "Hold up a second, I ain't as fast as I used to be."

Duke carried on walking, calling over his shoulder as he headed towards a small door cut into the barn's wooden wall. "Well you'd better be on your toes tonight, that's for damn sure."

Well aware of the close scrutiny he was under, Jake tried to look around surreptitiously as he hobbled awkwardly after his countryman. Walking a little slower than he really needed to, Jake began to wonder if maybe he'd been wrong from the start. Maybe the last big job of gangster lore really *did* exist, and it was unfolding right before his eyes. However, the arithmetic was troubling as he looked at the many crates of US Army equipment crammed into the confined space. No matter how he tried to divide guns by personnel, he kept ending up with a whole arsenal left over. "That's one hell of a lot of hardware for a bank heist," he observed.

Duke stopped at the side door and turned on his heel. "So you're an expert on strategy as well, huh?"

Jake was about to respond when he noticed that all activity in the barn had ceased and all eyes were fixed firmly on him. Sensing trouble, he hurriedly limped on, pretending to be oblivious to such frosty scrutiny.

Duke beckoned impatiently from the doorway.

Jake grimaced and limped a little faster, nodding to a man he recognised from Tooley's pub. The nameless gangster gave a surly acknowledgement before returning to his task of brushing several army and police uniforms hanging from a makeshift clothesline. Whatever was about to happen had been meticulously planned, and its potential size kept growing with each new observation.

The winter cold hit hard as Jake stepped out of the barn and back into the freezing December night. He quickly removed his glasses and tried to get his bearings. Turning a full circle, it became clear that Tooley had chosen his hideout with great skill as there were no other signs of civilisation nearby. Jake guessed there were probably a few similar farms dotted around the area, but they were invisible in the all obscuring mist. That swirling, freezing grey camouflage was a perfect co-conspirator for a big job like this, and Jake had to remind himself that Tooley couldn't possibly have organised the weather as well.

Duke's smiling demeanour grew sullen and serious as he pointed to the rundown cottage just a few yards from the barn. "The Guvnor's in there, and I'm betting he'll be mad as hell that you've hitched yourself a ride without asking."

Jake started forward again, eager to be out of the freezing damp. "Yeah well, I'm real sorry about that."

"You might be," replied Duke as he turned and made his way back towards the relative comfort of the barn.

Jake stopped and turned back. "Hey, where the hell are *you* going?"

The large deserter quickly vanished back through the small doorway.

Jake gave Duke's back a two fingered salute and limped on to the cracked and peeling farmhouse. He noted that for all its dog-eared appearance, the front door looked pretty solid and sported some new and substantial locks. He reached for the tarnished knocker before chiding himself for his own lack of confidence. He had some explaining to do, and he didn't want to start by waiting quietly like a chastened schoolboy outside the headmaster's office.

Jake had turned the door's new handle and stepped smartly into the farmhouse before he'd given himself time to wonder what might happen next.

54

The parlour was small and cramped, but it was also wonderfully warm. The shadows obscuring each corner of the room danced and swayed in time with the roaring blaze in the ageing fireplace.

Both George Tooley and Sam were seated at a chipped and ageing table, their faces shining in the glow of a stuttering hurricane lamp as they quietly discussed the imminent operation.

Tooley spoke without looking up. "For God's sake shut the bloody door and just wait there."

Jake did as he was told, grateful to be indoors even though the place smelled of dust, damp and neglect.

The two men continued their whispering, leaving Jake frustrated that his extraordinary abilities didn't include superhuman hearing. He thought of a smart comment about the house being warm while the barn was freezing, but instinct warned it wouldn't win him any favours. Maybe he was losing his nerve.

At last the hushed conversation ended and both men leaned back in their chairs. Sam looked completely out of place dressed in a flat cap and donkey jacket, although the ever-present glint beneath his workman's coat reminded Jake that he was still facing the very same hardened gangster.

For a while there was silence, save for the odd crackle of the fire until Tooley spoke at last. "You've got some bloody nerve showing up here, especially after telling me to sod off in front of my own men! By rights I should just let Sam here deal with you."

Jake flopped into a vacant armchair and fished in his pocket for his aspirins. "You know, I've had one hell of a day. I've been hunted, shot at, and I've probably killed one of the few people in this world I actually give a damn about; and that's just the stuff you might believe."

Sam pouted. "Poor you."

Tooley's expression never changed, and his unnerving stare seemed somehow more steadfast than usual. "Why did you change your mind so suddenly? Did Piggott persuade you?"

Jake felt himself relaxing into the dusty chair despite his precarious situation. "The old man's gone," he said simply, deciding not to elaborate on that factual statement.

Tooley sighed sadly. "Well, we all knew it was coming. You know he's the only reason you're not six feet under right now, don't you?"

"Yeah, and now that he's gone I figure you're even *more* in the market for a replacement. I've thought about what you said and I reckon you were right all along. A guy like me can't just go it alone, no matter *how* tough or smart he might be."

Sam interjected, and although his voice was quiet he wasn't able to hide his anger and frustration. "This is all a load of cobblers. You *must* know it, Guvnor. We're on the verge of the biggest job of our lives, probably of *anybody's* life, and this Yank just *appears* from nowhere." He looked pointedly at Jake. "I *still* say you're a plant, and you're clever enough to know that the only way to fool the Guvnor is to fool the old man...but you don't fool me."

Tooley tilted his head towards his top lieutenant. "Why shouldn't I take my trusted colleague's advice and just play it safe? We've got this far without you."

Jake stifled a yawn, the sudden warmth of the fire making him drowsy. "You change your tune more often than the goddamn radio. Early this morning you were practically *begging* me to work with you."

"That was *before* you decided you were too good for the likes of us, and now suddenly here you are again. You might not be a grass, but we're still just a last resort in those funny shiny eyes of yours, so why should I trust you now?"

"You trusted Piggott, and Piggott trusted *me,* at least enough to know that I wouldn't turn you over to the law."

Sam remained unmoved. "He's a risk we can do without. Like you said, we've got this far without him so I say we just put a bullet in his head and bury him out back. Nothing personal, me old china."

Jake returned Sam's icy stare. "I'm betting that *none* of you would be here tonight if it wasn't for that poor old man. Well he's gone now, and I'm the best pair of eyes you'll ever hire at *any* price. Hell, from what I've learned I've gotta be one of the best in the *world*."

Tooley drummed his fingers while he thought. After a lengthy silence he straightened himself in his chair. "Sam's right. When I think about it objectively, you haven't actually *done* anything except bollocks up a delivery, get my pub raided and cause me a real pain in the arse I could do without. You'd better just *show* me why I shouldn't cut my losses right now."

"I told you, I don't do parlour tricks."

Tooley's peculiar, unflinching gaze returned. "Well you'd better do *something* in the next five minutes or you won't be doing *anything* ever again; savvy?"

"You want a show, is that it? You want some table tipping, or maybe you want to talk to your great aunt Fanny."

"Don't insult our intelligence, Yank. You've now got four and a half minutes to show me why I should look after you the way I looked after Piggott, so you'd better get started."

Jake realised he was cornered and out of options as he stood up and awkwardly dragged his chair closer to the fire. "I need to be warm and it needs to be quiet."

Sam yawned and stretched. "No one to disturb us here, Yank."

Jake pulled a small wooden footstool closer with the toe of his boot. "Whatever happens just don't go prodding at me, I'll need some space to work."

Tooley glanced at his watch. "Four minutes, get on with it."

Jake quickly settled into the chair, thankful that it was fairly comfortable. He closed his eyes and concentrated on his breathing, trying to focus on the actual experience of his consciousness detaching itself from its earthly vessel.

Dammit! Jake was furious when he suddenly found himself standing in that twinkling twilight of the astral realm, with the instant of separation from his physical form remaining maddeningly elusive. He began to wonder if his disembodied consciousness would *ever* experience and remember the moment of transition between the corporeal and incorporeal. However, he did feel *some* satisfaction as he saw both gangsters' faces drop.

Sam looked at the Guvnor, his voice muffled in the peculiar underwater manner of that invisible realm. "Christ Almighty, that's bloody strange."

"Damn right it's strange," Tooley breathed softly as he stood up and hesitantly crossed the dusty room.

Sam followed, clearly shocked by Jake's sudden transformation. "Bloody hell! Last time I saw someone that colour it was my old aunt Dolly, and *she* was stretched out in the parlour."

Jake watched with a feeling of wry amusement as Tooley gingerly reached toward the empty body he'd left in the chair.

Tooley quickly withdrew his hand from Jake's neck. "Well I'll be jiggered, he's alive all right."

Sam looked around nervously, his former self-assuredness well and truly deflated. "He can't *really* be out there, can he?"

Tooley also glanced around reflexively. "Maybe; I suppose we'll have to wait and see."

Jake pondered his options as both men returned warily to their seats, their energies partially obscured by the fire's blazing orange glow, which spread across half the room on this hidden parallel plane. He'd already given them cause for doubt, but doubt was not the same as certainty. He knew he'd have to put on a show if he wanted to walk out in one piece, and he'd already decided on the best way to grab his small but sceptical audience's attention.

The disembodied deserter slowly skirted the walls of the room, coming to rest behind the two men as they gazed incredulously at his comatose body. He quickly brushed his glowing ethereal hand across the nape of Sam's neck, disrupting the unsuspecting gangster's glowing aura.

The distraction worked like a charm and Sam whirled round, his eyes darting in every direction while his voice had lost its coldly confident edge. "Jimmy, is that you?"

Tooley turned as well. "What?"

Sam glanced back at Jake's inert form, and then around the seemingly empty room. "Someone just walked over my grave."

I'm right here you pair of dumb-asses. I'm less than three feet away but you can't see or hear a goddamn thing. Jake waved sarcastically as both men squinted straight at him, yet saw nothing.

Tooley's voice was muffled, distant. "All right, I'm paying attention. If that really *was* you just now then let's see you do something else, if you can."

Jake smiled, or at least *felt* like he was smiling as he concentrated on a single stubborn memory that burned like a beacon among his increasingly unreliable recollections, a memory that steadfastly refused to vanish or fade like the rest of his personal past. *Welcome to my world,* was his silent greeting as he stepped forward and stretched out his glowing astral arms to embrace both unconvinced observers.

For a moment, Jake felt a little foolish as Tooley and Sam merely shivered and twitched...and then the explosion came. He *felt,* rather than saw the warning flashes streaking across the open sky of his consciousness before a kaleidoscopic blizzard of images and impressions suddenly overwhelmed him. Shadows of fear, triumph, sex, conflict, violence and absurd hilarity poured into the suddenly empty vessel of Jake's waiting mind, instantly displacing his sense of himself. That single, vivid image Jake had hoped to share with both men was instantly transformed from weapon to lifeboat as he desperately clung to it amid that roaring maelstrom of otherness.

Jake was more than a little relieved to suddenly find himself pushed back into the redoubt of his physical form, although he had no idea if his plan had succeeded as he suddenly felt the dusty chair beneath him once more, followed closely by the scents of coal and kerosene in his nostrils. He heard his heart pounding in his ears as he tried to lift eyelids still leaden with sleep, his jilted body resisting his clumsy attempt at a rapid reoccupation. Instead, it repaid his short absence with a bout of nausea that burned up through his throat and jarred against his chest along the way. His return to the physical plane was completed by a solid thump on the side of his head, accompanied by a bright flash of corporeal pain. The sudden smell of ancient dust confirmed that he'd somehow tipped himself out of his chair, probably as a result of trying to operate his body before being properly seated back at the controls.

Despite the pain and the vomit and the still raw recollections tumbling through his mind, Jake felt a surge of satisfaction as he heard Sam's voice somewhere in that dusty darkness.

"Jesus Christ! Just what the bloody hell was *that?*"

Jake didn't hear or feel anything for a while after that distant exclamation, until a foot finally jabbed him in the ribs. "You all right down there? Come on, wake up, this ain't no dosshouse you know." He recognised George Tooley's voice as the foot jabbed again.

Jake felt his eyelids, then his fingers, and then his limbs finally responding to his will. A sudden taste of bile confirmed that his other senses were settling back following their brief out-of-body excursion. At last he managed to groan and raise his head, his blurred vision confirming he had indeed fallen from his chair and thrown up over the musty carpet.

He suddenly felt hands beneath his arms as he was lifted none too gently back into his seat. A dented aluminium pitcher of water thumped hard onto the table, followed by an equally dented bowl.

"Clean yourself up for Christ's sake. Come on, hurry up." Sam displayed his predictable bedside manner as he perched on the corner of the table, his default expression of disdain unable to mask the paleness of his features.

Jake slopped some water into a bowl and wiped his face before using the remainder of it to rinse his mouth and quench his post-projection thirst.

George Tooley was back in his own chair, his face as inscrutable as ever despite the fact that his features were also a little on the pale side. He waited until Jake had finished washing and drinking before he spoke. "I think in a different time you'd have been hung from a tree or burned alive. Like Sam said, just what the bloody hell *was* that?"

Jake fished for his aspirins. "I thought I should introduce you to the kind of people I've been hanging out with, just so you know who's on my tail."

Sam looked first at Jake, then at Tooley. "Did you see something?"

The Guvnor nodded slowly. "Yeah I did, and so did *you* I reckon."

Sam's voice took on an unfamiliar and hesitant tone. "I'm not sure; I think there might have been something. Do you *really* think this Yank can make us imagine the same thing at the same time?"

Tooley thought for a moment before speaking. "I'm not telling you anything, and you're not going to tell *me* anything either, but if Jimmy's responsible for what we were thinking then it'll be easy for him to tell us *both* what we saw. Won't it, Jimmy?"

Jake wasn't sure if he'd managed to suppress the triumph in his voice, although he really did try. "If I did my job properly, then you'd have both thought about a dead German soldier swinging in a gibbet. I chose that charming image because it's something I saw not so long ago, believe it or not. Now I know you've both been around, but there's no way you guys could *ever* have seen anything like *that.*"

Both gangsters turned paler still.

Sam shook his head slowly. "It can't be. There's no way. It's got to be a trick, has to be."

"It's no trick," confirmed Tooley quietly. "Use your loaf, Sam. It turns out that that the old man wasn't the only one with some very special talents, even though you weren't supposed to know about *either* of my intelligence sources."

Jake spoke up. "There's something I should tell you about Piggott's information."

Tooley held up his hand for quiet as the farmhouse door opened and Yellow shuffled in, dragging Jake's kitbag with him.

Sam never took his eyes off Jake as he spoke to Yellow. "Anything?"

Yellow placed Jake's journal and his stack of fake identities on the table. "Yeah plenty, but nothing to tie him directly to the outside, unless you can speak German." He looked at Jake and shook his head. "Just who the *hell* are you, really?"

"Just a poor sap trying to save his own ass," was Jake's resigned reply.

Tooley nodded to Yellow. "All right then, we've still got a couple of hours until kickoff so make sure everyone's fed, and that *includes* your new friend here."

Yellow nodded and promptly left the house.

Tooley said nothing further as he looked through Jake's limited but convincing array of false documents.

"They'll hold up fine," confirmed Jake as he anticipated what Tooley was thinking.

Tooley slid Jake's journal across the table but made no attempt to return his assorted papers. "All right then, Jimmy, you've made your point. Get yourself over to the barn and get properly cleaned up. The lads will find you some spare clothes."

"He's coming with us, just like that?" Sam was still suspicious.

Tooley's voice was quiet, although it was obvious he was hanging onto his temper with both hands. "Don't start second-guessing me *now*, Sam. Piggott's gone and he was the *only* reason we've gotten this big and stayed this quiet. All the other mobs are too busy pointing fingers at their own blokes to do anything *really* special; and I'm not going to let that happen to us, not when we're this close to pulling off the job of the century."

Sam protested again. "Just cos he *says* his papers are good, that don't make it so. How do we know the rozzers, or the Snowdrops or God knows who else aren't out searching for every single one of these names?"

At last Tooley's face cracked into a smile and he winked at his right-hand man. "You reckon I haven't thought of that? We've got room on board for just one more, assuming our new man doesn't mind getting himself arrested."

55

Jake awkwardly wiped condensation from the window as the sleek Railton sliced through the freezing night. The fog had cleared unexpectedly ahead of their departure, allowing a large winter moon to paint the brittle countryside in glistening shades of silver-grey. They'd passed swiftly through several sleeping villages, only stopping twice for checkpoints at lonely rural junctions. As they climbed into the hills, the monochrome moon picked out a rolling landscape of fields and forest, punctuated by picturesque hamlets or the odd isolated farmhouse in the middle distance.

George Tooley hummed an ill-defined tune as he gently steered the car down an isolated lane. For a man setting out on what was obviously the most important journey of his life he seemed extremely calm, even jovial. Perhaps the irony of playing a fanatical lawman appealed to his sense of humour.

Acting as a counterweight to Tooley's good cheer, Yellow was anything *but* calm in the passenger seat as he lit his umpteenth cigarette. Clearly not a natural actor, he'd adopted the standard Hollywood monotone of Hoover's famous G-men when questioned.

Jake had played his part as well, adding to the deception by throwing curses and obscenities at anyone who dared to shine a light in his face. The cold and tired Home Guard were only too pleased to wave the tight lipped G-men and their villainous prisoner through their checkpoints and onto somebody else's patch. The implicit threat of retribution from above should oafish bureaucracy hinder their journey had also helped to oil the wheels of progress.

Tooley checked his watch. "Should be there very soon now."

Jake gazed at the picturesque but ultimately unremarkable landscape outside. "Couldn't you have dreamed up something better than my being a goddamned gunrunner?"

Tooley accepted the cigarette Yellow had offered him. "You should think yourself bloody lucky. We've had to improvise just to get you on board, and by the way it was a stroke of genius. Nobody wants to delay your journey to hard labour, or maybe even the gallows. Anyhow, we're clear now so stop whining and enjoy the peace."

"Strange thing to say in the middle of a war," observed Jake. "Where the hell *are* we anyway? And more to the point where are we going?"

Tooley cracked open his window and the swirling cigarette smoke was immediately sucked out. "We're just over an hour north-west of central London, up in the Chiltern hills. Beautiful countryside."

The moonlight vanished as they entered a wooded area, and suddenly Jake could see only a dim reflection of himself in the darkened glass. No matter how he twisted and tilted his head, the clustered shadows conspired to keep half his reflection hidden, lost somewhere in the endless darkness pressing in at the window. He shuddered and turned away. "Well that's real nice, but what are we *doing* out here in the middle of nowhere?"

"You know what's out here, Jake?"

"Sure as hell ain't the Bank of England."

Tooley chuckled as he slowed the car at a junction. "No, but the Bank of England's only about an hour away. The same goes for the War Office, Downing Street, the Admiralty and just about anything else you can think of. You'd be amazed at what's hiding out here, safe in the dark, out of rocket range but still close to London, and one another." Tooley turned left, this time heading uphill. "Chequers ain't far from here you know."

"Jesus Christ. You're kidding me!"

Now Yellow chuckled, and it was the first time his mood had lightened since leaving the farm. "Relax; you don't think we're *that* dumb?"

"I don't know, are you?"

Tooley changed gear as the hill became steeper. "Don't worry, son. There's no money in hitting a place like that. The point I'm making is that all kinds of people live quietly out here, tucked in between these green and pleasant hills. They don't like publicity and they sure as hell don't want anyone prying into their business. There's lots of shy people and places hidden down these little lanes and farm tracks, if you know where to look. Even more so since the war started."

Jake was mightily relieved when they finally left the shadowy woods behind, and as they reached the hill's sharp brow he was able to catch a glimpse over the trimmed hedges lining the road. The freezing moonlight revealed a rolling patchwork of wooded hills and open farmland spread across the valley below. He noticed a house perched on the opposite hillside with no obvious means of approach, then another, and then a third. With just that brief glimpse Jake realised that maybe Tooley wasn't quite so crazy after all. Whole battalions could easily hide in this gentle landscape while large, comfortable and discreet dwellings could be requisitioned for any purpose with no perceptible changes. He soon found himself wondering what might lie at the end of every darkened lane they passed. A farmhouse? Maybe; but who slept there at night, safely hidden from the dangers of the capital?

"This is it. By this time tomorrow we'll be living the high life, or not at all." Tooley's tone was only half-joking as they turned right onto a main road and then left again onto an even narrower, obscure and grit covered country lane.

Jake tensed as they rounded a sharp bend, to be confronted by another checkpoint guarding a substantial wrought iron gate set back from the lane.

Tooley turned in his seat. "Don't worry, I'll take care of this one."

Leaning forward for a better view, Jake watched Tooley exit the car and stride towards a lantern wielding Redcap. It was only when the two men shook hands that Jake realised the British MPs, their vehicle and the isolated roadblock were all fake. On closer inspection, Jake remembered that he'd seen those same soldiers leaving Tooley's barn about an hour before they themselves had departed.

Yellow sniffed the air. "Smells like freedom to me."

"Yeah, now that you've mentioned it," Jake jangled his handcuffs. "I'm done acting for the night."

"Not yet. Besides, the Guvnor's got the key."

Jake cursed inwardly and slumped back into his seat, using the short stop to study his surroundings more closely. Frost glistened on the gate's scrolling ironwork, making it almost shimmer in the bright, cold moonlight. He removed his glasses for a better look as the moon's glow was refracted through a million tiny crystals of ice, conjuring ideas of those other gates said to guard the entrance to paradise. However, Jake was pretty sure Tooley wasn't seeking admittance to the afterlife this night.

As he looked through the frosted metalwork, Jake's excellent night vision picked out a small gatehouse skulking behind a screen of trees. That gatehouse, coupled with a lengthy gravelled drive told him they were at the boundary of a substantial country estate. However, the obscure lane and lack of identifying marks also suggested that the estate's occupants chose to hide their influence rather than flaunt it. He was immediately reminded of Cedarwood House, and he fervently hoped that such a connection existed only in his mind.

After a brief and seemingly tense exchange, the fake Redcap jumped into his drab green Austin and backed it away from the gates while Tooley rapidly returned to the Railton.

Sliding into the driver's seat, the Guvnor tossed the handcuff key into Jake's lap before dropping a forty-five onto the seat beside him. "Time to start earning."

Jake rapidly freed himself and picked up the weapon, glancing around suspiciously as they bumped through the gates and halted once more beside the small gatekeeper's cottage. "Hey, where's my Browning?"

Tooley never took his eyes off the gatehouse. "We're all using the same ammo from now on, just in case we have to start shooting."

Jake's heart sank as he watched a second phoney Redcap frogmarching a prisoner out of the darkened cottage. Handcuffed, hooded and dressed only in pyjamas and coat, the bleary eyed watchman had stood no chance against the uniformed imposters.

"Badges on," said Tooley crisply.

Yellow tossed a piece of rolled fabric onto the back seat. "That's for you. Right-hand side and square on the chest."

Jake unrolled the mysterious bundle to reveal a linen square with a large number painted on it. With safety pins top and bottom, it was clearly a replacement for his name should conversation be necessary. "What's the point in this if our faces are showing?"

The sarcasm in Tooley's voice sounded out of character; maybe the stress was finally starting to show. "Well thanks for pointing that out, number Seven. I'm really glad we decided to bring you along. Got any other pearls of wisdom for us stupid Brits?"

Jake's response was cut short as the door opened and the second Redcap, who sported the number four, pushed his captive into the back seat.

Realising that he still needed to show willing, Jake immediately pressed the Colt's muzzle against the shaking man's head. "Get down in the foot well, hurry up! Just stay quiet and you'll be okay."

Yellow nodded approvingly. "Nicely done, number Seven."

"Go to hell, number Three."

"That's enough!" Snapped Tooley as he shifted into gear and accelerated smoothly away from the gates.

Jake quickly glanced through the back window just in time to see the stolen staff car reversing behind the gatehouse to hide from the deserted lane. He rested his foot gently on the prisoner's shoulder. "Just take it easy, buddy. There's no need for anyone to get hurt." He fervently hoped that was true as the car began to climb a gentle hill.

As they rounded a skeletal spinney of bare, glistening trees Jake got his first glimpse of their intended destination. He hadn't really known what to expect, but the entrance gate with its staff quarters had implied a grandeur which ultimately failed to materialise.

Although some details were lost even to Jake's night vision, the main house was something of an anti-climax. It was a rambling and homely looking pile of Victorian brick, although its proportions were far from palatial. Relatively modest and discreet, it was clearly a shy dwelling, despite the fact it overlooked countless acres of rolling park and farmland. Jake quickly concluded that location and privacy had trumped more grandiose displays of wealth and influence in the builder's mind.

Jake increased the pressure on his captive as the prisoner began to fidget in the foot well. "Just settle down, pal. Don't make me knock you out." He looked through the windscreen again as the Railton slid quietly up to the house, the hooded headlamps illuminating a solitary figure waiting beside a large front door that looked right at home sporting a Dickensian wreath of green leaves and red berries.

Although he was no expert in such matters, Jake felt that the combination of functional brick and the grey roof tiles suggested that the house had been built by a well-to-do country gentleman. Maybe a lesser landowner, a self-made man with a number of tenant farmers scattered across the valley. Although he had no idea of who they were about to meet, Jake was certain that Tooley and his band hadn't gone to such exhaustive lengths merely to discuss livestock prices. This place wasn't a jeweller's shop, a bank or even an obviously wealthy abode, so the true purpose of their painstakingly planned expedition was as much a mystery now they'd arrived as it had been when they'd first left Tooley's hideout.

The Guvnor didn't turn round as he issued his orders. "All right, this is it. From here on in I want everyone to pay attention and concentrate on what they're doing. I don't want to hurt anyone, but if somebody gets clever then I won't hesitate, and I don't expect *you* to hesitate either. Number Seven, you wait here with our new friend and I'll let you know when it's time to come in. Number Three, you're with me." He paused and took a deep breath before opening the car door.

Yellow followed suit.

The man beneath Jake's feet stopped squirming, his hooded head twitching this way and that as he tried to make sense of the sounds from outside the car.

Jake told his captive to keep still as he watched Tooley and Yellow flash their fake ID cards before disappearing through the door, along with the unsuspecting householder.

56

"Just take it easy and you'll get out of here in one piece." Jake reassured his bewildered prisoner again, even though he knew he was in no position to make promises. In reality he had no idea of what was about to happen, other than the fact it involved robbery with violence.

He looked back down the drive to where the winter moon's gentle, almost astral illumination stretched long shadows from the bases of trees to merge with darker patches of scrub scattered across the estate.

At any other time such a sight would seem beautiful, perhaps even magical, but the quiet countryside engendered no sense of peace or wonder within Jake's increasingly skittish mind. Rather than marvel at winter's serene and stately beauty, Jake found himself wondering what sinister spirits might lurk in those deeper shadows between the trees. He'd seen it before, and that recollection only increased his already strong sense of unease.

Suddenly filled with a superstitious desire to keep the clustering shadows at bay, Jake fished in his pocket and extracted his torch. Figuring there were no ARP wardens nearby, he illuminated the car's interior and looked down at his captive. He guessed that the gatekeeper was the wrong side of fifty and had grown accustomed to the sedentary life. Still clad in coat and pyjamas, the hapless warden looked as though he might've served in uniform once, but those days were far behind him now. Whatever this place turned out to be, Jake's portly prisoner was a far cry from the hardened professionals who'd patrolled the grounds of Section 12's HQ. That lack of serious security suggested the house had no real military or intelligence significance, which made Tooley's painstakingly planned operation all the more mystifying. On reflection, the place looked more like a target for common burglary than a tightly controlled and heavily armed raid. As he considered what little he *did* know, Jake was suddenly overcome by the wearyingly familiar feeling that something didn't quite fit. Something was missing.

Making a conscious effort to ignore the worry that something might be lurking in the woods, Jake made the mistake of glancing at his reflection in the Railton's window. The sheer shock of the ghoulish image staring back at him stopped his breath in his throat and chilled his very soul. Jake felt his heart lurch as he turned his head from side to side, confirming that he really was looking at *himself* and not some soulless wraith plucked from deep within the pages of a gothic novel.

Jake felt the final kernel of denial dissolving inside him as he was confronted by that inescapable, objective expression of his vanishing self. No matter how hard he squinted or tilted his head, the lines of his cheeks and mouth remained stubbornly smudged, poorly defined and unable to convey any meaningful expression. However, the eyes were the worst part, probably because they were entirely absent. The windows of his soul had simply vanished, to be replaced by two ragged and poorly defined pools of nothingness. Jake winked and blinked at himself but nothing stirred inside those fathomless smudges of dead darkness.

He quickly looked away and sought a second opinion. Sure enough, the face staring back out from the Railton's rear mirror was weary, unshaven and pale, yet it was thankfully solid, fleshy and alive.

With dread rapidly displacing unease, Jake slumped back into his seat and wondered how he could possibly overcome such a bizarre metaphysical malady. He knew that if he didn't find an answer soon then Sergeant Jacob Small might very well fade away altogether, to become little more than a misplaced shadow inside an unknown mind, the ghost of a dream chased away by the sun. However, that existential fear also begat its own resolve, and Jake knew he sure as hell wouldn't be checking out without a fight. This was *his* life, and he wasn't about to surrender it to a bunch of dead guys no matter *how* wise or powerful they claimed to be; and if a bullet through the head was the only way to beat them then so be it. Suddenly the idea of dying became far less terrible than the thought of living on indefinitely, trapped in the dark dungeon of stranger's subconscious, existing only as a fleeting sense of déjà vu. *Screw that!*

Jake was relieved when at last the front door to the house opened and Yellow beckoned him inside. He shoved the pistol in his pocket and opened the rear door. "Let's go, buddy. Nice and steady and nobody needs to get hurt." He waited patiently while the gatekeeper wormed his way out of the car before hauling him to his feet and guiding him towards the house.

Yellow handed Jake a rough woollen balaclava to match the one hiding his own features. "Here you go, this should improve your looks." He jabbed Jake in the ribs before bundling the prisoner over the threshold. "Get that on and get yourself in here pronto," he called out as they disappeared through a side door.

The mask itched and smelled somewhat greasy as Jake pulled it over his head and stepped into the panelled hallway. He felt ridiculous wearing both balaclava *and* sunglasses, but the glare from the oil lamps in the hallway was still too much to endure comfortably,

The house - whatever its name was - exuded an air of relaxed gentility. Tastefully trimmed for Christmas, the polished floors, soft rugs and gently ticking clock could easily belong to a retired surgeon or academic. It was a worn yet polished place; comfortably informal and steeped in the ambient odours of beeswax and cigar smoke.

A varnished door opened at the far end of the hall and Jake instinctively reached for the weapon in his pocket. He was only partly relieved when he recognised Sam in his workman's clothes, despite the fact his features were hidden by a mask much like his own. The Thompson high on his shoulder and the low number pinned to his donkey jacket left no doubt as to who was second in command tonight.

Sam quickly closed the distance between them and pointed to the side door. "Is the gatekeeper in there now?"

"Yeah, number Three just took him in."

Sam nodded and tapped Jake's own number. "Good boy, number Seven, you're quick on the uptake. Right then, let's get started."

"What the hell are we supposed to be *doing?*" Asked Jake, genuinely baffled as to what his role in the evening's events was to be.

Sam grasped the door handle. "Just grab that gun of yours and be ready. I don't think we'll have any trouble but I expect you to pull the trigger if anyone gets lippy." With that he pushed the door open and left the hallway.

With forty-five in hand, Jake followed Sam into a comfortable looking parlour. The orange light from the fireplace mingled with the dimmed, sulphurous glow of hurricane lamps glancing off picture frames and polished furniture. All electric lights remained emphatically off.

Two frightened figures huddled on a sagging couch. An attractive young woman sobbed quietly into a handkerchief, while a large matriarchal figure offered comfort and urged quiet. The captured gatekeeper and another man with salt-and-pepper hair sat cross-legged on the floor close by.

George Tooley turned up the lamps and stood in the centre of the room. "Ladies and gentlemen; first I'd like to reassure you that nobody will be harmed, provided you follow all instructions quickly and without question."

"Like bloody hell we will!" The gatekeeper's companion was quick to voice his dissent.

Tooley paced slowly across the room and stood over the defiant domestic. "You must be Mr Cartwright, the butler; or should that be, general servant?"

Cartwright said nothing as he stared up at his captor, his jaw jutting forward.

Tooley unexpectedly pulled a small stack of envelopes from his pocket and shuffled through them. "There's no need to attempt any deception here. We already know your names, and a great deal more besides." He handed one of the envelopes to the butler before distributing the others among the wide-eyed staff.

Cartwright quickly tore open his envelope scanned the contents, his face visibly darkening even in the dim glow of the fire. "How dare you! Who the hell…"

Yellow darted forward, the muzzle of his pistol hovering just inches from the butler's face. "Just take it easy, old fella. You'll be responsible if anyone gets hurt."

The older woman, presumably a cook or housekeeper, stared straight at Tooley with large, unblinking brown eyes. "My God. Just what kind of monsters *are* you?"

George Tooley returned to the centre of the room, checking his watch as the distant drone of an engine became audible. "I'd like to apologise for having dragged you all from your beds tonight, but let me reassure you again that we don't wish to harm you."

"No, just threaten our families instead. You're a cowardly bastard!" Cartwright's voice resonated with anger and bitterness.

Yellow pushed the muzzle of his forty-five into Cartwright's forehead with a solid thump. "I hate servants."

Tooley continued. "We know everything. We know your names, the names of your families, your friends and *their* families too. We know which pubs you visit and where you do your shopping. We can find you, or anyone connected to you at any time we choose."

The handcuffed gatekeeper finally spoke up. "I think we all understand the situation. What exactly do you *want* from us?"

"Nothing, Mr Forster. We want nothing from you, apart from your quiet co-operation for the next couple of hours. After that, we'll depart and you can just go back to fetching and carrying." Tooley began to gather up the letters and envelopes. "I shouldn't need to spell out what may happen to those close to you if the police or anyone else becomes involved in this matter, now or at any time in the future. If you *ever* discuss tonight's events with *anyone* I can guarantee you that we'll find out, and the repercussions may or may not fall on the offender's family alone. From now on, you're all responsible for each-other." He glanced across at Jake. "From time to time you might even receive a postcard or letter, just to keep in touch; and don't worry if you move house, we'll find you." He tossed the bundle of letters onto the fire and watched them flare brightly. "Just to be clear, any correspondence you might receive in the future is to be burned immediately. Once again, we'll find out if you fail to follow these very simple rules. Do not test our resolve."

The sound a heavy vehicle reversing on gravel filtered through the blacked out window.

Cartwright ground his teeth. "So we have to lie to the police or put our families in danger."

Tooley smiled beneath his balaclava. "You needn't worry about the police, Mr Cartwright. I promise that your employer won't be calling them tonight, or ever."

The parlour door opened and Jake immediately recognised the hooded figure of big Frank Tooley, although he didn't know the large man's companion. Each sported his own number, five and six respectively.

Tooley pointed to Yellow, Frank and his friend. "Three, Five and Six, you're on guard duty. If anyone gives you any trouble then shoot the whole bloody lot of them on the spot. Two and Seven, come with me." He made for the door.

Jake followed Tooley and Sam into the hallway, his breath suddenly showing in mid-air as all the warmth had rushed out through the open door. He noticed that the stolen GPO van had now appeared on the drive, and distant headlamps glanced off the trees as yet another vehicle approached.

Tooley checked his watch again, nodding with some satisfaction. "Only six minutes behind schedule, not too bad." He pushed open the door opposite the parlour and beckoned Jake inside.

For some reason, Jake wasn't a bit surprised to see either the comfortable panelled study, *or* the silver haired hostage gagged and handcuffed to an expensive looking office chair. This was obviously the homeowner and the operation's main target, but for what reason? Ransom? Assassination?

Sam strode forward and pushed the muzzle of his Thompson into the man's temple. "Now that we're all settled, I know you're not going to try anything heroic." He picked up the telephone receiver and held it to the man's ear. "See? Dead as a dodo. Nobody's coming to help, so let's not be stupid about this. We'd rather get what we came for with your help, but we but we can do without it. Understand?"

The silver haired captive licked his dry lips and swallowed hard as Sam roughly pulled the gag down. "What is the meaning of this outrage?" The prisoner's voice was well educated, and its origin was clearly European.

Tooley smiled. "I'm a disciple of Bacchus, and an avid reader too."

"I do not understand you."

"We've gone to a lot of trouble to view your private collections, Mr van Cortlandt."

57

Jake warily descended the last few cellar steps, his mind still reeling from the revelation of their hostage's identity. Personal experience and whispered folklore had showed him how unusually shy the van Cortlandts could be, and yet this was second member of that mysterious clan he'd run into in the past six months. There was no goddamned way it could be a coincidence.

He knew that he'd crossed the line when he'd fired on Ellie Parsons, and if the authorities caught up with him he'd most likely he'd face a severe "debriefing," possibly followed by a slow and undignified end in a secret laboratory somewhere. So with his life, liberty and perhaps his very soul at stake, Jake wondered why he should be at all worried about meeting the van Cortlandts again. But worried he was.

"Hey, wake up. This ain't a sightseeing tour." Sam snapped his fingers.

Jake recovered with a start.

"You all right, number Seven?"

Jake blinked rapidly. "Yeah, I guess so."

George Tooley studied the subterranean space for a few seconds before turning sharply to his handcuffed prisoner. "Just what the bloody hell is this?"

Van Cortlandt shrugged. "Just refrigeration and atmospheric control. Some of the vintages do not sleep well and they must be properly stored."

"Wait a second, something's really wrong here." Jake stepped forward to stand beside Tooley, both of them staring at the thick rubberised cables snaking around the cellar's walls.

Sam pushed their captive forward. "Never seen a fridge like *this* before, number One. Never seen a *cellar* like this before either, come to think of it."

"Me neither," agreed Tooley.

"That's because this is no fridge," Jake murmured as he cautiously stepped closer to the dividing wall slicing straight across the generously sized cellar. Clearly added after the house was built, that newer partition was all but covered by high voltage cables coiling across its surface, while a small and very sturdy looking door provided the only access to the chamber beyond.

Both Tooley and Sam were taken aback as Jake unexpectedly grabbed the prisoner and slammed him into the cold stonework. "Okay, Mr van Cortlandt, start talking. What the hell are you hiding down here?"

Van Cortlandt swallowed hard as the muzzle of Jake's pistol dug into the flesh beneath his chin. "As I said, it is just air circulation for our wine collection."

"We're wasting time, number Seven." Tooley's voice was calm but there was no mistaking his meaning.

Jake ignored him and jabbed his knee into van Cortlandt's crotch. The prisoner's strangled squawk was cut short as Jake shoved him still harder against the wall. "Don't give me that crap! This here's a Blank Space!"

The older man grimaced against the pain. "Who *are* you? What do you know of these things?"

"I met one of your relatives back in the summer. He taught me a lot."

Tooley and Sam exchanged glances.

"You are mistaken, sir. Whilst it is true that we are a large family, I can assure you that nobody else knows of this."

"Bullshit! What about Nero, or did you just kinda forget about him? What's in that room? What've you got that's so important you have to hide it from men like Peter van Cortlandt...men like me?"

Van Cortlandt shook his head sadly. "I'm sorry young man, but you have been misinformed. I assure you that there is nobody of that name living here *or* in Europe, if any of my kin are alive at all."

Jake pushed the muzzle still further into van Cortlandt's skin. "One more lie from you and I'll pull this goddamn trigger. It won't be the first time."

The older man's voice began to quiver. "You must believe me. There is nobody who goes by the name of Peter van Cortlandt, unless he is some kind of impostor."

"I'm warning you."

The older man's speech was almost a babble as he tried to explain. "I remember overhearing some stories about an Uncle Peter, but even if there was some truth to them he must've died while I was a child. I never met or even *saw* him, if he ever existed. I'm sorry to say that it wouldn't be the first time some pretender has used our good name for his own ends. I don't like to say it, but it's clear that somebody has convinced you there is more to our family history than just fireside fables and stories of sorcery."

Jake flicked off the safety. "Yeah, those stories are *so* much bullshit that you've spent a small fortune fitting this place out to keep guys like me from snooping around. What are you hiding down here?"

Tooley stepped in. "You'd better open that door before my associate *really* loses his temper."

"You don't honestly think I carry the key in my dressing gown?"

Jake continued staring at van Cortlandt, although his remarks were directed at Tooley. "Nobody's opening *anything*, not until we know what's on the other side of that wall."

"I *already* know what's on the other side of that wall, number Seven. Now just calm down and give Mr van Cortlandt a chance to remember where he put the key."

Sam weighed in. "Yeah, come on grandad, spill the beans. I'll even go and get it for you."

Van Cortlandt remained defiantly silent.

Tooley stepped closer. "Last chance to be sensible."

Van Cortlandt looked pointedly at the number pinned to Tooley's chest before meeting his gaze. "This is *your* last chance, *number One*. I will not be held responsible if you continue."

Tooley nodded. "Very well then. Number Seven, would you please escort Mr van Cortlandt back upstairs and make sure he's comfortable. Number Two, go and tell number Eight that we're moving to plan B."

Jake interjected. "Guvnor, this is a bad idea."

Van Cortlandt chimed in. "Your American friend seems to have some wisdom. You would do well to heed his advice."

Tooley closed his eyes for a moment before opening them and taking a deep breath. "All right, slight change of plan. Number Two, would *you* please take Mr van Cortlandt upstairs and tell number Eight he's needed down here."

Sam looked from Jake to Tooley. "All right, number One." He roughly grabbed van Cortlandt by the collar and shoved him back up the stairs.

Tooley waited till they were safely out of earshot before pointing at Jake's pistol. "Put that damned thing away before someone gets hurt. Just what the bloody hell's the *matter* with you? Do you think we're some kind of family outing, who wants this and who wants that? If you think I brought you along just to have you fall apart and bollocks this job up then you're in for a shock."

Jake rubbed his forehead, trying to ignore an overpowering sense of déjà vu. "Listen, you don't understand. Something's wrong."

"The only thing wrong around here is *you*. Pull yourself together! Perhaps Sam was right about you after all."

Jake took a deep breath and stuck the pistol back in his pocket. "Okay, I know how it looks but just hear me out."

"Make it bloody quick. I don't want the rest of my crew thinking this has suddenly turned into some kind of bleedin' debating society."

"Fair enough, Guvnor. For what it's worth you're right, I shouldn't have disagreed with you in front of anyone."

Tooley paced across to the studded door and gingerly touched the handle. "Too late for that now, so what's on your mind?"

"I was never a whiz at maths, but what are the chances of someone like me bumping into someone like the Reverend Piggott, and *then* coming across something like this?" Jake pointed at the electrically charged chamber. "Not to mention the fact that just a few months ago I bumped into a relative of our new pal upstairs." He jerked his thumb towards the ceiling. "I don't know how to figure it out, but the odds against must be in the millions. Hell, it's probably *billions.*"

Tooley pursed his lips as he thought for a moment. "What are you getting at, Jake?"

Jake took a deep breath, and then let it all rush out in a sigh of exasperation. "I don't know, I can't figure it out, but what I *do* know is that we're being set up. *You're* being set up."

Tooley shook his head. "Doesn't make any sense. Why would a man I've trusted all my life point me towards the biggest job of my career just to set me up, especially when he knew he was dying?"

Jake thought for a moment. "I don't know; I really don't know. All I know for sure is that we're wandering around the magazine with an open candle."

Tooley's eyes narrowed. "Jake, just what do you think is *inside* that room? If you know something then now's the time."

Jake grasped his forehead with fingers and thumb. "I've no idea what's in there, I *can't* know what's in there, and that's the whole idea." He pointed at the maze of electric cables covering the cellar extension. "You know that's not refrigeration, right?"

Tooley folded his arms. "Go on."

Jake paused for a moment as he gathered his thoughts. "Listen, I know that Piggott's been your point man for years. He hasn't just shown you *where* the best scores are at, but he's kept you tipped off as to who's least likely to call the cops *and* who's most likely to rat you out."

Now it was Tooley's turn to rub his forehead. "Jake, this might be amazing for an outsider to hear but it's hardly news to me, so what are you trying to say?"

Jake glanced around to check they were still alone. "I'm saying that your golden boy Piggott wasn't quite as hot as he made himself out to be, at least not for the short time *I* knew him."

"Jake, you're not actually *telling* me anything. Piggott was an extraordinary man, God rest him. He was never wrong, and he's not wrong now."

Jake resisted the urge to shake the Guvnor by the lapels. "Listen, I didn't know Piggott back in the old days, but by the time I'd met him he was losing it, high on laudanum half the time and too sick to really be any use."

"Go on," said Tooley slowly.

"At the end, Piggott wasn't doing it all by himself…I think he had help."

"From who, you?" Was Tooley's immediate question.

"Hell no, not *me*. All I know for sure is that it's some guy with a moustache who eats dead people."

"All right, I've heard enough." Tooley turned away.

Jake grabbed the gangster's elbow. *"He's* the one who put Piggott onto this place, and then Piggott told *you,* just like he always has. With his track record you never questioned him, why would you? Don't you think it's a bit strange that this last big score is protected against men like Piggott, men like me? Even if he *could* have found this place there's no way for him to know what's inside, so why bother to send you here?"

"I give up Jake, why? Pray tell, as you seem to be so much better informed than everyone else."

"That's just the point. We call these things Blank Spaces for a reason. I'm just as blind here as everyone else, so was Piggott, and so is the maniac with the moustache, but he must know *something* about it."

Tooley pulled his elbow free. "Now it's *my* turn to make a prediction. I predict that once we open that door we'll find a fortune the likes of which none of us has ever imagined before. *That's* what Piggott told me, and he's never been wrong in all the years my father knew him, and in all the years *I've* known him."

"This is a mistake."

The sound of footsteps and the clanking of tools interrupted the exchange as Duke lumbered down the steps. His smile flashed white as he dropped two large canvas bags and shook both Jake and Tooley's hands. "So, here we are. The big score, the mother lode. Man, I'm as giddy as a sailor in a whorehouse." He fell silent as he approached the dividing wall. "What the hell's this, an electric fence?" He turned and stared hard at Tooley. "Nobody said nothin' about no electrified strongroom."

Tooley stepped forward and grasped the door handle. "See? Now stop whining and let's get started, we're running late as it is."

"You'd better be right about this," Duke muttered under his breath as he delved into his tool bag. After a few blows with a lump hammer and some grunting on the end of a crowbar the door suddenly sprang open, pitching Duke into the darkness beyond with a curse and a clatter.

Tooley quickly suppressed a smile. "See if you can find a light switch in there."

"Got it, Guvnor."

Jake braced himself as the Blank Space behind the wall was finally filled with light.

58

Jake took a deep breath and clenched his fists as he stepped across the threshold and looked around the carefully concealed Blank Space. At first he was mystified, then even a little disappointed to discover that van Cortlandt had been telling the truth after all. The secret strongroom that so many had risked so much to penetrate was nothing more sinister or exciting than a wine cellar, albeit a very fancy one. Dusty bottles slept cosseted in wooden cribs covering every wall, as well as filling a pair of freestanding racks that dominated the room's centre. A muffled hum emanated from behind a small service hatch cut into the cellar's rear wall, presumably leading to a generator that powered the room's anti-Sensitive security.

Duke discarded his tools and grabbed a bottle from the nearest rack, wiping away the dust and squinting at the label. "You've gotta be fucking kidding me! I mean, no offence, but please tell me you ain't dragged us all out here for a bunch of booze I don't even *like!*"

Tooley held up his hands. "Will you relax, number Eight, you should have more faith in me by now."

Duke replaced the bottle and selected another at random. "So what gives?"

Jake felt his heart beating faster as a disconcerting sense of déjà vu crept through his consciousness, first diluting and then displacing his initial surprise. Without wanting to dwell on *how* he knew it, Jake already understood that an interest in valuable vintages was not the reason for their nocturnal visit.

Tooley quickly issued orders. "All right then. Duke, check that back room, and I mean *check* it. Then we'll have to empty every last rack and cabinet in this room."

A look of alarm appeared in Duke's eyes. "You're not serious, Guvnor? We won't have time."

"Then you'd better get bloody moving! Nobody's leaving until we've found what we came here for."

"Don't even know what that *is*," grumbled Duke as he made his way towards the generator room.

Tooley turned to Jake. "You'd better get a couple of blokes down here straight away." He tapped his foot against a freestanding cabinet, the bottles chuckling and chattering in protest. "These here fancy racks look custom-built so that's where we'll start. We're looking for some kind of safe or hidden compartment."

Jake wasn't listening as he paced slowly around the central storage racks, running his hands over the ageing vintages as a long-buried idea bubbled up through decades of dark sediment. He felt as though he was recovering a long lost memory, and yet his conscious mind knew that was impossible. Jake had never been near this place or anywhere *like* it, but that undeniable truth didn't prevent the intimate history of a long-dead stranger from dovetailing seamlessly with his own past. Jake experienced that mental fusion with such crystal clarity that he almost admonished himself for forgetting something which had never actually happened...at least not to *him*. He began to chuckle, his shoulders shaking uncontrollably as that chuckle quickly grew into a full-blown laugh.

Tooley frowned irritably and signalled for Duke to shut off the humming generator. He breathed a sigh of relief when the omnipresent electric crackle finally disappeared, although the dim electric lights helpfully remained on. Obviously the house was hooked up with more than one supply.

Duke returned from his recce of the generator room. "Nothing in there but a big old diesel setup. What's up with him?"

Tooley stepped forward. "You got some joke you want to share, son?"

Eventually Jake controlled his laughter before throwing back his head and speaking to nobody. "Thought you were pretty smart, huh? I guess you didn't figure on the likes of *me* ever setting foot in a place like this."

Tooley looked confused. "Jimmy, this is no time to start cracking up. We've got a lot to do."

Jake continued to address a crowd that wasn't there. "All your great big dead brains have backfired on you this time, that's for sure."

Tooley jerked his head.

Duke stepped forward and grabbed his countryman by the shoulders. "Come on, buddy, snap out of it. We ain't got time for this bullshit." He turned to Tooley. "Guvnor, just what the *hell's* going on? You said there'd be a safe."

"There might be one somewhere, but what *you're* looking for sure as hell won't be in it." Jake raised his head to the ceiling once more. "You're far too cunning for that aren't you, you bastards? You've really screwed up this time and there's not a goddamn thing you can do about it." He flung his arms wide and turned in a slow circle. "Well, what are you waiting for? Not gonna stop us? No bolt of lightning or fearsome phantom to chase us out?" He turned back to Tooley. "Just as I thought, there's no one here."

Tooley had finally lost patience. "Duke, take this idiot upstairs and get some manpower down here, we're wasting time we don't have."

Jake didn't hear what Tooley had said because he'd already started pulling bottles from the racks. "Forget about the safe, it's just a well-hidden decoy anyway. I remember what they used to do, it was camouflage right out in the open, although none of us was even *born* yet." He stopped and addressed the ceiling once again. "Didn't see *this* coming, did you? You thought you were so smart, you thought you had it all figured out, except that it's all come back to bite you in the ass, and now you're being cleaned out by a guy you've never even *heard* of. What do you think of *that,* huh?"

Duke tried to be diplomatic. "Come on, pal, let's go upstairs where it's warmer."

Jake ignored him, beads of sweat appearing on his forehead as he feverishly yanked bottles from the racks. "A red bird, I remember it like I was there...well not *me* actually, but someone else, and he's dead now. But then in another way I guess I *was* there, I mean if I can remember it then I might as well have been. Anyhow, we're hunting a red bird in here."

Tooley's tone was one of resigned sadness. "Just what the bloody hell are you blathering on about?"

Jake stopped and turned to face the Guvnor. "There's good news and there's bad news. The good news is that crazy old priest was right on the money, and this really *is* the last big score."

Tooley nodded cautiously. "And the bad news?"

"The bad news is, I know that Piggott can't have been up to the job for quite a while, and that includes him putting you up to *this* juicy little caper. My guess is that he added it on as a last stop before you guys sail away to the Emerald Isle, bejesus. I just couldn't figure out why you had such a huge arsenal for a simple job like this; but then you're not the *real* buyers, are you? I'm betting those guns are the IRA's going rate for sanctuary, at least until the war's over and you can move on."

"None of this sounds like bad news, Jimmy."

"Like I said, the bad news is that Piggott didn't dream up this last big job at all, he can't have."

"Then who *did,* and why?"

Jake rubbed his forehead. "I told you already, I don't know the guy's name but he's the real bad news. He must've convinced Piggott he was some sort of benign benefactor, and then the old man went and convinced you of the same thing. After all he was dying, you trusted him, and you couldn't pass up your best shot at every gangster's glorious dream, the final big score. I'll bet you didn't need *that* much persuading."

"Well, whoever this mysterious wizard might be, he's not here right now, so does any of this really matter?" Asked Tooley matter-of-factly.

Jake thought for a moment. "Maybe, if this guy comes looking for his slice of the pie later on."

Tooley's tone was philosophical. "Yeah well, he might just have to go hungry at this rate."

Jake opened his mouth to say something, then closed it, and then frowned as an intense expression overtook his features. "No wait, this is bullshit. It doesn't make sense."

"So says you."

Jake ran to the generator hatch and yanked it open.

Duke and Tooley exchanged glances as their nine-fingered accomplice vanished into the generator room, only to emerge half a minute later with a puzzled look on his face. "Where the hell *is* it?"

Tooley's tone expressed his increasing exasperation. "Where's *what*, Jimmy?"

"Whatever it is you came here for."

"We came here for the money that we ain't seen yet, remember?"

Jake shook his head. "No way. I know the money's *your* reason for being here, but that can only be *part* of the deal. What about the other half?"

Tooley's expression darkened. *"I'm* in charge around here in case you'd forgotten, and I've got plenty of questions I should be asking *you."*

Jake grabbed the central racking and leaned back, pausing for a few seconds as he marshalled his thoughts. "I'm looking out for *all* of us right now, which is exactly what you employed me to do. Look, we both know that you could've easily taken this house with just a single car full of guys. There's no way you need those heavy wheels for shifting money unless they're hiding bullion down here, but I'm betting you brought them along for something else."

Duke gestured around the dusty wine cellar. "I guess that don't matter now. There ain't nothing here anyhow."

Jake stared hard at Tooley. "What was the deal, George?"

Tooley folded his arms and also leaned on the racking. "What makes you think there was any kind of deal?"

A smile flickered on Jake's face as the pieces began to fit. *"You're* here for the money, the guns are for the Irish, so what's in it for the guy who helped Piggott put it all together the first place? I reckon you're not planning on splitting the profits with him. Hell, why *should* you after you put your ass on the line for it?"

"Well, I can't tell you how glad I am that you approve."

Jake didn't seem to notice Tooley's sarcastic response. "My point is this. Why should the man with the moustache just *tell* you where to find a ton of money without wanting something in return? What does *he* stand to gain from this adventure?"

Tooley's answer was three simple words. "Books and papers."

A look of understanding began to dawn on Jake's face as he nodded slowly. "Now I get it. You get the money, he gets the books and the guns buy you *both* safe haven in Ireland. Sounds like a great idea, except you'll have nothing for him when he finally shows up for real."

"Well that ain't my fault is it? You said yourself that neither you nor Piggott's mysterious pal could've seen inside this room, and it turns out he's guessed wrong about his precious books."

Jake grimaced. "I don't think he's the kind of guy to just accept the word of a notorious criminal. He'll probably think you're trying to screw him over, and you've got no idea what he could be capable of."

A smile twitched at one side of Tooley's mouth. "You might be right about that, but now we've got *you*. Seems I was right to give you another chance after all."

"Sure, and my advice right now is to find that red bird and get the hell out of here."

"You mean a bird like this?" Duke held up an especially dusty and ancient looking bottle.

Jake snatched it from the big man's grasp. "That's it! How many?"

Duke made a quick count. "A dozen or so."

Tooley pulled a second bottle from the racking. "You sure about this, Jimmy?"

Jake was sure. He was sure because he clearly remembered the van Cortlandts' preferred method for the discreet distribution of wealth. Even though that event had occurred long before he'd drawn his first breath, the recollection was clearer, sharper and more personal than much of his own increasingly cloudy history. "No corkscrew?" He asked as he glanced around the cellar.

Tooley's response was predictable. "Sorry, old chap, but we weren't expecting guests for dinner you know."

"All right then." Jake rapped the bottle hard against the racking, snapping off the neck and slopping the expensive vintage across the floor.

Tooley and Duke looked mystified as Jake slowly poured the bottle's remaining contents onto the swept flagstones. The air quickly filled with the fruity aroma of a good quality red as it slurped and gurgled down a drain hidden beneath the cabinets.

"Hold out your hands, and be careful."

Tooley nodded towards Duke. "You heard the man."

"Nothing like getting your hands dirty," quipped Duke as Jake poured the dregs of the wine into the big man's cupped palms. Duke's eyes widened as a number of small objects rattled into his waiting grasp.

"Oh dear Lord," breathed Tooley as he saw several cut gemstones glistening against Duke's dark skin.

Jake picked up one of the polished stones and shook off the last remnants of red wine, which looked uncannily like blood in the cellar's muted light. "Diamonds from Amsterdam."

Duke's shoulders shook as he chuckled. "Goddammit Jimmy, you really *are* the magic man. You can sniff out loot like a bloodhound on a skunk."

Jake was in little mood for congratulations. "Listen, right now I just want to get the hell out of here as fast as possible. I'm telling you this isn't the end; we're not safe here."

Tooley grabbed a shining gemstone with one hand and a full bottle of vintage with the other. "The cunning bastards. Jimmy, you and I are going to have a good long talk once we get clear and settled."

"Another one?" Jake replied acidly as he dropped the diamond back into Duke's trembling hands. "I'll send a couple of lads down. Any more than four and it'll get too crowded in here."

It was clear that Tooley's expression had darkened behind his balaclava. "And just where the bloody hell do you think *you're* going?"

"There's something I need to straighten out," was Jake's cryptic response as he made for the cellar steps.

59

Jake pushed the study door open with all the authority he could muster. "Number One needs you downstairs."

Sam pointed at van Cortlandt, who was handcuffed in his chair once again. "He said he wanted me to look after this one."

"Hey, I just work here. Don't you worry, I'll keep an eye on his Lordship."

Sam hesitated.

"It sounded pretty important."

Sam finally made his way towards the door, dropping the handcuff key in Jake's hand as he passed by. "Better leave you with this then, just in case."

"In case of what?"

Sam just stared hard at Jake before finally leaving the room.

Jake waited until the door had fully closed before he dropped the key in his pocket and crossed to the desk. "So, here we are, just you and me."

Van Cortlandt said nothing.

Jake half sat on the desk and folded his arms. "We don't have time for bullshit so I'll just get straight down to it. Why do you have a Blank Space in the cellar, and where have all the books vanished to?"

The older man's eyes flickered slightly before his face resumed its default expression of disdain.

Jake fished in his top pocket and produced the polished gem he'd palmed down in the cellar, the dim kerosene light winking brightly across its faceted surface. "You're in deep shit. We've cleaned you out, bankrupted you, and right now I'm probably the closest thing to a friend you've got."

"Friends do not rob one other at gunpoint," observed van Cortlandt quietly.

"Suit yourself. What *I* can't figure out is why you'd keep a bunch of books hidden away from a guy like me. I mean it's not like I can just go skimming through them, unless of course you're trying to hide the fact that they're missing. I'm betting those books belong to the Brotherhood, and I'm *also* betting they won't be happy when they find out their private collection has just walked off somewhere. Did you sell them or something?"

Van Cortlandt stared up at the Sergeant, a wistful smile spreading across his face. "You've been reading too many cheap novels, young man. It's true that the van Cortlandts have always been perceptive, after all, that's how we have prospered, but I assure you this so-called Brotherhood is a fable; a fairy tale peddled by those who must look to some mysterious force to explain life's disappointments."

Jake rubbed his forehead as a trickle of perspiration ran beneath his woollen mask. "Yeah, a fable that you've spent a ton of *real* money trying to hide from."

The older man turned his head away with a snort of contempt.

Jake felt the butt of the forty five in his pocket, and for a moment he was tempted to just beat the truth out of the guy. However, it began to dawn on him that maybe such crude methods wouldn't be necessary. "Let me spell it out for you. I'm just the sort of snooper your little setup downstairs was designed to fool, and if you keep playing dumb I'll have to get what I need by other methods. I reckon you already know what *that* means."

If the man in the dressing gown really *did* have any idea of Jake's meaning, he never let it show.

The American sighed sadly as he settled himself into a nearby chair and closed his eyes. "Okay, have it your own way. It's nothing personal." After a few deep breaths and some mental effort, Jake suddenly found himself standing in the astral equivalent of the semi-darkened study, just one degree and yet a whole world removed from the physical realm.

Silent and invisible, he moved a little closer to better study van Cortlandt's extra-physical form, although his captive's astral appearance raised many more questions than it answered. He wasn't surprised to see that van Cortlandt's aura was significantly stronger than average, although it lacked the searing ferocity of his now deceased kinsman. The older man was probably very shrewd, intelligent and highly intuitive, but he was no Sensitive of Jake's calibre; let alone that of Nero or Stryker.

He moved in closer still, reaching out to pass his glowing ethereal fingers through the outer edges of van Cortlandt's swirling aura.

The man in handcuffs caught his breath and shuddered as Jake's astral body invaded his personal space. "Is that you? Please say something."

Jake quickly withdrew his hand as he felt a surprising surge of fear and confusion. It took him a few seconds to understand that these were not *his* feelings, but an emotional echo of his captive's state of mind as van Cortlandt's consciousness somehow overlapped with his own.

He backed away from the frightened prisoner as he considered his next move. Although Jake didn't have the luxury of extended study and practice, he figured that such an intimate merging of minds must be something like the way Hammond had conducted his so-called "special sessions." Maybe van Cortlandt really *didn't* know anything useful, but there was only one way he could be certain in the short time available.

As he approached the older man once more, Jake consoled himself with the idea that it *should* be possible to conduct his enquiries and still leave his subject unharmed, more or less. After all, Hammond had been able to manage it...or so he'd been led to believe.

Relying purely on his instincts, Jake slowly reached forward again, this time placing his astral non-hands just inside the outer edges of van Cortlandt's aura. The hostage trembled and his eyes widened as he began to strain against the handcuffs biting into his flesh.

Jake reminded himself that the sense of rising panic he felt was not actually *his,* but merely a shadow cast by van Cortlandt's increasing agitation. Working through his intuition, Jake visualised his fingertips as miniature magnets, steadily syphoning a stream of energy away from van Cortlandt's ethereal form. Despite his incorporeal state, Jake soon began to feel an unmistakable tingle as he systematically gnawed at the edges of van Cortlandt's astral body, like a microscopic parasite attacking a single cell.

Sure enough, as Jake watched van Cortlandt's aura grow visibly weaker, his own ghostly form grew brighter and more substantial as he eagerly devoured the older man's very life energy. The glowing astral room began to blur and streak as a torrent of impressions, images and ideas began to tumble through Jake's consciousness, threatening to overwhelm his sense of himself like a storm surge swamping a trickling stream.

Within seconds Jake not only knew but also *felt* everything he'd wanted to learn as both their minds merged to form a third, new condition; like hot water pouring onto a sheet of ice.

The electrifying exchange ended far too soon when Jake was inexplicably flung back into his chair, with neither warning nor any sense of astral movement. He took a long shuddering breath, licked his dry lips and tried to ignore the post-projection dryness which always left his throat feeling like it was coated with sand.

As he waited for the rest of his body to regain consciousness, Jake was shocked to see the older man's limp and seemingly lifeless form slumped in his seat, with only his handcuffs preventing him from falling to the floor. He was relieved to see the prisoner's chest slowly rising and falling, but the fact that he hadn't finished the old guy off entirely did little to mitigate his own sense of unease.

As his living consciousness trickled back into its physical host, Jake began to feel nauseous, as though he'd gorged himself on a banquet of rich and unfamiliar food. Although he'd taken lives when he'd had little choice, this was an altogether different experience, and the forced exchange of energy seemed somehow sordid. Jake felt unclean, contaminated and even ashamed at having rifled through the most intimate secrets of another living consciousness with such complete abandon. He felt as though he'd committed an offence so unlikely and obscure that it didn't even have a name by which it could be condemned.

However, Jake quickly learned that retribution for such a cruel and unusual sin was swift, proportionate and entirely appropriate. He instinctively knew that just as he'd stolen some part van Cortlandt's very soul, so the old man had taken something from *him* in return. Although he couldn't say what that something was, Jake immediately saw the inherent danger of using his talents to forcibly extract information from others. He might very well learn what he needed to know, but there was every chance he might give away just as much, if not more than he brought back with him.

However, a simple and permanent solution to *that* problem rested heavily in his pocket, and Jake was shocked that he could entertain such a cold blooded concept even for a second. Could it be that his fight for both corporeal and spiritual survival was somehow making him less...scrupulous?

He chose not to dwell on such abstract ideas as he flexed his fingers and stretched his legs, before clambering slowly to his feet and shuffling hesitantly across the darkened study.

As he shook the older man by the shoulder, Jake found some comfort in the unspoken revelation that nobody, not even the shadowy and perceptive van Cortlandts, got their lunches entirely for free. "Where did they take it?"

Van Cortlandt's eyes fluttered as he mumbled something about a fat agent.

Jake couldn't decide if the older man was smirking or wincing as he shook him again. "The Collection, where did they take it to?" This time there was no response at all.

Frustrated but not wholly surprised by his subject's incoherence, Jake relented and flopped back into his own chair. The unspoken interrogation had confirmed his suspicion that the old man had bartered away the Brotherhood's private library in order to save both himself and his fortune, although that decision was beginning to look like a poor tactical choice. Jake had no idea of what was actually *in* the van Cortlandt Collection, but he knew it was important enough for the mystic with the moustache to break cover and strain every sinew in pursuit of it. Now that Collection was missing, confiscated by His Majesty's government in exchange for a fresh passport and a comfortable home, far from the horrors of Hitler's purges. It was understandable, kind of.

Jake was almost relieved when Sam finally returned, although number Two looked less than pleased as he quickly checked on their semi-conscious captive. He gave a groan of disgust as he realised their prisoner was literally dripping with perspiration. "What in the name of bloody hell's happened *here?* I've only been gone five minutes." He turned to Jake, his eyes narrowing. *"You* don't look too clever either. Listen sunshine, I don't know what your game is but you can be damn sure I'm gonna find out. The Guvnor might trust you but *I* still say you're trouble."

At last Jake felt the strength returning to his body. In fact it was more than just returning, it was roaring back! A buzz of electricity crackled through his system as though the very blood in his veins burned with the light of that uncanny astral energy. It seemed that his ethereal entanglement with van Cortlandt was coated with both sugar *and* salt, and he briefly wondered which would turn out to be the stronger of those two flavours. "Listen, I won't be cruel and ask you to *understand* anything, but just do as the Guvnor says and you'll be fine."

Sam bristled behind his balaclava. "Yeah well, the Guvnor says it's time to go, and that means all of us, so hand over that key, sharpish."

Jake slowly stood up, fighting a growing urge to dance, run and laugh out loud all at the same time as he fished in his pocket and returned the handcuff key. "What do we do with him? I guess the Guvnor's got a plan for getting out of here."

Sam expertly freed van Cortlandt from his restraints and draped one clammy arm around his shoulder. "Of course he has, you moron! Now just bloody well help me with this old geezer."

Jake fought a new urge to just punch Sam straight in the face as he crossed the room. "He's coming with us?"

"Of course he is, you great tit. We're not in the clear yet."

60

Jake leaned forward and squinted through the Railton's windscreen as it bumped down the drive towards the farmhouse. The return journey had seemed a lot quicker, so he figured they'd taken a more direct route back now that that job was completed.

He leaned across and checked on van Cortlandt's pulse to find it weak but regular, its earlier fluttering now seemingly settled. The old man was still alive in the sense that his heart was still beating, although Jake was becoming increasingly worried about the prisoner's mental condition.

It was only when the car slid to a halt in the darkened farmyard that Jake started to think about his *own* unusually upbeat psychological state. Perhaps it was just the simple exuberance of a man who'd escaped with his loot, but deep down he suspected it was something more significant than that. The only thing Jake knew for certain was that his initial misgivings had evaporated and he felt good, *really* good; better than he'd felt in a very, very long time. His mind was alert, nimble and superbly focused, as though the wheels and cogs of his consciousness were spinning at a much higher speed than the clumsy, cumbersome world stagnating around him. The stolen energy illuminating his mind bestowed a renewed sense of direction, purpose and even a little peace. It had been a long time coming, but Jake at last began to acknowledge the possibilities of his full potential. However, he was far *less* keen to acknowledge the risks of trying to realise that potential.

Sam killed the engine and nudged Tooley before addressing Jake directly. "Take those bloody stupid glasses off, you must be nearly blind."

Jake's response was simple and short. "I ain't seen this good for a real long time, maybe never."

Tooley stuffed two large drawstring bags into his coat before opening the passenger door. "All right, let's get moving, the lads will be here any minute and we still have a lot to do."

Jake stepped out of the car and looked around, increasingly aware that his perception of the world had subtly changed, becoming somehow deeper and more profound in a manner that almost defied verbal description. He couldn't shake the idea that the veil between the physical and astral planes had been stretched tissue thin, allowing the invisible energy from one to shine perceptibly through the other, like the dawning sun behind a stained-glass window.

Sam quickly opened the rear door and began heaving van Cortlandt's dead weight out of the car. "Damn you, Jake! This bloke should be able to walk, so either wake him up or help me *pick* him up."

Jake rounded the car. "You leave him be, I'll take him."

"Suit your bloody self," was Sam's churlish response as he dropped the old man back in his seat and followed Tooley into the farmhouse.

Jake grumbled as he hoisted the old man onto his shoulders and stamped towards the house. Only when he reached the creaking front door did he realise that Thomas van Cortlandt felt no heavier than a small child. He'd gotten used to the idea of improved night vision, but this sudden surge of strength, clarity and confidence was something new, and he liked it. However, a tremor of trepidation chimed its warning as he realised he could easily get to like it *too* much. Suddenly the forces driving his mysterious astral tormentor were a little easier to understand.

"Feeling better?" Was Tooley's rhetorical question as he watched Jake deposit their unconscious hostage in a chair beside the fireplace.

Jake groaned and puffed to give the impression he was a man straining hard. "It's okay, I'll just lift this old guy all by myself." He stood up and squinted against the glare of the fire that Sam was busy reviving. Even with his smoked specs the glow was becoming uncomfortably bright. "So, what's the plan? Don't tell me he's coming with us." He pointed to van Cortlandt.

"Don't be daft!" Replied Tooley as he deposited the priceless bags on the battered table. *"Nobody* touches those apart from me!"

Jake looked first at the bags, and then at Tooley and Sam. It suddenly occurred to him that in his current state he could probably overpower the pair of them and vanish into the night, with a king's ransom casually stuffed in his pockets. Maybe it was the smartest thing to do as he suspected that Nero had been right all along, and that the Guvnor would inevitably come to see him as a liability. Sooner or later the wily London gangster would realise that a man to whom no door was ever locked could never be anything *but* a potential security risk. Eventually the balance of that argument would be tipped by the weight of a single bullet.

The sound of an approaching engine interrupted Jake's train of thought and he quickly crossed to the window, shielding his eyes as a flare of headlamps heralded the next vehicle returning to base.

Tooley pointed at Sam and then to the front door. "Let's get those lads sorted out and changed, then we need to get the rest of the kit loaded; and for God's sake keep them quiet! We're not home and dry yet."

"Right Guvnor." Sam made his way out of the house, leaving Jake and Tooley facing one another across the room.

Eventually it was Tooley who broke the silence as he pointed to the unconscious man slumped beside the fire. "Want to tell me what *this* is all about?"

"Not really." Jake stared out through the window to see a second vehicle bumping down the track towards the barn.

Tooley continued. "You're a strange man, Jacob Small. Some folk might even call you a miracle, but *I* know that deep down you just can't be trusted."

"What?"

The Guvnor shook his head ruefully. "Keeping that old man safe and silent was an important part of the plan, but *now* look at him. What's to stop the staff from singing their heads off once they find out we've broken our word and all but executed their employer? Now they'll feel safer talking to the law than they will by keeping quiet, all thanks to you."

Jake turned his head slightly, unwilling to look Tooley in the eye. "You'd still be trying to crack an empty safe or loading crates of booze if it weren't for me."

Tooley nodded and jammed a cigarette in his mouth. "That's true, but we'd have loaded them just the same, and we'd have shot that peter just the same. It would've taken more work and more time but we'd have still arrived at the same place we're at now, and our main bargaining lever would still be in good health. It's taken *months* to plan this final job, and you've put us all in danger for the sake of your own selfish and unnatural agenda."

Jake homed in on that single word and retorted angrily. "Unnatural? Just wait a minute..."

Tooley pulled out his forty-five and levelled it at the American. "I know you're something very special, but that's just not enough. I'd sooner have a hundred loyal men of average intelligence than a single loose cannon like you."

Although Jake felt charged, strong and agile, he still didn't fancy his chances of dodging a bullet. "What *is* this?"

There was genuine sadness in Tooley's voice. "It's my own fault really. I let the idea of a brand-new and ready-made Reverend Piggott run away with me. I forgot my own rules, and that's always a recipe for disaster."

Jake watched another vehicle vanish into the barn. "Listen, you're not thinking straight. You said it yourself, if I was any kind of snitch then Piggott would've sniffed me out."

Tooley fished for his lighter with his free hand. "I know you're not a grass, but you're still a dog, and I never do business with dogs."

Jake winced when Tooley's lighter flared brightly. "Listen, George, we really don't have time for this."

The gangster continued. "If you lock a man in a room with a freshly cooked chicken, he might resist the temptation to eat it if you tell him not to, but a dog never will."

Jake frowned. "What the hell?"

"You see, if I lock a dog in a room with a fresh chicken, it's really *my* fault when that chicken gets eaten. The dog's just being a dog, and it doesn't know any different. *I'm* the idiot for thinking that a few stern words are going to overcome that dog's true nature."

Jake removed his glasses and rubbed his eyes. He still had his own gun tucked in his waistband but there was no chance of reaching it, even *with* his heightened awareness. "Well that's a real interesting bit of philosophy, Guvnor."

Tooley jerked his head at the unconscious man beside the fire. "You're a frightening man, Jacob. I've got no idea what you're really capable of, and I don't think *you* do either, but that's not my concern. *My* concern is that you were left alone with that prisoner for five minutes and now he's half dead. You're following your own instincts and your own impulses, even if you don't want to, and that can't work in a group like mine."

Jake replaced his glasses, stepped away from the window and played his last card. "Do what you want, but I'm telling you there's a guy ten times worse than me just waiting out there, and he's played us *all* for suckers. Christ knows what he *really* wants but my guess is you'll be finding that out pretty soon, especially when you tell him his books have gone missing. You guys are so damned crazy you might even *make* it to Ireland after all, but do you really think our mystery man won't turn up sooner or later? Do you *really* want to face him by yourself, without someone like me in your corner?"

"We'll overcome, we always do."

Despite his imminent execution, Jake's attention was drawn to a sudden movement outside the window. Time froze as a small object drew a slow arc towards the house, winking in the moonlight before it struck the outside wall with a metallic clunk.

Training took over, and Jake just had time to hurl himself to the ground before the phosphorus grenade spewed its murderous contents across the front of the house. He covered his head as the window caved in and the mildewed curtains burst into flames. Within seconds the room was a featureless field of stifling, blinding and stinging white smoke. There was a muzzle flash and a loud report as Tooley fired off a round, although Jake couldn't be sure of just who he was shooting at. In any case, he figured it was safe to move when he heard the Guvnor clatter out through the parlour's rear door.

Ignoring the shattered glass around him, Jake quickly crawled towards van Cortlandt's chair, his abnormal night vision rendered useless by the thick phosphorous fog. It only took a few seconds to find the old man's unconscious form and hoist it back onto his shoulder, but Jake knew he was running out of time as he fought hard to prevent a choking fit from flooring the pair of them. He only had seconds left before he started losing consciousness.

Jake heard fresh gunfire and grenades outside as he reeled into the rear hallway. Kicking the parlour door shut behind him, he laid van Cortlandt down on the threadbare rug, hoping the already comatose prisoner might avoid the worst of the smoke. He quickly ran his hands through his hair and over his head before methodically checking his body to ensure there were no chunks of that deadly searing chemical lodged in his clothes, eagerly eating their way towards his skin.

Jake couldn't actually *see* who was attacking the farmhouse, but it didn't take a genius to figure out that Mr Digby, Major Clarke and their pals were closing in. He was confident that the raiders couldn't just rush into that smoke-filled front room, unless they had gas masks, so Jake guessed he had maybe half a minute to make it out through the back door. He just hoped they weren't already waiting outside.

He bent down and heaved van Cortlandt's dead weight back onto his shoulders before grabbing the wall to steady himself. The toxic smoke had made both his head and stomach spin as he yanked the Colt from his waistband and stumbled towards the relative safety of the back garden.

Jake briefly wondered where George Tooley had got to as at last he staggered into the freezing December night. His unspoken question was immediately answered by a muzzle flash and a sudden hammerblow to his right arm. He caught a glimpse of Tooley's silhouette vanishing into the night as his legs folded beneath him.

The only thing Jake could do was clamp his jaw shut to save his tongue as the ground rushed up to meet him.

61

Jake opened his eyes, for a moment unsure of where he was or how long he'd been unconscious. The numbing pain in his arm, the stink of phosphorus in his nostrils and the dead weight of the old man on top of him confirmed that he'd only blacked out for a few seconds. No out of body experience this time, just a simple loss of consciousness.

Using his good arm and scrambling backwards, Jake managed to roll the unconscious van Cortlandt into a weed-choked flowerbed. He'd done enough to keep the old man alive and he didn't seem too badly hurt, at least not in the physical sense.

Jake quickly hauled himself into a sitting position, grateful that his thick winter clothes had taken at least some of the sting out of the forty-five slug that had knocked him down. However, the tear in his jacket and the blood flowing freely from of his sleeve confirmed that he'd suffered more than just a flesh wound. He was bleeding badly.

He gritted his teeth and growled against the pain as he clambered to his feet and blinked away smoke-induced tears as he tried to assess the situation. Judging by the gunfire echoing through the freezing night, it was clear that George Tooley's hideout had been raided by a substantial force, most likely army or perhaps military police. He wasn't sure why they'd launched their attack before properly surrounding the house, but he wasn't about to let that mistake go to waste.

Jake knew he had to move fast, but to where? Behind him stood the house and that was no good. To his left was the barn and to the right loomed a high and thick looking hedge, ruling out both of those directions. Quickly realising that straight ahead was his only real option, Jake awkwardly picked up his weapon with his left hand and set off into the night.

The dilapidated farmhouse's dilapidated garden was largely overgrown, with only the remnants of a path showing beneath a layer of freezing mist that hugged the ground and obscured his feet. Within seconds Jake was across the treacherous lawn and into an even *more* tangled orchard, where neglected fruit trees competed for space with rampant nettles and brambles.

Jake set off after George Tooley, who was vaulting over a crumbling and partially collapsed wall separating that half-strangled orchard from the surrounding fields. He'd only taken a few steps before he slid to a halt, losing his footing on the icy grass when Tooley suddenly popped up from behind that very same wall with his pistol held level and ready to fire. Jake fell painfully onto his back, the impact forcing the wind from his chest and releasing a wave of agony to radiate out from his wounded arm. Lying there momentarily stunned, he could only watch as three quick muzzle flashes illuminated the orchard like lightning, followed by the thunder-crack of Tooley's automatic.

Jake braced himself for the impact, only realising he was not the intended target when a burst of automatic fire from the house sent the gangster diving for cover amid a shower of brick shards. The trap was closing, and Jake knew he had to make a break for it before he was completely outflanked.

The cold, numbing pain in his arm made it hard to concentrate as Jake rose to his knees and squeezed off three rounds of his own to send the pursuers diving for cover. He wasn't really sure if he was aiming at anyone or not, although he had no time to consider the point as he staggered to his feet and stumbled after the fleeing gangster. The bullet wound and the sudden smoke attack were beginning to take their toll as he felt a soaking sweat breaking out across his body, despite the sub-zero conditions.

At last he reached the boundary wall and half-vaulted, half-fell over its lowest point, the effort leaving him lying in a freezing wet field. Although he was certain his endurance was enhanced by the energy he'd recently stolen, Jake also knew that unnatural boost didn't make him anything *close* to some sort of indestructible superman. He was weakening fast.

Jake struggled to his knees again and looked up to see George Tooley about thirty yards ahead of him, panting, caked with mud and taking aim once more. He instinctively dropped back into the mud, trying to keep his wounded arm above the frozen wet soil. He still couldn't be sure if Tooley was aiming at *him* or the raiders swarming through the overgrown garden, but he was sure that the Guvnor wouldn't shed any tears regardless of *who* he hit.

Hoping he was hidden by the low-lying mist, Jake watched Tooley disappear once more, this time vanishing behind the brow of a gentle rise. He began to wonder if blood loss was causing his brain to misfire as he immediately thought of that dead, grey nothingness marking the boundary between a Sensitive's multi-faceted realm and that silent, nameless, other place that lay far beyond the reach of the living.

Pushing that grim association out of his mind, Jake rolled onto his back and loosed off a couple of rounds at the advancing soldiers who were cautiously peeping over the orchard wall, grunting with satisfaction as he heard bullets ricocheting off brickwork. With any luck, the prospect of two desperate men willing to open fire might caution their would-be captors against charging headlong into the darkness after them.

Jake clambered breathlessly to his feet once more, his every movement an exhausting effort. His right arm had lost all feeling and dangled uselessly as he fought against the cloying, sucking mud that turned his boots to diving weights and sapped the strength from his already trembling legs. His leaden feet vanished beneath the low-lying mist with every shuffling step, only adding to the idea that the ground itself was eager to pull him beneath the surface.

Wounded, hopelessly outnumbered and growing increasingly tired, Jake knew it was just a matter of time. It was almost a relief when his knees finally folded and he collapsed into the freezing mud once more. As he rolled onto his back for the last time he heard a familiar voice, although it sounded distant and muffled as he drifted towards the painless oblivion of unconsciousness.

"I knew it! I *knew* you were a grass, no matter what the Guvnor *or* that cancer riddled old duffer told me. I should've trusted my guts and sorted you out while I had the chance. Still, it's never too late."

Jake feared the worst as a silhouette loomed large across the darkened sky above him. He braced himself for some kind of otherworldly assault as the physical plane slipped further from his perception, like a radio signal fading to a distant static hiss.

In the end it was no mysterious astral energy but a pursuing soldier's torch beam that revealed Sam's rage-twisted features. Only then did Jake understand he was experiencing no metaphysical revelation as he stared straight up the barrel of a gun held by a man who'd never liked him, and now had nothing to lose.

Soaking wet, with a bloody nose and a half-closed eye, Sam looked like he'd done some hard fighting to make it out of that barn and into the fields, and it was painfully clear who he held responsible for the surprise raid on Tooley's hideout.

With his vision dimming and the sounds of the world fading into the distance, Jake raised his own weapon and even managed to fire off a left-handed shot before the Colt slipped from his grasp to squelch onto the sodden ground. He had nothing left.

Facing his last moments, on this plane at least, Jake's mind spontaneously replayed the highlights of his early training and deployment to England, followed by that bloodied bocage slog through France and ending with his bizarre adventures back in Britain. Who would've thought it could end up like this? No crack German sniper would be the author of *his* demise, just an angry Englishman who wasn't even a soldier.

If he'd had the strength left, Jake would've laughed as Sam cursed with rage when the last round in his American gun stubbornly refused to fire. However it was only a short reprieve as Sam quickly cleared the jam, reloaded and took aim, savouring one last moment of defiance and retribution before his inevitable capture.

Jake's world was fading fast, and he distantly realised that his life's last memory would be watching a reluctant American gun being fired by an eager Englishman. Whatever else might follow his passing, he was doubtful if anything would ever top *that* kind of absurdity. He'd miss the world for its sense of the ridiculous if nothing else.

He never even felt it when the final shot came, in fact he barely even heard it. As the darkness quickly closed in, Jake was vaguely aware of some muffled voices nearby, although he couldn't make out what they were saying. It was upsetting to think that perhaps the last sensation he'd ever experience in this world was one of feeling so very, very cold.

62

After a moment of silent darkness, Jake became conscious of himself and his surroundings once again. The ethereal glow of the sleeping hedgerows and the brighter luminescence of the approaching soldiers confirmed that he'd escaped his battered body and slipped unnoticed onto the astral plane. However, his brief respite from physical torment brought little comfort as he inspected his own supposedly resilient astral form. Stuttering weakly and entirely absent in places, it looked to Jake as though his very *spirit* was bleeding out right before his disembodied eyes, and he was mortified to think of what his abandoned corporeal shell might look like.

Jake knew he had to look, and yet he was terrified of what he might see. If he refused to look then he might miss a vital chance to save himself, but on the other hand he could end up facing the absolute certainty of his own imminent demise.

Knowing that in the end he had very little choice, Jake mentally steeled himself, turned and looked across the field to where his empty physical frame lay slumped in a waterlogged farmer's furrow.

It was everything he'd feared.

Jake had sometimes wondered how he might meet his end, especially since the Cedarwood episode had made his day-to-day existence that much more precarious. He didn't fear death, as he'd learned first-hand that there could perhaps be *some* kind of afterwards, at least for him. What he hadn't anticipated was breathing his last in a frozen English field just a few days before Christmas. It just somehow felt so *wrong* that the final result of all that fighting and running and struggling was the stark, gothic terror of watching his own life seeping into the sodden, uncaring earth. He felt a tide of anger and resentment building inside as he bore silent witness to his own demise. It just *couldn't* end here, like this, not after everything he'd been through.

He knew he needed to bolster his astral form quickly if he hoped to salvage what little remained of his physical life, and it didn't take long for his gaze to focus on a most unlikely and yet entirely suitable saviour. Sam was still very much alive, although his right leg was shattered by a rifle bullet and his aura stuttered between agony and rage as he tried to crawl away into the darkness.

Jake was both amazed and appalled at the new ideas suddenly springing from his increasingly unruly imagination, however the more he thought about the radical plan forming in his mind the more it made sense, kind of. After all, he'd already died and returned to the living world once before, so why not twice? Although Peter van Cortlandt was no longer able to help him, Jake figured he had a slim chance of repeating such a feat on his own if he moved fast. The afterlife would surely welcome him one day, but he planned on spending as much time in the physical world as he could before he was finally evicted.

He briefly forgot about Sam as half a dozen young, healthy and undamaged soldiers finally advanced to surround the injured fugitives sprawled across the sodden ground. For more than a couple of seconds, Jake wondered if he could oust one of those more sprightly soldiers from his physical form and simply take over. After all, why re-occupy a wounded and weakened body when perhaps he could overrun a fit and healthy one? Nero had displaced *him* once, so why shouldn't he try his luck for himself?

At length Jake turned away, trying not to dwell on whether he himself had come up with such a morbid idea, or whether some long dead Sensitive had whispered it deep in the shadows of his own subconscious. Whatever the case, in the end, those young men swarming through the freezing night were really no different to him. They were just a bunch of guys doing a job, and trying not to get killed while doing it. Jake's disgust at his own selfishness only increased as he watched his pursuers administer first aid to a nine fingered stranger about whom they knew nothing, except for the fact that he'd been trying to shoot them down just minutes before.

As he watched the drama of his own slow death unfolding, Jake began to think of a more practical reason to leave the healthy soldiers well alone. He himself had been injured in an explosion and Piggott was eaten alive by cancer when they'd both been ousted by astral intruders. Maybe the link between physical and incorporeal had to be weakened before even the most gifted Sensitive could launch a successful assault. Maybe it was more than simple cruelty that had driven Stryker to hang his victims out like fish in a smoking shed.

As he was in no position to start testing theories, Jake retuned his attention to the second weakest man in the group. As he silently closed in on Sam, he tried to console himself with the idea that his actions were the moral equivalent to eating a rat or a skunk. It was repulsive idea, but the normal rules of civilised behaviour were relaxed in a survival situation. At least, that was what Jake told himself as he slipped between the surrounding soldiers and plunged his hands into Sam's still bright and defiant aura.

It began with a flash, a jagged bolt of brightness that transformed the glowing astral world into a smeared and over-exposed negative. With the barriers between the two of them dissolving fast, the entirety of the man known as Sam swirled unchecked into the already muddied stream of Jake's own consciousness.

Within seconds Jake's view of the world and everything in it had vanished as the sum total of Sam overwhelmed him. Distorted images, stolen memories, and hand-me-down emotions flashed across the empty screen of his mind like a maniacal slideshow narrated in tongues. Jake's most fundamental sense of himself was briefly subsumed as what remained of Sam carved its way through his already compromised consciousness, leaving new, deep fissures in an increasingly unfamiliar mental landscape.

Although Jake felt confident that his sense of self would triumph against Sam's weaker consciousness, he also knew he'd have to pay a price for stealing this wounded and angry man's very life to save his own. Soon the tide of Sam would begin to recede, but it would still leave him soaking wet and shivering on the coastline of his own mental kingdom, forever stained by those strange and tainted waters.

At last the stampede of Sam's consciousness began to subside, allowing Jake to corral the now dead gangster's unruly recollections into some sort of psychic stockade. It was only when the entirety of Sam was successfully fenced in that Jake realised he'd only understood that uncompromising criminal in a very superficial way, although his newer and deeper insight did nothing to help him warm to the man.

Sam believed...no, that wasn't it. Sam had *discovered* at an early age that ideas like morality, compassion and civility were simply devices used by both the weak *and* the strong to justify oppression or cowardice. It was an astoundingly simple philosophy, and the proof of that fundamental truth was everywhere, woven through both the natural world and human history. Sam had never seen himself as any sort of starry eyed idealist, but rather as a man acting according to a nature and upbringing beyond his control, and with which he was fully reconciled. The dead man had long accepted that if he'd been born under different circumstances, he'd have applied his talents and energies to defending the established order. However, the fates had decreed that he was to spend his life working against those who displayed no greater courage, strength or wisdom then he had himself. Thus Sam had concluded that nearly all authority was a matter of happenstance and was therefore illegitimate. Boiled down, Sam knew full well that those at the top had just gotten lucky.

As Jake's sense of himself returned, he was somewhat surprised to understand that Sam didn't actually *hate* authority or the Establishment. He just didn't care enough about those values, or any others, enough to feel either empathy *or* antipathy. For Sam, morality was just another facade of falsehood and self-justification, and just another problem to be managed in the pursuit of one's own personal goals.

With the balance between the two streams of consciousness swinging back in his favour, Jake was more than relieved to see the glowing astral world swimming slowly back into focus. He had no idea how long he'd been absent from himself, but the steadily growing crowd in the field suggested it was more than just a few seconds. He watched with interest as a soldier felt Sam's neck and grimaced, wiping his hand on the dead gangster's clothes before beckoning to a civilian who'd look more at home standing guard over the farmer's crops.

Even here, in this glorious glowing reflection of the physical realm, Mr Digby's spiritual aura somehow managed to look tatty. Stuttering purple, green and red, its edges were jagged and ill-defined, looking almost creased as though his crumpled attire was somehow reflected by its ethereal equivalent.

Jake didn't know if he felt angry when he learned that the scruffy intelligence agent was the author of Tooley's downfall, although he certainly wasn't surprised. He kept his distance as he watched Digby pick his way to where the bewildered soldier squatted beside Sam's bloodied and rapidly cooling corpse.

The young man's voice sounded distant and flat in the usual, underwater manner of the astral plane. "I don't understand this. He only caught one in the leg but just *look* at him. He looks more poisoned than shot."

No more than five feet away and completely invisible, Jake felt like he was grinning as Digby pulled a face and glanced furtively around the field. *Yeah, you know I'm out here don't you? You can't see or hear me, but you know I could do you in right now. Hell, maybe I should.* Jake knew he couldn't utter any sort of sound in his disembodied state, although just mouthing those words provided some satisfaction.

Digby straightened up and gestured for the soldier to cover the corpse. "Get a stretcher down here pronto, and for Christ's sake get some gloves on before you handle him."

The younger man swallowed hard. "What is it, sir, some kind of chemical?"

Digby was only half listening as he gazed across the marshy field. "Yeah, some kind. You'll be okay, kid. Just get this guy back to the farm and we'll have the experts take it from there."

Jake thought back to the man he'd dispatched down at Cedarwood during the summer, then forward to van Cortlandt and now Sam on the same night. Although he was reluctant to admit it, he was forced to concede that despite his internal debating, he'd had far fewer qualms about committing such an act *this* time around. Maybe he was getting used to it. When he looked down at his newly strengthened ethereal form he had to concede that maybe a part of him was even beginning to *like* it.

Although he felt both sickened and invigorated in equal measure, Jake also knew that he couldn't afford the luxury of soul searching. His physical form grew colder and closer to the point of no return for every extra second he lingered on the astral plane. It was now or never.

He started by remembering the pain in his right arm, using that sensation as a kind of mental signpost to guide him back to his frozen and bleeding body.

No change.

He began building around the agony in his arm by recalling the unpleasant sensation of sodden clothes clinging to his ribs, thighs and shoulders, but still there was no shift. Once again Jake found himself stranded as his disembodied consciousness remained resolutely outside its corporeal home.

Jake tried hard to control a rising tide of fear as he wondered if he'd left it too late and his body was already beyond all healing. Maybe this was it; maybe he really *had* died, and there could be no return to the warmth of the flesh this time. Although that was a real and frightening possibility, Jake also knew there could be another, equally likely explanation for his continued exile from the physical plane. His hunch was confirmed as he watched two soldiers gently lifting his own empty carcass onto a field stretcher, blissfully unaware of the perfectly black and featureless shadow which had silently materialised close by.

Standing just beyond the gathering group with arms outstretched and hands limp, Jake's relentless astral tormentor looked the perfect parody of a farmer's scarecrow. Or was it something else? Jake didn't know why, but he was struck by the strange idea that perhaps that visual pun portrayed some other meaning, a whisper of darker, deeper things than merely mocking helpless puppets of wood and straw. Suddenly those centuries of folklore surrounding the Reaper receiving the dead didn't seem nearly so far-fetched.

Whatever the case, Jake knew he was at a serious disadvantage, exposed on the astral plane and forced to face his adversary at the wrong time and on the wrong ground. He quickly thought back through their earlier encounters, rapidly running through a mental checklist of all he'd learned about his accomplished adversary. It took him about a second to realise that his first ignorant, unscientific and illogical gut instinct had been the right one all along.

So Jake turned and ran once again.

63

Uncomfortably aware that escape was still his only strategy, Jake set off at speed across the sodden countryside. The cloying, sucking soil of the physical plane was no impediment to his flight through its twinkling astral equivalent, and within seconds his momentum was such that entire fields flashed by in a single leap as he accelerated faster still.

He had no idea how far he'd travelled when he spotted a wooded hill up ahead and made for cover. Jake's reason counselled that those dense, solid trunks obscuring the skyline were no real danger as they hurtled towards him at a terrifying speed, but a life lived in the physical world had instilled instincts strong enough to overcome faultless logic. He had to slow down.

Time froze, and Jake felt like he was hanging in mid-air as he searched for a suitable landing spot. Having quickly made his choice, he executed a rapid descent towards a patch of untilled ground separating wild woods from orderly farmland. He pitched himself forward as his non-feet connected with the uneven ground, rolling and sliding across freezing wet grass as he tried to somehow dissipate the momentum he'd so rapidly built up.

Jake winced as he passed painlessly through a barbed wire fence before finally coming to rest beneath the boughs of an ancient, slumbering oak. Gnarled, and leafless, that venerable tree somehow reminded him of a sentry keeping silent vigil over the borderlands of that ancient forest. It might say nothing; but it remembered everything.

He quickly righted himself and looked around, relieved but also suspicious when he saw that his silent stalker wasn't hard on his heels. In fact, the faceless Projector who'd pursued him through city, countryside and even the surreal constructions of his own nightmares was conspicuously absent.

Jake was surprised to see just how far he'd travelled as he turned his attention to the confusion unfolding in the valley far below. A plume of glistening heat billowed high into the night as a group of soldiers struggled to quell a fire which had broken out in Tooley's barn. That burning column of chaotic colour seemed like a sinister echo of the organised and mechanised destruction he'd witnessed in that other, nameless place not so very long ago. His disembodied eyes instinctively traced the course of that dazzling energy discharge as it climbed and tumbled high into the clear, freezing sky, before streaking down into the shadowy woods behind him like a cloud of coloured iron filings marshalled by a powerful magnet. Jake instantly saw that something was wrong when he observed that obviously unnatural dispersal pattern, and it wasn't difficult to guess what was causing it.

He spun round on the spot. Having fled so far and so fast, Jake had no idea how his astral tormentor had managed to get into the woods before he'd reached them, but there he was nonetheless. Standing stock still between two large oaks, Jake's seemingly unshakable stalker stood with arms outstretched and fingers curled to harvest the raw astral energy whipped up by the drama of Digby's raid.

As he watched his nameless nemesis gorging on life's invisible excess, Jake was reminded of another forest in another land, and a much simpler time before Cedarwood, Colonel Stryker, Section 12 or any of it. Those memories felt like the distant, hazy days of a fading childhood summer, when he was just another doughboy trying to make it back home with body and soul mostly intact.

As the two Projectors stood face to face in the frozen forest, Jake was struck by the disturbing idea that he'd always assumed it was Colonel Stryker's astral shadow he'd glimpsed stealing between those trees in faraway France. What if he'd been mistaken? Could the terrifying truth be that this gifted lunatic had been keeping tabs on him far longer than he'd ever thought possible?

If the figure in the woods could somehow sense Jake's confusion it gave nothing away as it feasted on the banquet of fear, pain and confusion swirling up from the valley below.

Jake knew he only had one option left, and that was to face the foe about whom he *still* knew next to nothing. Already isolated from his dangerously weak physical form, he knew there could be no further retreat if he was to stand any chance of seeing the world through his own eyes once again. He also knew that he had absolutely no plan whatsoever as he moved out of the open countryside and into the darkened woods.

Silver-grey shafts of moonlight lanced between the frosted trees as Jake looked around, fearful of a surprise attack by a slavering Shade; but there was nothing and no one else to be seen. They were quite alone on that wooded hilltop, and Jake got the distinct impression that the other guy wanted it that way. This was it. This was a reckoning.

Standing no more than twenty feet from his ravenous persecutor, Jake tried not to think of two desperate gunmen facing each other down in a dusty western street. There were no six-shooters in this place, and if his opponent *did* make some kind of move then he had little notion of how to respond.

As both Projectors stared silently at each other, Jake was struck by the idea that it was the first time he'd been able to really study the man who'd hounded him throughout the Place Removed and beyond. He'd always been too busy running and hiding to understand just what he was running and hiding *from*.

Jake swallowed down the urge to flee and ordered himself to pay close attention as his ethereal stalker luxuriated in the energies overflowing from the drama down at Tooley's hideout. He had no doubt that his silent stalker was well aware of his presence, and he also had no doubt that the featureless phantom felt little fear of anything, even when faced by another naturally gifted Sensitive.

He moved a little closer as the dark truth about his ethereal opponent finally began to dawn. Jake mentally kicked himself as he began to understand the series of clues he'd been handed; clues that he'd spectacularly failed to piece together. Now, in the quiet solitude of those sleeping woods, the answer was finally revealed by the stream of colour vanishing into the dark oblivion of his sinister pursuer's astral form.

Suddenly that old song hummed by Peter van Cortlandt echoed loud and clear in Jake's mind, and as he stared at that dark and unfathomable phantom, he finally understood that he'd actually been fleeing from a man who wasn't really there. Just as van Cortlandt's huge astral presence had once crackled and burned so very fiercely, *this* Projector's absence was perfectly reflected by the absolute darkness of his ethereal form.

Jake still wasn't certain if he could show a smile in this place, but he sure as hell *felt* one spreading across his face as the realisation finally dawned on him. He wasn't looking at a man, a Shade or any other Projector like himself. The thing that hovered between the shafts of moonlight was nothing more than a man-shaped hole torn into the twinkling fabric of the Place Removed.

As Jake's disembodied mind finally grasped the troubling truth about his pursuer, he saw a slight distortion begin to ripple around that absent, otherworldly shadow. It was a distortion he'd never really noticed before, and he watched apprehensively as the trees surrounding that black silhouette began to stretch out of shape, almost as though he were observing the astral world through a poorly made lens.

As the revelation of his relentless pursuer's true nature became clearer in his mind, so too did the distortion created by Jake's ethereal rival. The sleeping forest creased and buckled still further as it began to vanish into that lightless, limitless hole punched into the astral plane.

Although it was all very confusing, Jake intuitively understood that he was on the threshold of some new and important understanding, although he had no time to put his hard-won knowledge to use as he felt an all too familiar pulling and pricking sensation in his non-existent stomach.

What had started as a slight visual distortion quickly grew into a dizzying ethereal whirlpool as the surrounding forest began to streak and run like a painting left out in the rain. The slumbering trees' glittering forms were picked apart grain by glowing grain as they splintered and tumbled into that man-shaped nothingness at the centre of the Place Removed.

Jake tried to back away as his own astral form began to disintegrate and his thoughts became increasingly disjointed and directionless. Knowing he had little time left, he made one last effort to visualise that freezing field beneath his back, the smell of his own blood and the pain coursing through his broken physical form. In the end, all he could conjure was a vague feeling of regret as the ground beneath him fell into that infinite nothingness impossibly constrained inside a human form. With his faculties failing, Jake struggled to picture the soldiers gathered around his body in the frozen December night, but his mental processes just stumbled into dark cul-de-sacs of fog and confusion.

Soon the Place Removed and everything in it had vanished completely; and without form, location or direction to guide him, Jake clung stubbornly to the idea of himself as expressed by the few strongest memories he could still trust as his own.

While he tumbled, or perhaps flew, through a vast and timeless nowhere, Jake began to wonder if even his most basic instincts really were *his* any more. Was it really *he* who defied that insatiable eater of worlds by holding fast to the lifebelt of himself, or was that solution simply a lesson whispered by a long dead stranger, now reborn to masquerade as his own, original idea?

Jake didn't know how long he'd been falling, or waiting, in the darkness of non-being before he saw the first glimmer of something other than nothingness. It had only felt like a minute, but he knew that a corporeal concept like time had little meaning in such a non-place. For all he knew, he might've been stranded out in the middle of nowhere for years on end, although his instincts told him that was unlikely. Jake reckoned that the stranger who'd chased him through this world and the next didn't have years in which to execute whatever plan he was hatching. He was a man in a hurry.

Streaking smears of grey began to flash from all directions, at first random and dizzying, but soon coalescing into a pattern suggesting direction...and direction suggested a destination.

Jake felt his faculties sharpening as the sense of movement decreased and the nowhere surrounding him was gradually displaced by a somewhere that grew increasingly familiar.

He should've guessed.

64

Jake felt as though he'd journeyed a million miles and travelled nowhere as he surveyed that oddly ashen copy of St John's crypt once again. The place - if it could really be called a *place* - somehow felt different this time around, and it looked different too.

The neat row of curiously re-designed caskets still remained, although the sparkling astral fire within them had faded to leave those detailed renderings of the dead that much darker, colder and lifeless, as he supposed tombs ought to be. Jake instinctively knew that symbolic dimming of life's light was significant, and he fervently hoped that those colourless coffins were not a sign that he himself was ready to remain in the empty and pallid kingdom of the dead. He glanced down and was immensely relieved to see that his own astral body still glowed with the chaotic hues of life, although his form still seemed a little blurry and badly defined. Jake quickly concluded that he was still alive, for now, and he decided not to dwell on whether his eleventh hour reprieve was entirely thanks to a dead gangster sprawled somewhere out there in the frozen darkness.

He quickly pushed all philosophical and ethical considerations aside, instinctively understanding that time was short if he was to escape this outpost of infinity once again. He didn't know if he had any real chance of success, but he consoled himself with the knowledge that at least he knew his way home this time around.

Jake turned his back on those darkened vestiges of the dead and crossed to the gate guarding the exit, he quickly pushed between the metal bars and glanced up the steps. His heart sank when he immediately noticed that the world above ground looked dimmer than he remembered, and he knew it wasn't due to any earthly explanation like the sun setting. A slight flicker and twist in that eerily active sky confirmed that he wasn't alone as he cautiously climbed the steps and entered the churchyard.

They were waiting for him just as he'd feared, and for a moment Jake thought that God himself had just switched off the lights as that befuddling fog of the forgotten dead eagerly enveloped him. For a few long seconds Jake knew only confusion as that mist of nothingness rushed in to tear at his glowing ethereal form like scavengers encircling carrion. Jake was immediately reminded that his lack of any physical presence granted him no immunity from pain as he felt a thousand tiny pinpricks stabbing at his incorporeal form like a flock of very tiny, but also very hungry birds.

Jake felt a rush of familiar dread as he watched faces, hands and even full apparitions snatching at glowing morsels of his astral body before collapsing back into the restless, roiling fog from whence they'd so briefly arisen.

As that mindless mist of death clustered ever more tightly around him, Jake sensed a tortured tangle of voices whispering from a distant place beyond the grave, eager to taste the sweet fruits of life once again. Like dormant seeds in the desert, those restless revenants had waited for the precious rains of self-awareness with infinite patience as one year of drought stretched seamlessly into the next. That mindless, lightless mass knew only that it had once been something more than just a faded memory, that it had once been something tangible, something constant and something aware of itself. Just as those twisting shadows knew only one thing, they also *felt* only one thing; a burning want for something more, something greater than just a glimpse of the light before sinking back into oblivion's dark and endless ocean. Their urgent, unspoken desire for a return to something and somewhere might one day be fulfilled, if only they could remember enough of themselves to make the arduous journey home from nothing and nowhere.

Jake shuddered to think that in the unknowable times to come, some new and as yet unborn explorer might one day glimpse *his* face peering out from that very same charnel smoke, eagerly awaiting a release from oblivion's timeless darkness.

Whatever the abstract, mystical truth of his experience might be, Jake knew he had little choice but to proceed according the psychology of the physical, and that meant not just standing there and letting himself be systematically eaten alive, even though he might already be dead.

With a sudden flash of clarity and understanding, Jake knew exactly how to deal with his immediate problem, although he couldn't be sure if it was his own idea or whether that seed had been planted by the shadow of some forgotten mystic, hidden away in the darkened depths of his own mind. Whatever the case, the wind that he began to imagine whirling out from his own centre was an instant success, and Jake felt a definite smile on his face as he watched that rolling miasma scatter and retreat, while fleeting faces howled their silent rebukes.

For a moment Jake almost surrendered to hope as that dark charnel fog began to fall back and dissipate, however his feeling of triumph was soon crushed as the mists parted to reveal a new and hitherto unseen degradation.

It was immediately clear that the mad architect of this colourless parallel plane hadn't been at all idle during Jake's absence, and the full extent of his dark ambition was finally revealed as those empty wraiths finally retreated to a more respectful distance. The leaning Victorian headstones of the "real" churchyard remained, but something else had also been crowded into that already gloomy, monochrome landscape. A new and eldritch crop had sprung up between death's desolate markers to make an already dangerous wilderness demonstrably darker, more hopeless and literally soul destroying.

Jake found himself both appalled and oddly unsurprised as he watched the formless undead whirling and hurrying among the just plain dead. Suddenly the memory of a strange visual joke in a farmer's field was writ large in his mind as he stared dumbfounded at the stuttering, glowing fruits of the Reaper's grim harvest. Painstakingly prepared and then displayed in a mocking parody of that most famous of martyrs; an immeasurable multitude of tortured ethereal carcasses were offered up not for the redemption of the living, but simply as sustenance for the insatiable undead. Jake tried to count the macabre, flickering scarecrows crowded into St John's already expanded and now gruesomely shimmering necropolis, but the rolling and twisting fog made a true reckoning impossible.

Jake had seen blood on the battlefield often enough, and he'd always reconciled the sight of the corrupted dead with the comforting knowledge that they had passed beyond all pain. Such an idea was especially important out there in the field, as he knew only too well just how swiftly nature despatched her outriders to reclaim the flesh of the fallen. It was those very same sickening scavengers that sprang to mind as Jake watched the unholy spectacle unfolding before him, and he wondered if he was being personally mocked as the cold comfort of death was cruelly exposed for the falsehood it plainly was.

As that tasteless and morbid drama was played out, Jake finally understood that neither an eternal afterlife *nor* the peace of oblivion were guaranteed destinations for the departed. It seemed that the dead could quickly slip back down the food ladder among the more abstract planes just as easily as in the physical realm.

As he stared at the weak and unstable astral forms scattered all around him, Jake wasn't sure if it was his own memory or the whispers of those formless wraiths stalking the churchyard that pushed the word *purgatory* to the forefront of his mind. Could it be true? Could he *actually* be standing in a "real" place described long ago by mystics and clergymen? Had he somehow fallen through a forgotten side door and into a place that was neither Heaven nor Hell; a place where the dead simply waited for something to happen? Shaking his non-existent head, Jake silently chided himself as that damned Catholic education suddenly made its presence known once more, unexpectedly resurrected to provide a voice and vessel for thoughts and ideas that constantly tested the limits of rational description.

Jake put the wave of anger, despair and revulsion welling up inside him to good use by flinging those feeding revenants still further across the grey, soulless space of St John's, and he felt some small satisfaction when that dark fog of the restless dead rolled back as he stepped forward. He couldn't be sure whether those mindless shadows truly feared him, or merely sensed his difference as he cautiously approached one of the many emaciated offerings to that formless, writhing miasma.

A twisted face suddenly leered out of the fog and Jake angrily pushed it away, only to be sickened still further when that dark, smoky mass quickly dispersed into tiny fragments as though mimicking a cloud of flies on a bloody summer's day.

A part of Jake wished he hadn't looked so closely as he finally came face-to-face with the formless dead's food, only to discover that he was looking at the emaciated astral body of a long departed soldier.

Worse still, it was a soldier he recognised.

65

Jake wondered if his imagination had finally broken loose and run amok as he stared at a dead man who still clung tenaciously to the last, feeble colours of life. "Ohlson?" Jake mouthed the word uselessly as the enormity of what he was witnessing began to sink in. He knew nothing of advanced theology or metaphysics, but his raw gut instinct told him that he was trapped in the middle of something wholly unclean, a blasphemous insurrection of life and death's natural and supposedly unassailable order. PFC Fred Ohlson, if this really *was* him, had been killed in action some months ago, but now it seemed that the mere destruction of a man's corporeal life was no guarantee of peace in the hereafter.

Jake had always rationalised his nightmares of Ohlson and the others as merely the shadows of his own guilt stealing through a disturbed and slumbering subconscious, but what if he was wrong? What if Ohlson, Dillard and the others were more than mere shadows conjured by his own troubled conscience? What if they really *had* reached out from beyond the grave with both a stinging rebuke and a desperate plea for help? What if his mistakes had done them an even greater disservice than simply getting them killed? What if he'd unwittingly abandoned them to this slow and agonising humiliation as sustenance for those formless phantoms stalking the shores of eternity? What if the men in his care really *had* grown even madder at him now that they were dead? Maybe they had a right, but maybe this was also a chance to make amends. Maybe it wasn't too late.

Just like van Cortlandt's coffin down in the crypt, Jake's glowing non-hands could grasp and even feel the stakes supporting Ohlson's half-eaten astral corpse; and just like van

Cortlandt's coffin, they too were as solid as stone and indifferent to his best efforts. At length he relented, realising that physical force was not the road to triumph in this ethereal cul-de-sac. This was a place created by the iron will of another mind, stronger than his, and so it figured that the normal rules of action and reaction had been re-written to suit their creator's purpose.

Confident that his reasoning was sound, Jake took a step back and concentrated hard on the frayed but sturdy ropes securing Ohlson's tortured astral form, imagining them crumbling to dust as a thousand years of decay was compressed into a matter of seconds.

Nothing happened, and the dead man's feebly fluttering form remained stubbornly lashed to its unyielding supports. Frustrated, Jake turned and vented his fury on a swirling cluster of spectres that had gathered nearby, just for the sheer hell of it.

That dark revenant fog rippled and curled angrily as Jake forced it to retreat once more. Those ragged wraiths betrayed a measure of sentience and purpose that he hadn't witnessed before as they railed against the insolent stranger in their midst. Responding to a sudden hunch, Jake made a conscious effort to contain the imaginary wind swirling out from his centre by instead imagining a calm, silent summer night.

Immediately the dark, smoky miasma rolled forward, reaching eagerly for both Jake and the man he'd failed to protect in life. Twisted grins and silent howls of triumph leered out of the fog as it rushed to in feed on the bright luminescence of life itself.

As Jake had feared, it seemed that those shapeless shadows of the dead were growing steadily stronger. Inch by painful inch, that which was formless and mindless was beginning to recall that, once upon a time, it been something more than just nothing.

Could it really be true? Could Stryker, van Cortlandt and a host of others he'd never even heard of *really* be waking from death's very own dark and dreamless slumber? It seemed absurd, blasphemous even, but as images and ideas of rebirth and resurrection suddenly swarmed through his disembodied consciousness, Jake knew that such a preposterous idea might just be possible.

Although his mind bubbled and burned with a hundred questions for every half-answer, Jake was absolutely certain of one thing; the dead stayed dead for a reason, and any subversion of that fundamental fact could never end well. He didn't know quite what the Brotherhood, or even his own shadowy nemesis were planning, and nor did he care very much. Pure instinct told him that he was standing inside a grave inversion of all that was self-evidently right and true.

As he stood and watched the most basic laws of nature running in reverse, Jake began to wonder if he'd made a terrible mistake for all the right reasons. Perhaps he should've been *helping* the likes of Clarke and Werner all along, lest the madman with the moustache should succeed in whatever misbegotten plan he was cooking up. Jake already knew that the war would be won without him, but perhaps a more important and fundamental struggle was just beginning. He had no idea what strange ambitions a group of men who'd cheated death might harbour, but he sure as hell didn't want the waking world to find out the hard way.

Jake couldn't tell whether it was his own meandering mind or the echoing whispers of the departed that guided his thoughts back to that flat grey, mirror-like ocean; an ocean that the dead seemed unable or unwilling to venture near.

Mirror! That single word resonated deep inside Jake's being like a funerary bell as the truth of what was right in front of him finally revealed itself. That endless, impassable, impenetrable expanse of grey reminded him of a mirror because it *was* a mirror; a mirror that reflected the projections of both the living *and* the dead straight back to their points of origin. That was why it had flung Jake back into the realm of the living, and that was why those slowly awakening spectres feared it so.

Jake knew the clock was still ticking, and that every second he wasted in some abstract ethereal nowhere reduced his chances of waking up alive. He also knew there was no way he could leave Ohlson and the others just strung up as tasty morsels for those insatiable, ravenous revenants. If he couldn't help them now, then maybe he could return again soon...maybe.

Silently mouthing some words about not leaving men behind, Jake blew those meandering husks of the dead as far back as he could manage as he readied himself to make a break for freedom. He didn't know if Ohlson had even heard or understood him as he set off at speed, making straight for the silent grey expanse that he fervently hoped could still send him home.

Poorly formed hands reached out eagerly as Jake carved a course through that swirling fog of the damned, with each fetid touch leaving a thousand pinpricks in its wake as he flashed by. He did his best to ignore the swirling dead's instinctive scrutiny as he knew he'd be passing beyond their grasp very soon, and he even smiled when he glimpsed the parade of angled gothic headstones marking the outer limits of the departeds' dominion. He pushed his feet deeper into the oddly elastic flagstones underfoot, planning to clear that final hurdle and plunge straight back into the comforting pain of the physical world with a single leap.

Jake didn't see any warnings as he approached, but he soon learned that *something* was wrong when the washed out world around him suddenly vanished into darkness, while a crackling cacophony exploded inside every light-filled cell of his ethereal form.

Mercifully, the impossible electric shock was short lived, leaving Jake curled on the colourless ground and wondering just how it was that he'd ended up right back beside the church again. There was a simple explanation, but Jake refused to entertain the idea that he was trapped among the unquiet dead because he'd already joined their ranks.

Instead he picked himself up, pushed the eternally circling spirits away and nodded to Ohlson as he considered his next move. Perhaps a slower and more deliberate approach was all he needed, like pushing his astral form through a wooden door back there in the real world. Maybe the mysterious, invisible barrier was weaker at some points than others, so maybe straight up the path and out through the front gate was the way he should go.

As he knew nothing for certain, Jake figured it was worth a shot. Anything to keep his mind off the very real possibility of his having died out in the mud of George Tooley's farm.

With his new strategy quickly settled, Jake cautiously began skirting the pallid reproduction of St John's church. The place suggested a picture copied or a story retold a thousand times. Details were missing, edges blurred and what little colour had showed through London's real winter gloom had long since been lost. It was a soulless, godless place that inspired only an overwhelming urge to flee from its silent scrutiny, and Jake briefly wondered if this place was where the uneasy feeling pervading the "real" St John's originated from. It made sense in an odd sort of way, like casting a shadow, or maybe it was more like an echo reverberating down through the planes to distort perceptions back on those dreary, drizzle soaked streets.

Jake had barely set off towards the front of the church before he rounded a corner and stopped dead in his tracks.

66

Those suffocating, swirling shades of the departed were suddenly forgotten as Jake gazed up at one unlucky soul who'd clearly been singled out for special attention. It seemed the master of that nameless realm at the edge of nowhere had been working on a great deal more than merely feeding the forgetful dead.

Broken, emaciated and clad in filthy ragged stripes, the last vestige of that anonymous casualty's spiritual life stuttered in weak defiance as he twisted helplessly between the gnarled branches of a scorched oak tree. Suspended only by a stout noose tightened around the right ankle, the inverted victim's left leg was bent at the knee and lashed behind the opposite thigh to form a kind of cross or figure four.

Jake instantly knew that he'd seen something very similar before, although he had no idea where a whole tree might have suddenly sprung from, or why. Perhaps he was thinking of a picture in an old book somewhere, but he couldn't pin down the exact memory he was searching for.

Although that dreadful humiliation's deeper esoteric meaning eluded him, the memory of a different dead man swinging gently in the summer breeze was only too clear in Jake's disembodied mind. At the time he'd dismissed that abhorrence in France as the unfathomable cruelty of a truly deranged intellect, only to learn much later that suffering endured in the physical realm could sometimes reverberate throughout other, more remote planes of existence.

Jake angrily shoved the ever-circling spirits away from their sinister feast and kept a wary eye on those restless wraiths as they twisted and writhed around that makeshift gallows, eagerly awaiting the chance to feed again.

Trepidation swiftly replaced revulsion in Jake's mind as the studied the sinister fruit of that slow torture, followed by death, followed by yet *more* slow torture. Such systematic barbarity had taken a terrible toll on this particular prisoner's ravaged expression, and Jake could easily see that those terror-twisted and half-eaten features were beginning to bear an uncanny resemblance to the empty, cadaverous glare of a deadly astral Shade.

Jake didn't understand the mystical process by which a Shade was born, but he knew the warning signs when he saw them. He also knew that he no intention of being trapped on the shores of forever with one of those shambling, insatiable fiends for company. There was no Peter van Cortlandt waiting to save him this time, and so his only chance was to act *before* the lengthy process of spiritual degradation was completed.

Had that hapless, nameless soul been mortally wounded on the battlefield, then a medic or an extra dose of morphine might have eased his suffering as he passed over, but it was far too late for that now. An altogether different kind of solution was required for *this* particular problem. Jake looked down at his own glowing yet smudged astral form, and then back up at the makeshift gallows once again. It only took him a few seconds to solve the riddle of how to neutralise a threat posed by a man who was dead already. He was learning fast.

The encircling wraiths suddenly shuddered as one, their movements becoming skittish and more urgent as though they sensed a change in the atmosphere, like exotic plants hunkering down before a storm.

After a little more hard thinking, Jake had even convinced himself that if the nameless stranger could still speak, he would surely beg him to get the hell on with it and end his suffering. Better the eternal silence of nothing than eternal enslavement at the hands of a man who fed his own dark dreams with the devoured souls of the departed.

Jake knew that he wasn't an evil man, just an ordinary guy trying to do the right thing in a world he barely understood; and right now it was literally dog eat dog, kill or be killed...and he just wanted to go home.

It had been a heroic mental effort, and Jake had almost managed to persuade himself that altruism drove his line of reasoning, but deep down he knew his own motivations were so much simpler and more selfish. Whilst he was sure that ending a stranger's suffering was a moral good, he was also growing accustomed to the after-effects of consuming another man's very essence. Maybe he was finally beginning to accept his strange and twisted spiritual evolution, and maybe was even learning to embrace his exotic new identity.

Preferring to think more of his victim's release than of his own darker desires, Jake concentrated his thoughts on the dead man still swinging from the half-dead tree. Remembering his unearthly adversary's stance back in the underground shelter, he spread his fingers wide and imagined a stream of astral energy flowing out of that proto-Shade's stuttering spiritual form and into his own. For a while nothing happened, and he started to feel a little foolish just standing there with his hands outstretched.

Then it started.

A tingling buzz spread quickly from Jake's non-existent hands to fill his entire ethereal body, while pinpoints of stuttering, stolen light twisted themselves into a weak ribbon of energy to nourish and strengthen his own luminous astral form. It was only after the feast had begun that Jake realised he was powerless to prevent himself from draining the man dry as a wave of impressions, memories and ideas overwhelmed his defences to swamp his self-identity. For a short while Sergeant Jacob Small was gone, swept aside by the remnants of a man whom he'd never actually known in life.

The onslaught didn't last long, as most of whoever the dead man had once been was already lost, consumed by the restless shadows prowling that strangely silent plane of existence.

As he became dimly aware of himself once again, Jake struggled to comprehend the tattered collage of ideas and impressions which had been poorly pasted into the scrapbook of his own past. It seemed that the would-be Shade had once been a sailor...no, not a sailor, but something connected with ships. Maybe some kind of clerk, although he'd definitely lived by the sea. He'd lived by the sea with his family, and that family had somehow managed to escape the death squads and the deportations. At least, that was the belief he'd stubbornly clung to in the knowledge that he'd probably not live long enough to learn the truth. In the end it was a tragic tale of an ordinary life defiled and wasted in the most unimaginable and extraordinarily cruel way.

At last the battle was won, and what remained of the man who'd lived by the sea was condensed down to an odd anecdote hidden inside the mind of Sergeant Jacob Small. The man once known as Johannes Meyer was gone forever, and yet something of him remained as yet another echo of the dead inside Jake's increasingly crowded consciousness. The worst part of it was that while he could often forget the most basic facts about himself, Jake would forever know the name of the man whose very soul he'd just devoured. Perhaps that was the way it *should* be.

Jake glanced back up at the scorched oak and was surprised to see that Meyer had vanished completely, the last remains of his spiritual form utterly consumed during the one-sided exchange. He'd like to have entertained some notion of Herr Meyer travelling on to the paradise so often promised by faith, but Jake knew that if such a place existed, Meyer was one man who could never reach it now. On the other hand, he'd managed to do some small good by delivering a stranger from the tortured fate of a slavish Shade.

That single ravenous, dangerous word was catapulted to the front of Jake's mind as he realised just how much extra trouble he might have landed himself in. Shades didn't spontaneously spring from the ether, in fact quite the reverse; and despite their seemingly shambolic appearance, those immensely strong astral beings were in fact painstakingly produced spiritual slaves.

Jake was no wise and wizened mystic, but he needed no arcane knowledge to understand that such a feat couldn't be easy, even for a guy like the one who'd been stalking him across one world, into the next, and then beyond even that. Whatever the man with the moustache was planning, Jake reckoned he'd just thrown a large wrench in the works.

Despite his huge innate talent, Jake knew full well that he'd gone and gotten himself way out of his depth. He possessed neither the training nor the weaponry to fight effectively in a non-place such as this, and so finding his way home should remain his priority now that the immediate danger had passed. A swift return to the reassuring pain of a broken body might at least let him live to fight another day, and he figured he might still stand a chance of escaping if he moved fast.

He turned his back on the empty, half-charred tree and cautiously began making for the silent grey infinity that lay beyond the reach of the restless dead. He felt nervous, on edge, all the while expecting to see an angry shadow bearing down on him from some unlikely angle. Jake knew that nameless harvester of tortured souls would be mad as hell when he finally learned that his prize pet was no more, and every one of his instincts warned him there would be a price to pay for what he'd just done.

His instincts were right.

67

Jake had expected his astral tormentor to descend in a blaze of burning darkness, or perhaps for the colourless sky to crack open above his head, or maybe the very ground might heave, shudder and suddenly swallow him up.

In the end, none of those things actually happened. It started with a singularly unspectacular experience, an experience that he'd once assumed to be impossible in such a disembodied state; and like many events that change lives forever, Sergeant Jacob Small's date with destiny began with a trivial and very physical inconvenience.

He started to feel sick.

There was little time to ponder such an unlikely turn of events as a very real bout of nausea quickly tightened into a burning knot of bile-spitting agony. Jake doubled over and slumped to the ground as a surge of white-hot liquid rapidly rose up through his chest and spilled onto the soulless grey of the ground.

He was amazed and horrified to see a pool of flawless black spreading beneath him as his ethereal body rejected whatever it was he'd just assimilated into himself. There was just enough time for him to see that he'd thrown up a large puddle of dead and lightless astral matter before his vision began to blur and stutter, like a movie reel jumping its sprockets.

Jake tried to rise but found himself paralysed by the physical pain wracking his incorporeal body. His mind screamed danger but he was defenceless, unable to move as he watched the shattered silhouette of St John's church blur and dissolve like a cube of sugar in hot coffee. The unearthly landscape juddered and streaked as he watched his world melt into a swirling stream of sounds and images stolen from a life he'd never actually lived. With his disembodied form paralysed by that impossible corporeal pain, Jake was once again a captive spectator as Meyer's strongest memories somehow replayed and merged with that rapidly liquefying landscape.

Curled into tight ball somewhere in a dark corner of his own consciousness, Jake figured that his astral ingestion, absorption or whatever the hell it was called must be running in reverse. It kind of made sense that his ethereal form would immediately reject the corrupted astral body he'd just devoured. After all, who in their right mind would contemplate consuming the rotting and diseased flesh of the physical dead, let alone the spiritual?

As the furnace in his stomach burned hotter still to punish his transgression, Jake wondered if it were possible to die out here in this obscure astral backwater, and what would such a concept actually *mean* anyway?

It wasn't long before the shores of eternity had faded from view altogether, leaving Jake to tumble helplessly through a confused collage of images culled from the mind of a man who'd seen far too much of the here, and yet would never see anything of the hereafter. The smell of fear and stagnant water filled his nostrils as fragments of Meyer's past whirled around him like a box of forbidden photographs tossed into a roaring tornado. Somewhere inside that maelstrom of dead ideas, Jake thought he might have glimpsed the man with the moustache through the blurry lenses of Herr Meyer's own lifeless eyes. It was hard to be certain as his shadowy nemesis was there and gone in an instant, somehow swelling and bursting to release a billowing cloud of flies into a damp concrete chamber; a chamber that Jake recognised all too quickly.

He found it hard to marshal his ill-disciplined thoughts as he felt a new and novel idea steadily pushing itself to the forefront of his mind, a growing perception of a place very different to that twilight peninsula on the edge of never. Something was wrong. In fact *everything* was wrong as Jake felt his consciousness finally overflowing with an awareness of a new, dark and cold location that smelled of damp and...Jesus Christ, what the hell was that *stench?*

At last Jake's growing mental fear was manifest in flesh as he felt his eyes burning and the breath rattling in his throat.

The fire in his stomach had faded at last, or perhaps it was simply overshadowed by a far greater pain busily gnawing at his right ankle. It was a shrill, screeching, excruciating agony which grew louder still as the physical plane slowly solidified around him.

Eventually the world came to a stop, more or less, and Jake even felt some sense of relief as he licked those wonderful, parched and cracked lips with his strangely swollen tongue. He had no idea how he'd escaped from the edge of infinity, but he'd never felt so grateful to be back among the living. He didn't even mind the fact that his mouth felt oddly misshapen and ignored his commands to speak.

Being a practised Projector, he knew it would take a while for his senses to settle back into their customary home, but those first distant and incoherent sounds that reached his ears were a welcome confirmation that he'd somehow escaped his silent exile. Not bad for some snot nosed kid from the ass-end of Motor City.

The agony in his ankle grew increasingly urgent while Jake was forced to wait for his equilibrium to return. He wondered if maybe he'd been shot, or perhaps he'd broken something during his escape from Tooley's hideout. For all he knew, he was still lying in a freezing wet field as his body slowly succumbed to simple hypothermia. Or worse still, he'd been absent much longer than he'd thought and he was already back under the dubious care of Section 12, or whatever they were calling it now.

With his eyes stubbornly refusing to open and his mouth failing to obey his will, Jake felt a nagging sense of unease slowly seeping up through layers of sleep to spill over into his gradually waking consciousness. Perhaps he was paralysed! Shot through the spine while attempting to escape. That terrifying thought streaked through his mind like a lightning bolt, finally jolting his errant senses back into gear.

As his faculties finally returned, Jake quickly dismissed fears of paralysis as the agony spreading through his right leg assured him that everything important was still connected. So why in God's name couldn't he *move?*

Jake's relief at having escaped from exile on the shores of eternity was quickly dampened by an ever increasing awareness that something had gone very, very wrong indeed.

He began to realise just *how* wrong everything was when he heard an educated voice whispering from somewhere close by.

"Welcome to the edge of the world."

68

Jake knew exactly who that thoroughly British voice belonged to.

"If I were you I'd confine myself to consuming the living. The dead are very much an acquired taste and the risks are great for the uninitiated."

Jake tried to formulate some kind of response but his mouth was an alien and lumpy landscape inside his own body.

The voice continued. "It's like feeding caviar to a toddler; a shameful waste which always ends with same predictably messy results. Mind you, the way you gobbled up that complete stranger out there was very impressive, and it's long overdue in my opinion. The more a man denies his true nature, the more unhappy and unsuccessful his existence will become. Surely you agree."

Again Jake tried to say something, and again he failed.

The British voice lowered in pitch, sounding just a little more serious. "It's all right to admit that you like it, at least to *me,* although I'd keep up the pretence of moral outrage while you're among the ignorant. Men don't like to think of themselves as food, it upsets their sense of divine superiority, and theology becomes *very* tricky, what with one soul effectively eating another. That's why the wizards and vampires of the ignorant peasantry still delight and enthral us so, despite our cerebral desire to leave them behind. Never forget that for all his mediocrity, the average man shares our insight on an instinctive level, which is why he so often fears those things that his emasculated intellect no longer permits him to accept. You see, despite his pretence to reason, the modern man's untamed intuition correctly recognises these things as signposts on the path to those hidden truths which he secretly hopes never to learn."

Jake tried to ignore the agony burning through his leg and the awful stench burning in his nostrils as he concentrated on cranking his eyes open. He desperately wanted to swallow, but even that simple reflex eluded him and his eyes remained resolutely shut.

"This will be a new and confusing experience, so you're bound to find it difficult at first. I assure you it's only a temporary inconvenience as you'll be dead again very soon."

Jake tried to ignore the sandpaper in his eyes as he concentrated on getting them open, but still they refused to obey his will. Then he was sick again, but this time the episode was all too physical as he felt hot bile bubble from his mouth to clog his nostrils and foul his face.

The voice in the darkness spoke again, this time a little less distant and a lot more irritable. "Now that really is quite revolting, although it's understandable. I remember the first time *I* returned; I could barely control *my own* body, let alone a diseased and rotted lifeboat like yours. Here, let me help you."

Jake heard a metallic scraping just before a torrent of icy water slapped across his face, choking him as it washed away the stinking vomit and anchored his mind that much more firmly to the physical plane.

At last he felt his eyes flicker open, although they weren't much help as the world appeared dim and hazy, as though he were gazing through a heavily misted window. Although Jake's eyes were less useful than he'd hoped, his sense of balance woke with a start and immediately warned him that he was hanging upside down. The shooting pains in his leg confirmed that he was somehow suspended by his right ankle, while his left leg felt oddly immobile. His fingers clutched vainly at thin air as he realised he was twisting in empty space.

The disembodied voice spoke again, this time closer, more immediate and more real. "Don't waste time trying to make it yours. You've crossed the Rubicon and entered an entirely new world, governed an entirely new book of rules. You'll just have to work with what you have, not what you're *accustomed* to having."

Jake suddenly felt a blow across his cheek, although the sensation was strangely dulled. "The kindest course would be to dispatch you back to where you came from and let you find your own way home, but I see no reason to show kindness in your case." There was a second, equally dull and oddly distant blow. "Wake up! I *shall* have an answer before you die again."

Jake finally managed to blink rapidly, his eyes adjusting to the gloom of a chamber that felt oddly familiar, despite its frozen and featureless anonymity. Although his vision was still blurred, it had sharpened enough to at last recognise the owner of that educated voice. He wasn't surprised to see the Sensitive who'd hounded him halfway across London, although this time he was dressed as a Private in the German Army. Jake smelled cigarettes on his captor's breath, although his sense of touch remained oddly detached as his captor slapped him across the face once more.

He glanced around with some difficulty as the man who'd invaded his most intimate dreams sauntered back to an ostentatious chair set at the centre of his cold, stinking concrete kingdom.

As he twisted in empty space, Jake was only partly relieved to see that the macabre carpet of the dead and dying had vanished since his last visit, although the flies scrambling over every surface testified to their recent removal. He got the impression that this nameless necromancer was about to shut up shop for good, but alas it seemed there was time for one last piece of unfinished business.

Although he'd made a valiant effort to ignore reality, Jake had seen all he could see and thought all he could think to stave off the wave of terror and revulsion that finally flooded through his mind and forced him to confront the unbelievable yet undeniable truth. He tried to form a few words, but all that escaped his unfamiliar mouth was an incoherent moan.

The Sensitive in the chair smiled, his teeth gleaming white as he luxuriated in Jake's terror and incomprehension. "I suppose this is where I'm supposed to say something grand and profound, but in all honesty I'm surprised that we should meet so soon. You don't have very much time left, so we really should make the most it before that worm-riddled raft finally gives up the ghost." He snickered at his own mirth. "Gives up the ghost. Oh dear me."

Although still blurry, Jake's vision had little cleared a little more as he twisted his head first one way and then the other as he tried to better understand his surroundings. He failed to swallow down a crying groan of disbelief when he looked up and caught sight of the painfully thin fingers protruding from a striped and filthy camp uniform. His last redoubt of denial was swept aside when he realised those skeletal digits were a full set of ten, just like the late Johannes Meyer's had been. Jake felt his stomach convulse when at last he learned that his own body was the source of the gangrenous stench filling his nostrils. He retched and shuddered as he felt the taint of fetid corruption flowing through his pathetic, wasted limbs, despite the fact that they'd never been his before now. He desperately willed his captured consciousness to slip its leash and free itself from that living horror as at last he focused on the flies and larvae busily crawling through the late Johannes Meyer's tattered clothes...*his* clothes.

The man in the chair waited patiently, drumming his fingers on the carved arms as he watched his guest struggling inside a prison of rotted flesh. "To be perfectly honest with you, I see no practical reason to hang them upside down, and neither did the Colonel. But unlike him, I'm a sentimental soul and so I defer to the aesthetics of tradition. I do like to think it adds a dash of superstitious terror to the whole process, which is all fuel for the fire in the end."

Jake clenched his unwieldy fists against another cycle of empty retching as he struggled to think clearly. Perhaps it was a fitting punishment that he should know something of Herr Meyer's true suffering, although being trapped inside the body of a dead man whose soul he'd just eaten felt like a serious perversion of some fundamental natural laws. Surely there would be a price to pay for such a transgression, whether wilful or otherwise.

Watching his prisoner with an expression of wry amusement, Jake's nameless captor unexpectedly reached behind his chair and produced a wooden bucket. Flies billowed into the air as he crossed the echoing concrete floor and held a ladleful of cold, clear water to the dead man's cracked lips. "I assure you it's quite safe."

Jake resisted the urge to drink.

"A gesture of faith then." Jake's sinister host quickly gulped down the water before dipping into the bucket and offering another helping. "It's long been our custom to offer water to all returning explorers. It's a tradition that stems from the legends of our ancestors crossing the Styx to commune with the Dark One. Just as witches and cunning women were said to bear his mark, so it was reckoned that those returning from the fires of Hell still carried that fire inside themselves. Upon waking, the suspected astral traveller was plied with water from the font, and if they couldn't keep it down then it was a sure sign of a tainted soul."

Jake greedily sucked up the water, coughing and choking as he tried to swallow as much of the blessedly cool liquid as possible.

The man in the suspiciously new and creased uniform offered Jake another drink. "As this is clearly your first Displacement, you'll need some practical instruction. The shell you now occupy is terribly weakened, long dead in parts but the spirit remained strong, at least until *you* happened by. It will require your full attention if you're to operate that mouth and tongue competently. I assume you *do* want to talk; you must have so many questions."

Jake gulped down the second helping of water, feeling it roll into his eyes and across his forehead as he coughed and choked again. At length he managed to gasp out his first few words. "What you want? Why me?" He shuddered inwardly as he heard the pitiful voice of a stranger close to death in his own ears.

"Introductions are always the best way to start, Jacob. My name is Morgan Jones. You've probably heard of me by now."

Jake tried to concentrate, although it was difficult with the agony in his leg and the constant swaying movement. "My name, how?"

Jones gently put the bucket down, folded his arms and cocked his head as he observed his captive more closely. "The old priest told me your name, or rather, I chanced upon it while he was busy stumbling around in places he had no business being."

Jake looked at the emaciated arms that had briefly become his own, then thought of that astral body trapped and twisting in some ethereal non-place that defied explanation. It was at that moment Jake finally saw the full extent of his own ignorance, both of his well-spoken tormentor, and perhaps even of himself.

However, one thing Jake *did* know was that he had little time left as he felt his tenuous toehold inside that borrowed body beginning to slip. Sounds were receding and the shooting pains pervading that diseased flesh were beginning to fade, feeling oddly abstract and detached once again. As Jake's mind started to lose its grip on its surroundings, it took a great effort to form only a single word. "Why?"

A sly smile appeared on Jones' face. "You mean why are you here? Or perhaps you're asking why I steered Piggott and his pack of hungry dogs towards van Cortlandt's fortune." He bent forward and placed his soft, closely shaven cheek against Jake's borrowed face to whisper in his ear "This is not the implausible plot of some cheap novel where the villain reveals all to his helpless captive, who promptly escapes to foil his plans."

Jake felt a drool of spittle run between his uncontrollable lips as he tried to reply. In the end all he managed was an incoherent gurgle.

Jones chuckled and gave his victim a firm push to send him swinging, disturbing the flies busily crawling through his soiled and tattered prison clothes.

Jake groaned as the world rocked and plunged, the renewed agony in his leg reminding him that although his grip on the physical plane was weakened, he still remained trapped for the time being.

Jones clasped his hands behind his back and began pacing in a slow circle around the stinking chamber. Squadrons of flies took to the air as he advanced, his breath misting as he neared the sulking electric lamps screwed to the streaked walls. "Your hip's been dislocated for a while now, although you're fortunate that it isn't really *your* hip. In fact I've heard tales of subjects losing whole limbs or feet during the process, but I've never seen it myself."

Jake tried to keep Jones in sight as he disappeared behind him, gritting his teeth against the agony and hissing out a few more broken words. "What you *want?*"

Jones completed his circuit and stood in front of Jake once more. "Where do you come from?"

Jake was in no mood for small talk, and he lacked the energy to form a coherent response.

Jones resumed his pacing, looking down at the flies avoiding his feet as he followed his circuit once again. "Your cavalier Displacement of the soul who once inhabited that form means that he's suffered in vain. He'll certainly be dead by now, and by *dead* I mean dispersed, gone, deceased in the most fundamental and final sense of the word. Such a casual disdain for the soul of another betrays a marked lack of character, but then I must concede that morals are the preserve of those with a roof over their head and food in their belly; don't you agree?"

Jake licked his dry lips and concentrated on forming his words, although they still grated out in a stuttering jumble. "Don't know, accident. Not planned. No plan."

Jones shook his head ruefully and returned to slouch in his chair. "People think it's all so simple. Just mix the potions, learn the magic words and abracadabra, just like that." He sighed wistfully and rummaged inside his tunic. "If only it were so. Life of any kind cannot be *manufactured* by the likes of us, despite whatever lies that sodomite Burton might tell you. Life can only be nurtured, guided and nourished with great skill and care. Tell me, how did it feel to just fling this pitiful wretch into eternity's darkness? It's all right to admit the truth, and I won't judge you for following your instincts. How could I?"

Jake's cracked lips stung as he forced a smile. "Did him a favour. Better to be nothing at all than what *you* had in mind." He took another deep breath and forced out his next sentence. "Is Piggott trapped like the others? Is he in the grey place?"

The man in the chair produced a silver cigarette case. "This is total war and we all have to make do with what we have, so it would be immoral to let all that valuable sustenance go to waste. There are so many hungry mouths on short rations these days, not that you Americans would understand that."

Jake could only muster up two short words as he thought of those formless phantoms dishonouring the dead. "You're sick."

Jones lit a cigarette and stared hard at his adversary. "Sick? No, not me...I'm the cure."

69

Jake felt his eyelids fluttering as he struggled to stay awake. "What cure?"

Jones slowly stood up and walked across his flyblown concrete kingdom once more, the orange glow of his cigarette reflected by Jake's paper thin skin as he leaned in close.

"The higher planes are dangerous places, Jacob. If you'd had any kind of proper schooling then you'd have known better than to go swimming in a pond full of leeches. To be frank, I'm amazed you can even remember your own *name* with the noise those restless souls must be making." He paused to blow smoke into his captive's face and tap him on the temple. "You can't keep them out forever," he said quietly.

Jake had some idea of what this Jones guy's cryptic warning referred to, but he lacked the strength to make a meaningful response.

Jones looked wistfully at the floor. "In their present state they're more like those broken, shambolic shells I string up for them than the collective wisdom of ages past. You must know that it's the height of cruelty to present a starving man with a banquet, which is exactly what you've done. God knows how many we may have lost forever thanks to *your* untimely appearance." Jones rubbed his forehead and blew out a long stream of expensive cigarette smoke. "They must've sensed you blundering around out there and seen what their addled, dead heads thought was a little light of hope shining through that unending darkness. I suppose it's understandable really. After all, I should think a drowning man would grab at the very first thing he sees, although *you* resemble a piece of discarded luggage more than a bona fide lifeboat."

Jake tried to summon the strength to say *screw you,* but failed.

Jones continued, a slow smile spreading across his face as he took another draw on his cigarette. "Yes, that's it. You're a suitcase, a hatbox which has bobbed to the surface long after the ship has gone down."

Jake just managed to croak out two words. "Van Cortlandt."

Jones blew smoke in Jake's face again, smiling wickedly as his prisoner coughed and spluttered. "You have it, although we must think of the late Peter van Cortlandt as both ship *and* passenger in this particular case."

Despite the blinding pain, burning thirst and light-headedness, Jake was becoming weary of his captor's obfuscation. "What do you want?"

"Believe it or not, I want to help you." Jones smiled and nodded as he saw how Jake's borrowed expression had darkened. "You have my word, although I'd like to be clear and explain this has nothing to do with any misguided sense of loyalty or morality. The simple truth is that you've involved yourself in important affairs that do not concern you."

"Real sorry."

Jones flicked ash at his opponent's face before bending closer still, his lips almost touching Jake's ear. "You see, now that both the Colonel and van Cortlandt have passed over, *I* am the only living candidate who is competent to lead what remains of the Brotherhood. Make no mistake, I will stop at nothing to ensure that our ancient rights are restored as mankind embarks upon a wondrous and terrifying new epoch."

Jake thought of a pithy comment about there being nothing left to inherit, although he lacked the strength to form the words. Instead he had no option but to hang there, swinging in that freezing, stinking, fly-filled space.

Jones turned away from his captive and clasped his hands behind his back. "Who trained you? Who *found* you?"

Jake just shook his head, his neck grating like rusted gears.

"I left you a million miles from anywhere, so how did you manage to crawl back here?"

Jake tried to speak but only managed a dry gasp.

Jones turned to face his rival once more. "None of us has very much time, and you least of all. If you think you can just drag those unquiet souls back into the darkness with you then I'm afraid you've been misinformed." He dropped his cigarette on the floor and ground it out with the sole of his boot. "I suppose Dr Werner has spun you some fairy tale regarding his knowledge and expertise. Be warned; Werner's a butcher, a schoolboy with a frog and a biology book. Stryker never trusted the Werners and neither should you."

Jake groaned and closed his eyes, praying he would wake up in that glorious sodden English field.

Jones smirked. "Did you know that the Hanged Man is a special favourite of ours? Not wholly of this mortal realm and always upside down when he's the right way up, although *his* position is a lot more enviable than yours." He stepped forward and slapped Jake hard across the cheek. "Wake up! How did you follow me here? Who's your handler? Werner? Burton? Who is it?"

The sharp blow had barely registered, and Jake lamented that he lacked the strength to tell Jones what to do with himself as the room began to dim.

Jones prised one of Jake's borrowed eyes open and sighed heavily. "I *had* hoped to show you of the truth of your own best interests, but you're too far gone already. So be it." He blew on his hands and rubbed them together before carefully placing his fingertips on Jake's temples. "This will certainly be painful...and fatal. But you're a talented man so I've no doubt we'll meet again soon, assuming you can find your way home in the darkness." With that Jones took a deep breath and rested his own forehead against Jake's inverted one.

Jake was more than ready to make his escape as that stinking torture chamber finally vanished from view and he braced himself for the strange sensation of falling in every direction at once. It had been a bizarre experience, but he knew he couldn't dwell on it as he mentally prepared for a return to the desolate shores of nowhere. However, it soon became clear that Morgan Jones had other ideas.

This time there was no sense of falling, flying, leaving or arriving. There was no sinister astral copy of any real place, and no haunted shadows of those who had passed that way before. There was none of that. In fact there was nothing at all save for a perfect, flawless and endless darkness that somehow seeped through his very being to obscure ideas that had once been simple and clear. The only thing Jake could be sure of was that he had travelled nowhere and existed in no place, not even a wild ethereal abstraction created by an unhinged, cigarette smoking demi-god.

The one idea that *did* shine clearly in that infinite darkness was the human mind's extraordinary capacity for triviality, even amidst the most profound metaphysical crises. Despite his best efforts to focus, Jake grew increasingly frustrated with himself as his inner dialogue stubbornly centred around his regret at missing the chance to tell this Morgan Jones character that he was completely nuts.

Hanging motionless amid that flawless, directionless emptiness, Jake began to wonder if he'd finally passed beyond all human experience and all hope of rescue. However that deep, existential anxiety soon passed when he began to hear a faint rumble coming from nowhere, or perhaps it was everywhere. It was an alien sound, unlike anything he'd ever heard before, and yet it reminded him of water rushing over some distant, invisible cliff as it grew rapidly louder. Or was that nearer? Jake didn't know what was about to happen, but he was certain it would be unpleasant because, just like Dr Hammond before him, Jones had convinced himself he was facing a foe who was driven by an ideology far greater than simply saving his own ass.

If he'd possessed any kind of a face, Jake would've smiled as the memory of his old pal Jimmy Partridge unexpectedly popped into his head. Jimmy was kinda bookish but he was smart as hell, and Jake suddenly found himself wondering where his boyhood friend was now, and whether he was rich or poor, dead or alive. He also wondered why his mind had turned to his previously forgotten childhood at such a dangerous moment.

Jake found it hard to concentrate as his meandering thoughts left Jimmy Partridge behind and turned towards that damned dead soldier back in France. *Sacrifice* was a word that sprang unexpectedly to mind when he thought of that corrupted corpse, twisted and ravaged by death's decay as he himself had been just minutes before. In fact, now that he thought of it, a corpse in a gibbet and a mysterious Frenchman called Pierre were where it had all started.

The skittish flock of Jake's fleeting thoughts suddenly wheeled and turned again, this time settling on the man he'd killed down in Kent. He really regretted learning that guy's name, and he especially wished he hadn't found out that he'd had a kid; and whatever happened to the blind soldier he'd met down there? Williams! That was his name, the guy who'd fried spam at Cedarwood...

Jake scolded himself for allowing his mind to drift at such a crucial moment. He felt like he should be focused on something important, something immediate, although he couldn't recall what that something actually *was*. He'd had it a minute ago, but now it was gone. It was hard to stay focused with such a disjointed jumble of images streaming across the blank screen of his mind, and it grew harder still as that poorly spliced newsreel of his past dissolved into a nauseating blur of colour and sound.

By the time Jake realised that *he* was not the author of that chaotic internal narrative it was far too late to act. Instead he could only watch helplessly from afar, oddly separated from himself as the stream of his consciousness somehow slipped away from him, to be rifled like a sagging shelf crammed with dusty, neglected and often embarrassing volumes. If he'd been married for thirty years, there was no way his wife could've known him in the same intimate way that Morgan Jones had just gotten to know him. All pretence and deceit were ruthlessly stripped away, leaving him with alone in the darkness with the same feeling of violation that Thomas van Cortlandt had undoubtedly experienced such a short time ago.

The single comfort Jake could draw from his intimate humiliation was that Morgan Jones could be certain he was nothing to do with any Brotherhood faction, and little to do with the security services either. It was almost worth the feeling of infantile helplessness for that most dangerous Sensitive to finally grasp just how clueless he really was.

Therefore Jake found it strange that although he'd never expressed any real loyalty to them, he still felt like some kind of traitor as he silently confessed all he'd learned about Major

Clarke, Section C and the mysterious Mr Digby. That was *before* starting in on his tangled ideas surrounding the alluring, dangerous and probably dead Ellie Parsons.

Without warning, the unspoken inquisition abruptly ceased and a seamless, crushing silence descended around him, leaving Jake alone in the darkness with only his shame and an unexpected understanding of his adversary for company. As he struggled to focus on those new and unbidden intuitions, it became increasingly clear that not even a man like Jones existed *completely* outside the rules of cause and effect. Although Jake could feel his self-awareness dimming rapidly, he was just able to appreciate that his new yet nebulous knowledge of the man called Morgan Jones was derived from some kind of mental residue or fingerprint his inquisitor had left behind at the scene of his crime.

Jake felt oddly deflated to learn that he'd actually got it right. Jones saw himself as the rightful heir to every aspect of the Brotherhood's legacy, and that *especially* included the mysterious van Cortlandt Collection. Tooley, Piggott and even the IRA had been cleverly exploited to deliver that celebrated body of work into the hands of a man who was busy preparing...*something*.

It was a frustrating experience as Jake knew the answer was right in front of him, but he just couldn't bring those increasingly cloudy impressions into sharper focus. What he knew for sure was that Jones had a plan, and it centred around those empty wraiths swirling in the metaphysical aquarium he'd so painstakingly prepared somewhere out there, at the very fringes of sentient life itself.

As the presence of his consciousness was watered down by the absence of oblivion, Jake's final thought was a sudden intuition that he might *not* end up as a forgetful ghost stalking those desolate, colourless shores of nowhere.

It might be far, far worse.

70

Major Giles Clarke squinted up at the horizon as a bright December dawn broke over the muddy farmyard. He'd finally achieved his goal of locating Jacob Small, as well as helping to prevent a shipment of the latest American weaponry from reaching the IRA. A messy firefight in the Buckinghamshire countryside was admittedly embarrassing, but a cover story about Nazi suicide squads would keep everyone guessing, even if they didn't really believe the official line.

Two serious threats to national security had been contained, and yet Clarke couldn't shake the feeling that he'd only just scratched the surface. The Major had spent most of his adult life analysing intelligence and concentrating on hard facts, so he found it ironic that he wondered whether those many years of precise analytical work hadn't sharpened some other, more subtle and less easily explicable instincts. Clarke just hoped he could put the pieces together before time ran out. It wasn't over, whatever *it* eventually turned out to be.

He sucked hard on his pipe to keep it burning as he looked across to the dilapidated barn. Now guarded by two cold and tired soldiers, it had been requisitioned to serve as both a makeshift medical post and temporary stockade. Clarke would've preferred it if his apprehensive prisoners were corralled on the front lawn in their underwear, deprived of sleep and under close supervision. However, they were still in the heart of the English countryside and so discretion was paramount. There would be plenty of time to question each captive in turn and at length.

Clarke watched as Digby slipped out of the barn's side door and walked towards him. Their rapport had grown steadily throughout the war, despite the conflicting pressures of serving different masters. Dependable and ruthless when it was required, Digby possessed an intuitive understanding of what they both fought for and why, although Clarke sensed that this time things were different. Digby had failed in *his* mission, and the Major wondered how much the man blamed himself, and how much he blamed the British intelligence machine for that failure.

Digby waved Clarke's tobacco smoke away with his hat before producing his crumpled Lucky Strikes. "You want to know what I think, Major? I've been in intelligence most of my adult life, and looking around at this mess, I can't figure out whether we've done the world a favour or screwed up real bad."

Clarke continued to stare at the tilting wooden barn, his breath merging with tobacco smoke in the early dawn mist. "I feel as though we've searched so very hard for the right platform, only to discover that that we've gone and caught the wrong train."

"Yeah, kinda like the one we wanted left already."

"That's it." The Major sighed heavily and turned to his American counterpart. "So, what's the butcher's bill?"

Digby replaced his hat, lit his cigarette and stared at the frost covered ground. "Four dead, including one of ours; five wounded, including *two* of ours. We've got six Yanks and the same number of Brits in there, so I guess you could call this a triumph for transatlantic co-operation. By the way those numbers *exclude* Jake Small, and your guy in there." He pointed to the sullen and smoke-damaged farmhouse.

For a while both men stood in silence, each preoccupied with his own problems. Eventually that silence was broken by the distant rumble of approaching engines.

Digby spoke again. "You know, my inside source told me the strangest story."

"There's very little that seems strange to me these days." Clarke watched as a drab green field ambulance appeared in the lane skirting the farm, its driver conferring briefly with the guard at the roadblock before swinging the large vehicle between the stone gateposts. A few seconds later, a similar ambulance and an army truck also appeared in the lane to form a convoy, bouncing down the rutted and waterlogged track leading to the barn.

Digby also watched as the vehicles cautiously approached. "Yeah, I know what you mean. Anyway, my source told me that this George Tooley's got a real reputation for sniffing out snitches. Almost kinda supernatural."

"I'll bet he does," said Clarke quietly.

The American rolled his shoulders inside his shapeless coat. "Just what the *hell* is going on?"

Clarke ground his teeth as the first ambulance shuddered to a halt. Immediately the barn doors swung open and a stretcher bearing the first blanketed corpse was carried out. "I'm really not sure, but the more I discover about this Brotherhood the more disturbed I become. Just look at what George Tooley achieved with the help of one talented man who wasn't even a true Sensitive, at least in the way that *I've* come to understand the term."

Digby took a long draw on his cigarette as he watched another stretcher being carried to the ambulance. A mud-caked hand flopped from beneath the blankets. It only had four fingers. "Where will you take them?"

"The nearest mortuary I suppose."

The American's response was quiet yet determined. "My orders haven't changed, and I *still* want Jacob Small."

Clarke turned to look directly at his friend and colleague. "I really am very sorry about your chap, but perhaps the fewer men like him running around the place the better we can all sleep a night. As for his worldly remains, I think you may have to take that up with the coroner. To be honest I'm not sure whose jurisdiction takes precedence at the moment."

"Christ I don't want to think about this any more, just for a while."

Clarke watched the first ambulance bump away carrying the dead while the second reversed to receive the living. "I don't blame you, it's enough to shrivel a man's heart. Let's change the subject."

Digby needed no prompting and pointed back at the farmhouse. "How's your guy doing in there?"

"He's certainly not *my* guy. In fact, I think it'll take a while to work out exactly *whose* guy he really is. But to answer your question, he's suffering from smoke inhalation, as well as being very shaken and upset. He claims the last thing he remembers is conversing with the late Sergeant Small, before waking up outside this miserable little hovel. Werner's still trying to keep him settled and get some sense out of him." Clarke paused for effect. "Whatever your man did to him, it left a lasting impression."

"Not half as lasting as the impression all those sparklers left on *me*. You reckon the priest put Tooley onto that lot?"

Clarke frowned as he thought for a second. "Must've been, there's no other explanation that makes any kind of sense."

"How are you going to handle him?"

Clarke sent a cloud of blue smoke rolling into the freezing dawn. "Assuming Werner gives the all clear, I'll put him in a car and take him straight home."

Digby squinted up at the golden winter sun breaking low over a nearby hill. "You know, some folk say that war either toughens or mellows a man, if it doesn't kill him first. I guess I know which club *you* belong to."

Clarke also squinted at the sun. "Once we're safely back at Mr van Cortlandt's house, I'll have a team of engineers dismantle it brick by brick. Meanwhile, he and I will discuss how a band of well-organised, well-armed and highly motivated cutthroats just *happened* to learn that he keeps a fortune in cut stones stashed away in his private abode."

"You reckon he'll roll over just like that?"

Clarke chewed his pipe and nodded thoughtfully. "I'm sure he'll see sense in the end. If he's a solid sort of fellow then it may not be necessary to raise the matter of his private collection with the Exchequer."

Digby watched as the second ambulance pulled away and bumped back up the uneven drive. "I'd appreciate it if one of your guys could drop me at the nearest town, I've got some calls to make."

Clarke nodded but said nothing, seemingly deep in thought as the army truck took its turn and slowly backed up to the barn.

Digby yawned, stretched and flicked his cigarette onto the frozen grass as the remaining prisoners were hustled into the back of the truck. "Keep 'em warm for me and I'll arrange to have our guys transferred, although I doubt they'll ever see an open court martial."

"It may be good for morale a living embodiment of the very rule of law for which we fight; that sort of thing," observed Clarke.

"Maybe for you, but I can't see any upside to a story about American liberators arming an Irish insurrection. If *that* leaks out then it's just a matter of time before some smarter than average reporter starts asking about gunfights at an English farm, and before you know it you'll be reading stories about a mad priest in a bombed out church. You know the rest."

Clarke turned away from the searing winter sun as the sound of yet another engine disturbed the idyllic country dawn, although this one revved much higher than the rumbling trucks. "It's a complicated business all right, and if I'm not mistaken the waters are about to be muddied still further."

Digby muttered a profanity under his breath as an Austin staff car swerved into the driveway and slithered down the rutted track, sending sprays of stagnant water high into the air as it bounced towards them. "That who I think it is?"

"I'm surprised you haven't met sooner," was Clarke's tightlipped response.

The Austin swerved past the waiting truck, almost clipping it with its rear end as it shuddered to a halt outside the farmhouse. Immediately the rear doors flew open and two large, stern and heavily armed Redcaps emerged, one of them opening the front passenger door for a much smaller, rotund figure to clamber out.

Once the passengers were clear, the driver quickly reversed the car, spinning it round as the Redcaps took up position behind the small civilian puffing his way towards Digby and Clarke.

Clarke extended his hand. "Good morning, Mr Thorndike. You really didn't need to bring your friends with you."

Thorndike fumbled as he unwound a long scarf that smothered his beetroot red face. "It was the least I could do, considering the courteous manner in which our last meeting was conducted."

Digby stepped forward. "Hi, the name's Digby, but I guess you already know that. The Major here was just saying how he was surprised we haven't met sooner, seeing as how we're all working together. Still, I'm pleased to make your acquaintance."

Thorndike ignored Digby's offered hand just as he'd ignored the Major's. "Well I'm pleased to finally have a face to match with the reputation that precedes you, but you must understand that *I* am in charge here, Mr Digby."

Neither Clarke nor Digby responded.

Thorndike draped the scarf around his neck and began unbuttoning his woollen overcoat. "Did you know I've been up all night, dealing with wild rumours of paratroopers and firefights in the hills?" He pointed over his shoulder. "You *are* aware that Chequers is just a few minutes by car from this very spot? I've had to spend the last few hours convincing my colleagues this wasn't some kind of full-blown assault by fifth columnists or Nazi suicide troops. Why did you see fit not to inform me of your intentions before you embarked on this embarrassing debacle?"

Major Clarke's response was as frosty as the December dawn. "We didn't have time for such...courtesies, and we were bloody lucky to catch them here. Added to that, none of us has an address or telephone number where you can be contacted."

Thorndike sucked on his thick lips as he thought for a moment. "Very well. So what exactly do we *have* here?"

It was Digby who responded. "We've got the arms shipment and we've tracked down Jake Small, although he got caught up in the firefight."

Thorndike looked into the air and closed his eyes. "Don't tell me."

Clarke's answer eventually came after an awkward silence. "Those lads were being shot at in the dark and simply returned fire. Any of us would've done the same thing."

The portly mandarin removed his hat and used it to fan his reddened face. "I suppose there's no possibility this is just some kind of terrible clerical error."

Clarke's jaw jutted forward. "No error, and in my opinion it may not be the disaster you think it is."

"Major Clarke, it is not clear to me how the death of the very man we've been straining every sinew and breaking every law to locate is anything *but* disastrous."

"Let's just say that the more I've learned about him, the less convinced I am of where the Sergeant's true loyalties lay. He's left a trail of dead Sensitives and lost research in every place he's ended up, and none of us here believes in accidents."

Thorndike continued looking absentmindedly into the lightening dawn sky. "Your assignment was to quarantine Jacob Small, to aid in tracking and neutralising the party responsible for some serious security breaches. As you have spectacularly failed in your primary mission perhaps you can at least tell me this; are we dealing with some sort of imminent attack or merely an intelligence gathering operation?"

Digby weighed in on his friend's behalf. "It's a bit more complicated than that, Mr Thorndike."

"Well do feel free to explain. Just the bare bones will do for now as I know I'll receive every detail in your imminent reports, eyes only of course."

The American smiled for the first time that morning. "What makes you think I'll be writing reports for *you?*"

Thorndike ignored the question. "This business has gotten out of control. People are dead and seriously injured, our security is *still* being probed and yet we are no closer to finding any sort of lasting solution. What with policemen being shot at on London's streets, firefights within earshot of the Prime Minister's residence and plots to supply Irish Republicans with American equipment, questions have been asked at the highest level."

Clarke's eyes narrowed as he thumped out his pipe, the hot tobacco sizzling on the frosted grass. "What exactly does that *mean?*"

Thorndike's complexion reddened still further. "Both the JIC and I concur that although it has served us well in the past, Section C has now become a liability." He held up his hand, cutting off the Major before he could protest. "First Cedarwood and now this. The press are already asking questions, but we'll discuss how *they* might've gotten hold of anything later."

Clarke's reply was straight to the point. "So shove a D-Notice down their throats, that's how we usually handle these things."

Thorndike dabbed his forehead with his handkerchief. "Is it me or is it getting much warmer?"

Neither man responded.

Thorndike shrugged and continued. "D-Notices may see us through to the end of the war, but what about the next ten years, and the decade after that? As yet we have no idea where this business with these bloody Sensitives is leading us, so the less noise and the fuss the better. In the past, now, and into the foreseeable future."

Digby seized on Thorndike's assessment. "Hey I'm with you, buddy, so I'll just pick up the garbage and get out of your hair. To be honest I'm looking forward to getting back Stateside. It's been fun, but jolly old England ain't exactly what I thought it would be."

"Things seldom are," observed Thorndike. "However, until I am satisfied we have a full strategic understanding of the situation, I'm not authorised to release *anyone* from security quarantine. It's only out of professional courtesy that you don't find *yourself* there at this very moment."

Digby stepped forward and jerked his head towards Thorndike's escorts. "Listen pal, your goons don't scare me, and you might want to think about a little thing called the Visiting Forces Act, in case you'd forgotten."

Thorndike's response was cool and menacing, despite his diminutive stature. "Neither Jacob Small nor any of those other wretches is in uniform, and they have all been implicated in a conspiracy to provide arms and assistance to enemies of the Crown. The survivors of this rabble are now classified as hostile agents and are subject to all the restrictions and penalties of Defence Regulations and the Treachery Act."

Digby turned to his friend and colleague for support. "Major, please tell Mr Thorndike how it is; tell him we're friends and tell him I've already put my neck on the block to help this goddamn country more than once, and it's something I'm beginning to regret."

Before Clarke could respond, Thorndike reached into his coat and produced a slim brown envelope. "Major Clarke, as of this moment you, Section C and all associated resources are under my direct control. There will be no more of these cavalier off–the-books, backstairs operations." He handed the envelope across.

The Major's face darkened as he quickly opened the envelope and scanned the single sheet of paper inside.

Thorndike's voice softened a little. "I assume you recognise the signatures."

"All very impressive," replied Clarke flatly.

Digby looked first at Thorndike, then at Clarke. "So that's it? You guys kiss and make up and I get the shaft? Is that how it works?"

Clarke pulled a resigned face. "It's all above board, and as of now I'm under new orders."

"Screw your orders! We had a deal, Giles!"

Thorndike waved the two large Redcaps forward. "Gentlemen, would you be so kind as to ensure Mr Digby reaches Amersham police station safely. I'm sure he can find a telephone there."

Digby thrust his hands in his pockets, making sure that his jacket was pushed back far enough to reveal his automatic. "You're not the only guy around here who can collect autographs. You're starting a fight you can't win, Mr Thorndike, or whatever the hell your name *really* is."

Thorndike's face was impassive. "Thank you for all your assistance and goodbye, Mr Digby, or whatever the hell *your* name really is."

Digby pushed past the small man and stamped towards the waiting staff car.

Clarke refolded the letter and slid it into his pocket as he watched Digby slam the front passenger door, followed swiftly by his escorts. "I believe this is a mistake, Mr Thorndike. Digby's a good man whom we've twice prevented from carrying out his orders, and if you think that's the last we'll see of him then you're very much mistaken."

Thorndike gave an overly cheery wave as the Austin slithered up the rutted track and vanished through the farm gate. "You just let *me* worry about Digby, *you've* got more than enough on your plate."

Clarke rummaged in his pockets for his tobacco. "So, what are your orders?"

Thorndike looked up and smiled at the smoke billowing from the farmhouse's chimney. "Let's go inside where it's warmer, and quieter."

71

A bluish haze of lingering coal smoke swirled and eddied as Major Clarke opened the farmhouse door. "Good morning, Mr van Cortlandt. I hope you're feeling a little better."

Sitting in a dusty chair and wrapped tightly in an army blanket, Thomas van Cortlandt seemed oblivious to the winter cold sneaking through the hurriedly boarded window as he stared fixedly at the glowing coals in the grate.

Wilhelm looked up from his own seat beside the fire. Pale, drawn and huddled inside a greatcoat several sizes too big, he wore the look of a man in desperate need of some rest and recreation as he tended his latest patient.

Clarke tried again, beckoning his companion to enter the room. "This is Mr Thorndike. He's come up from London especially to see to you. I'm sure you realise we have a lot of questions."

Still van Cortlandt didn't respond.

However, Thorndike *did* respond as he stepped forward and offered his hand to the weary physician by the fire. "It's a pleasure to finally meet you face-to-face, Dr Werner. I had the honour of talking with your father on a few occasions; such a tragic irony."

Wilhelm's eyes narrowed. "I do not recall my father mentioning your name, Herr Thorndike."

"Alas we live in times when fathers must keep secrets from their sons, and that's a great shame." Thorndike stamped his feet against the cold before crossing to the dining table. His composure evaporated as he stared stupefied at the vast fortune spilling out of two rather muddy drawstring bags. His mouth fell open and he emitted a sound somewhere between a sigh and a groan as he held a polished ruby between his fleshy fingertips.

The room was quiet for a while before Thorndike eventually thought of something to say. "Either the Irish have gotten very generous of late, or we've stumbled into the middle of something entirely different."

"We're at an early stage in our enquiries," was Clarke's simple and not very helpful response.

Thorndike was quickly turning a shade reminiscent of the valuable gem he was holding. "Major Clarke, a word if you please." He jerked his head towards the rear passage and waddled out of the rundown lounge.

Clarke sighed heavily and followed.

Thorndike just managed to contain his anger long enough for the yellowed parlour door to squeak shut. "Just what the bloody hell is going on here, Major? Why is Thomas van Cortlandt sitting in a notorious gangster's hideout along with a fortune in cut gems? I assume they *are* his."

Clarke raised his eyebrows and folded his arms. "And you wonder where I got the idea that you can't be trusted. Secrets are our stock in trade, but they also get good men and women killed in the field. You weren't nearly surprised enough to see van Cortlandt, and you immediately assumed that king's ransom is tied to him. *I* should be the one asking *you* just what the bloody hell's going on."

The smaller man fished for his spotted handkerchief and dabbed his forehead. "You're on a need-to-know basis, Major."

Clarke produced his pipe from his own pocket. "Fine then, have it your own way. You may consider my resignation immediate."

"You're a commissioned officer in time of war, Major Clarke. You do not have the luxury of simply walking away and abandoning your duties."

Clarke looked at his pipe before shoving it back in his pocket. "No, but I think I'd be more use back in uniform. Who knows, they might even give me a nice comfortable office like yours, wherever it is."

Thorndike perspired still further and turned a shade brighter as he considered Clarke's not-so-veiled threat. "I can't go into the details regarding Thomas van Cortlandt because in truth I'm not privy to all of them."

"Just the bare bones will do for now," was Clarke's sarcastic response.

"You must understand that I've never met the man before, but I have known about him for some time now."

Clarke chewed his own lips in an effort to control his temper. "And you never thought to mention any of this to me, not even while I was investigating Section 12?"

Thorndike's voice took on a matter of fact, business-like tone. "There was no reason to think there was any connection between the two, and besides, you didn't seem to need any assistance with the Cedarwood business. I myself have received assurances that Thomas van Cortlandt was thoroughly vetted and given a clean bill of health. My understanding is that he settled here a short while before Kristallnacht; not that the van Cortlandts are German, or Jewish as far as I know. He was questioned at length regarding the more, shall we say, exotic legends surrounding his kinsmen but there's never been any evidence to suggest he's a Sensitive, or even *believes* in this so-called Brotherhood."

Clarke's response was scathing. "At least I've learned how the fabled van Cortlandt Collection found its way into the country, and I have no doubt that family's control of Radnage Investments was given its proper weight during your deliberations."

Thorndike stuffed his handkerchief back in his pocket. "I needn't remind you that those were difficult years for everyone, and everything was above board. Our chaps have checked in from time to time but they've never found anything to arouse suspicion."

"Except for a secret fortune in gems and his being related to the Brotherhood's erstwhile leader, or grand master, or whatever the bloody hell they call him."

Thorndike drew himself up to his full, if short height. "Now you listen to me very carefully, Major. I don't much care for your tone or your sudden pious attitude towards this issue. It was a different world back then. Peter van Cortlandt had been dead for decades, or so we thought, and Dr Theodore Burton was languishing in Dartmoor, discredited as a fringe lunatic and a pervert to boot. Nobody was taking the notion of these Sensitives seriously."

"Except the Sensitives themselves," observed Clarke.

Thorndike relaxed a little. "Quite so. Today is a whole new can of worms as the Americans say."

Clarke shook his head and gave an exasperated sigh. "The more I hear about these dangerous lunatics, the more I think we've all been asleep for years."

"So it would seem, Major. I assure you that I dislike being made a fool of just as much as you do, and it is my avowed intention to find out *exactly* what Mr van Cortlandt's been up to whilst he's been enjoying His Majesty's protection. To my knowledge, this is the *second* time a member of that increasingly notorious family has crossed us and abused our hospitality. Such duplicity will not go unanswered, and I would very much value your experience and expertise during the investigation."

Clarke reached for the door latch. "We'll need to question van Cortlandt very thoroughly, then question him again, and then again once more. And we'll need to put George Tooley's mob through the mangle while they're still confused and apprehensive."

Thorndike's face brightened as he beamed a fleshy smile. "That's the spirit! I knew we'd see eye to eye eventually. I'll dispatch a team to van Cortlandt's home to start a thorough search. We'll dismantle the place brick by brick if we have to, but I want answers just as much as you do."

Clarke smiled approvingly. "That's exactly what *I* had in mind. Now what about Radnage Investments?"

"Nothing. For the time being we shall do nothing, except issue a cover story regarding Mr van Cortlandt's sudden illness. Radnage Investments is firmly off-limits unless and until we encounter firm evidence of impropriety. Is that understood?"

The Major nodded. "Very well then. So, for the moment our best source of information is probably our friend in the living room."

Thorndike nodded his agreement. "Let's start gently with just a few simple questions. Who knows, he may be only too pleased to cooperate."

"It may be better to wait," observed Clarke.

"Oh really, how so?"

"He's under sedation."

"Why?" Thorndike's single worded question was long, drawn out and suspicious.

Clarke finally released the latch and pushed the badly fitted door open. "Let's just say I don't think Mr van Cortlandt is quite all there."

Thorndike pushed his way back into the lounge and beckoned to Wilhelm, keeping his voice low once the psychiatrist was standing beside him. "Major Clarke informs me that you've administered a sedative to Mr van Cortlandt."

"That is correct, Herr Thorndike. It was necessary as he became very agitated and confused during the night."

"Mr van Cortlandt sits on the board of a small but highly respected investment company, he's hardly the kind of man to suddenly become agitated and confused."

Wilhelm glanced back the man staring determinedly into the glowing coals. "It is difficult to be precise, but my best guess is that he has been in close contact with Jacob Small."

Thorndike raised his eyebrows above his thick glasses. "When you say *close contact,* you mean..."

The younger man stared hard at Thorndike. "Are you familiar with my father's work?"

Thorndike needed no further prompting as his face broke into boyish smile. "Displacement? Really? Right here?"

Wilhelm held up his hands. "Not exactly, Herr Thorndike. Not in the sense that *you* mean, but nonetheless I believe that Jacob Small's shadow has fallen across Herr van Cortlandt. Alas we cannot know how long it may linger before it fades."

Clarke pushed the lounge door closed and crossed to the broken window. "I'm familiar with the concept, and I think I may even have seen Displacement for myself, but I'm sceptical in this case."

"Why so in this case?" Wilhelm's eyes never left his patient.

Clarke watched the soldiers bustling in the farmyard. "In the light of everything I've experienced, I'm forced to concede that there are some extraordinary people in this world, people who can perform feats those in a less enlightened age might describe as magic."

"But..." Wilhelm nudged the Major's train of thought.

"But Mr van Cortlandt here is no Sensitive. Bright yes, intuitive I've no doubt, but we're still talking about the difference between a county sports team and an Olympic champion."

"At this point I can only speculate," was Wilhelm's less than scientific response.

"Speculate away, Dr Werner." Thorndike urged excitedly.

Wilhelm lowered his voice. "Although Thomas van Cortlandt is not a confirmed Sensitive in his own right, he shares a common ancestry with the most gifted line ever recorded. He's already told me that Jacob Small has used his abilities to extract information, and I believe that process has left a weak stimulant effect. Think of it like a needle retaining a mild charge after exposure to a strong magnet."

Thorndike's whisper matched Wilhelm's. "Then we're looking at Transference rather than Displacement, and your father's notes clearly state that it's only temporary, when it happens at all."

Clarke's frown deepened as he looked from one man to the other, although he remained silent.

Wilhelm continued. "That is the conventional wisdom, or tradition if you like. However, if the iron content is high enough and the magnet is strong enough, who knows what might happen."

Thorndike could barely contain his excitement. "You realise what this means?"

"Possibly, Herr Thorndike."

"It means that Hammond may have been right all along. Perhaps we *can* train our own cohort of invisible watchers."

Clarke's contribution was less than optimistic. "I hate to be the fly in this jar of increasingly unlikely ointment, but Section 12 was hardly a resounding success."

Thorndike was quick to counter. "Section 12 was overseen by entirely unsuitable management, and I assure you that mistake will *not* be repeated." He turned back to Wilhelm. "This could be a great opportunity for all of us, if you can show me something verifiable."

"Very well." Wilhelm stepped across the room and reached into the shadows above the mantelpiece. He produced a Colt pistol and crouched in front of the permanently distracted banker. "Thomas, do you remember what we did earlier?"

It was a few seconds before the man huddled in the blanket responded. When at last he did, his face wore the look someone who'd lost his place in the middle of a sentence. He looked down at the pistol, frowned and shook his head slowly.

"What's he doing?" Thorndike whispered to Clarke.

The Major murmured his response. "If Wilhelm hasn't dosed him up too much then you may see something interesting, although I'm not sure it qualifies as evidence."

Wilhelm held out the pistol by its barrel. "Thomas, you know this is more than just a parlour trick. It's very important, and it should still be very easy for you."

Van Cortlandt turned his head back towards the glowing coals, as though they held some inexpressible fascination from which he could not escape. Although his eyes remained fixed on the fireplace, his hands grasped the weapon and dismantled it with a casual, almost flippant familiarity. Magazine, main spring, barrel and frame were all arranged in the banker's lap within seconds.

Wilhelm quickly grasped the pistol's components, changed their order and dropped them back into van Cortlandt's lap.

With a swift series of clicks the weapon was reassembled in the same offhand manner before being passed back to the psychiatrist.

Wilhelm rose and crossed to the men standing beside the table. "Herr van Cortlandt claims not to have handled so much as a shotgun in his entire life. However, we know for certain that Sergeant Jacob Small was an expert with this weapon."

For a while there was silence as the full implications of Wilhelm's statement hung heavily in the air.

It was Thorndike who spoke next. "Do you believe him? About his knowledge of firearms, or rather his lack of it?"

Clarke interjected. "That was *my* first question, and I have to say I'd have been utterly unconvinced were it not for this." He fished in his pocket and produced a folded piece of paper. "Van Cortlandt insisted on drawing it, said he had to get it out of his head so that he could see properly. Shortly after that he became very upset and Wilhelm had to sedate the poor man."

Thorndike snatched the sheet of paper and unfolded it, glancing towards the window as the sound of a new vehicle approaching grew louder by the second. "Well, that could've been better..." He tailed off mid-sentence as he stared at the skilfully rendered pencil sketch of five prefabricated huts against a backdrop of cracked and broken glass.

Clarke also glanced out of the window before returning his attention to the paper between Thorndike's increasingly clammy fingers. "Either two men who've never met before have held a detailed discussion about a Section C's HQ, or van Cortlandt and Jake Small somehow shared that information by other means. You already know which is the more likely."

Thorndike carefully folded the paper and placed it in his jacket pocket. "All the available research suggests this Transference effect is temporary, so we'll have to move fast if there's anything else Jacob Small unwittingly revealed before his death. We might yet salvage something useful from this almighty balls up."

"Agreed," said Clarke simply.

Thorndike scooped the fortune in gems into their battered bags and then into his pockets. "All right, Dr Werner, let's get our man outside. You look like you both need some fresh air."

Clarke helped Wilhelm prise their very distracted patient from his fireside chair.

Wilhelm smiled reassuringly as they made their way to the front door. "It's all right, you're among friends here. Nobody is going to harm you."

Thorndike opened the front door, sighing sadly as a drab green Bedford ambulance rocked to a halt and two army medics jumped out. "I've had this ready and waiting for a while now, although its intended passenger won't be needing it."

Van Cortlandt stopped at the sight of the ambulance and turned to Thorndike. "Are you taking me home?"

Thorndike beckoned the drowsy and confused man out of the house and towards the waiting ambulance. "Better than that. I'm taking you somewhere very safe, both in this world *and* the next."

72

"It should be just up here," said Wilhelm reassuringly as the draughty staff car lurched down yet another pothole.

Jake grimaced and held onto his arm as it bounced in its sling, with every jolt somehow translating to a blank frame in the movie reel of his mind. Although Wilhelm had recently supplied him with some new and even darker glasses, the low winter sun made it impossible to see properly as he shielded his eyes and glanced out through the grime spattered window. He wasn't sure *why* he'd insisted on this personal pilgrimage, but since his second death he'd been unable to shake the nagging feeling that it was essential.

Wilhelm continued to chatter amiably and usefully beside him. "It's a pity I didn't get to know Herr Piggott before he passed away. I understand he was a promising subject, at least in the beginning. I think *late bloomer* is the correct phrase."

"Yeah, he was," agreed Jake absentmindedly. He pulled the collar of his new coat tighter around his neck as he returned to the sketch in his journal.

Wilhelm leaned over to look at the American's work. "Is this something you remember? What can you tell me about it?"

Jake spoke short, distracted sentences as he continued shading in a detailed drawing of an ornate but neglected looking iron gate. "It was winter; there were still patches of snow on the ground and the horses were steaming. There was the smell of horses, and damp leather."

Wilhelm prodded verbally. "Good. What else do you recall?"

Jake stopped sketching and wiped the mist from the inside of the car's window. "I was sad, and afraid. I felt like I was going to school, but I knew it wasn't *really* a school, more like an education. It's hard to explain."

"Don't try to explain it. Just let the memory reveal itself as it will, whether that be through words, images or perhaps even music."

Jake's looked down at the drawing in his journal. "I know for sure this *isn't* one of mine. *I* can't tell one end of a horse from the other so that place must've left a lasting impression on someone. I wonder where I...where *he* was going."

The psychiatrist peered at the scene taking shape on the page. "That's very good work, Jacob. It looks like a respectable sort of place so who knows, perhaps that garden gate is still out there somewhere."

The American suddenly stopped sketching. "I don't want to know."

Wilhelm was quick to reassure. "It's a difficult and complex problem, but there's no need to talk about it now."

Jake returned to his work while Wilhelm wiped the mist from his own window and stared out into the brilliant winter morning.

At length it was the young psychiatrist who broke the silence. "This must be it."

Jake leaned forward to get a better view through the windscreen. His heart sank, leapt and turned to ice all in the same moment as the low, golden sun cast a ghostly aura around St John's irreparably shattered silhouette.

Wilhelm shook his head as the driver brought the car to a stop and killed the engine. "Such a tragedy. I do not think our collective memory will *ever* recover from this conflict. I am afraid to think of what Amsterdam or Munich might look like."

"Not thinking about Berlin?"

"I can *easily* imagine what Berlin might look like."

Jake said nothing as he opened the rear door and stepped into the crisp winter morning. He didn't look round as the other doors opened and Wilhelm also emerged from the car, followed by their two plain-clothed escorts, or *shadows* as he'd jokingly christened them.

The American's arm throbbed as he slowly made his way to the low wall surrounding what little still remained of the churchyard. Both stunned and yet accepting, Jake stared down at the water-filled crater which had taken a huge bite out of the building during his short absence. A great many of St John's departed lay drowned beneath the motionless, icy grey surface that taunted him with its silent reminder of another place so far away from nowhere. "When?" He asked simply.

Wilhelm's voice was quiet and measured. "Two days after the raid on the farm, while you were still in a coma. I think there's an old expression about lightning which has just been disproved."

Jake continued to stare, somehow lacking the strength to utter anything more than a few words. "Was it a rocket? Forget that, I already know." He decided not to elaborate on the half living, half dead tree that was missing from this "real" version of the place. The young psychiatrist would no doubt ask a thousand questions, for which he had nothing even resembling an answer.

Wilhelm motioned for their minders to keep a respectful distance. *"How* do you know?"

"I was here before."

Wilhelm's response was slow and deliberate. "Yes, but not since this more recent explosion."

"I'm telling you I've been here before. Not actually *here,* but out there, in the Place Removed, I think. It's hard to remember. I was sick and I'd passed out. Yeah that's right. The first time I saw this, I mean as it is *now,* was the first time I ever saw Morgan Jones. At least I *guess* that was him." Jake glanced across at the young psychiatrist. "Not gonna jot all this in your little book?"

"No, not today. Somehow it seems...inappropriate."

"Well I guess that's something."

For a while neither man spoke, they just stared into the murky grey water filling the crater. Eventually it was Wilhelm who broke the silence. "Jacob, you must surely know that I need to ask you some questions."

"About what?"

There was a pause of several seconds before the half-German exile continued. "Where were you?"

"How do you mean?"

Wilhelm never took his eyes off the water's inscrutable surface. "I know you're not a fool, and you make a poor attempt at passing for one. You were declared dead at the farm, then you were unconscious for three whole days; and after *that* you drifted in and out of this world for the better part of a week. It's obvious that you weren't really here with us, so where were you?"

Jake thought for a while before answering, and in the end he confined himself to a simple, factual statement. "I was nowhere."

Wilhelm looked up at the church's open carcass. "I have just said that I know you're not a fool, Jacob. I trust you do not think that *I* am one."

Jake didn't respond.

There was another protracted silence before Wilhelm tried again. "It would be better to just tell me as much as you can. I promise I will listen, no matter how strange your story may be."

"Better for who?"

The young psychiatrist persisted. "Jacob, you were pronounced dead by an experienced doctor, and now you are not only alive, but your wounds are healing at a disturbingly rapid rate. Questions have been asked."

Jake maintained his mysterious silence, mostly because he wasn't really certain of anything.

Wilhelm glanced over Jake's shoulder as a second staff car rounded the end of the cobbled street. "I'd advise you to be much more open, Jacob. Things have changed, and in my opinion not for the better."

The American was barely listening as he turned to watch the car approaching. "Who's this, a friend of yours?"

"Not exactly, Herr Small."

Jake was filled with both curiosity and foreboding as the car parked beside the church and two more security men climbed out. They quickly looked around before one of them opened the rear door to let a squat, plump and red-faced man heave himself out of the back seat.

Jake watched the small civilian closely as he puffed across the short distance between them. No way was this guy combat fit, and neither was he some wily intelligence officer like Clarke or Digby. The staff car ruled him out as an underworld kingpin, but it also suggested that he was an official of some kind.

At last the mysterious visitor wheezed to a halt, unbuttoned his coat and unwound his scarf. For a while he said nothing as he studied the wounded American with the expression of a man trying to discern the meaning of an abstract canvas.

Jake said nothing either as he stared back. He sensed trouble, although he couldn't figure out what kind.

When the short man eventually spoke, it wasn't to Jake. "Dr Werner, would you please be so kind as to wait in the car. Sergeant Small and I have some important business to discuss."

Jake watched as Wilhelm made his way back to the staff car, closely followed by his two minders. "What have *we* got to discuss? Who are you anyway?"

The round man pulled a spotted handkerchief from his pocket to mop his brow and waited until Wilhelm was back in the car before speaking again. "I trust your arm isn't giving you too much trouble. The doctors tell me that you've made a remarkable recovery, especially for a man who was legally deceased for several hours. I'm not sure that poor mortuary assistant will ever be quite the same."

Jake stared up at the short man's tall minders. "I'm guessing you didn't follow me here to ask a dead man about his health. What do you want?"

"Quite right, I *didn't* come to enquire after your health. All the same I'm glad to see that you're still with us, or at least a *part* of you is." At last the stranger raised his hat in greeting. "My name is Thorndike, and I shall be your new handler."

"Well then, Mr Thorndike, you can just go and screw yourself. I ain't your goddamned dog."

Thorndike's companions stepped forward as one, but he quickly waved them away. "I think I should make true nature of our relationship crystal clear from the very beginning."

Jake theatrically rubbed his forehead. "Well, let me just put my advanced powers of premonition to the test. I sense that you're about to tell me you want to help realise my potential, and all in the service of good and righteousness."

Thorndike stuffed the handkerchief back in his pocket. "It's really much simpler than that, Sergeant. I'm here to arrest you."

Jake couldn't stop a smirk from appearing on his face. "And people say *I'm* crazy."

Thorndike didn't smirk, and neither did he frown. In fact his expression remained fixed in every aspect.

It took a little while, but Jake eventually felt his own smirk vanishing as he realised that Thorndike was quite serious. "What the hell am I being arrested *for,* Mr Thorndike? And you don't look like any kind of cop to me."

Thorndike began re-buttoning his coat. "I won't bore you with all the technical legalese, but we'll start with conspiring to aid an insurgent group in time of war, handling stolen goods and robbery with violence. There's also a strong suspicion of espionage, and that's before we even *mention* poor Miss Parsons."

Jake swallowed down a sudden surge of anger as he felt both fists tightening. "Bullshit! I want to talk to Digby right now."

Thorndike raised his eyebrows. "Really? I thought you disliked the man, and anyway it's irrelevant now. I'm afraid your countrymen have declared you killed in action and abandoned you to your fate."

"What the hell does *that* mean?"

"The Americans have grave misgivings as to where your true loyalties lie, and by the way, you can thank Major Clarke for that. They're more than happy to keep you as far from any programs they may, or may not, be operating as they possibly can. In short, you're damaged goods, persona non grata until and *if* we can give you a clean bill of health."

For just a moment, Jake fantasised about taking to his heels and making another escape. He knew it was folly though; he was still weak and his squat inquisitor's shadows were highly trained and fighting fit. Instead he confined himself to a simple but far reaching response. "So, what happens now?"

"I'm taking personal charge of your debriefing, and I strongly advise you to cooperate fully as it's the only way you might have *any* kind of future."

"And supposing I just tell you to go pound salt up your ass, what then?"

Thorndike sighed heavily as he looked over the wall bordering St John's churchyard. "It's such a shame. I'd have enjoyed meeting the Reverend Piggott. I hear he'd become quite a talent in his later years, although his gifts were too erratic for regular use."

Jake also leaned against the low wall. "Listen buddy, if you think these Gestapo tactics are gonna work on me then you've got the wrong guy."

Thorndike looked back at the American. "I don't know whether that sudden display of bravado is rooted in your culture, upbringing, or is driven by your new-found abilities. The truth is that you've been pampered and indulged by the likes of Hammond and Clarke for long enough, and the results have been meagre at best. We've squandered huge resources on these dubious, arm's-length operations and gotten absolutely nothing in return. Outcomes have been entirely unsatisfactory if not downright counter-productive, and I'm here to tell you that the free ride is over. I've been authorised to take this entire matter in hand forthwith."

"Jesus! If that was a free ride, I'd hate to be around when you guys get serious."

Thorndike remained unmoved. "Keep up the gung-ho facade if you wish, but it's my duty to inform you that you're potentially facing the noose should your account of yourself be less than satisfactory."

Jake finally understood the reality of his situation and responded appropriately. "So you're telling me that *my* life depends on keeping *you* happy. Like I said earlier, go and screw yourself, you lardy little bureaucrat!"

Thorndike ignored Jake's insult. "I've sent someone to the hospital to pack up your personal items, and Dr Werner will accompany you to your new billet. You should be there some time after nightfall, and we'll begin formal debriefing tomorrow."

Jake swallowed inadvertently. "And just what the hell is *formal debriefing* around here?"

The smaller man beamed inappropriately. "Don't worry about that. You won't be subjected to any mediaeval vulgarity, nor will you be left at the mercy of your good friend Dr Hammond."

"That bastard is *not* my friend, and besides, there's nothing to tell that you don't know already."

Thorndike clasped his plump fingers together. "You know, I wanted to be a soldier when I was young, but alas my body is just not equal to the challenge."

"I don't know how His Majesty has got by without you."

The rotund official continued despite Jake's obvious hostility. "When I was a boy I owned the most wonderful battalion of toy soldiers. Hand painted and each with his own unique features; they were truly magnificent and I loved them so."

Jake yawned, and made no attempt to hide it.

Thorndike's voice took on a wistful tone. "I've always been a rather fastidious sort, I suppose I take after my mother in that respect. Every night those soldiers stood guard around my room, and each had to be in precisely the right place, watching over me and also protecting his brothers in arms."

"Lucky you didn't grow up where *I* did or you'd have gotten your ass kicked real good," Jake observed.

"I've always been a stickler for details, Jacob. Everything in its proper place and everything in order. Even as a small boy I just couldn't sleep if those soldiers weren't all present at their posts, or even if I just *thought* they weren't. I can't count how many nights' sleep I lost getting out of bed to check they were still patrolling properly, only to repeat the whole process over again about an hour later."

Jake wrung his hands. "I'll be good, I promise. I'll answer all your questions and help in every way I can. Just don't tell me any more stories about yourself when you were a fat kid. I just can't take it."

Thorndike's expression hardened. "Mock me if you will, Sergeant, but my fastidious nature has served me well in my adult life, and that same instinct for order now tells me that you've been playing fast and loose with the truth from the very beginning."

"You're a very strange man, Mr Thorndike."

"We're going to document the story of your life, Jacob. We're going to record everything you *claim* to remember, and we're going to account for every hour you *claim* to have forgotten. You see, none of this sits well with me, not at all. In fact, so many of the pieces of the puzzle are missing that I'm having trouble sleeping."

"Tell me about it."

The plump civil servant's gaze returned to the grey water filling the enormous bomb crater. "There are so many unanswered questions, but right now I'm *especially* interested in how you escaped detection following the Cedarwood incident. I have no doubt that you're a tough and resourceful soldier, but I find it hard to believe that you managed to stitch your own head back together."

All Jake could offer was an honest answer. "I forget things, and then I remember *other* things that the dead forgot about years ago, so your guess is as good as mine."

Thorndike remained silent for nearly a minute as though lost in thought. At last he turned and began waddling back to the car while his minders fell in behind him. "Your escorts will ensure your safety while you settle into your new quarters. You've made the most remarkable recovery, but you still bear the pallor of the dead. I'd recommend lots of fresh air and a pint of best stout each day. My old great aunt used to swear by it, and *she* lived to be a hundred."

Jake called after the overweight inquisitor. "Wait a second, just where the hell am I *going?*"

Thorndike continued waddling. "Somewhere safe, quiet and a lot more comfortable than your recent bevy of flophouses. You should regard yourself as very fortunate, all things considered."

Jake called after the plump man again. "Don't forget that maniac's still out there, and I'm the only hope you've got of stopping him from doing...whatever the hell it is he's gonna do."

Thorndike turned as a bodyguard opened the car door for him. "I almost forgot something. You know I sometimes think *my* memory's worse than yours." He smiled broadly and tipped his hat to the American. "A very happy new year to you, Sergeant Jacob Small."

Author's Note

Thank you for purchasing The Cronus Equation. The continued support of readers like yourself is the lifeblood of independent authors, and we certainly appreciate it. Remember that it's never been easier to share the good news when you find an exciting new book.

Visit www.charlesnaton.com or find me on Facebook to stay in touch and help spread the word.